Long Time Gone

## Also by Denis Hamill

*Stomping Ground*
*Machine*
*House on Fire*
*3 Quarters*
*Throwing 7's*
*Fork in the Road*

# Long Time Gone

## DENIS HAMILL

a novel

**ATRIA** BOOKS
New York  London  Toronto  Sydney  Singapore

**ATRIA** BOOKS
1230 Avenue of the Americas
New York, NY 10020

Library of Congress Control Number: 2002104624

ISBN: 0-7434-0709-1

First Atria Books hardcover printing August 2002

10   9   8   7   6   5   4   3   2   1

**ATRIA** BOOKS is a registered trademark of
Simon & Schuster, Inc.

For information regarding special discounts for bulk purchases,
please contact Simon & Schuster Special Sales at 1-800-456-6798
or business@simonandschuster.com

Printed in the U.S.A.

For my brother Brian,
bravest guy I know, who always came
when "they" were chasing me
through the jinglejangle mornings

# acknowledgments

I would like to thank Celina Shevlin for her invaluable research into the year 1969; she unearthed details I didn't even ask for but somehow knew I needed. I'd also like to thank Esther Newberg, my friend and agent, for her valued ideas and making this happen. And thanks to my daughters, Katie and Nell, who read a first draft and gave me keen and honest notes. Ditto for my brother Joey, one of the smartest guys I know, who reads like a convict studying an escape plan. A special thanks to my editor, Mitchell Ivers, who believed in this book from the first lunch and made it a better one by the time he paid the tab. And, finally, to the survivors of Hippie Hill—peace.

*"I'm a long time a-comin', babe,*
*An' I'll be a long time gone."*

> —*Bob Dylan,*
> *"Long Time Gone"*

*"If you can remember the sixties, you weren't there."*
> —*Dennis Hopper*

Long Time Gone

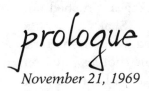

# prologue
*November 21, 1969*

Danny Cassidy couldn't remember if he'd killed the cop.

The night before was a blackout. Acid, goofballs, booze. Smashed.

Ankles, the cop who'd rousted him from his dirty crash pad mattress a half hour earlier, now pushed him up the hill to view the bloody pile that had once been a NYPD detective named Vito Malone, nicknamed Boar's Head.

"So long to the sixties, Danny," Ankles said. "Peace, love, and fuckin' hom-i-cide, man."

Now Danny knew why the cops had tossed his crash pad for muddy and bloody clothes. They didn't find any. *But what the hell happened to my old clothes,* he wondered, *the clothes I wore the night before?*

Detective Anthony "Ankles" Tufano had dragged him from his tenement on Fifteenth Road into his Plymouth Fury detective car as Brendan hurried up the block with fresh rolls and orange juice. Brendan told Danny to say nothing, that he'd get O'Dowd the lawyer.

"Better get him a priest, too," said Ankles. "He's gonna do a lot of confessing."

Then Ankles drove Danny up to Prospect Park.

Crime-scene tape was lashed from trees to bushes to lampposts to park benches, securing the killing ground. Two guys in hospital-green jumpsuits leaned against a coroner's station wagon, smoking cigarettes as they watched crime-scene cops from a police station wagon marked FORENSICS do their jobs. Techs snapped crime-scene photographs, made plaster molds of footprints, elbow and knee indentations, and placed little numbered paper tents over shell casings, measuring the distance between bullets and tracking a trail of the dead man's blood.

Three patrol cars with dizzying twirling lights were parked on the pathway of hexagonal paving stones that was strewn with empty manila pot envelopes, Bambu rolling-paper packs, crumpled

Marlboro, Kools, Pall Malls, and Winston packages. Crushed and discarded beer cans—Rheingold, Ballantine's, Shaefer, Schlitz, Knickerbocker—overflowed from two mangled wire-mesh Parks Department trash cans. Drained cheap wine bottles—Twister, Lemon Rock, and Boone's Farm—littered the grass. Leaky takeout cardboard beer containers from nearby Foley's tavern lined the bases of the Totem Poles, the Grecian columns that stood like marble sentries at the entrance to Prospect Park. And Danny knew this was only minor late-fall clutter compared to the debris field of roaring summer nights on Hippie Hill, the sloping, shady hillock inside the mouth of Prospect Park, when hundreds of young long-haired freaks converged for the daily be-in.

Two cops allowed a *Daily News* photographer to take three pictures from different angles and then escorted him behind the crime-scene tape.

Danny's LSD-heightened sense of smell of the wet garbage, stale beer, and cheap wine churned his stomach. The scratchy drone of police squawk boxes became exaggerated in a psychedelic blare, making Danny's temples pound and pulsate. He swallowed through a painful sandpaper thirst, and his skin itched and stung as if smothered by a giant jellyfish. As he shivered on Hippie Hill, the twirling police lights triggered mini hallucinatory flashes before Danny's eyes, some horrific and filled with guns and blood and violence, some slapstick goofy and pratfall comical. When he closed his eyes he was blinded by a brilliant cone of light, like the one where angels escorted souls from purgatory to heaven in the second panel of Hieronymus Bosch's *The Blessed and the Damned.* This *was* like a Bosch painting, Danny thought. A nightmare. *Beyond my control.*

Danny stared down at the corpse, trembling. The LSD residue gave everything he saw a Day-Glo, color-saturated cartoony look. Detective Vito Malone lay on the muddied yellow grass, the bullet hole in his forehead like a red dot on a Hindu. Cordite-powder burns surrounded the wound. Much of the face was scorched, indicating he'd been shot at very close range. Danny flashed on Bugs Bunny's charred face after being blasted by Elmer Fudd's blunderbuss. He looked at Ankles and was tempted to ask, "What's up, doc?" He stifled a laugh. A snicker escaped and he camouflaged it with a cough. But this wasn't a fucking cartoon, he thought. This wasn't funny. This was real—very, very real.

One gun blast in the dead cop's groin had been fired at point-blank range and made a big purple mess. Four other bullets perforated Malone's ski jacket. Burnt down feathers shivered in the late November wind as gray dawn seeped across the cold Brooklyn sky over Prospect Park.

"Poor Erika," Danny said. She wasn't even over the other horrific trauma in her life yet, he thought, and now her father was dead. Murdered. *Maybe by me.*

"Why the fuck did you do this to him?" Ankles asked. "To her? He knew you knew about Wally Fortune, didn't he? Talk to me, you little motherfucker."

"I didn't do it," Danny said, although he had no idea if he was telling the truth.

"Six shots," Ankles said. "You must have been pretty fucking pissed off, kid. What are you? Seventeen, just eighteen? Figure you'll be eligible for parole just in time to collect Social Security. If you're lucky."

"You think I did this?" Danny asked, teeth chattering, hands jammed in the front pockets of his brand-new stovepipe corduroys. His boots were also new. So were his leather jacket and his Giants sweatshirt. He had no idea where these new clothes had come from. And he was a Jets fan, loved Broadway Joe Namath, not a Giants fan. The only thing that wasn't new was the Mets cap pinned with a peace button. He'd worn the hat since the Mets won their first World Series the month before and got the button while staggering in the 250,000-strong Moratorium march on Washington on November 15. But why was he wearing these clothes? And why was he a prime suspect in a cop killing? He removed his hat and felt his squeaky-clean hair. He examined his spotless fingernails and realized that he didn't remember showering or shampooing before going to sleep.

"Whaddaya think I think?" Ankles said.

"I think I wanna talk to my lawyer, who my brother Brendan went to get when he saw you drag me outta my pad."

Danny stared at Malone, licked his dry cracked lips, his head banging like the church bell up in Blessed Virgin Mary.

Ankles stamped his thick-soled size-14 cordovans on the damp earth, a White Owl cigar smoldering in his thick dry lips. A yawning, skinny crime-scene cop named Mackin handed him a brown paper evidence bag containing the dead man's wallet, stuffed with at least fifty $100 bills that bulged behind the gold NYPD detective shield. Ankles didn't need to run the shield number or read the police department tax ID card. He already knew the dead man was Detective Vito Malone. The local longhairs on Hippie Hill had nicknamed Malone Boar's Head because of his snarling resemblance to the angry swine in the cold cuts logo.

Ankles grabbed Danny, once a rippling halfback, by his methamphetamine-atrophied bicep and led him halfway down Hippie Hill to the parked Plymouth Fury detective car. He opened the back door, and shoved Danny in. Ankles rolled down the back window, making sure Danny could hear what was going on outside of the car. He also wanted Danny to see and be seen. He was a stage prop in a murder investigation.

"Sit here and dummy the fuck up, unless it's to confess," Ankles said, slamming the door. "Blab word one and you'll be shittin' Chiclets."

Danny shivered on the cold plastic seat. He peered down at the small crowd that was gathering behind the yellow crime-scene tape near the entrance to the park as word spread on the neighborhood tom-toms and most of the uppie and speed freaks who hadn't slept all night came to watch the drama. Danny's pals—Timmy O'Toole, Kenny Byrne, Eddie Fortune, and Brian Walsh—were there. So were Hippie Helen and Christie Strong and Dirty Jim Dugan. A harmless psycho named JoJo Corcoran, who had been experimented on with psychedelic drugs in the army before they discharged him on a 100 percent psychiatric pension, paraded back and forth, trying to ignite a chant: "Free Danny Cassidy! Free Danny Cassidy!" But two uniformed cops made a move toward him and he ran off. Danny wondered what was keeping Brendan with O'Dowd the lawyer.

His friends waved to him. Danny nodded, scared now.

Danny watched Ankles stalk ten feet back to Mackin, motioning for him to tell him what he knew. "They didn't rob him, Anthony," said Mackin.

"I wish it was that simple," Ankles said. "And don't call me Ant'ny in fronna the punk. And tell the uniforms to keep those skells away from the crime scene."

"Just our piss-poor luck," Mackin said. "Liver temp says he was shot during the downpour, which washed away most of the footprints. Which fixes the time at about two forty-five, according to that Tex Antoine on the morning weather. Rain fell all night on top of the scene. He kept bleeding for about a half hour. But it looks like he fell and crawled some. He didn't die until he took the one in the head."

"The rest were in anger," Ankles said, glancing at Danny. "Looks to me like a forty-five caliber. A vet's gun, maybe. Some kid's older brother's maybe, just home from Nam."

Danny swallowed. He remembered taking his brother's Nam-issue .45 from Brendan's army footlocker the night before. *Jesus Christ,* he wondered, *did I use it? Did I kill the son of bitch? Did I shoot Boar's Head? Could I actually have killed a cop?*

Danny had almost no memory of the later part of the previous night. He recalled only bits of the early evening: dressing in his old raggedy bell-bottom jeans, John Jay High sweatshirt, his scuffed brown Frye boots, and his army jacket. He remembered taking Brendan's gun from his father's apartment, gulping shots of Hennessey cognac for balls, planning on meeting Boar's Head here on Hippie Hill at two A.M. He remembered thinking that he might even kill him if he couldn't reason with him. Because Boar's Head wouldn't miss one meal if he killed Danny. The way he didn't skip a bite over killing Wally Fortune. Maybe even Wally's sister, Mary.

But the night before, somewhere between his crash pad on Fifteenth Road and Hippie Hill, Danny had stepped through an unseen door into an inky void. A memory vacuum. And because of the total blackout he had no alibi. *What the hell did I take?* he thought. *Goofballs? Acid? Thorazine? Booze? All of the above? Think! Jesus Christ, try to remember. Where the fuck did I get these new clothes?*

Danny closed his eyes. He tried to squeeze memory out of the wrinkles of his brain. But all he could see was that blinding beam of light. Like the cone of light in the Bosch painting. That kind of amorphous memory. There were no concrete images. No memory of doing anything good or bad. Just a complete blank. Just that white light. Then total blackness. Nothing else until Ankles dragged him off his bare mattress on the floor and out of the dreamless abyss at a little past six A.M. and told him he was the prime suspect in the murder of Vito fucking Malone, who also happened to be the father of Erika Malone, Danny Cassidy's first love, and the girl he knew would be his last love.

Danny watched Mackin hand Ankles two plastic evidence bags filled with thousands of amphetamines, Seconals, meth, LSD tabs,

THC capsules. Danny's eyes widened; he licked his lips with a cottony tongue. Ankles did a quick eyeball estimate. "Maybe ten Gs street value," he said.

"These were in his coat pockets," said Mackin, handing him two rolls of hundred-dollar bills bound with rubber bands.

"Thicker than a thoroughbred's prick," Ankles said.

"And this here. . . ."

Danny watched the cop hand Ankles another plastic baggie containing a small .22-caliber handgun. "This was in his left hand," the cop said. "Serial numbers drilled out and burnt with acid so it can't be raised in a lab. It looks to me like a . . ."

"I know a fuckin' drop gun when I see one, Mackin," said Ankles, referring to an untraceable gun crooked cops sometimes planted on suspects or at crime scenes to frame suspects or shift blame away from themselves. At thirty-seven, Ankles was ten years older than the other cop, and a detective for nine of them. Danny watched Ankles widen his eyes, re-creating the crime to Mackin as he paced the outline of the corpse. "Malone was here to kill somebody. Maybe over drugs. Maybe over something bigger. Like Wally Fortune's murder. Maybe here to kill a witness to that earlier murder. But that dealer, or that witness, that somebody, killed him first. Which means Malone had to know him, too. In order to get that close. To take one right in his face like that. This was personal. The last thing Malone saw alive was his own murderer. Or someone killing him in self-defense. Too scared to stick around and try to explain away a cop killing."

"Didn't you have a beef with Malone once? Coldcock him over something?"

"That was personal and a long time ago," Ankles said. "He's still a dead cop on my stomping ground."

Ankles stared at Danny, who watched, listened, and shivered, wiping a frozen diamond of mucus from the tip of his nose. "And whoever it was wasn't satisfied with one in the head," Ankles said. "They wanted to kill him a few times. One in his head, one in his chest, one in his balls, even. Whoever did this wanted him to die in pieces. Personal. Without a doubt, someone he knew."

Jack Davis, Malone's partner, arrived on the scene, parking a BMW in the parking lot down from Hippie Hill. "Corruption-mobile," Danny heard Ankles mumble to Mackin. Davis was dressed in faded jeans with frayed hems, dry-cleaned and starch-pressed with a razor crease; brown Italian boots; and an expensive skintight leather bomber jacket. He wore his hair in a shag cut that Danny recognized as the one invented by a Brooklyn guy named Tony Rossi in Paul McGreggor's salon in the East Village.

"Couldn't have taken Davis two hours to drive in from Mill Basin," Ankles said to Mackin. "Probably talked to a PBA lawyer first."

"When a dirty cop is found murdered it never looks good for the partner," Mackin said.

"Or maybe he hadda convince his wife to bring the deed to the house to a bail bondsman," Ankles said.

In the interim Ankles had rousted Danny Cassidy from his skanky hippie crash pad mattress. Before leaving the crash pad, Ankles had let Danny take a piss. With his LSD-heightened aural sense he'd overheard Ankles and another cop mumbling, discussing Davis's personnel folder: married, two kids—girl, five, boy, three—house, and a boat on Mill Basin. Second place in the Poconos. Some good arrests in Bed Stuy, Bushwick, East New York. Now working undercover narco for Brooklyn South. Partners with Malone for two years, lots of arrests but mostly nickel-and-dime. Ankles had said, "Behind every cop's second house there is a crime."

Now Danny watched Davis mope up Hippie Hill from a BMW. He recognized him. He'd been there the night Wally Fortune was murdered. Davis was about five-eight, with an overdeveloped upper body, like he was trying to make up with biceps and pectorals what nature had denied him in height. "Lift enough fucking dumbbells, you become one," Ankles said. Mackin snickered. Davis walked stiff-legged, his big arms extended away from his sides, moving like a statue on wheels. He reminded Danny of a robot toy called Garloo that he'd once gotten for Christmas. "I got no time for fucking around," Ankles said. "I'm going for his jugular."

Davis squished toward Malone's body, his handsome face sloping to horror, trying to control his gag reflex with desperate little breaths. Ankles nodded to Davis and said, "So, who had the six-shot hard-on for your partner?"

"It was my night off," Davis said. "Believe me, I'll find out who did this."

"This is my case. You, you're under the lamp."

Davis glanced at Danny in the backseat of the Plymouth Fury, his eyes skittering. "You arrest the kid?"

"Not yet," Ankles said. "But he's a treasure trove of information, Davis. Speed freak. Never stops talking, like a fuckin' ticker tape machine. Talks about all kinds of stuff. He yakked all about Apollo 12 landing on the moon last night. What's with you fuckin' guys and the moon, anyway? The last time someone was murdered in the park was July 20 when Armstrong took his lunar stroll. And that kid over there saw what happened that night. And he's talking about it. Second moon walk, second murder. Fuckin' loony, you ask me."

Ankles dangled the drugs and money in front of Davis. He didn't show him the drop gun. Yet.

"Speaking of loony, you know anything about this crazy shit?" Ankles asked.

"No," Davis said, his nervous eyes darting to Danny again. "Vito was probably after someone big. He was always looking to make the big score. He was tired of rousting two-cent hippies."

Ankles, who had earned his gold shield by working five tough years undercover in narcotics, knew the value of street drugs. He also knew the temptation they presented to cops who loved the power and respect of the badge but resented scrounging by on a cop's shitty salary.

Ankles knew that the NYPD narcotics division would have no record of Malone ever vouchering out this many drugs and that kind of money for a buy-and-bust operation. Not for working a small-potatoes target like Hippie Hill, this scroungy grassy knoll just inside the mouth of Prospect Park at Veteran's Memorial Square in Prospect Gardens.

"Between the cash and dope, must be twenty-five large here," Ankles said. "Or about nine grand more than Malone's annual salary. Maybe enough to keep up the payments on his nice brownstone, his Caddy, and to keep his beautiful wife in furs and jewels, and a juicy college fund for his beautiful daughter. Who just happens to be swiping that skelly Cassidy kid's joint, which couldn't have made Vito a very happy Papa Bear."

"What are you insinuating?" Davis said, a clicking sound coming from deep in his throat. He tried clearing it. But Danny heard it continue to click like the clicker Sister Kevin Therese used to use to make kids stand and kneel during First Holy Communion practice up in Blessed Virgin Mary.

"Davis, I'm a cop, you're a cop; stop gagging on the truth here," Ankles said. "This kind of fuckin' cash and weight would have a lieutenant attached to it. There would be a backup team following every dime. Nobody here on Hippie fuckin' Hill had thirty-five extra cents to buy a slice of Mom's pizza never mind this kind of weight. Hippie Hill is a collection of out-of-work skells, long-haired mopes who strum guitars, toss Frisbees, and fuck like minks when they're stoned. They're all assholes. Kids. Or adults who never grew up. Maybe a few aging Greenwich Village beatnik types who might have pushed a little grass, five-dollar bags and a few joints. Maybe an O-Z here, another ounce there, and a couple of Pilgrim State outpatients who sold acid one tab at a time and their prescription Thorazine to take kids down from bad trips. But there ain't a big-time hard-drug dealer among them. And only the real desperados are even still around this time of year, harmless homegrown bums with no place to even eat Thanksgiving. And none of them had the reason, the inclination or the motherfuckin' balls to kill a cop, Davis. Even a dirty one."

"Somebody did," Davis said.

"You're a fucking marvel of observation, Davis," Ankles said, pointing at Malone's body. "A real fuckin' bloodhound. Figurin' all that out on your own, like."

"Hey, watch your mouth, Ankles, I don't let nobody talk to me like that—"

"Somebody offed your fuckin' partner, Davis, " Ankles said. "Use the muscle between your fuckin' ears to tell me who. Because, the way this is gonna look when Captain Bush gets IAD involved is that this money, this dope, it came from somewhere very D-I-R-T-Y. The badge on your kid's cowboy hat will be worth more than yours if you don't have good fucking answers. And my guess is you don't have any good answers. Malone was the brain; you were the horse-flesh. He was your rabbi. He shitted his way through the PD. He could walk you through walls. He could con his way out of quicksand. But you, Davis, you can't bench-press your way outta this. Malone's dead. Murdered. This is dope and dirty money, buddy. Headline news. You're his partner. You both ran hard. Big dough from lowlifes. But the fuckin' run is over. His blood is on your hands. So stop dickin' around and tell me: Where'd Malone get the weight? And what about this drop gun? Who the fuck was he gonna use it on?"

Ankles dangled the drop gun in front of Davis as the morgue crew from Kings County Hospital arrived. "And what does it all have to do with the murder of Wally Fortune last July 20?" he asked the stunned Davis. "The murder that kid over there knows all about. The one he's gonna sing through his nose about like another Bob Dylan on the stand."

Danny's heart raced as Davis glanced at him like a desperate man in a steel trap. Davis swallowed hard. His eyes skitted to Malone's corpse, to the bloody grass, and back to Ankles. *Doomed*, Danny thought. *Just like me.*

"I was you, Davis, I'd start singing myself," Ankles said. "The way it looks right now, those kids of yours—you ain't gonna be there to help them blow out any birthday candles until they're in their thirties."

As the sun poked through the sky, Danny thought Davis was starting to look more like a suspect himself than a cop.

"Talk to me, brain box," Ankles said. "A detective making sixteen Gs with two kids can't even afford that hairdo and the boots never mind the house and the boat. Your only hope is to turn state's."

Davis gazed at Malone, who looked even more grotesque in the hard unforgiving light of morning, his blood-drained face an arctic blue, the sun refracting in the shiny arterial purple bullet hole in his forehead. Davis shivered, blinking, glancing at Danny, his frosted breath spurting from his nose like an old horse's.

As Danny watched Davis tremble, gaping at the morgue guys covering his partner's face and loading him onto a gurney, he felt sorry for him. He knew Davis was a dirty, corrupt cop, that he shared responsibility for Wally Fortune's murder—maybe Mary Fortune's, too—but he still felt sorry for him. The guy had a wife and little kids. . . .

"Davis, listen to me. You're a big muscle-bound guy," Ankles said. "But I don't think you're mentally built for all of this."

"You have any kids, Tufano?"

Ankles was rattled by the question. He didn't answer. Danny thought Davis looked even more frightened now.

"Look, I think Malone found out that the Cassidy kid knew about Fortune," Ankles said. "That maybe he even witnessed it. But the kid had a very good reason not to dime on Malone because he was his girlfriend's old man. So maybe Malone planned to meet Cassidy here last night. Maybe he was gonna off the kid, the way he offed Wally Fortune, right here in Prospect Park. See, I think Fortune also knew Malone was dirty. So Malone wasted him. And you were there.

Which would make you an accomplice to a murder, wouldn't it, Davis?"

Ankles paused as Davis grimaced at the sound of the word, taking two steps backward, gulping for air like a drowning man.

"Some word that, *murder*, ain't it, Davis," Ankles said, sensing he'd hit a raging nerve. " 'Specially when you're accused of it. In some ways it's worse than being the victim. Every letter of the word—M-U-R-D-E-R—eats at you every waking hour of every day. Like cancer, chewing you up inside. All you hear, think, eat, piss, shit, and breathe is M-U-R-D-E-R. At night, head on the pillow, all you think about is M-U-R-D-E-R. And if you can't sleep, instead of sheep, you count the times nothing-left-to-lose-lifers will try to M-U-R-D-E-R a cop in the can. And so maybe Malone decided he was gonna murder the Cassidy kid to keep him from ever talking about what he knew about the Wally Fortune murder. How the fuck could he let some little skinny speed freak like that over there in the back-seat of my car hold his life in his hand? So he planned on icing him. But maybe the Cassidy kid got to Malone first."

"No way that kid could take out Vito Malone," Davis said, his voice growing high-pitched.

"Well, I'm gonna keep talking to that Cassidy kid," Ankles said. "And if he knows what I think he knows, well, we both know what that means to you, Jack. IAD will be taking a very hard look at how you bought that fifty-thousand-dollar house in Mill Basin, with the boat dock, the swimming pool. They'll learn whether you paid cash for the boat tied to the dock. And the BMW and the red Fiat con-vertible in the driveway. Oh, and for the place in the Poconos. The place where you keep the pickup and the motorcycles and maybe where you take your broads for fuck-a-thon weekends when your wife thinks you're off hunting with the fellas. So, you wanna tell me what you know, Davis? My advice? Turn state's. Tell me who you and Malone were dealing all this weight for. Tell me all about Wally Fortune. Tell me about the Cassidy kid. And I'll help you cut a deal with the DA. You might get man two—ten years, out in seven. Maybe even five."

Davis looked deep into Ankles's eyes. "You know what they'd do to a cop and a rat in prison," Davis said, his baby-blue eyes unable to hold a stare with Ankles. "I can't have my kids growing up visiting me in the joint, where I put a hundred skells."

"They'll put you in Punk City, not general pop," Ankles said.

"Spare your wife and kids a messy trial. Go for a deal. Cop a plea. Fall on the grenade. It'll be a one-week story in the papers. Then history. You'll still be in your forties when you get out."

"I'm no angel," Davis said, looking Ankles deep in the eye. "But I heard plenty of talk about you and a bastard kid with another guy's wife. A war hero's woman. And I never laid a hand on a prisoner in my career. Never once. Which is something you can't say. So don't act so damned high and mighty, Tufano. And don't worry about my kids. Jack Davis's kids'll never have to visit him in jail."

Danny watched Ankles's eyes fill with rage. His fists balled. But he said nothing. He tossed away the nub of his cigar. "Cop a plea," Ankles said one last time. "Turn state's."

"Fuck you," Davis said.

Davis lurched down Hippie Hill toward the parking lot, the big arms dangling at his side like ballast. He stopped and stared right into Danny's eyes. Danny's heart pounded as Davis clutched the handle of his gun, which was jammed into his belt.

"Sorry, kid," Davis said, pulling out the pistol and stealing a glance at lifeless Vito Malone.

"Davis!" Danny heard Ankles shout. "Drop the fucking gun, Davis!"

Danny cowered, held up his hands for protection. He saw Ankles whip out his own service revolver and aim it at Davis. "Davis!" But Davis never turned. He descended the rest of the hill like a man resigned to walking a plank into shark-infested waters. He climbed into his BMW.

"No, Davis! *No!*" Ankles screamed as he raced down Hippie Hill, passing Danny, skidding in Malone's blood and the mud.

Then Danny watched Davis power down the driver's window, spit, and take a deep gulp of cold air. Then Danny watched Davis take a pair of dangling rosaries from the rearview mirror and loop them around his neck. He heard Davis turn Jimi Henrdix's "Purple Haze" up full blast on his stereo tape deck system. Davis spit again and powered up his driver's window, locked the door, leaned his head back onto the leather headrest, and closed his eyes tight. Then Danny saw a powder blue Plymouth station wagon pull off Park Drive into the lot and approach the BMW, horn honking. A pretty blond woman sat in the front seat next to a bald middle-aged man in a business suit. Two very young kids, a boy and a girl, sat in the backseat. The station wagon pulled abreast of the BMW, the pretty woman driver still honking the horn to get Davis's attention. But Danny knew Davis could not hear the horn. Or Ankles's pleas. Hendrix drowned out his desperate world outside.

"No!" Ankles shouted again, running down Hippie Hill, his feet sliding in the wet grass, startling the crime-scene cops and the morgue crew as he tried to make it to the BMW. "No, Davis! No! Jesus Christ, Davis, no! Your wife! Your kids! No, Davis. . . ."

Danny watched Davis make the sign of the cross with the barrel of his .38-caliber service revolver. And as Davis's wife leaned on the horn and turned to try to shield the kids in the backseat from view, Danny watched Davis push the muzzle of the .38 to his temple. He saw him mouth the lyrics, "Excuse me, while I kiss the sky!" Danny watched him squeeze the trigger while Jimi Hendrix, Davis's thick wet brain, and the closed windows muffled the sound of the shot to a small pop. Danny saw a large amoeba of blood splatter against the driver's window like the design of a tie-dyed shirt, obscuring Davis from sight. Danny spun his head and gaped at the horrified wife and kids in the pale blue station wagon. Gun smoke billowed inside the BMW.

And as "Purple Haze" thumped into the cold morning, Danny Cassidy knew that Ankles was right: The sixties were now over.

# one

After four loud rings he lifted the receiver, mumbled hello, and then Danny heard a gruff voice say, "Your father's dead."

Eleven months before, on his forty-ninth birthday, Danny Cassidy had decided that before he turned fifty he would stop running. He had lived like a fugitive for thirty-two years. Haunted, rather than hunted, he always expected a knock on the door in the middle of the night—followed by handcuffs, trial, jail.

Maybe even the death penalty for killing a cop.

With the sixth decade of his life looming, Danny Cassidy was no longer going to skulk through life looking over his shoulder, afraid of the ghosts of 1969. He was determined to confront the nightmare of that year head-on before he turned the proverbial big five-oh.

But even with that commitment made, Danny had procrastinated most of his forty-ninth year. He got up each morning in his one-bedroom apartment in West Hollywood, determined that this would be the day he would take the old knapsack out of the big trunk in the back of the closet and confront the year that had ended in horror—a year from which he had been on the lam ever since.

But as Labor Day approached, he still hadn't opened the trunk, still hadn't worked up the balls to take out the knapsack, which he'd carted across the country and through the decades, and once and for all piece together the broken shards of his life.

The dirty canvas knapsack was what most of the hippies in the late sixties called a head bag, carried on the shoulder and covered in peace signs and smart-ass protest buttons. Danny had carried his head bag through all of 1969 in Brooklyn—filled with Bambu rolling papers; hash pipes; roach clips; pill boxes; incense; eight-track tapes of Dylan, Donovan, and the Doors; a copy of Francois Villion's collected poems; and a trade paperback on the life of Hieronymus Bosch, replete with color plates of the Flemish master's nightmarish paintings.

There were also several handwritten letters from Danny's older brother, Brendan, written from Vietnam, and eleven marble-design copybooks, one for each month of 1969 through November, which served as Danny Cassidy's detailed and drug-addled journals of the worst year of his life.

To Danny the head bag was the decade itself, sealed in a trunk like a vampire in his coffin. He was afraid of opening it and releasing the monster that used to be Danny Cassidy.

Now in his forty-ninth year, Danny found that the phone call about his father sent him skipping through time, forever changing his life.

"What did you say?" Danny said, reaching past the digital clock that said it was 4:59 A.M., for the pack of Vantage.

"I said your old man bought the farm," said the now familiar voice of Ankles Tufano. "Sorry, kid."

Danny hadn't seen Ankles in over thirty years but every two or three years, always on November 21, the anniversary of Vito Malone's unsolved murder, Danny would receive a long-distance phone call from him. Just a dirty little middle-of-the-night-piss call to let Danny Cassidy know that there was still an open homicide file on Ankles's desk—and that Danny's name was still in that file as the prime suspect.

Ankles reminded Danny again that there was no statute of limitations on murder. Every time he called, Ankles said he had every intention of solving this case before he retired. He would ask Danny to come back to Brooklyn to cooperate. Danny would always refuse, and then Ankles would tell him that he always knew where he was, what he was doing, and whom he was doing it with. Just a shout-out to tilt Danny's life off-kilter, to keep him from ever having a good night's sleep.

Danny tried to live a low-key, normal existence, but Ankles popped out of the past every once in a while just to add melodrama and angst and uncertainty to his life. Just enough of an intrusion to keep Danny smoking, eating junk food, suffering from insomnia and an occasional case of hives. It helped wreck his marriage and helped strain his relationship with his only daughter, Darlene. The calls from Ankles were out of a past that kept him distracted enough so that he could never break out of the grind of the daily newspaper life into the broader world of the novel, movies, or theater. He chose to stay under the radar, afraid that any kind of high-profile success or fame would add heat to the old murder case. Years ago he even switched from the hard-news beat of the front of the paper to middle-of-the-book entertainment features, just so he wouldn't have to cover homicides, which always caused him to turn the blood-stained soil of his own past. He even turned down most freelance magazine assignments, except for occasionally agreeing to write a short story for one of the skin mags, and always under an assumed name.

With 1969 always simmering like a low-grade fever in his veins, Danny developed a kind of ADD that kept him from concentrating on anything longer than a newspaper article. Any writing that required sustained concentration shattered into bloody images, fragmented flashbacks, thoughts of a fierce but ruined first love. Sometimes a song triggered one of these unsettling episodes. Or a movie. Or a TV or radio broadcast reference to 1969. Sometimes a newspaper story about an old sixties radical like Brinks robbery suspect Kathy Boudin, or anti–Vietnam war firebomber Howard Mechanic or Symbionese Liberation Army would-be bomber Kathleen Soliah being busted after decades on the run made Danny too nervous to sleep. Even prosecutions he applauded scared him, like the arrest in the murder of the four children in a Mississippi church bombing that was prompted by Spike Lee's documentary *Four Little Girls.* Or the indictment of the mayor of Yorkville, Pennsylvania, for a race-motivated murder dating back to 1969.

But most times his fears were in direct response to the occasional phone calls from Ankles.

What made the anxiety worse was that after three decades he just couldn't *remember* whether or not he'd done the murder. He was so stoned on drugs and booze that long-ago night that he'd suffered a total blackout. The night of November 20 was like a page from an FBI file with all the important sections Magic-Markered out.

Danny once even paid for a private lie detector test that came up as inconclusive. Try as he might with the help of shrinks and hypnotists in the years since, Danny could bubble up no memory of that awful night. He read once that a killer lived inside of every man. *But am I a* murderer, Danny wondered.

Now, as he approached fifty, he decided that even a yes answer would be better than not knowing.

But there was never any solid indictable proof that he *was* the killer. He might have had motive, means, and opportunity, but there were no witnesses, no smoking gun, and not one shred of forensic evidence—not enough to arrest or convict Danny at the time, or in the years since. The dead cop had been dirty, so from the beginning NYPD tried to downplay the case, hadn't put on the usual cop-killer full-court press. An embarrassment. But Ankles had never given up. He had never even liked the dead cop in question, but the murder had happened on his watch, on his stomping ground, and ever since it had nagged him like a dent in his otherwise flawless gold shield.

After Danny witnessed Malone's partner, Jack Davis, kill himself in front of his wife and kids, he hit the road, facing possible jail. Danny never returned to Brooklyn. He ran from that night, that year, that Brooklyn neighborhood, and that dead cop. He ran from a fractured family, a shit father, a dead mother, and a first love. And he ran from that murder, across the decades, across a continent.

Now he was being confronted with it again in his bachelor pad on Sweetzer Avenue in West Hollywood.

"Who is this?" Danny asked, pretending he didn't recognize Ankles's unmistakable voice.

"You know who this is," Ankles said. "Don't play fucking games, Danny. Big-city reporter. Married. Divorced. Kid in Harvard. Fifty-six hundred and change in the bank. Over twenty large in debt. Turning fifty next month—"

"Which gotta make you seventy."

"Sixty-nine," Ankles said.

"I thought NYPD gave you the mummy walk," Danny said.

Danny knew that after his NYPD mandatory retirement at age sixty-five Ankles had signed on as an investigator at the Brooklyn District Attorney's Office, the elephants' graveyard where a lot of old detectives too active for Florida golf went to beef up their city pensions.

"How . . . Why do you know all this about me, Ankles?"

"What, I'm too fuckin' stupid to use a computer? Even before computers, I knew where you were every day, all these years. From Boston to Fort Myers to Vegas to Los Angeles. Your ex-wife got a guy living with her in the house you bought. Your daughter is doing great in school, needs help with math, though. You work out every day in Gold's Gym, pumping iron. Maybe you wanna make sure you're in shape when I snap the cuffs on you. You should cut down on the smokes, though; they banned them in prisons in New York State. Your eye doctor says you need prescription glasses now. But you never got them filled. Not on your lousy medical insurance anyway."

"Why are you calling me now?" Danny asked, his mouth dry, his palms damp, his heart thumping, biting a smoke out of the pack, switching on the green desk lamp on his wooden night table, pulling on a pair of nonprescription magnifier glasses with a 200 intensity. He was ready for 250s. "It's the day before Labor Day weekend, Ankles. You're not due to call and pester me till November 21. My old man was nothing to you."

"Your voice sounds a little high-pitched, there, Danny," Ankles said. "Nervous? Palms sweaty? Heart pounding, pal? Mouth dry? Reaching for your first smoke of the day? Bet your asshole's puckering, too, like it will be in a jailhouse shower. These tough young cons love turning middle-aged baby boomers into jailhouse Maytags. Washing socks and sucking cocks."

Ankles laughed as Danny lit a Vantage with a match from a Hamburger Hamlet matchbook. "Still smoking, huh?" Ankles said. "Me, I quit. I intend to keep collecting my pension for twenny years after I clean up this last piece of unfinished business."

"Unless you got something else to say I'm gonna hang up," Danny said.

"Look, I thought you might have enough class to come home and bury your old man. And we could talk. Clear some things up."

"What did he die of?"

"Whadda you give a shit? You haven't spoken to him in over thirty fuckin' years."

"Did someone hurt him?"

"Nah," Ankles said. "Who'd kill him? Just a neighborhood guy, veteran of the forgotten war. Widower. The only enemies he had were his two sons. And his liver."

"Where is he now?" Danny blew out a stream of smoke, hacked.

"Drawer nineteen, Kings County morgue with a tag five-six-seven-two on his toe. I called Dunne's planter to go get him. I know he got a plot next your mother in Evergreen. He bragged about owning it whenever he had his lump on up in Foley's. All he owned at the end was his goddamned grave. Some fuckin' legacy."

"Foley's Bar, Dunne's Funeral Home. Out of another life."

"One keeps the other in business," Ankles said. "But Dunne's needs a family member to sign the papers, and a check."

"That neighborhood is a time warp."

"Lotta changes, Danny, but a lotta things are still here," Ankles said. "Fact, front of me on my desk, there's a thirty-two-year-old file folder on a homicide. Still open. Like his daughter Erika's legs always were for you."

Danny's heart fluttered at the sound of the name: *Er-i-ka*. Her flag-waving father picked the name because it rhymed with Amer-i-ca. All these years later, Danny had never gotten over her. *And Ankles is wrong,* he thought. *The funny part is she was a virgin in a time when young people shared sex like a hash pipe.* But not Erika. Not sweet, beautiful, brilliant, sexy, wacky Erika. Erika, in her skintight hip-hugger bell-bottoms with the Native American–design stitching on all the seams and hems. Erika was such a noncon- formist that in the hedonistic free-love summer of Woodstock she thought it was rebellious to stay clean, sober, and a virgin. Erika had her innocence stolen from her on one awful, bloody night, only months before her father was also robbed from her. Erika, he thought, was another very big piece of unfinished business. *Christ almighty, I might've murdered her father.*

"Maybe Vito Malone didn't want a skinny long-haired speed freak like you porking his daughter," Ankles said. "And there was that business about Wally Fortune, and maybe he wanted to whack you, but you got to him first."

"You run the same spiel every time we talk, Ankles," Danny said. "You having a senior moment, or what? Find a new case. I didn't kill Vito Malone. And I was smashed the night Wally Fortune was mur- dered."

"That's what you say now," Ankles said. "That's what you said then. But I always suspected you don't even know for sure. Maybe you just hope that's true. You were so shit-faced that night—on your uppies, acid, booze, Dristan inhalers, and maybe a few Seconals. All that shit you freaks shoved down your throat, in your nose, up in your ass, and in your arm—you have no fuckin' idea if you killed him or not. And that's why you never stepped foot in Brooklyn since. You've been run- ning from that night, and that murder, ever since you were eighteen. You may be turning fifty, but you're still a scared little kid, Cassidy."

"I never used a needle."

"Congratulations, Mr. Clean, but guess what?" Ankles said, without skipping a groove in his rant. "The state can use one now. For cop killers."

"So what is this?" Danny asked. "A courtesy call about my father's death or an interrogation about a thirty-year-old murder? You want to grill me, I'll get a lawyer."

"I liked your old man," Ankles said. "He fought for his country, he worked for a living, he paid his fuckin' taxes that helped pay my salary. He minded his business. . . ."

*He drove my brother to that dirty fucking war,* Danny thought, still as cold about his father as the day he'd left. *Which drove my mother into her grave at forty-two.*

"Call me old-fashioned," Ankles said, "but I want to see an old neighborhood soldier get a proper send-off."

"I don't mourn his death," Danny said. "But my mother would have. So I'll come and bury him next to my mother. So *she* can rest in peace."

"You're all fuckin' heart, pal," Ankles said. "Call your brother. Last I checked, which was last month, he was still living in Saigon, teaching English and American history to Coca-Cola workers."

"Are you going to leave me alone when I come back?"

"Nah. As a matter of fact, I've built enough circumstantial evidence over the years to at long last sell this one to my boss here at the Brooklyn DA's office. No one wanted an arrest on this in the old days because the trial would have been too embarrassing for the PC and the mayor. It was better left unsolved. But since then the cliché is that they can indict a ham sandwich. In fact, a famous judge coined that line. He was later indicted himself for stalking a teenage girl. So indicting you now, in my boss's election year, will be easier than indicting a ladyfinger. It'll be sexy in a close race. My boss would love the headlines about indicting a big-city reporter for a thirty-two-year-old cop killing, whether he can convict you or not. The trial won't come up until after the election anyway. And the only profession John Q. Voter hates more than lawyers is the press. It's a win-win for him. It's a no-lose for me. Except I believe in a fair ball game. I don't wanna retire with any doubts in my head. I don't want someone reopening your case and proving me wrong. And if you get convicted, I don't wanna see an innocent man behind bars, even if you are a dickhead."

"Why are you telling me all this now? If you're going to give the case to the DA to bring to a grand jury, what would stop me from running to South America?"

"Because you love your daughter," he said. "For her alone you'll want to clear your name instead."

"You're still convinced after all these years that I did it," Danny said.

"Convince me you didn't and I'll leave you alone, Danny," Ankles said. "A little cooperation, even thirty-and-change years late, can open or close a door."

"Look, Ankles—"

"Jeez . . . no one's called me that in twenty years," he said.

Danny remembered the six-foot-three cop had gotten the nick-name as a uniform cop and later with the Youth Squad when he used to roust the beer-drinking hooligans in the neighborhood, kicking them in the ankles with his size-14s, confiscating their six-packs. After a night of an Ankles rampage half the kids along the parkside of Prospect Gardens hobbled and limped home, often side-lined for an entire weekend. If they fucked up a second time, they wouldn't be able to outrun him. It was how Ankles maintained order on his beat.

Now the old cop had outgrown the nickname he once cherished. Time changed everything.

"If you can't remember your name, go ask the nurse, she'll know what it is."

"There's nothing funny about M-U-R-D-E-R," Ankles said. "In fact, you should know, a DT named O'Rourke from the Cold-Case Squad is working this case, too. Asking all over the place about you. Ready to try to make a sale on this one to my boss come Tuesday morning. I'd sort of resent CCS breaking this case instead of me after all these years. So I'm ready to beat them to the punch. But how come you never tried to find out who did it, if it wasn't you? So I'm not convinced it wasn't. My advice, come back, bury your old man, help me piece together that night, and convince me not to dump my file on my boss's desk on Tuesday morning. Otherwise you'll be dealing with a young, hungry cold-case cop looking to nail you regardless of the truth just for a cheap promotion."

Danny sat in silence, imagining another young cop burning the midnight oil trying to put him in the can. Danny had always hoped the case might die with Ankles. Now some new son of a bitch would haunt him to the grave.

"So that's why you called me this time . . . you want my help after all these years of making me feel like a piece of shit. Look, I'm too old for this sixties nonsense, Ankles. Like you said, I'm gonna be fifty, and you're ready for mothballs. But OK, I'll be back to bury my father. Maybe I can put 1969 in the ground with him. If I learn any-thing new in those few days, you'll be first to know."

"I'm gonna cling to you like ringworm," Ankles said.

"I'd like some answers, too," Danny said. "Once and for all."

"No matter how the chips fall?"

"Yeah."

"You ready for her, too?"

"Who?"

"Erika Malone," Ankles said, and Danny's heart thumped again, remembering the long red hair, the skintight bell-bottom jeans that fit like another epidermis, the Catholic high school uniform.

"I hear she still comes around once in a while, to visit her mother. The old lady still lives in the same brownstone on Garvey Place."

Danny was silent for a long moment.

"Some things don't change," Ankles said.

"I have," Danny said and hung up.

# two

Danny called Sue Newberg, his managing editor at the *Los Angeles Chronicle,* and told her he had to take a one-week funeral leave.

"I'm sorry to hear but this couldn't have come at a worse time, Danny," she said. "They're in the middle of drawing up a list here. Like every other newspaper in America, we're downsizing. They're offering buyouts to everyone who will be fifty by the end of the year. Those who don't take them might be laid off anyway. I'm fighting like crazy to keep you off that list, Danny. For selfish reasons. I like your work. I like your work better than I like you. But you've taken so many fucking sabbaticals and bullshit sick leaves over the years, man . . . for books you never finished, for your goddamned divorce, to try to mend fences with your daughter . . . your work is great, one of the best writers on the paper. But on a bean counter's list you come off as a high-priced malingerer. Now you tell me your father died. You told me you didn't even have a father."

"Well, we didn't talk in thirty-two years, but somebody's gotta bury him, Sue."

"OK, by all means, go home, bury your dad. But my advice is, get your ass back here on Wednesday morning. I can't fudge it more than that. Not a single day. And to be honest with you, Danny, if you lose this job, I don't know where a guy like you finds work in this business at your age anymore."

"Thanks, Sue."

"And when you come back get a pair of real fucking glasses, will you," she said. "While you still have medical insurance. You're a half a century old. Admit you need them. Admit you're old. Get your shit in order."

She hung up.

Then Danny tried calling his brother at the Coca-Cola office in Saigon. An Asian clerk who spoke broken English with a Brooklyn accent said Brendan Cassidy was in Japan for two days. But he took Danny's detailed message about their father's death and funeral. Nice accent, Danny thought. Must be one of Brendan's students.

Then Danny called Dunne's funeral parlor in Brooklyn and made arrangements to have his father's body collected from Kings County for a two-day wake in Dunne's, a funeral mass in Blessed Virgin Mary, and burial in Evergreen Cemetery on Tuesday. The funeral director said there were no burials on holidays. She also said Dunne's would place an announcement in the *Daily News* so that his father's friends and family would know about the wake. Danny thanked her, hung up, and booked a coach seat on the American Airlines red-eye into LaGuardia.

As he packed for the funeral he felt an eerie coldness like Meursault in Albert Camus's *The Stranger,* which he hadn't read since high school. Danny couldn't summon a nickel's worth of loss or dread or remorse or grief over his father's death. Not even pity for the lonesome end of the man who helped give him life. His father had caused too much pain, done too much harm, helped end his mother's life much too young.

Danny packed a small carry-on bag.

He dialed a number in the 617 area code. He heard Darlene's voice on an answering machine say she was away white-water rafting until Sunday and was unavailable at the moment. Danny left a message saying that her grandfather, whom Darlene had never met, had died. He said he didn't expect her to come down to Brooklyn for the funeral, but that if she were looking for him, Danny would be staying in the new Marriott Hotel in Downtown Brooklyn until Tuesday, when his father would be buried. "And if you need any extra dough for a math tutor, let me know," he said. "Love ya, pussycat."

Then Danny walked to the hall closet and pulled out the old steamer trunk and opened the lock with a key he kept on his key chain. He removed the musty old green canvas head bag, dangled it from one hand. It was heavy, a good seven pounds. Inside was his past. Inside was his future. Inside was Brooklyn 1969.

He sat in a window seat as the plane sailed east over the Rockies. He lifted the head bag from under the seat in front of him. The middle seat of the row was vacant and on the aisle a pretty, frosted-haired woman, about thirty, wearing a cream-colored pants suit, sat tapping on a PalmPilot. Her perfume was subtle. She was as clean as a nun's bed. Danny noticed her watching him as he plopped the head bag onto his lap, opened the seat tray, and placed it on top.

Danny intended to use the fly time to Brooklyn to immerse himself in memories. Sue Newberg was right. He was going to be fifty. Time to get his shit in order. In order to do that he had to think clearly about events in his past. The head bag might help trigger some of the memories he needed to conjure up.

The yuppie woman glanced at the bag, looked back at her screen, and then did a double take of the peace signs and sixties slogans scrawled in Magic Marker on the dirty green canvas: HEY, HEY, LBJ, HOW MANY KIDS DID YOU KILL TODAY? WAR IS NOT HEALTHY FOR CHILDREN AND OTHER LIVING THINGS. NIXON SUCKS! HELL NO, WE WON'T GO! UP AGAINST THE WALL, MOTHERFUCKER! PULL OUT, LBJ—LIKE YOUR FATHER SHOULD HAVE! REMEMBER CHICAGO!

Pinned all over the bag were peace and love buttons, signs of the dove, and other faded and cracked buttons with more witticisms of the sixties: I AM A HUMAN BEING: DO NOT FOLD, SPINDLE, OR MUTILATE. DRACULA SUCKS! TUNE IN, TURN ON, DROP YOUR PANTS. DON'T TRUST ANYONE OVER 30.

His favorite button read: BELLY.

Whenever a chick had asked what it meant Danny said it was his belly button. It would get a laugh and he'd ask to see hers. Which sometimes led to getting laid.

Danny looked at the young woman, embarrassed by the corny slogans of yesteryear—every dead decade always seems corny in ret-rospect—and in the close quarters of the plane he recoiled from the rank smell emanating from the old bag. It stank of mold and must, a foul and dank odor like something dragged up from a tomb. The smell reminded him of dirty hallways, tenement cellars, and clammy nights on the paranoid speed-freak scrounge, the grubby, unwashed stench of that unromantic part of the sixties that had faded in Danny's memory but which now came wafting back.

The frosted-haired woman crinkled and rubbed her small cute nose, reached in her pocketbook for a Kleenex, and did a polite half blow. Danny looked at her and hefted the bag. "My kid's bag," he said. "She's an actress. It's a prop in a revival of *Hair.*"

"Oh," said the pretty woman, wiping her nose and returning to her work, which consisted of a series of debit and credit columns. *Bet she's drawing up a buyout list,* Danny thought, *for people turning fifty.* Then he laughed at himself and realized that the PalmPilot was the head bag of the new century. Yuppies carry them around with all the phone numbers and E-mail addresses that keep them stoned on the latest stock quotes, Dow and Nasdaq counts, inflation rates, consumer price indexes, forecasts from the Fed, 401-K and Roth IRA balances, quotes on all the money markets. And lists of aging baby boomers to be downsized.

Danny unfastened the two snaps on the head bag and opened the flap. He had opened it and rooted around inside it at home before leaving for the airport to make sure there were no drugs or weapons in the bag. There weren't. And the security guys at LAX had sent it through the X-ray machine without suspicion. But the smell from inside the bag was so strong that the woman squirmed in her seat as if she were being forced to sit through an exhumation. Danny reached in and pulled out a pair of love beads and a wad of cardboard concert ticket stubs held together with an old rubber band. The rubber band broke and crumbled as he unfastened it.

Danny pulled on his magnifiers and shuffled through the ticket stubs. Some were from Madison Square Garden, some from Forest Hills Arena, one or two from Lincoln Center, but most of them from the Fillmore East—the Doors; Poco; the Chambers Brothers; the Mothers of Invention; Cream; Blood, Sweat and Tears; Creedence Clearwater Revival; Country Joe and the Fish; Arlo Guthrie. He'd gone to every single one of those concerts with Erika. He fingered one from January 16, 1969: John Sebastian at Town Hall, four dollars. He took out the first of his eleven soft-backed marble-designed copybook journals, marked January 1969.

He leafed through the scratchy entries of the dog-eared copybook until he found a poem he had written to Erika Malone on the same day as the John Sebastian concert: Once you and I are at long last one / Your virgin blood will make kingdom come. . . .

It was something he'd tried hard to forget, but now he touched the concert ticket stubs and the poem, trying to resurrect the memories the way a bloodhound takes a scent from a piece of clothing and chases it. . . .

*January 11, 1969*

*Erika bounds down the steps of Blessed Virgin Mary at two-thirty P.M., her long wild auburn hair swinging, her tall lean body moving with a flawless confident grace. She rolls the waistband of her blue-and-gray-checked Blessed Virgin High uniform until the skirt is hoisted halfway up to her perfect little bubble ass that is kept hard and firm by her star status on the swimming and track and cheerleader teams. And from eating health food—vegetables, fresh fish, fruit, pasta, no meat. Danny is waiting a half-block away, hidden behind a lamppost so the nuns won't see him.*

*But before Erika reaches Danny she runs into Father O'Keefe, emerging like clockwork from his rectory, which Danny calls the "erectory" because the old rumpot priest has a perpetual boner for Erika. Father O'Keefe is a graying black Irishman in his late fifties, a notorious rummy, whom Danny knows from his altar-boy days, when O'Keefe would make him put vodka in the water and wine cruets before pouring them into his golden chalice at the daily six-fifteen A.M. mass. The booze gave him the courage to flirt with the young girls. These days O'Keefe always goes out of his way to stop and say hello and chat with Erika. Touching Erika's shoulders, arms, hands, sliding his nervous hand under her thick mane of hair, massaging her bare neck, and drawing her closer, whispering into her ear. Erika flirts right back. Knowing she's tantalizing the old priest, also aware that Danny is watching, as jealous of the man of cloth as he is of every other guy who dares look at Erika.*

*Danny walks Erika to the pizza parlor, buys her a slice and an orange juice, the only junk food she'll eat. And as they eat Danny gloats seeing the other envious neighborhood guys gape at him with the beautiful Erika at his side, throwing back her head, laughing at his jokes, whispering to him in her deep sexy voice that reminds him of Janis Joplin's.*

*Then he walks her home, double-timing to her family's brownstone on Garvey Place, between Eighth Avenue and Parkside West, her saddle shoes skipping along the sidewalks. He tells her about the tickets to the John Sebastian concert. She says she can't wait. He tells her about the latest books he's read, Jack Kerouac's* On the Road *and Capote's* In Cold Blood, *and how he loves both of them but how both writers hate each other.*

*Erika talks about biology, how one day diseases will be conquered when the genetic code of DNA is cracked. She stumps him with chemical formulas, abbreviations of the elements, math equations. Then as they approach her house, Danny smells her mother's simmering garlic floating through the windows that are half covered with shades bearing a print of American bald eagles. They enter the street door of the brownstone vestibule.*

*In Danny's mind this is a five-by-five-foot chamber of pure unadulterated sexual danger, the most erotic little cubicle on the planet.*

*Inside, with the street door closed and the inside house door locked, the two teenage lovers are alone. Safe from the world, enough raging hormones in this little box to melt the steel buckle on his belt. But on the other side of the house door is her mother, Angela, dark, Sicilian, still beautiful at forty-two, overprotective of her daughter. On the other side of them is the street door through which her cop father walks every day after work at 4:20 P.M.*

*Danny has never laid eyes on Erika's father, doesn't want to meet him, in case he ever recognizes him out in the street. Danny and Erika have never been caught together in the vestibule, but her mother almost always seems to lurch toward the house door just as Danny is about to come in his pants from a furious grinding dry-hump with Erika.*

*This episode in the Grindbox, as Erika calls it, starts much the way as all the others. Erika stands on her tiptoes, grabs Danny by the back of his hair, kisses his face, neck, ears. Danny runs his big hands over her small breasts, groping them through the sweater, his hands tracing the raised letters of BVM, and makes out with Erika, her tongue exploring the ridged roof of his mouth, the gully beneath his tongue, gliding over his perfect white teeth.*

*When she starts to simmer she sucks on his lips, kneading the bulging football muscles of his arms and shoulders and back. He knows this is a permission slip. Now he can go up under her sweater and blouse, to cop a hot fleshy feel, rolling her nipples between his thumb and index and middle finger, like he's rolling a joint. And then his hands drift down her hard flat belly, where he tries to get one hand down the front of her panties. But she grabs it just as he touches the moist crinkle, stops him. "Pig," she whispers, her beautiful smile splitting her face, her eyes dreamy with arousal. Then she pinches his erection with her left hand, thrilling him. And then glides his right hand to the small of her back. And he slides it over the tight butt, under the short pleated skirt, back up over the nylon knoll of her behind to the waistband of the pantyhose, and down into the forbidden land "Where Alph, the sacred river, ran / Through caverns measureless to man / Down to a sunless sea." He grabs the bare cheeks, pulls her closer against his stiffness, and then she buries her tongue in his ear and they dry-hump as she crushes herself against him, her skirt hiked all the way up now. And then she loops her arms around his neck and scissors her swimmer's legs around his hips and rides her cloth-covered vagina up and down him in a frantic rhythm.*

*"Erika, that's you, love?" her mother shouts from inside the house.*

*Danny ejaculates in his underwear, hopping around like a man being electrocuted, just as he hears her mother shouting louder. "I want you to get some experience," Erika whispers to him, the same thing she says every day, meaning she isn't ready to surrender her virginity. But she wants him to go out and fuck other girls, free-love hippie chicks, so that when she finally does it with Danny, he can teach her all he's learned. He always tells her that he only wants her, that he doesn't need experience. In the twisted, convoluted rites-of-passage logic of the Brooklyn neighborhood, Erika tells him, "A guy needs experience from at least three other girls, at least one older than you, before he can cherry-bust the girl he loves. Jesus Christ, Danny, how embarrassing would it be to give up my cherry to a guy virgin?"*

*"Won't you be jealous if I screw other chicks?"*

*"Not if you're doing it for me," she says. "For us."*

*"I'll meet you at six-thirty at the subway to go to the concert," he says.*

*"I'll be there."*

*Then as the house door opens Danny bolts through the street door. He half runs, half limps, trying to straighten his diamond-hard seventeen-year-old friction-burnt penis as he makes for the green leafy sanctuary of Prospect Park, where he searches for a hippie chick to take his cherry so he can in turn take Erika's.*

*But first he sits in a thicket of rosebushes just inside the park from which he can spy Erika's house. And with his underwear wet and sticky, he takes a copybook from his head bag and writes yet another love poem, trying to ape Coleridge, Donne, Villon, or Dylan Thomas, the man from whom a young man from Hibbing, Minnesota, named Robert Zimmerman borrowed the name. To Danny, of course, Bob Dylan is the greatest living poet in the universe, the poet laureate of his generation, a troubadour with hidden messages on the meaning of life itself in the lyrics of songs like "Mr. Tambourine Man" and "Love Minus Zero/No Limit" and "Desolation Row." He has all his albums and bootleg tapes, even knows by heart the lyrics of early obscure songs like the haunting "Long Time Gone," which Dylan wrote but only recorded on a 1963 Witmark Demo that Danny had purchased through a classified ad in* Rolling Stone.

*Every love poem Danny writes is for Erika, the girl he loves.*

\*        \*        \*

In the airplane, Danny put down the notebook, shifted in the seat, and came out of the trance, aching for a smoke.

He realized he was partially aroused from the Erika reverie. The woman on the aisle glanced down at the ticket stubs as Danny scooped and gathered the crumbled bits of the rubber band. "Your daughter likes the real oldies, huh?"

The remark made him fidget.

"Yeah," he said. "I was at Woodstock. My daughter went to Woodstock '99."

"God, you were actually there at the first one? My mom and dad met there. I guess you could call me a Woodstock baby. But I must admit, it kind of skeeves me to think I might have been conceived in all that mud and muck and general nastiness. I always wondered why nobody rented motel rooms."

"In the sixties, the whole world was a hot-sheets motel," Danny said, exploring deeper into the bag.

"I'm sorry," the woman said, shrugging. "I'm distracting you. Don't mind me, I have work on liquidating a dot-com to do."

The yuppie woman returned with her stylus to the mini keyboard as Danny put the concert tickets back inside the bag. He scooped his hands around the paperback books and the eleven copybook journals and located a few letters Brendan had written to him from Vietnam, addressed to him at their parents' old address on Prospect Road in Prospect Gardens.

He took them out, this rubber band also breaking into dozens of shriveled rubber links, and he wondered if there was a link for every year that had passed since last he read the words his brother sent him from the war.

Shuffling through the letters, he realized that 1969 really began for him on November 23, 1968, the day Brendan left for Vietnam. No, he thought. Maybe it began in December 1967, when Brendan first joined the army. *That was the prologue to the year that fucked up my entire life,* Danny thought. It was a blur. . . .

*December 1967*

*Brendan has graduated high school and has just finished his first semester at Staten Island Community College, where he met Maria, an accounting student. He'd gotten straight As, astounding his literature and history professors with all the reading he had already done on his own. Brendan is as familiar with history as current events. As an elementary school kid, when most kids were reading* Archie *and* Marvel *comics, Brendan was home reading* The Iliad *and* The Odyssey *and* Huckleberry Finn. *As a teenager, while most kids his age were reading* Rolling Stone *and "the good parts" of Harold Robbins, Brendan was reading that shit too, but he was also reading the* New York Times, The New Yorker, The Village Voice, The Wall Street Journal, I.F. Stone's Weekly, Ramparts, The Realist, *and* Evergreen, The Sporting News, *and* Ring *Magazine.*

*Brendan is seventeen now. He'll get a student deferment from the draft when he turns eighteen. He's enjoying college life when Maria announces she no longer wants to go steady with him. As steeped as he is in classic literature—*War and Peace *and* Madam Bovary *and* The Brothers Karamazov—*even* Romeo *and* Juliet *didn't prepare Brendan for his first teenage broken heart. And at home, at the breakfast table, their father, Mickey Cassidy, proud ex-Marine, veteran of Inchon, a Camel-smoking, Four Roses–belting steamfitter by trade, continues his endless harangue against Brendan for being "a longhaired pinko sympathizer without enough balls to go fight for his fuckin' country like I did when I was your age."*

*Brendan counters, calling his father a walking-talking hard-hat cliché, saying that the war is wrong, that history will be unkind to those who sent kids to kill and die in it. "Besides, you aren't interested in what the war is about," Brendan tells him. "You just want to be able to go up to Foley's, get shit-faced, and brag about your son over in Vietnam killing commies."*

*"You bet your fuckin' beatnik peacenik ass, I do," Mickey says. "I wanna be proud of my son. My son the patriot. Not my son the commie fag."*

*"You're not proud that I'm a goddamned A-student?" Brendan asks.*

*"Karl Marx was a fuckin' A-student," Mickey says. "Ho Chi Minh was a fuckin' A-student. Timothy Leary was an A-student. Fuck being an A-student. Be a fuckin' A1 soldier for the good old U. S. of A.!"*

*"Easy on the kid, Mickey," says their mother, Maggie, on this cold morning in late 1967. "Brendan's not the soldiering type."*

*"The men in this family serve their country," the father shouts. "Or they get the hell out of the family and my house."*

*"Easy, Mickey, I'm warning you," says the mother.*

*"The long hair, the peace buttons, the protest rallies, I'm fuckin' embarrassed of him," Mickey shouts, hoping the neighbors would*

*hear.* "*Any kid who won't serve his country in a time of war is a fuckin' coward. No wonder that little guinea broad gave you your marching papers.*"

*Brendan takes the first swing he's ever taken at his father. He misses. And his father drops him with a hard, short right hand to the chest. Maggie slaps Mickey hard across the face.* "*Come on and hit me, you son of a bitch, and prove how brave you are,*" *she shouts, jutting her jaw out at Mickey, who balls his fists. Danny, a halfback for John Jay High, every inch the jock, jumps in front of his mother and hits his father with a right hand on the chin. Mickey Cassidy staggers backward, tilting the pictures of the Sacred Heart of Jesus and JFK that hang on the kitchen wall, but does not go down. The father rubs his chin and smiles.*

"*At least one of you ain't a commie fag,*" *he says, before leaving for Foley's.*

*An hour later, sixteen-year-old Danny steps off the F train with Brendan out in Coney Island, where Brendan enters the United States Army recruiting kiosk located in the parking lot outside of Nathan's Famous hot dogs. And over Danny's teary-eyed protests Brendan joins the army. He wants to prove to his father that his broken heart does not beat in the chest of a coward.*

"*I always wanted to write history,*" *Brendan says.* "*What better way than to be part of it? Besides, if I become a medic I can do more to save lives over there than I can over here.*"

"*I hate him for making you do this,*" *Danny says.*

"*Don't,*" *Brendan says.* "*I was thinking about it anyway. I want to go and see the history happen.*"

*Which Danny knows means Vietnam.*

*Except for the release of* **Sgt. Pepper** *and* **Monterey Pop,** *the rest of 1967 is a blur. After boot camp Brendan volunteers for medic training and then for the Airborne Rangers. And after the "gentle brother" is stationed in Texas and Georgia for several months, he volunteers for Vietnam, gets his wish and a final two-week leave just before Thanksgiving. When he comes home on November 10, Brendan watches Danny score the winning touchdown against Lincoln High. And over those two weeks, every day after school, as the leaves fall in the season of the witch, with winter chilling the city and the Christmas lights swaying across Parkside West, the two brothers take a football up to the park. Without mentioning it, in those two weeks they try to relive their youth together, in case the inseparable brothers never see each other again.*

*They recall all the pitched battles they've had playing cowboys and Indians, cops and robbers, Japs and Americans. They walk past Blessed Virgin, where they'd gone to grammar school, and down to the Ansonia clock factory on Twelfth Street, where, as little kids when their father was on strike, they had collected soda bottles, rinsed out the roaches that'd drowned in the syrup, and cashed them in for the two-cent deposits, so they could buy Spaldeens for stickball and a Popsicle from Bob the ice cream man who held contests where you could win a free fifty-cent crewcut from Joe the barber.*

*They retrace as many of their footprints as they can find, smoking weed, drinking beer, and hanging out up in McCaulie's bar on Sixteenth Place and Tenth Avenue, goofing with Wally Fortune and Bird the bartender, who even serves underage Danny because in that neighborhood you always got served if your brother was going away to war.*

*They drink with some of Brendan's older classmates, guys named Tommy Ryan, Mike O'Brien, George Brady, and Eddie Fortune, who is a Green Beret and leaving for Nam the same day as Brendan.*

*Wally Fortune is Eddie's older brother, the funniest guy in the neighborhood, who many think could have been a stand-up comedian. Wally is also a con man who could get a cripple to trade his wheelchair for roller skates. At twenty-two, Wally is older than most of the other guys and has some kind of psychiatric deferment from the draft. Wally uses his powers of persuasion to convince an older, hot-looking barfly nicknamed Susie Blowjob, who is twenty-six and divorced, into giving both Brendan and Eddie Fortune hum jobs in the back room of McCaulie's the night before they leave for Nam, because it's the patriotic thing to do. "C'mon, Susie, for Old Glory," Wally says. "These poor kids are going over there to make sure you live in the home of the free and the land of the brave. You owe them at least fifteen minutes each of duty to your country."*

*Danny's heard that Susie Blowjob got her nickname after she came home early from work one day and busted her unemployed husband getting a blow job from her best friend. She then decided that the best way to get even with him was to go shopping, buy the sexiest clothes she could find. And then she stalked her best friend's husband and blew him first. In her best friend's bed, with a secret tape recorder spinning. Then one by one Susie isolated and sucked off every single one of her husband's friends, tape-recording every one of them, asking each guy if he was enjoying her sucking his dick. Then she sucked off two of her husband's brothers. Then she played these tapes for her husband until he was so mortified that he moved to Florida. Susie moved to the last stool in McCaulie's, drinking beer and popping amphetamines and living up to her neighborhood moniker that stuck to her like a tattoo.*

*Wally pins an American flag and a WWII poppy on Susie's blouse and gives her two blackbirds—and two Seconals for the crash—and has Bird bring her a steady stream of Budweisers. Once the amphetamines hit her in a wave of euphoria, she says, "OK, I'll do it, but only if they wear their uniforms."*

*Brendan races home, changes into his uniform, runs back, and Susie BJ leads him into the back room as Wally leads the bar in a rendition of "Halls of Montezuma." Danny pops a boner just thinking of his brother getting blowed in the back room. Brendan comes out, grinning, as the whole bar salutes and breaks into applause. Then Eddie goes back. And they all drink beer until Bird calls last call at four A.M.*

As the plane taking him back to Brooklyn hit a patch of turbulence, Danny remembered the exact date that his brother, Brendan, left for Vietnam, five years to the day after Sister Margaret Timothy entered his fifth-grade classroom to announce that everyone should kneel as she led the class in a rosary for President John F. Kennedy, who had just been assassinated.

*November 23, 1968*

*Then the morning comes.*

*Their father, Mickey, sits at the table, smoking Camels, drinking coffee, and staring out the window in cold, unflinching silence. Maggie, their mother, makes bacon and French toast and as the dawn breaks and the clock ticks toward six-thirty when Brendan will have to leave, she says she is going out for more orange juice.*

*"You're the greatest, Mom," Brendan says, because he knows she isn't coming back until after he's left.*

*Maggie pulls on an old gray wool sweater, her woolen overcoat, and stands behind her son for a long moment, holding his face in her strong coarse hands as she glares at Mickey Cassidy. She kisses the top of Brendan's head, tells him she'll be right back, and rushes out into the cold morning. Danny knows that their mother—who had read the great books to them every night at bedtime, filled with Irish legends and Greek myths, stories about knights of old and astronauts of tomorrow—doesn't know how to say good-bye to her gentle son who is going away to war.*

"She's running to Blessed Virgin Mary church to catch Father O'Keefe stumble through the six-fifteen mass," Brendan says. "With all the prayers she'll offer up to the Holy Souls in Purgatory for me, I can't possibly go wrong."

Danny and Brendan select their Thanksgiving Day football picks from the list in the Daily News. They talk about the Beatles Magical Mystery Tour, and Tom Wolfe's Electric Kool-Aid Acid Test, and the new TV show called Laugh In. They talk about what a horror four years of Nixon will be like. Then after finishing his breakfast, Brendan rises from the table and pulls on his Airborne hat.

"See ya, Dad," he says.

"I'm . . . I'm very proud of you, son," Mickey says. He looks like he wants to say more but doesn't know how.

Brendan nods, grabs his duffel bag as Danny grabs a Wilson football and slams it into his brother's gut. He yanks the bag off Brendan's shoulder, insisting on carrying it. Brendan hurries down the stairs as Danny pauses in the apartment.

"I hate you. I hate your fucking guts," Danny says quietly and then he follows his brother out the door. Danny walks him to the subway station at Veteran's Memorial Square, a widening void in his guts, shouldering the duffel bag. Brendan spins the football in his hands as he walks in silence. They stand on the corner for a few minutes, smoky breath scattering in the November wind. They look over at Prospect Park, where they both had played in the sandbox, sliding ponds, and monkey bars of the Eleventh Street playground. Where they'd learned how to ride two-wheelers, played guns in all those make-believe games of war, hit Little League home runs, kissed girls who wore training bras, and played endless games of football. Together. Brendan and Danny. Always inseparable.

Now Brendan is going away to war. A real one. And maybe he isn't ever coming back.

"Careful over there," Danny says, dropping the duffel on the sidewalk, grabbing the football from his big brother.

"Yeah," Brendan says. "Make sure you write."

Danny feels something enormous drop out of his soul as he looks deep into his brother's kind dark eyes and buries the football in his gut and races for a long one, across Parkside South, into the mouth of Prospect Park, their childhood Sherwood Forest. Brendan drops back, *along the bus stop where the B-75 grunts to the curb, and hurls the football high and deep into the park, above the leafless skeletal trees, up onto the far reaches of the grassy knoll nicknamed Hippie Hill. Danny chases the towering spiral and hauls it in on the run for what would be a winning touchdown. He brandishes the ball over his head. When he turns to flaunt it to Brendan, his brother is gone.*

*And so is their childhood.*

The woman next to him said, "Excuse me, your snack is here, mister."

Danny, his head in the clouds, snapped out of his reverie, as a flight attendant handed him a tray with a turkey sandwich and a Diet Coke.

"Thanks," he said, picking at his food.

"You were sure lost in thought," the yuppie said, pouring herself a glass of zinfandel wine from a small bottle. "That stuff all your daughter's research? Sixties stuff?"

"Yeah, I'm helping her research it," he said.

"I'm glad I didn't live then," she said.

"Why?"

"What was the Dow, like, less than a thousand?" she said, clicking the keyboard, speed-dialing an Internet database with her built-in phone, and coming up with an instant answer. "Yikes! The Dow was as low as five-sixty-six in 1960 and the highest it went in 1969 was nine-fifty-two. No wonder you people ran to ashrams! I mean, I guess the Beatles were OK, but it looks to me like a grubby decade. Drugs, dirt, war. I don't see what there's to be nostalgic about—people who lived like homeless people. Or on communes, hog farms, spreading STDs. Personally, I like a guy with clean short hair, girls with long hair. Give me an in-shape guy in a pair of jeans and a starched white shirt, sleeves rolled up, nice watch, clean white sneakers or polished Botticelli loafers. Who the hell found dirty nasty bell-bottoms and flip-flop sandals and wilted flowers in dirty stringy hair on a *guy* sexy? And tie-dyed shirts! Give me a cyanide pill before you give me a guy like that. Ronald Reagan described a hippie as someone who 'dresses like Tarzan, has hair like Jane, and smells like Cheetah.' But that's who my mom fell in love with. I've seen the pictures. Don't get me wrong, I love my dad, but yuk! What a difference a new century can make. Thank God."

"It was all that," Danny said. "And worse."

"Don't get me wrong," she said. "I think it's great that you're helping your kid understand where you're coming from. Even when it sucks, history is important, so we don't repeat it. It's kinda sweet to see a father so involved with his daughter. It must make for great father-daughter bonding."

The words stung. Because they were all false. Worse, he had used his daughter as a convenient prop in an idle conversation with a girl on an airplane, pretending that he even had a cordial relationship with Darlene. The truth was they hadn't spoken more than a dozen times in five years since he and his wife, Tammy, divorced. She accepted his calls on birthdays and Christmas, but she never called him on Father's Day. The only accurate part of the story was that his daughter was an aspiring actress, studying at the Harvard drama school, where she had once done a production of *Hair*. But he had never seen it. Darlene had not invited him.

She never forgave him for walking away from the family when she was a confused teenager, telling Tammy—a photographer for a Los Angeles weekly newspaper—that he didn't love her and that he never had. He admitted to her that when she had become pregnant with Darlene, he respected her Catholicism and her personal opposition to abortion. Like Tammy, Danny was pro-choice but found abortion repugnant. As a social option it needed to be legal; as a means of birth control it was grotesque. Although she had not pressured Danny, he asked her to marry him as much out of loneliness as obligation. After years of bouncing around the country alone, running from the law and his past and the specter of Erika Malone, never dating anyone for more than a few months, with no sustained friendships, he had an aching desire for long-term companionship.

After watching his own family die and splinter in 1969, after a ten-year estrangement from his only sibling, he craved the warm safe cocoon of *family* back in his life. He'd ached for a child, hoping that he would also learn to fall in love again. With his baby's mother, with Tammy, the best woman he'd ever known.

The marriage gave him sweet, amazing Darlene. It blessed him with a father's lifelong love. But it did not bring him true romance. He longed to love Tammy, wished there were some magical bromide that could make love bubble in his veins. There wasn't.

He'd married a beautiful, smart, talented, funny, sweet woman. Had a great kid. Bought a nice little three-bedroom house in the San Fernando Valley. But love just didn't happen. Not love as he remembered it with Erika Malone, anyway. Which was his first love, and whether he liked it or not—and he didn't like it at all—the love by which he measured all subsequent passions of the heart.

With Tammy he had never experienced that raging, uncontrollable, absurd obsession with a member of the opposite sex that he'd felt as a teenager for Erika. Not that illogical, almost mystical sensation of fusing with another human heart. Nothing that corny, dizzying, or wonderful happened with Tammy. Nothing that made him write sonnets and bad poetry. Their marriage had been a sturdy union, a generous sharing, an intellectual parity, and there was very good sex in the king-size bed where Darlene had been conceived. He'd felt deep affection for Tammy. He still did. He would have died protecting her. He even missed her, often pining for her kindness, understanding, comfort, the smell and touch and reliability of her. He envied the idea of another man having her.

But with Tammy, for fourteen long years, it had never been love. And it never would be.

And so five years before, after another of Ankles's middle-of-the-night calls on the anniversary of Vito Malone's murder telling Danny that he was still the prime suspect in the murder for which there was no statute of limitations, Danny knew it was time to end it.


*November 21, 1996*

*At first Tammy says nothing. She just stares at him, thunderstruck, the wind and the sea roaring between them.*

*Danny fills the awkward moment by saying that she should of course keep the house, the car, and the cat. That he will pay her a fair alimony and child support. He won't contest anything she thinks is fair.*

*Tammy stares out at the Pacific, her hair whipping in the sea wind, as the waves rush and run from the shore. Her pale blue eyes squint, tiny crow's-feet etching her eyes, and he watches her swallow and moisten her trembling lips. Then she turns to him, beautiful and wounded and betrayed.*

*"You don't even know the meaning of the word fair," Tammy whispers, her eyes like rain-beaded glass, her bare toes curling into the retreating surf. "I get the house but you take my fucking heart and soul? You did me wrong, Danny. You deserve the past you've been running from. For dumping it into my life. And Darlene's. It wasn't fair*

marrying me back then. It wasn't fair having a baby with a woman you didn't love. It isn't fair leaving me now."

"I always told you I had a hard time feeling love," he says, realizing how lame he sounds. "I can't explain it, Tam. It's like the veins to my heart are clogged. Love can't get through. Does that make any sense? Jesus, Tam, I told you I had a ton of baggage in my life. I'm sorry, but I just can't shake my fucked-up past. There's too much unfinished business in my life. You're right, I was wrong to marry you. But it would be more unfair to you to continue this. I just can't give you the love you deserve. I'm just not good enough for you, Tammy. Please, forgive me."

"No."

She turns, walks across the hot sand, past the new homeless bums of the nineties that remind Danny of the skankiest of the sixties, skanky like he was, just with higher-octane drugs. Tammy never looks back. He's never come as close to loving her as he does in this instant that he loses her. But then she and the marriage are gone.

That night, explaining his leaving to Darlene is even more painful. It's all too convoluted and painful for a brokenhearted kid.

"How can you say you don't love Mom," she asks. "Isn't Mom faithful?"

"Yes."

"Doesn't she love you?"

"Yes, but that's unfair because I can't give her that same love back."

"Why?"

"You can't fake what you don't feel, Darlene."

"Isn't Mom a good wife? A good mother?"

"The best."

"Then why are you leaving her? Leaving us?"

"Because your Mom deserves better than me. And I'm not leaving you; I'll be your father forever. I just won't be your mom's husband."

"Are you leaving her for another woman?"

"No."

"Swear?"

"Swear."

"Then it must be because of me."

"No, sweetheart, don't ever say that."

"If you don't love my mom, then I don't love you."

"Please, don't say that, either."

"In fact, I hate you for destroying our family . . . I fucking hate you."

*He looks at her, knowing that this was how he must have looked to his own father when he'd told him the very same thing all those years ago.*

He didn't speak to Tammy again without the presence of a lawyer. Afterward, Tammy had been fair, very fair. She offered unlimited visitation with their daughter, so long as Darlene wanted to see him. She kept the house but assumed the mortgage payments herself, and declined alimony. She asked only for child support. She didn't want another minute or penny of his intrusive life.

The counseling sessions that followed never helped. Then Darlene refused to go to any more shrinks.

In the months after the separation Danny called Darlene every day, but she wouldn't take his calls. As she got older and more mature the anger turned to aloofness, distance, and silence. He had become a legal father. Later, when she needed him to pay for her schooling, airfares, clothes, and other needs, they were civil to one another. They smiled together for pictures at her high school graduation. He suspected that most times when he phoned her and got her answering machine that she screened her calls. She took them when there was family business to discuss.

But the blood bond, the family cocoon, the unqualified love had been drained from his relationship with his daughter. His ex-wife didn't even speak to him. She was no longer angry, just indifferent. She had found a way to make Danny not matter anymore. Nothing made you feel more finite.

Now as the American Airlines pilot announced they were passing the Mississippi River, Danny looked down at the great waterway and took a deep breath, trying to gather enough oxygen to get him over the guilt and sadness that came from his fractured relationship with Darlene.

The flight attendant collected the trays. Danny declined coffee. And as the plane hit a pocket of turbulence, he fastened his seat belt and put his head against a tiny pillow wedged against the window. He closed his eyes, pulled the small blanket over him. He began to doze, aware that he was leaving consciousness, and hoped he would dream of Erika. . . .

Instead he went into a half trance, more a scattered rehash than a dream, filled with dark images, blurry fragments, like jagged pieces of a shattered mirror.

*November 21, 1969*

*Brendan demands that Danny flee. Packing a bag. Grabbing the head bag. Visiting Mom's grave. Saying good-bye to Erika. She cries her eyes out. And as Brendan waits, she kisses him. She offers herself to him. He says there is no time. Then a clumsy, frantic, urgent, weepy final kiss.*

*And then leaving. Begging Erika to come with him, but her saying it's good-bye. Forever. Then Brendan dragging him down the subway. Riding in silence to Ninety-fifth Street in Bay Ridge, to catch the Verrazano Bridge bus.*

*"Did you kill him?" Brendan asks.*

*No.*

*"Are you sure?"*

*No.*

*"My army issue forty-five is missing."*

*I took it.*

*"Did you use it?"*

*I had every intention. But I can't remember.*

*"This much is for sure," Brendan says. "You killed any chance of us having a life together. I'm going back to Asia. You're going to America."*

*They catch another bus in Staten Island because they're afraid Ankles will have Port Authority, Grand Central, and the airports watched. They ride the bus out to the end of the island, to a truck stop near the entrance to the Goethals Bridge.*

*"This is good-bye, bro," Brendan says. "Don't even write. I saw enough dead people over there. I didn't need to come home for more, with you involved. This is worse than fucking Nam, bro. Killing there was legal."*

*Come with me, Brendan, we can start over. . . .*

*Brendan gives him a wad of cash. "Peace," he says and runs for a bus back toward Brooklyn.*

*The last time he ever saw him.*

*Danny hitches a ride with a trucker, heading into America and leaving behind Brooklyn, his father, Ankles, Erika, and the sixties. . . .*

"Mister, we're gonna land in a few minutes," the frosted-haired woman said.

Danny popped awake. Yanked his seat into an upright position.

He snapped the buckles on the head bag. He glanced out the window at the city of New York, the plane gliding in over Staten Island and then over the Verrazano Bridge and over the borough of Brooklyn. The flight path passed over Bay Ridge and Borough Park and Prospect Gardens, which was sandwiched between Evergreen Cemetery, where his mother lay, and Prospect Park, where so much of his childhood was buried. And where Vito "Boar's Head" Malone was murdered.

Down there in that compact twenty-square-block neighborhood of sturdy limestones and prewar tenements his father would be in a coffin by now, in Dunne's, waiting to be waked. Down there in that cruel little self-sustained hamlet of Brooklyn, where he hadn't been for more than three decades, there was a detective named Ankles waiting to put him in a cage for the rest of his life. Down there in Brooklyn he might be reunited with his long-estranged brother, Brendan, for a few short days. He might see some forgotten friends down there in Brooklyn. Who knew, maybe his daughter, Darlene, would appear down there in Brooklyn for her grandfather's wake.

But as the plane banked toward LaGuardia airport the thing that frightened Danny Cassidy most was that down there in Brooklyn he might once again come face-to-face with Erika Malone.

# three

Danny rented a Toyota Camry at the Hertz counter and drove like a homing pigeon toward Brooklyn on the Brooklyn-Queens Expressway. After three decades on the glass-smooth highways of Florida, Nevada, and Los Angeles, he was shocked as he jolted along the moonscape of the BQE.

He signaled to change lanes, checking his rearview and side-view mirrors. He saw the car behind him, a forest green Crown Victoria, slow down and also blink on its turn signal. Danny had spent three decades looking over his shoulder and in his rearview mirror until paranoia had become as much a part of his life as morning coffee and cigarettes and fear of cancer. He noticed the green Crown Victoria, made a mental note of it, and then stored it in the paranoia compartment of his skull.

He exited at the Civic Center–Brooklyn Bridge off-ramp and as he made his way toward Downtown Brooklyn was amazed that Fulton Street, where he had shopped with his mother for back-to-school clothes as a kid, was now a pedestrian mall, crammed with black and Latin and Asian faces. Dozens of stores displayed odd signs that read: WIGS, PERFUME AND GOLD SOLD HERE. The A&S department store, Korvette's, Martins, and Mays were all gone. A McDonald's replaced the old Nedicks.

He drove down Adams Street and spotted the Marriott Hotel, which was only a few years old, rising fourteen floors above the busy street. The hotel was adjacent to a new sprawling business center called Metro Tech, where big banks and Wall Street firms were now headquartered in the once backwater but now booming borough of Brooklyn.

Weird, he thought.

The look and smell of Downtown Brooklyn had changed so much that for Danny it was like being in a foreign city for the first time.

He drove slowly down Adams Street, horns still blaring behind him as he searched for his bearings. He recognized the old white stone main post office on the corner of Tillary Street. But most of the courthouses were new, as were the city buses that didn't look anything like the round-nosed green-and-white ones he remembered from the sixties. The new buses were now flat-backed, unlike the old, uneven ones that were so easy to hitch onto for a free ride.

He stopped for a red light and glanced at a campaign poster on a lamppost: REELECT JUDGE MARVIN "THE MALLET" LEVY JR. TO THE NEW YORK SUPREME COURT.

Danny knew the name and the face looked familiar. He figured it was the son of a once infamous Court Street lawyer who used to represent local neighborhood criminals like Tommy Ryan and a guy named Dirty Jim Dugan. The old man made a bundle from common crooks like Dirty Jim and used the money to make his son a judge. That was the corrupt Brooklyn Danny remembered.

As Danny glanced along the six-lane Adams Street he noticed that old-fashioned historic lampposts had replaced the aluminum phalli of the sixties. When he left Brooklyn in 1969, an aluminum invasion of bland, smooth-planed, unclimbable lampposts had replaced the ornate wrought-iron light poles of his youth.

He remembered that the lamppost control boxes at the base of each pole used to be covered by a steel-plate door that could only be opened with a special key. And a resourceful Dirty Jim Dugan had a lamppost master key. Dirty Jim carried it on a large ring that also included keys to every subway vending machine, pay phone, parking meter, emergency subway exit gate, schoolhouse, Parks Department supply room, firehouse, sanitation garage, public swimming pool, bus depot, public bathroom, and police vehicle in the neighborhood of Prospect Gardens.

"Fuck the mayor," Dirty Jim was fond of saying as he rattled his keys. "I got the keys to the city."

A modern Artful Dodger, Dirty Jim had spent years pickpocketing city workers who slept off roaring drunks in the back rooms of bars like Foley's and McCaulie's. He never took their money or their wallets, just their keys, often making copies and returning them before they awakened and knew they were missing. Some people collect stamps, some coins, baseball cards, pepper mills, and model trains or old cars. The passion of Dirty Jim's life was keys. "Keys open doors," he was fond of saying. "Keys unlock the future." "Broads love a guy with keys." "Keys get you rich, keys get you laid, keys set you free." "Life is one long series of locked doors and I got the keys."

Keys got Dirty Jim locked up more than a dozen times. But when the cops confiscated his keys, he always had a second set available when he got out.

Dirty, as he was called for short, was also an amateur photographer, a lascivious Peeping Tom, and ruthless blackmailer. A nocturnal creature, like a two-legged roach, Dirty Jim zigzagged the neighborhood of Prospect Gardens at night, using special high-speed and infrared film, or sometimes popping flashbulbs, chronicling the dirty doings of the neighborhood.

Shooting from factory windows, rooftops, doorways, or from the front seat of stolen vehicles for which he had the keys, Dirty Jim caught cheating lovers, disloyal spouses, car thieves, burglars, crooked cops, closet homosexuals, and dope dealers on film. "I got the dirty on you," he was fond of saying.

It was how Dirty earned his nickname. Like his keys, these photographs empowered the weak, emaciated, unhealthy Dirty Jim. He was not beneath blackmailing sexual favors from a pretty cheating wife when she was presented with the dirty pictures. "It's like this, honey," Dirty would whisper, shuffling through the dirty photos. "Blow me or your husband blows your fuckin' brains out." And as the compromised woman got to her knees to comply, Dirty Jim would grin and rattle his key ring in her ear. The only reason Dirty had not been murdered was that most neighborhood people knew he had a dossier on almost everyone. And if anything happened to Dirty he had on retainer a young Court Street lawyer named Marvin Levy—Danny'd never forget his name because he was considered the best, if sleaziest, in Brooklyn back then—who would release his "dirt" to the appointed spouses or proper authorities.

So Dirty Jim survived, a grinning, rodent loner, scurrying through the neighborhood with a ring of keys jingling from his belt loop and a camera strung around his neck.

Dirty Jim always had a wad of money on him, which often meant he had a pretty gum-snapping neighborhood bimbo along for a night out, exchanging sex for pot, pills, acid—even cocaine, long before it became fashionable.

Before he would pull a score in one of the municipal garages or civil service supply rooms, Dirty Jim would use his master lamppost key to unlock the control panel and switch off every lamppost in a three-block radius. Then he'd unlock the doors to a half-dozen public buildings, triggering the burglar alarms, so that the cops from the local precinct would be left scrambling in the dark, rushing from one alarm to the other. Meanwhile, Dirty Jim would be doing his score four blocks away, in the light, with a special key to switch off any alarm, often making his getaway in one of the vacated police cars, the trunk of which would be loaded with hot property that he'd sell in the saloons of Park Slope, Bay Ridge, Windsor Terrace, and Prospect Gardens.

Jesus, Danny wondered, could Dirty Jim still be alive? Nah, someone must have killed him by now. *Why the hell am I even thinking about him? I haven't thought of him in thirty years.*

But Dirty Jim was more than a vague memory. Danny had always suspected he might be part of something more important, maybe something vital to that final night in Brooklyn, and that was why he was bubbling to the surface. Maybe something to do with a neighborhood drug pusher named Christie Strong, a messianic sixties guru who had a flock of young bimbos and a herd of drug mules and even dirty cops on his payroll. Dirty Jim and Strong were part of that night—they were there behind the crime-scene tape the morning after. Danny wasn't sure what, if anything, Dirty Jim and Christie Strong had to do with the murder but he was determined to find out.

As he sat at the long red light he tried to fit Dirty into that blank canvass. He didn't know where Dirty fit, but he could see him, silhouetted against a blinding cone of white light, like the one from the Bosch painting.

A barrage of horns blared behind Danny as he realized the traffic light had turned a New York insanity-provoking green. He looked in his rearview mirror and saw a *New York Times* truck driver banging on his horn, his face a balled fist. Danny signaled to change lanes and glided through the light, into the right lane. In his rearview he saw a green Crown Victoria appear from behind the *Times* truck, which thundered past him like a landslide of lug nuts.

*There's more than one green Crown Vic in New York City,* he thought before turning into the carport of the Marriott and handing his keys to the uniformed valet. As a bellhop grabbed his only suitcase, Danny watched the green Crown Victoria pass the new hotel. Danny held on to the head bag, which the bellhop regarded with the same curious disdain as the yuppie woman on the airplane.

*It's weird,* Danny thought, following the bellhop into the lobby. *I was born and raised in this place called Brooklyn. Why do I feel like an interloper?*

A doorman pulled open the glass door of the hotel and in the mirrored reflection Danny saw the Crown Victoria make a U-turn at Tillary Street. It swung back along Adams Street on the other side of the traffic island, slowing and parking at a free meter across the street. Danny could not see the driver behind the tinted windows.

Ankles, he thought.

After checking in, Danny showered, dressed in fresh black chinos, black socks, black loafers, and a white shirt. He let his curly salt-and-pepper hair dry naturally and walked to the window overlooking the downtown bridges. The skyline of Manhattan was as startling as he'd first seen it as a kid from his top-floor walkup tenement window, when all the kids of Brooklyn called it the City, as if it were some mystical Oz on the other side of the Yellow Brick Road. The skyline was one of the few things that didn't seem smaller with age. If anything, after the low-to-the-ground earthquake architecture of Los Angeles, it looked even bigger than he remembered. Massive. Magnificent. Intimidating. Like nothing he'd seen in thirty-two years.

Across the East River he spotted something called Pier 17 and assumed it was part of the South Street Seaport he'd read about a few times in the national edition of the *New York Times,* the upscale version of the mob-ruled Fulton Fish Market.

His eyes searched the spot at the parking meter across Adams Street for the green Crown Vic. It wasn't there.

He lifted the phone and called Dunne's Funeral Home. "Is Mickey Cassidy laid out yet?" he asked, using the phraseology everyone had used when he was a Brooklyn kid.

"Yes. Mr. Cassidy is in repose starting today," said the voice on the other end.

"What're the hours?"

"Two to five," said the woman. "And seven to nine."

"Thanks," Danny said, glancing at the digital clock radio that told him it was just ten-thirty A.M.

Which gave him time to reconnoiter the old neighborhood.

Before he left, he dialed information and asked if there was a number for Erika Malone on Garvey Place in Brooklyn.

"I'm sorry," the operator said. "The only listing for a Malone on Garvey that I have is for a Vito Malone, but it's an unpublished number."

"Vito?" he said, startled that all these years later the number was

still under the murdered man's name. The number was so old he figured it might still have the ancient phone-company letter-and-
number exchange from the 1950s, when Erika's mother and father
were newlyweds. As he hung up the receiver, he was startled to
realize that he still knew the number by heart—Sterling-8-0571. It
popped out of the foggy past like a little buried treasure. It was like
remembering that Mickey Mantle was number 7 and Roger Maris
was number 9 and Yogi was number 8. Or that Erika's address was
962 Garvey Place. And that her bra size was 34-B, waist 22, hips 34.
Without straining, he even remembered Erika's Social Security
number. He'd been with her down here on Adams Street at the
Social Security office the day she first got it, so she could take the
after-school job at the Brooklyn Public Library on Evergreen
Avenue.

He wondered what Erika looked like now. She'd be forty-nine.
She had always been athletic, ate healthful food, shunned drugs.
Her mother had remained an attractive woman into her forties. A
lot of the women in that neighborhood went on the doughnut diet
right after their first pregnancy, using marriage and housewifery as
an excuse to eat anything they wanted, lots of red meat, bacon and
eggs and butter and Entenmann's cakes. They stood outside the
schools at three o'clock, smoking cigarettes, like a herd of bison,
waiting for the kids to come out, so they could go with them to the
pizza parlor for a snack before the big red-meat dinner. Erika's
mother, Angela Malone, ate a Mediterranean diet of fish and pasta
and salad and had aged like Sophia Loren, whom she resembled. In
the neighborhood the teenage guys used to have three fantasy
lists—the Virgin List, the Busted Cherry List, and the MILF List.
Erika was always on top of the Virgin Lists. Hippie Helen led the
Busted Cherry List. And Erika's mother, Angela, was always the
number one MILF—Mother I'd Love to Fuck.

He dialed Erika's old phone number.

"Vito, that's you?" said an old woman on the other end. "Come
home, it's Friday, I have your dinner waiting. Vito, that's you?"

Danny didn't respond. The voice came to him as if he were
standing in the vestibule, dry-humping with Erika. "Vaffanculo," he
heard her say before she cradled the phone.

*Ankles was telling the truth*, Danny thought as he left the hotel.
*Her mother is alive. And still living in the same house. Stoned or nuts.*

\* \* \*

Danny drove up Atlantic Avenue, passing the burgeoning Arabic population that had begun settling there in the sixties and had now become the largest Islamic enclave in the nation. He passed the Brooklyn House of Detention, where so many of the kids he'd hung around with had done time for drugs and gang wars when gangs with names like the Golden Guineas used to battle the Skid Row Boys with bats, knives, car antennae, Garrison belts, and chains. One guy, Skinny Muldoon, who went into the House of D on a pot bust, wearing his hippie hair down to his ass, had hanged himself after being passed around like a party favor in a jailhouse gangbang. Danny had spent two nights in there on a drug charge in, of course, 1969. . . .

He searched his mirrors for signs of the green Crown Victoria. There was no sign of it. Danny made a right on Flatbush Avenue and drove south toward Grand Army Plaza, where the monument to the Civil War loomed over the outskirts of Prospect Park. The park was built right after the war between the states, most of the land donated by a railroad lawyer named Edwin Clark Litchfield and designed by two tortured landscape architect geniuses named Frederick Law Olmsted and Calvert Vaux, who, of course, could never have known that one small hillock in their emerald master-piece, nicknamed Hippie Hill, where Vito Malone was found murdered in the fall of 1969, would be the "grassy knoll" of Danny Cassidy's life.

He didn't think it was possible, but the New York traffic was even worse than he remembered it. More speeding cars, so many of them SUVs, rocking over the potholes as he tried to gather his bearings. He felt like an astronaut writhing through decompression. He stopped for a light in the center of the frenzied plaza, glanced left at the magnificent main branch of the Brooklyn Public Library, where Erika Malone used to work the overtime shift on weekends. He remembered sitting in there on his seventeenth birthday, waiting for Erika to get off, because she said she had something very special for him for his birthday. . . .

*November 12, 1968*

*Danny's seated at a large table in the hushed literature room reading* One Flew Over the Cuckoo's Nest *by Ken Kesey, shattering the silence with his uncontrollable laughter, rooting for McMurphy's mad rebel-*

lious bus trip with the lunatics, when Erika, still wearing her hiked-up-at-the-waist Blessed Virgin Mary High skirt, signals for him to follow her down a back stairwell to a book-sorting room.

"How much do you love me?" she asks, when she is sure they are alone in the rear of the big room, surrounded by overflowing bookcases and carts piled high with hardcover books.

"More than all the words all the poets in this building could ever express," he says.

"You know I don't believe in free love," she says. "Just complete love."

"I have complete love for you."

"Promise?"

"Promise."

"Sit there," she says, pointing to a stack of books. "I collected all your favorite poets and authors."

He checks the names—Byron, Coleridge, Yevtushenko, Auden, Blake, Yeats, Robert Browning, Dylan Thomas, John Donne, Francois Villon, Allen Ginsberg, Kerouac, Mailer, Chandler, James M. Cain, Twain, Emerson, J. P. Donleavy, Shakespeare. All of the books Brendan had read first and recommended to Danny.

"My favorites," he says, smiling.

"Am I your favorite girl?"

"My one and only."

She smiles, walks closer to him, and nudges him to a sitting position on top of his favorite authors. It's intimidating, scary, like sitting on a literary land mine.

"Then I'm gonna let you touch it for your birthday," she says.

His dick grows along his leg as she stands over him and takes his hand and guides it up under her skirt. She's not wearing panties. He begins to sweat.

"Don't you dare push it inside," she says, her whisper like an incantation. "Just pet it. And tell me that you love me."

"I adore you," he says as she leads his finger to a bald, stubbled patch on her pelvic bone.

"Know what that is?" she asks.

"You shaved?" he says, swallowing, trying to gather saliva and control the pounding in his pants.

She hands him a small translucent wax paper bag containing a coiled lock of her auburn pubic hair. "You always said you wanted a lock of my hair," she says.

*"I never thought it would be this hair!" he says, excited, opening the envelope and smelling it.*

*"I shampooed, idiot," she says, laughing, giving him a shove.*

*"I wish you hadn't."*

*"Keep it in your wallet," she says. "With a rubber with my name on it for when we do it. Happy birthday, Danny. I love you."*

*"I couldn't have asked for anything better," he says.*

*"I'm not finished yet," she says, pinching his erect penis.*

*She crouches down and pulls down his zipper. She takes it out through the metal brass teeth of his Wranglers. She gawks at it, squeezes it, examines it. She winks at him. And as he pants she gives him the first hand job she'd ever given him. "It's like churning butter," she says, her strong athletic arm never tiring, as he watched the U.S. Navy ring her father had given her glide up and down in a silver blur. "Dicks are funny-looking but I like the way it feels."*

*His flesh catches in the metal teeth but there is no anesthetic like lust so he let her continue.*

*Sitting on a literary treasure, he is finished in less than a minute. She helps him clean himself off.*

*"Next time, if you still love me, maybe I'll kiss it," she says. "Once."*

*"I love you, Erika."*

*"Take me to see* Romeo *and* Juliet *and maybe I'll put it in my mouth in the balcony," she says.*

*"As soon as it comes out, we'll go to the first show."*

*"When I turn seventeen, if you still love me, I want to go all the way," she says.*

*"I'll go all the way to the grave with you," he says.*

*"Promise me you'll get experience," she says.*

*"I only want you."*

*"Promise?"*

*"Promise, but—"*

*"I don't want to know who, when, where, or how," she says. "Just do what you're supposed to do as a man. And then you can make a woman out of me."*

*"Promise. . . ."*

Horns blared behind him again, this time a city bus driver leaning on the horn as Danny stared at the facade of the library. He hit the gas and turned onto Parkside West and realized that the old madonna residence was now part of NYU Medical Center. Jesus

Christ, he thought. Where do they put all the old people in the neighborhood? When yuppies move in, the first to get pushed out were the old. Then their working-class children.

He drove along Parkside West, through Park Slope, noticing that not many people were out sitting on their stoops like they used to when he was a kid. Most of the park benches were empty, but joggers and power-walkers, all them yuppies and health-conscious baby boomers wearing $125 sneakers, crossed paths, squirting $4.50-a-gallon designer water into their mouths. Fiftyish women with blond-frosted hair, personal-trainer-sculpted behinds and augmented breasts walked pedigree dogs, picking up shit with folded pages from the *Wall Street Journal* and the *Times*. Black women pushed white children in expensive strollers. Mercedes, BMWs, and Lexuses were squeezed together along the curbs.

Passing Garvey Place, he slowed to a crawl, glancing down at the gas lamp still flickering in front of number 962. The Malone house had been the very first one on the block to get a gas lamp. Now almost every house had one. But there was no sign of anyone entering or leaving the Malone home. He'd only been in it once, on Erika's seventeenth birthday, and her father had taken him down to a subbasement bomb shelter where he threatened to kill him if he ever so much as felt up his daughter. That had been some dick-killer of a night.

But right now Danny got a quick cheap thrill knowing that a few feet in from the gate was the Grindbox, which had sizzled in his fantasies for three decades. Now here it was. Just down the block. A physical three-dimensional reality. Cars whizzed around him, horns blaring, motorists shouting obscenities.

"Ass-fuckin'-hole," a road-rager bellowed as he sped past Danny, blowing through a red light. Danny stopped for that same light and realized that there wasn't a single construction worker with a lunch pail or a folded tabloid at any of the bus stops. He didn't recognize a single face. None of them even had the DNA-branded familiarity of enduring neighborhood clans. In the old days you could look at a kid and just know he was one of the Brennans, Daverns, Burnses, Montfortes. Families were like tribes then, six and seven strong, some even larger, all in the same church pew on a Sunday morning, wearing each other's hand-me-downs.

Now there was a new and different vibe in the air. None of the people who strolled along the parkside looked homegrown to

Danny. Blow-ins, he thought. And they didn't even have that hungry-to-fit-in demeanor of new immigrants. No, these were people with a monied arrogance in their step, a smugness in their carriage that suggested they had bought their way in, like memberships to an exclusive tweedy brownstone club.

The old tenements that rose above the park were cleaner, the pointing perfect and sure, the areaways swept and immaculate, cornices gleaming with fresh enamel paint. Shiny new Andersen storm windows sealed into modern aluminum frames. Polished brass knobs, knockers, mail slots, and hinges adorned gleaming oak doors. Even the two copper lions on their pedestals above the Third Street entrance to the park had been stripped of their Lady Liberty–green tarnish. Danny thought the whole panoramic sweep of the tree-lined avenue now looked more like Central Park West than Parkside West. It was as if it had been Manhattanized with a great big cosmopolitan airbrush. The unique disheveled elegance that had made Brooklyn look like, well, *Brooklyn*, had been power-washed into the sewers and relacquered with an upscale patina of respectability. The Brooklyn that Danny remembered had gone from a kind of dangerous film-noir beauty to the bright high-gloss slickness of a Mercedes commercial. The buildings were the same buildings. The granite wall bordering the park was still there. Even the trees were all the same as Danny remembered them. But the neighborhood looked like Litchfield's old estate had been sold to rich new owners, overhauled, reimagined, and refurbished, and then a whole new and different list of guests had been invited to stroll its grounds. Natives were made to feel like trespassers.

A commercial for a beta-blocker heart drug called Lopressor came on the radio, the pitchman extolling its miracle-drug qualities for arrhythmia and ventricle tachyacardia and then rattling off a host of side-effects that included fatigue, dry mouth, nausea, diarrhea, and temporary impotence or sexual dysfunction in the first sixty days of use. *Great miracle drug,* Danny thought. *Save your heart, shit in your pants, and kill your dick all with one little pill.*

He parked the car in a no-standing-anytime zone in front of the monument to the Marquis de Lafayette, a large peach-colored marble rectangle depicting the great French statesman who had supported George Washington's colonial army.

Danny had first kissed Erika sitting on the rear base of the monument, still in his football uniform, she in her Blessed Virgin Mary cheerleader uniform. . . .

*September 24, 1968*

*The day she got kicked off the cheerleading squad for cheering for Danny, pom-poms flailing, when Danny scored the wining touchdown to beat her own team.*

*"I couldn't help it," she tells him later. "You had the cutest butt I ever saw. I'd been watching you on the sidelines, with your helmet off, your hair all sweaty, intense, pacing like a savage. Then watching you run, strong legs pumping, breaking tackles, refusing to go down, made me want to jump up and fucking cheer. So I cheered. And I got kicked off the team. And here I am. So what are you gonna do about it, Cassidy?"*

*She shoves him, her big dark eyes searching his, trying to look behind them into his brains. He clutches her face in his dirty hand, kisses her, and thinks for sure he'll also score with her. Any chick who comes on this strong must put out, he thinks.*

*She doesn't. But she wins Danny's sixteen-year-old heart. He falls so hard for impulsive wacky Erika that it scares the shit out of him. . . .*

Meanwhile, a cop car pulled abreast. Danny looked over at the young cop, maybe twenty-five, chewing gum in a slow I'm-in-charge rhythm. His silent female partner sat in the passenger seat, staring his way through a pair of sunglasses with tiny lenses. She chewed her gum the same way as the guy cop.

"Yo, you have a high school diploma, ace," the cop asked.

Danny nodded. "Sign says 'No Standing Anytime.' "

Danny nodded to the cop and pulled away from the curb. The cop car passed him. When Danny crossed Ninth Street he was in more familiar territory. In the old days Ninth Street was the neighborhood "tracks." The Cassidys lived on the wrong side of Ninth Street.

He slithered along the avenue, pretending to look for a parking spot but just refamiliarizing himself with the lay of the land. A city was an ever-evolving entity, and Danny was curious to see what a three-decade glacier of new money had left in its wake. Danny approached "the Bench" on the corner of Twelfth Street, where he had hung out for years with his neighborhood pals. Sometimes twenty-five of them—guys and chicks—gathered on hot summer nights, smoking a little reefer and guzzling beers, always looking out for Ankles the cop. Ankles so terrified the neighborhood that Danny often called the local precinct asking for him, pretending to be a relative, to see if he was working that night. If he was, they often stayed down in their friend Gordon's house, whose father worked nights, drinking indoors. If the desk sergeant said Tufano had the night off, they'd all head up to the Bench for a parkside party.

As he pulled abreast now, two yuppie women who looked like they might be a lesbian couple sat on the bench sipping coffee from cups from someplace called Yankee Doodle Danish, playing an intense game of chess. He double-parked the car to stare at the Bench, remembering carving his and Erika's initials inside a heart into the stone retaining wall behind it with a Rhinegold beer-can opener. He was sure it had faded by now. The two women looked up at him, the thin pretty one smirking and making a comment to the heavier pleasant-faced one. The heavy one grinned, looked back at her chessboard, and calculated a move.

Danny recognized a familiar neighborhood face. Skinnier, more twisted and ravaged by booze and other toxins, grayer, unshaven, rumpled, and missing several front teeth. But he was certain it was JoJo Corcoran, the neighborhood lunatic, who had once saved several passengers from a burning bus, winning himself a write-up in the *Daily News*. But when he joined the navy to avoid the draft, the military made him for a guinea pig. It was later proved that after he was sent to the brig for various infractions, most of them because he was nuts, they had experimented on JoJo with LSD, other mind-altering drugs, and sensory deprivation tanks. After he was given a "medical" discharge, JoJo spent ten years in and out of Kings County, Bellevue, and Pilgrim State mental asylums getting electroshock and more chemical bombardments.

But do what they may have to his brain, JoJo was one of those guys who was a walking trivia trove and could tell you what Ed Kranepool's batting average was in his first year as a Met. He could tell you what movies Paul Newman did every year of his career. He remembered the dates of all the great New York Mafia hits and what the weather was like when they happened. He knew the birthdays of almost everyone in the neighborhood.

JoJo was a harmless soul but loud, always speaking in raspy capital letters. His hair was wild, gray, and stringy, and a scrub of beard clung to his face as he approached the two yuppie women.

"Hey, ladies, this is your unlucky day," he said. "I'm straight, single, clinically schizophrenic, unemployed, on Thorazine, Stellazine, Zoloft, Methadone, and in need of a jug of Night Train. If you give me a quarter I'll flip to see which one of you I leave alone first."

"Do I have to call a cop?" the thin austere-looking woman asked.

"Nah," JoJo said, turning to the pleasant-faced one. "Do me a favor, just move king's pawn to bishop's four, and you got fart face in checkmate."

The pleasant-faced one looked at the board and sat bolt upright, astonished at his suggestion.

"JoJo," Danny yelled.

JoJo turned and looked. "Excuse me, ladies," he said, shambling over to the Camry, and without missing a single beat, as if three decades had never passed, he leaned on the car. "I know I still owe you a deuce since the night *The Intruders* played in the band shell, Danny," he said, pointing to the modernized outdoor concert band shell stage in the Eleventh Street playground. "But I could use another two bucks. That is, if you're working. If not, meet me here on the Bench tonight by eight and I'll see if I can hustle up the deuce I owe you."

Danny handed him five bucks. He watched the pleasant-faced woman in the background make JoJo's move and declare check-mate, pointing at him in dumb show, laughing.

"That's one tenth of the best handout I ever got, which was fifty clams from Dirty Jim a long, long time ago when—"

"Where is everybody?" Danny asked.

"You're looking at him," JoJo said. "Unless you count Swifty Magee, who's still huffing glue. When they ask where have you gone, Joe DiMaggio, they mean it now. Game called on account of dark-ness. The Bench has been benched. The only people you still know are waiting for you up at Dunne's."

"Thanks," Danny said and put the car in drive, about to leave. "Hey, JoJo, you mentioned Dirty Jim. He still alive?"

"Computers," JoJo said. "Plus, he still takes pictures. Seen him in July, the seventeeth, 2:35 P.M., on Church Avenue and East Eighth Street, getting his Lexus washed at Hollywood Car Wash. I was on my way to Silverrod Drugs to get my chlorpromazine scrip refilled. Reminds me, I owe Dirty Jim five, too. I feel bad because he gave me that fifty once just to keep my mouth shut, which is the most I ever got for dummying up. So if you see Dirty tell him you ran into me and I said to say you haven't seen me. If you're looking for me, you know where to find me, same hole in the ground I've been living in for thirty-four years."

Of course, Danny thought, figuring Dirty Jim was now a hacker. The keys of the modern age were passwords. He would threaten to put his dirty photographs on-line.

"Sorry to hear about your old man," JoJo said. "I owed him six bucks. Add it to my tab. Say hello to Erika for me. I don't think she recognized me last time I said hello because I had dentures from the VA dentist then. I sold them to a tourist in Strawberry Fields in Central Park, told them the uppers belonged to John Lennon and the lowers belonged to Mark David Chapman. Twenty-five bucks. But when I saw Erika I still had 'em in."

"When was that?"

"Eight months ago. January fourth, 2:55 P.M., outside the bank on President and Seventh. Raining. . . ."

"How'd she look?"

"She looked like ten million, which is about a hundred mil less than she's worth."

"Haven't seen her lately, huh?"

" 'Course I have. I didn't say I haven't seen her. I just didn't say hello. Christ, Danny, I still owe her the ten she gave the last time I said hello when she didn't recognize me with the dentures in the pouring fuckin' rain but I was afraid she would recognize me this time, without my teeth. Without the teeth I figured she'd make me and I didn't have the tensky to give her back. . . ."

"She's still around, though?"

"No, still skinny, not round. I owe you thirteen, counting the deuce from 1968, and the six I owed your old man since two Halloweens ago, and the pound you just give me. You better give me another dollar before the thirteen brings bad luck. I'd give you back one, to make it twelve, like the Apostles and the Angry Men, but I don't have change."

Danny smiled, amazed and even a little frightened that he could still follow and make half sense of JoJo's legendary stream of con- sciousness all these years later, and handed him another single. JoJo did a pirouette, never said good-bye, and hurried to the two women on the bench. He creased the dollar bill, dropped it on the chess- board, and curtsied. The two women looked up, bewildered.

"You can owe it to me," he said and marched off along the park-side, bent at a forty-five-degree angle, heading toward the liquor store on Sixteenth Street across the street from Foley's.

JoJo had made Danny feel better. JoJo was Brooklyn without the Scotchguard. Before it had been turned into www.newbrooklyn.com.

He drove three more blocks and saw that the old Sanders Theater was now called the Paragon, a multiplex. The last movie he'd seen there was *Easy Rider.* . . .

*April 1969*

*With Erika, in the middle of the week, last row of the balcony, and during Peter Fonda's acid-trip sequence, she unfastens his zipper, bends down, and springs out his thumping hard penis and kisses it.*

*"Get any experience yet?" she whispers, rotating a fingertip on a hot dime of leaking lubricant on the head of his dick.*

*"Some," he tells her, but not wanting to elaborate about the generous lessons he'd received in the back of a VW bus and the water bed of a local earth mother known as Hippie Helen.*

*"Good," she says, kissing it again, a long lingering nibble, her full lips so hot they sizzle. "Because I'm getting closer to wanting to do it with you. . . ."*

Danny saw a blue Ford Escort pulling out of a parking spot near the corner of Fifteenth Road. He darted for it, parked the Camry, and climbed out. He stood on the sidewalk and looked around, saw that the old Parkhouse Diner was now a restaurant named Pie Squared. He took his time turning around. He watched the line of moviegoers file into the theater. He didn't recognize a single person.

Then he turned and walked into Prospect Park, into the mouth of the lion, and started climbing the small rise called Hippie Hill.

*I'm home,* Danny thought.

# four

Danny stopped on the small hillock on the spot where Vito Malone had been murdered, his soft-soled Bally's stepping on a thousand disjointed memories. But not the memory he needed. He took each step as if eluding land mines, trying to remember if he had taken these same calculated steps on that November night in 1969, with Brendan's army-issue .45 tight in his fist.

He crouched, scooped up a small clump of dirt, attempting to will up the images from the hard-packed earth. He felt a soft breeze blowing across the park drive from the ball fields and the bridle paths, tickling the leaves of the trees that would soon be drooping with fall. He closed his eyes, took a breath, tried to force the memories. But he summoned only a white blur. Was that the white cone of light in the black night, he wondered, or was it just a patch of erased memory?

No other clear images of that night surfaced.

Thirty-odd years later he noticed that the bushes along the fence of Parkside South had been allowed to grow wild, a Parks Department sign explaining that it was part of some new forestation program. The same big Norwegian elm towered over the shady slope where the sixties had come to Brooklyn. Here on Hippie Hill, where young people from all over the borough had flocked when the first buds of spring appeared on those bushes. Carting wine skins and water pipes, spreading multicolored blankets on the grass, passing joints, and playing four- and eight-track tapes of the varied folk and acid rock music of the age, the women bared their breasts and had uninhibited sex with multiple partners in those bushes, and everyone got stoned as Brooklyn tried to catch up with Greenwich Village and Haight Ashbury.

But no matter how hard Brooklyn had tried to act sixties the blood-soaked fifties kept blasting through with eruptions of street violence and flag-waving right-wing backlashes. Battles often broke out between the long-haired freaks of Hippie Hill and the hard hats and buzz-cut right-wing denizens of Foley's Tavern a block away. Many of the WWII and Korean War veterans of Foley's were the fathers and big brothers of the draft-evading longhairs. As the hippies smoked dope on Hippie Hill, listening to Dylan sing "Blowin' in the Wind," the Foley's brigade guzzled beer and booze, wore NIXON'S THE ONE buttons, and stood at attention when the national anthem played before every Mets and Yankees game on the two color TVs.

By the time the sun went down on any given weekend night in Prospect Gardens during the late sixties, the animus between the two groups was palpable in the night air. Sometimes fathers and sons duked it out in the center of Veteran's Memorial Square. Sometimes a few of the twisted juiceheads from Foley's would do night raids on the sleeping hippies, a few chicks zonked on barbiturates raped in their sleep. Zombified necrophilia, Danny thought.

They were tense and hairy times, not conducive to meditating and grooving on a Sunday afternoon. Danny came to think of Hippie Hill as a microcosm of an America torn apart by the *war* and silly shit like the length of your hair, or whether or not you got stoned on four reds or Four Roses. Danny didn't remember much of that last year of the sixties and none of the last night that he spent in Brooklyn.

But now that he was back he knew that if he committed this murder, there had to have been a slow, steady escalation to the crossing of that line. There had to have been a specific action that triggered that reaction.

Somehow, he suspected, it was all tied to Wally Fortune and the drug dealer Christie Strong. But Boar's Head Malone had many other enemies. Maybe his partner, Jack Davis, killed Malone and then ate his own gun out of guilt. Maybe he double-crossed his pusher, Christie Strong, and got iced for it. Maybe it was someone Boar's Head had planted drugs on. Maybe he rousted the wrong dude on the wrong night. Maybe it was Wally Fortune's brother, Eddie Fortune, a Green Beret fresh home from Nam, seeking revenge for the bludgeon murder of his brother, Wally, and the suspicious overdose death of his sister, Mary. It could have been a lot of other people. Boar's Head had more enemies than friends.

*It could have been me,* Danny thought.

When he looked to the parking spot where Jack Davis had ended his life, an involuntary shiver scurried down his spine. Parked in the very spot was the forest green Crown Victoria with tinted windows, motor running, air-conditioning frosting the windshield. With the sun mirroring off the tinted windshield, Danny could not make out the face of the driver. But he was certain he was being watched.

*Ankles,* he thought again.

He checked his watch. It was a little past noon.

Danny walked down Hippie Hill, stopping to toe tap the very spot where Vito Malone had leaked his life into the soil. When he looked up the Crown Vic was backing up and speeding away.

*What the hell,* he thought. *Come out and at least say, "Fuck you."*

He turned and strolled along the winding blacktop path on the southwest edge of Prospect Park, toward the Elephant Steps, remembering that it used to be hexagonal cobblestones. He stopped and stared over at the inlaid metal access door to Sewer 7, Pipe 11, the neighborhood nickname for the big dirty underground subway generator room that all the guys used to hang out in on cold or rainy nights. You could gain access to the room from the metal subway plate set into the ground in the bushes near the fence bordering Parkside South.

The Transit Authority workers gained access to Sewer 7 by unlocking the big heavy lock, opening the metal plate, climbing down a twenty-foot metal ladder into the roaring subterranean machine room.

Dirty Jim, of course, had keys to the lock on the metal plate and Christie Strong had made Dirty give copies to his drug dealers, who often evaded cops by escaping into Sewer 7, fleeing into the labyrinthine subway tunnels. The keys got duplicated, and soon the local winos and homeless hippies got copies. Whenever anyone on the Hill needed access to the subway, instead of paying thirty-five cents for a token all they had to do was climb down into Sewer 7, walk down the tunnel catwalk for fifty yards, and climb up onto the platform of the Prospect Park station on the F line.

When it was cold or rainy or when the cops were busting balls—like on the night of July 20—you popped down to Sewer 7 to drink beer, smoke weed, get a blow job, or crash for the night with the rats, who for the most part didn't like the noise or the vibrations of the generator room. It was the neighborhood Bat Cave.

Danny shuddered at the thought of all the sleepless speed-freaked nights he'd spent in Sewer 7, breathing in the dirty air that was alive with airborne bacteria, fungi, and hanta viruses from rodent droppings. *Between all that and the drugs, cigarettes and alcohol, lack of food and sleep, how the fuck did we survive?* he wondered.

He walked on, gulping the good clean air. He approached the
Elephant Steps, the lonesome white-granite stairwell that ascended
one side of a steep hill from the northern side, reached a flat
twenty-foot landing at the summit, and then descended to the
southern side like the steps of a pyramid. Danny climbed the wide
stone steps that were big enough to support the hooves of elephants. At the summit the lush foliage shielded the surrounding
streets from view, promoting a rustic refuge in the big city. At night
it was a moonless sanctuary, a favorite spot for underage drinkers,
kids smoking joints, young lovers knocking off a quickie. Most
times it was desolate and silent, the only sounds coming from
small foraging animals and the anonymous drone of cars whizzing
past on the park drive.

Danny tried to evoke the images of an awful night on this very
spot. He checked his journal.

July 20, 1969

Moon day. All the lunatics should be out. Dropped a tab of
mesc. Round nine. Grooving on the stars. Looking for Apollo
11. Overcast. Walking through the park. Another fight with E.
She busted me on mesc. Eyes dilated. Cotton mouth. Too many
blackbirds to get a boner in the Grindbox. "Clean up your
fucking act, man," she said. Slammed the door.

Mots and Bowles have chicks over for moon-landing party.
Ask me to scram. Later, BH and Apeshape Davis dispersed
everyone on the Hill. Midnight curfew. No answer at HH's
pad. Up for three nights. No sleep. No eat. Sittin' here in
Sewer 7, Pipe 11, with JoJo. Should write to B on historic
night. Gotta patch it up with E. E wants me to meet parents.
Get shave and haircut for birthday. Says she'll give me her
cherry in exchange. Gotta do it. Gotta see if she really is a
virgin. Or if she's been banging the other guys. Is she banging
CS in his penthouse pad? Is she banging LA, the pretty boy
from Bay Ridge who always stops to talk to her when he sees
her? HH taught me all I need to know. Is pretty boy LA E's
teacher?

Dyin' for a smoke. JoJo is sleeping. I'll go to Burgarama
and write B letter in the light, get a smoke. Swap a blackbird
for a smoke and a container of tea. Later, I'll go stand in the
bushes by Garvey Place and see if CS or LA come to ren-

dezvous with E in the night. Life is faster than a speeding speed freak. . . .

The entry ended there.

Fucking profound, Danny thought. He shuddered, thinking of himself in that mental and physical condition. Squatting in Sewer 7, Pipe 11, with JoJo Corcoran, grinding his teeth like a cudding cow, scribbling paranoid, jealous nonsense into a dog-eared journal. The entry was written after three nights of no sleep. And yet it was a touchstone. He could almost taste the foul gluey metallic taste caused by the amphetamine-induced dry mouth. Like a mouthful of subway tokens, he thought. He remembered that on mescaline he had experienced a heightened sense of smell and sound and taste and touch. Everything he saw was in movie 3-D. As he strolled toward the Elephant Steps he could recall vivid images from that night now. . . .

*July 20, 1969*

*Danny walks in the bushes on the edge of the park, always out of view of the "oinks," while carrying drugs, a sweaty, itchy, unwashed watcher in the night. Then, as he climbs the grassy hill alongside the Elephant Steps, he spots Wally Fortune, standing on the summit. He's about to call out to him, hit him up for a smoke and a dollar, when he hears the squealing brakes of an automobile. The slamming of a car door. Footsteps. He sees Boar's Head's green, unmarked Plymouth Fury. Danny's overworked heart races even faster. . . .*

Right over there, Danny thought. By the stone pillar. As he stood on the Elephant Steps in a new century, Danny climbed over the railing and nestled himself into that same stand of scrub pines where he remembered standing thirty-two years before. He looked north, then south, then straight ahead to the stone pillar where he thought he remembered seeing Wally Fortune. He tried to evoke the images of that historic moon-walk night, the same night he was almost sure he'd witnessed a man murdered here in Prospect Park.

Whether he had in fact witnessed it, or only thought he did, that incident had happened. Wally Fortune was murdered right here, he thought. *And it changed my life.*

That murder had sent Danny reeling into paranoid decline and became forever intertwined with the murder of Vito Malone. Which followed him through life like a second shadow. So he stood in those same bushes, looked again, imagining himself flying on speed and mescaline, remembering that his 1969 journal said he hadn't slept for almost three days, his body a frazzled instrument panel of spasms, twitches, and tics. But even in his short-circuiting condition, Danny was almost sure now that he had seen the murder.

*But was I hallucinating?* he wondered. *I was up for three days.* No real food for days. Beer and wine and weed and speed and uppies and mescaline. No sleep. It was dark and cloudy.

Danny's journal suggested he was in a state of mind in which he imagined that Erika Malone was banging half the neighborhood. And she was still a virgin. A July 10 entry in his journal showed that Danny thought Christie Strong was planning to have him killed so he could make Erika one of his growing flock of hippie bimbo flower girls. Danny thought his own father was going to have him shanghaied, and he'd wake up, head and beard shaved, as an enlisted man in a United States Marines boot camp.

*I was a total fucking mess,* Danny thought. *A basket case. Any defense lawyer would have ripped me more assholes than a proctologist sees in a leap year.*

But as he stood here now on the Elephant Steps, he tried to use the surrounding tactile elements as triggers for his memory. Tried to summon the details.

Wally arrived first, Danny remembered. Agitated. Smoking. Pacing. Checking his watch. *I was about to approach him. Then . . .*

*July 20, 1969*

*Boar's Head arrives. Danny stands in the scrub pines, watching the narc car pull up at the bottom of the stairs on Wally's right. Davis comes running up from Danny's left, after being dropped off by Boar's Head, who'd then looped around the other side of the Elephant Steps. Wally Fortune turns to run left and here comes Boar's Head, stalking up the stairs, slapping his nightstick against his open palm.*

*"I'm waiting to talk to your ghee," Wally says, jailhouse jive for headman.*

*"I'm the fuckin' ghee," Boar's Head says.*

*"I need to talk to him about my sister, Mary," Wally says. "She was*

*hot-shotted, man. I know that. You know that. Your ghee knows that.
I wanna know why."*

"Who gives a fuck what you want," *Boar's Head says.*

"Lemme talk to the ghee, to Christie. . . ."

*Without another word Boar's Head smacks his baton across Wally's
face, knocking Wally to the ground. Danny sees blood. Hears Wally
whimper. Danny trembles, adrenaline percolating in his veins. His
heart pounds. His mouth's so dry he can't swallow. As Boar's Head
kicks Wally in the right temple, then the groin, Danny's testicles
retract. His dick shrinks even smaller than the meth-nub.*

"No, please, man, I got a kid bro in Nam; he ain't got nobody else to
come home to, man," *Wally says.* "Please, no, I'll dummy up. Tell
Christie I'll dummy up. . . ."

*Wally clutches the stone railing, hoisting himself to his feet. Boar's
Head runs at him, smashing his baton across the bridge of Wally's
nose. Danny hears the blood lash across the meaty summer leaves.*
"Uhhhn," *Wally groans.* "No, man, no—"

*Boar's Head hitches up his pants, circles a cowering Wally, squats
into a hitter's stance, grasps his nightstick with two hands, arcs it over
his head.*

*Davis grabs the nightstick.* "No, enough."

"Don't you fucking dare," *Boar's Head says.*

"You're gonna kill him. No more. It's not part of the deal."

*Wally tries to crawl away, crying, babbling, the words garbled with
blood. Danny stands frozen, his body rattling now, his matted beard
and scalp itching. Impotent.*

"Get out of my way before I tell your missus on ya," *Boar's Head
says, pushing Davis and smashing Wally as he crawls, leaving a trail
of dark blood, the club crushing the back of his skull. It sounds like a
Louisville Slugger on a melon. Wally's body jerks. His hand grasps for
something, anything to hold. There's nothing there. Davis turns, his
hand over his mouth, ready to barf.* "Stop it! Don't hurt him any
more! Stop it, stop it, stop it!"

*Boar's Head rears on Davis like a horse:* "Fucking sissy. I'm doing
this for you, too. Remember that."

*Davis pulls his gun, aims it at Boar's Head.* "I said no more!"

"Go ahead, let's see if you're man enough to pull the fuckin' trigger.
C'mon. You're already balls deep in everything, let's see if you have the
balls to go a little deeper still. C'mon. . . ."

*Davis shivers. Holds the gun with two hands. Cannot shoot. Danny watches Boar's Head chuckle, then laugh, then turn and beat Wally again and again and again. Maybe a dozen blows to the head. Until Davis staggers Danny's way, gasping for air. Danny can no longer stand it.*

*"Pig! You fucking pig motherfucker," he screams.*

*Davis hollers in fright, covering his ears, dancing in a circle, vomiting on himself. Boar's Head turns. Danny sees Davis look his way. He knows Boar's Head has seen his silhouette, a bearded long-haired hippie. Boar's Head flings his nightstick at Danny. Misses. It rattles down the Elephant Steps like a boy running in wooden Dutch shoes. And the chase begins. Danny runs faster than he's ever run before. Across the Park Drive. Past the ball fields. The cops chase him, but Boar's Head and Davis are no match for Danny's speed on meth. Danny runs into the Quaker Cemetery through a hole he knows of in the fence and disappears into the necropolis of mausoleums and headstones, passing the one bearing the name of Montgomery Clift and scores of markers of slain Revolutionary War soldiers and colonial burghers.*

*The chase lasts about five minutes because Boar's Head and Davis just run out of wind. Danny exits Prospect Park, enters the subway at the Fort Hamilton stop, waits until a train comes roaring into the station, hops the turnstile to the shouts of the token clerk, rides the F train back one stop, gets off at the Prospect Park stop, negotiates the catwalk to Sewer 7, and sits there until the dawn. He has no intention of ever telling anyone what he's seen. He's not even sure he's in fact seen what he thinks he's just seen.*

*Who would ever believe a speed-freak kid accusing two cops of murder? . . .*

Danny wasn't sure if the memory was any good. *How much of what I remember from that year is real,* he wondered. *How much is drug-induced paranoia, hallucination, or delirium?* Danny'd seen a recent TV magazine show about a normal man who on a return flight from Mexico went completely berserk, hallucinating, delirious. He broke into the cockpit, threatening to take down the jumbo jet. Five passengers had to subdue him before he killed everyone aboard. Months later, it was discovered that he was suffering from encephalitis. What he had imagined in his mind still seemed real. The hallucinations, the delirium were permanent memories. *Am I remembering a hallucination,* he asked himself. *Or am I recalling reality?*

Danny stood on this second killing ground, listening to an industry of winged insects, bees on kamikaze missions as the summer died. A chorus of birds sang; startled rodents scurried in the dense underbrush. The smell of horse dung wafted across the park drive from the corral of the bridle path where Wally Fortune's younger sister, a sassy little knockout named Mary, had been found OD'd a few weeks before Wally was murdered. Wally was convinced she had been given a hot shot, street slang for poisoned speed. Her death sent Wally on a revenge mission, and it got him killed. Danny had a vivid memory of that murder but couldn't be sure it was a real or an imagined memory. There wasn't even a mention of it in his journal. *Why*, he thought. *Was I too scared? Did I try to block it out? Or was it because I hadn't seen it and had pieced together my own version of events from bits and pieces reported in the newspapers and on the local grapevine?*

He sighed, kicked the soil. Then he remembered that the very next day had been a nightmare. . . .

*July 21, 1969*

*In the morning he runs into Christie Strong, dressed in flowing robes, silhouetted against the bright sun.*

*Strong tells him he looks nervous, asks why he's so jumpy. Danny doesn't let on about witnessing Boar's Head killing Wally Fortune.*

*But Strong says Danny doesn't look well. He has a hippie chick give him a tranquilizer to relax. But the tranq turns out to be a tab of STP, a ferocious eighteen-hour trip of synthetic LSD that sends Danny reeling through the streets, hallucinating, paranoid, hysterical.*

*Everyone's face is a chisel-jawed character from Dick Tracy. He picks up a pay phone to call his mother. But the phone is an unshelled peanut. He looks at his own reflection in the phone-booth glass and he is Mr. Peanut, wearing a top hat and a monocle. He yanks a dime from his dungarees pocket, gapes at it. It looks and feels enormous, the size of a manhole cover. FDR winks at him from the face of the dime and says, "Heads I win, tails you lose!" Danny tries jamming the giant talking dime into the phone but there's bubble gum over the coin slot and FDR starts to laugh, biting his cigarette holder. "Christie Strong is taking Erika's cherry," FDR says. Danny runs amok. The neon* SAM'S LIQUORS *sign drips loud, splashy blood from the tail of the letter* Q *onto Seventh Avenue. The* Q *is for questions. People are gonna ask me questions that will get me killed. All the cars squeal with steel subway wheels, faces pressed against foggy side windows, drawing letter Q's in the steamy windshields.*

*Danny covers his ears and runs and runs until he comes to the rectory of Blessed Virgin Mary Church, where he was once an altar boy. He rings the bell and bangs on the door at a little past three A.M., bangs and bangs and bangs, until Father McBride answers the door, eating cherries, the juice sluicing down his face like the blood of Christ. Pissed off, half stewed, McBride asks what Danny wants. Danny kneels in the threshold of the rectory. "Bless me, father, for I have sinned," Danny says and confesses that he's witnessed an awful, violent murder. But he doesn't name names. Just rants on in a disjointed acid rampage. And then runs off into the terrifying night.*

*Father McBride calls Danny's mother, who searches the neighborhood and by dawn she finds Danny huddled behind the garbage cans in the back of their own tenement hallway. Mickey Cassidy comes in from Foley's, half in the bag, laughs at frightened Danny. " 'Smatter, can't hold your drugs," he says, smacking Danny on the back of his head. "Already on probation for the marijuana, now you're on the LSD. Time to join your brother in the fuckin' service, asshole." Danny's mother calls a car service, rushes Danny to the emergency room where a Filipino doctor shoots him with a syringe filled with Thorazine.*

*Father McBride also calls Ankles, hinting that one of his old altar boys, a dirty hippie named Danny Cassidy, might've witnessed the recent murder in Prospect Park. Ankles appears in the ER, all over Danny. Danny says he's seen and knows nothing, which is what every young person always says to cops in the neighborhood. Ankles says he knows Danny is on probation for a February pot bust. He says that he can have him violated just for being high on LSD. Danny says he was dosed, slipped it in his soda over in Greenwich Village. Ankles tells him he suspects that a bad cop might have been involved with Wally's death. He tells him he understands if he's scared. But he says he can protect him, even from a rogue cop.*

*Danny's saved by the doctors, who tell Ankles that Danny needs sleep. And to be left alone. Danny's mother takes him home to her house that night, July 21.*

Two weeks later she dropped dead cooking hamburgers at the stove. Danny remembered that he dodged Ankles for most of that month.

Ankles kept his distance in the time of his mother's death. Then Danny ran up to Woodstock for four days. He crashed in other people's pads. He knew that Ankles would track him.

And then Danny learned that Boar's Head was Erika's father, and he knew he was fucked. Ankles soon found that out, too. And he put the full-court press on Danny to testify against the father of the girl he loved. Which would've meant that Danny would lose Erika. When he refused to testify, Ankles threatened to cite him for violating his probation that was due to run out in September.

Which would've meant jail, and also losing Erika. He thought killing Boar's Head was an answer. He was a kid in a squeeze, not thinking clearly, intoxicated by first love, stoned on every drug of the sixties, threatened by jail or maybe murder.

*Maybe I did it*, he thought, thirty-two years later, as gold coins of sunlight dropped through the overhanging trees onto the same stand of pines where he had stood watching a man get beaten to death. The strong smell of those pines overpowered the odor of dung in the hot air like a natural disinfectant. The sounds and smells and sights of life clashed in vivid juxtaposition to the two scenes of murder, and in life-brimming contrast to his father, who lay in a casket in Dunne's a few blocks away. For which he still felt no surge of emotion—no sadness, no joy. Nothing.

He clopped down the last flight of the Elephant Steps, walking out of the thicket of trees into the bright light from the big Brooklyn sky that reflected off the mirror-topped Big Lake of the park. As he passed the refurbished Vanderveer Playground, also now filled with children of white yuppies and their Caribbean nannies, he stopped short.

Idling on the traffic exit ramp was the green Crown Vic, just sitting there, the tinted window obscuring the driver. Danny held up his hands, gesturing to the vehicle in an exasperated pose. "What?" he shouted.

Several mothers and nannies gawked at him, clutching their kids.

The car sat there, gray exhaust blowing out of its tailpipe, a bold and silent intimidation. When Danny approached, the Crown Victoria again crept out of the park, nosing north.

Danny headed in the same direction, toward Dunne's, where his father lay dead.

## five

It was twelve-thirty P.M. when he entered Foley's, which in the old days the Hippie Hill freaks referred to as Fort Foley's because of all the combat vets that hung out in there. He had thought of walking to Dunne's to have a private moment alone with his father before the doors opened for the wake at two P.M. But he could not think of anything he wanted to say to the old man. Even in death.

So he decided to pop into Foley's for a beer.

The place was half full. Most of the customers were old-timers clinging to the wooden rail at the foot of the L-shaped bar, facing Parkside West, feet propped up on the brass footrest. There were no stools, a policy implemented by old man Foley when the bar opened right after Prohibition, on the theory that if you could not stand you had had enough to drink.

The place hadn't changed much at all since 1969. There were no cushions, drapes, or hanging plants. There was nothing soft in the tavern. Even the crowd was hard. The whiskey roar reverberated off the tin ceilings and bounced off the cracked-ceramic tile floors, making it sound like lions trapped in a steel drum. Smoke billowed in front of the cut-glass mirrors behind the thirty-foot mahogany bar. Old-fashioned silver cash registers gleamed in the slats of sunlight that lanced through half-drawn wooden shades on the front and side windows. The registers made *ka-ching* sounds every time Houlie, now a man in his late fifties, wearing a starched white shirt and white apron, rang up a sale. Young guys and women in their twenties stood in a loud loop at the back end of the bar, watching ESPN on a TV set mounted high on the beige-colored wall. That was new. Women were not served in the bar back in 1969.

Danny shouldered out a spot at the bar. Houlie studied him with a silent laser stare as he plopped a Budweiser coaster in front of him. Danny placed a twenty-dollar bill on the bar and said, "Beer."

Houlie didn't utter a word, walked to the glass rack, grabbed a gleaming seven-ounce goblet, pulled the beer tap, and delivered the foam-topped lager to the coaster in front of Danny. He knocked the bar wood next to the beer, indicating it was on the house.

"Sorry about the old man, there, Danny," Houlie said.

A few conversations stopped at the end of the bar, as the old-timers studied Danny Cassidy. Low murmurs replaced the loud booze gab.

"Thanks, Houlie," Danny said and lifted the beer and took a sip.

"He was a good guy," Houlie said.

Danny didn't respond. That was pantheon praise from a cynic like Houlie.

"Balls, he had," Houlie said. "Took shit from nobody till the end. He was in here last month, still smoking and drinking Four Roses. How old was he, anyways?"

Danny wasn't sure and said, "Younger than his liver."

Danny leaned closer to Houlie who also bent toward him now.

"He ever talk about me?"

"He always bragged how good his sons were doing," Houlie said. "Showing off your Los Angeles write-ups with the movie stars. Ally McBeal and like that."

Danny was shocked, stared at Houlie, blinking. He took a deep gulp of the cold beer, washing the nervous morning out of his mouth.

"How you doing?" Danny asked.

"I own a piece a the place now," Houlie said. "Old man Foley died. What the fuck else am I gonna do? Sing and dance?"

The loud saloon conversations resumed at the old-timers' end of the bar and in the general din Danny found the privacy he needed to pry a little deeper.

"Houlie, you remember the Vito Malone murder," Danny asked, almost whispering.

Houlie pulled a beer for a customer who was reading Mike Lupica's column in the *Daily News*. " 'Course."

"I'm thinking of writing about it. . . ."

Houlie looked at him with a fixed stare and said, "Bullshit."

"Huh?"

"You ain't writin' shit about it," he said. "You're askin' because Ankles always thought you were involved. Me, I never believed that. You mighta been an asshole, but you weren't a bad kid. But I do think it's outta line you askin' about Malone, dead thirty-whoozis years when your own old man you ain't seen in all them years is laid out up Dunne's, not even cold yet. Shit like that gives me itchy balls. But that's just me."

Danny looked at him, the conversations raging around him. He took a sip of his beer and tugged his earlobe, nodded his head to the others. "On the Erie Lackawanna, Houl, huh," Danny said, meaning this was just between them. "Main reason I've never been back is because of that murder."

"Why didn't you come sooner, when the old man was still kickin'?"

"That's personal," Danny said. "Family business, inside baseball."

Houlie stared at him, his blue eyes probing for bullshit in Danny's eyes. He didn't find any. If there was one thing people in that neighborhood respected as much as God, country, and Foley's beer it was the sanctity of private family business. People in the Brooklyn he remembered had never used the all-purpose catchphrase "dysfunctional family." A family might be "shanty," or "ugly," or "welfare artists," or "thievin' cocksuckers." But no family was ever called dysfunctional. Because no one knew anyone who came from a functional, or problem-free, family. If anything, Danny thought of his native stomping ground as a dysfunctional neighborhood. Everybody had been to night court at least once to bail out the family fuckup.

"That fucking war tore this whole neighborhood apart," Houlie said. "They were sad times, them sixties. Watching it from here, behind the stick, sober, I seen the guts ripped outta families. I seen father-and-son cops pull guns on each other over that My Lai thing. Seen families busted up for good. I seen grown men like your father, fuckin' United States Marines, fuckin' weep."

Danny said nothing. There were no words to add. In his own inimitable way Houlie, with his tortured Brooklynese, was a sage. He watched Houlie serve the entire group of old-timers at the end of the bar, beer and shots, some had both. Danny tapped his twenty and nodded toward the old men. Houlie grabbed his wet twenty, slapped it against the side of the register where it would stick until it dried and fell off, and rang up twelve bucks and rapped the change on the wet bar. "Round's on Danny," Houlie shouted. The old men lifted their glasses in salute to Danny. One of them, a wizened old guy with one eye half closed from an old stroke, said, "To Mickey Cassidy, USMC." And they all raised their glasses and drank. For show, Danny joined the toast.

"I served Malone that night," Houlie mumbled, leaning closer to Danny. "He had a full shitter on."

"You remember what he was talking about that night?"

Houlie walked to the other end of the bar, filled six goblets of beer, three in each hand, as Danny drained his own glass. Houlie delivered the beers, walked back, grabbed Danny's glass, refilled it, and pointed to a man who looked to be in his early seventies who stood in the corner near the front window at the end of the bar.

"That one's on Horsecock," Houlie barked, doing a loud whinny toward the old man and pantomiming him swinging his dick.

"I'll rock it up in your fat fuckin' ass," Horsecock shouted to Houlie. Houlie laughed, whinnied again, and rang up the one-dollar beer.

Danny lifted his glass and toasted it toward Horsecock, who raised his glass. "Your father was a great fuckin' American," the man said and saluted.

"Thanks," Danny said.

Houlie smiled and leaned closer to Danny. "That old guy got a cock bigger than his fuckin' old nightstick," he yelled. Then, hunching closer to Danny again, Houlie whispered, "He was Malone's captain at one time."

Danny took a sip of beer, letting the data register. Horsecock might know a few things about Boar's Head.

"You were saying Malone was in here getting stewed the night of the murder?"

"Yeah, he was in here that night," Houlie said. "I tole alla this to Ankles back then. And to that other cop the other day, there. Malone said he had to take care of some business. I asked him for his keys, because he was in no shape to drive. But he refused to hand them over. Said he hadda clean up some family business. I thought maybe it had something to do with his wife, or his kid. He was always worried about his daughter. It was like an obsession. He was afraid the Black Panthers were gonna deflower her, or something. He was fuckin' nutty like that."

"What was he like when he was with friends?"

"I don't wanna talk bad about the dead, Danny, know what I mean? You might run inta them in the aftalife and have to listen to their shit for eternity, like."

"I need to know, Houlie," Danny said. "I think you know why."

"If it was me I woulda dealt with it back then," Houlie said. " 'Stead of followin' the Dodgers west."

"I was eighteen, Houl," Danny said. "Me and my old man weren't talking. My mother was dead. Ankles was trying to pin the murder of my girlfriend's father on me. My brother was just home from Nam and he shoved me on a bus. You sure you would have stayed, Houlie?"

Houlie gave him the Brooklyn-polygraph stare again and nodded. "Not many people liked Malone." Houlie said. "I was young, remember, but I thought he was full a himself, too. Thought who the fuck he was, like. Loud. What I call badge-and-gun loud. Loved to let everyone know he was cop, that he was packin' a gun. Nasty when he drank. A fuckin' monster when he went on the Hennessey highway. The cognac brought out the fuckin' demon in him like that Incredible Hulk. But he tipped good. Always had a wad, which who the fuck knows where that came from. A lot of the other cops in here thought he was a bagman. But that was pre–Knapp Commission. No cop ever said nothing about another cop back then, not like today, where they do a fuckin' Olympic hundred-yard dash to the DA's office to rat to avoid jail. Hole on a minute. . . ."

Houlie watched a youthful-looking man in his mid to late fifties dressed in an Armani suit walk in through the back door. His steel-colored hair was so perfect that it looked like it was cut one hair at a time. He wore a dark silk tie with red stripes and polished black Botticelli loafers. His fingernails were trim and buffed. He looked familiar around the eyes. Eyes like a Doberman, he thought. Devil eyes. Familiar eyes. . . .

But Danny couldn't fit the face into the puzzle of time. The man checked his Rolex watch, and Houlie delivered him a quart-size Styrofoam container of beer to go. Foley's was famous for its take-away containers of draft beer.

The dapper man handed Houlie a twenty-dollar bill and told him to keep the change. The man caught Danny's eye and he nodded through tiny gold-rimmed, rose-tinted glasses. He whispered into Houlie's ear, handed him another bill, and turned to leave.

"Sorry about your troubles, Danny," the man said, tilting his beer and leaving through the back door. Through the side window Danny watched the man hop into a double-parked silver Jaguar. A bumper sticker on the car read: BE STRONG, VOTE STRONG. Danny returned to the bar, starting to place the face. Houlie came back over.

"Millions of dollars, three joints of his own, and he still comes in every day for his noon container," Houlie said, refilling Danny's goblet. "He bought you a beer."

"Who was that? Looked a little like—"

"Christie Strong," Houlie said.

"You're fucking kidding me, right?" Danny remembered when Strong was boffing some hot little Jewish hairdresser chick named Stacy from Avenue X, and every two weeks he'd bring her to Blessed Virgin Mary Church, make her sit with him through mass. Afterward Strong would stand in front of the large oil portrait of Jesus Christ that hung in the vestibule, and he would make Stacey trim his shoulder-length hair and beard in a perfect replica of the painting. Strong would then stroll to Hippie Hill in flowing robes, a messianic counterculture figment of his own imagination, with a loyal flock of guy dealers and hippie flower bimbos in his wake. One of them was Mary Fortune, Wally's sister.

Now in the new century Strong's 1960s gentle redeemer look had been replaced by all the images of alpha-male money—designer clothes, tight shave, supple skin, indoor tan, power glasses, Jaguar wheels, steel hair.

"Or, I should say," Houlie said, affecting a proper King's English accent, "Christopher Strong, real estate baron and restaurateur, and city council candidate. Made a fortune over the years buying up shit houses in the neighborhood. Everybody thought he was wacky, like in his Jesus days, that maybe the LSD finally caught up to him, buying rat-trap tenements on Eighth Avenue, Seventeenth Road, the parkside, Prospect Road, across from Evergreen Cemetery. Firetrap tenements, rat nests, shit houses on all them little dog-patch side streets. Strong bought 'em and rehabbed alla them, using Mexicans and Guat-a-ricans and alla them other imports, and made them inta beaut-i-ful one- and two-family homes. Made luxury condos outta Roach Motels. And when the yuppies spilt over Park Slope and came around looking for rooms in Prospect Gardens he stuck them up like counter kids in 7-Eleven. Made more money than Merv Griffin. Got a restaurant called the Strong Arms up near Gorman Place, fuckin' wine costs more than dinner for two anywheres else on earth. But packed every lunch and dinner. All yupped up with Wall Street whiz kids and money honeys."

Houlie excused himself while he went down to tap a new keg of beer. Danny nodded and thought hard and long about Christie Strong.

Strong was the guy who first turned Danny on to hard drugs. Speed, acid, barbiturates. In 1969, Danny remembered, Strong was the biggest drug dealer in the neighborhood, but he was slick enough never to be in personal possession of so much as a pot seed. He had legions of dealers pushing for him all over Prospect Gardens, Park Slope, and Hippie Hill. Including two of Danny's own roommates in his Fifteenth Road crashpad, Lefty Mots and Harry Bowles. Danny wondered if they were still alive.

Strong had two pads back then. One was in the apartment house that towered over the entrance of Prospect Park and Hippie Hill, the place where he had his free-love sexcapades and legendary sixties orgies. But his primary residence was two blocks from Erika's house, a penthouse pad in a doorman building in the fashionable brownstone end of Park Slope near Grand Army Plaza.

Danny had always suspected that Boar's Head and Jack Davis were on Christie Strong's payroll. Strong also had a hungry eye on Erika, watching her move in her skintight hip-huggers, asking when she was going to join his flock.

Erika told him, "I already have one ass in my pants, I don't need another one."

Strong liked to toy with people, play mind games with men, manipulate women. Danny saw him do it many times. One day, while passing a bong in his pad overlooking Hippie Hill, Strong casually mentioned that Harry Bowles must be very tight with his roommate, Lefty Mots. Bowles said, yeah, they were best friends. Christie said, "Must be to share your chick Nancy with him like that." Bowles, tripping and speeding, asked what the fuck he meant. "Oh, shit . . . nothing," Christie said. "Maybe I wasn't supposed to say anything. But when you were crashing here last night I went by your pad to look for Mots and . . . look, man, I figured you *knew*. Sorry, man . . . but she does have one incredible body naked, so who can blame him . . . at least you share her between best buddies, instead of a stranger, right?"

Bowles raced out of Christie's pad searching for Mots and Nancy. He found Nancy first, slapped the shit out of her, and threw her and her clothes out of his pad. And bruised and bloody and with nowhere to go, Nancy came sobbing to Hippie Hill. Where, of course, Christie was waiting, offering to take her in. Meanwhile, Bowles caught up with Mots a little past midnight, and they went to savage blows in the middle of Seventh Avenue. Both got locked up while Nancy spent the night in Christie's bed.

In the morning Christie bailed out Bowles and Mots. And then they both owed him. And as a payback he used them to deal his drugs or carry out some of his other devious schemes, to work off their debts, like indentured servants of his drug industry. Nancy became a loyal member of Christie's flock, available for cooking, cleaning, dealing, and sex on demand in exchange for drugs and lodging.

Christie was older than Danny, but all anyone knew about him was that he blew into town when he was about seventeen. Strong lived in Brooklyn but hung out in the Village and was one of the first guys to import hippiedom to Brooklyn, bringing flower chicks to hang out on the sweeping knoll they then called Hippie Hill, strumming guitars, and baring their breasts. His flock would turn people on to the great weed, acid, mescaline, and pussy from the Village. Soon people came from all over Brooklyn to score on Hippie Hill. And Christie seemed to grow richer by the month.

He started to believe his own mythology, that he was a sixties guru of sorts, a go-to swami whenever you were down on your luck and needed help.

And once you needed help, bared your weaknesses, Strong owned a piece of you.

Danny knew that no matter how respectable he might be now, Strong had made his fortune selling drugs in the sixties. But he never knew him to take anything stronger than a beer or wine and a joint for himself. Danny remembered when a sizzling-hot nineteen-year-old hard-to-get Italian chick named Ella that he fancied thought she was buying three amphetamines from Christie so she could dance the night away at the Electric Circus, Strong ordered Nancy to fill the gelatin capsules with LSD. Just to see how stuck-up Ella reacted when she swallowed three trips at one time.

Then he paid Dirty Jim to follow Ella around with a camera, to take pictures, leaping out from between parked cars or from behind trees, flashbulbs popping in the night. Ella freaked out, went so over the edge that she stripped naked and ran through the streets, screaming for her mother.

And Strong appeared in front of her out of the terrifying night, dressed as Jesus in his flowing white robes, hands aloft like a saint giving a blessing. He was a real-life mirage of salvation to a young girl whose mind was exploding with demons. Strong told Ella that he had the antidote to the devil's bad trip. All she had to do was come with him to his pad to make the devil-monsters go away. In his pad, long before "roofies" and other date-rape drugs became popular, Strong gave Ella a cup of hot sweet tea and three Thorazines, which were known as straitjackets in a pill. Hours later, after she awakened, Ella found herself stretched on his bed. Naked.

"Now, for saving you, you must kneel and worship at the altar of my cock," he said. Ella, Stacey, and two other chicks had told Danny almost identical stories about Strong.

Other times, if he fancied a hot chick and wanted her right away, he'd have his dealers give her downs instead of ups, Seconal barbiturates in the amphetamine capsules, so she would be zonked out cold by the end of the night. And then Christie would take her to his beautiful penthouse apartment, furnished with Manhattan-bought antiques, a king-size brass bed, Persian rugs, original art and signed prints, suede coaches, soundproof walls, and his prized five-thousand-dollar sound system, and she would wake up naked in his bed. Often with another naked chick like Nancy or Ella whom she didn't even know. And before she left, Christie Strong would have her convinced he found her naked and OD'ing in the park. And he saved her life. And she would "worship" him and become a member of his cult-harem. They flocked around Christie because he had wads of money, a great pad, tickets to the best concerts in town, and the best drugs in the city.

Christie Strong was every parent's sixties nightmare, a messianic guru who reminded Danny back then of the sinister bird-faced monster who ate people whole and farted them into hell in the hellish third panel of Bosch's *Garden of Earthly Delights*. Strong was like a mad Third Reich medical experimenter, Danny thought. He used human beings as guinea pigs.

If the sixties were about flower power, Danny thought, Christie Strong was a fucking funeral wreath.

He'd always believed it was Strong who gave him the megadose of acid that had sent him reeling on a bad trip on the night after he'd witnessed the Wally Fortune murder. Which had always made him suspect Strong must've been somehow involved in that, too. Even earlier, when he had refused to be a dealer for Strong, Danny thought Strong had even set him up for that 1969 pot possession bust that put him on probation.

He thought about all of that, back in the days when he ran through the night streets into the grim dawn, a paranoid speed freak, a boy who cried wolf so many times even Little Red Riding Hood wouldn't have believed him.

*Strong is the kind of guy who would have put me into this situation for cheap laughs,* Danny thought. *But even Strong wasn't crazy enough to kill a cop. Unless he had to. And needed me as the fall guy.*

Houlie returned from the cellar and filled the empty glasses on the bar, leaving Danny's for last. He filled it. Danny took a swig and said, "Strong always seemed to have the world by the balls."

"You gotta hand it to the guy," Houlie said. "He don't like some of the real estate zoning laws, he wants to build high-rises, so he's running for the local council seat, on the Independent ticket. Bet he wins, too, with his money. Some people say he changed the neighborhood, saved it from going down. Everybody's property values are up, and they point to him as the main guy to thank for it."

*Prick scrambled more local brains than Sun Myung Moon and Timothy Leary combined and he's gonna be a councilman,* Danny thought. *I'm running from the law and this shit heel is gonna be the law?*

A snatch of a song played in his head: "Something is happening here / what it is ain't exactly clear. . . ."

A stampede of firemen dressed in formal uniforms burst through the front and back doors, arriving from an early-morning funeral for a firefighter who had died in the line of duty. Foley's swelled to three-deep at the bar, Houlie swamped with beer requests.

Danny finished his goblet of beer, and when he caught Houlie's eye as he filled a long succession of glasses, he asked, leaning on his hand that shielded part of his mouth. "Houl, the other cop who's been asking questions about Malone, you have a name?"

Houlie placed three beer pitchers under three running taps, turned, rummaged around in a cigar box located next to the cash register, shuffled through a stack of business cards, and came up with the one he was looking for. He handed it facedown to Danny.

"Keep it," he said. "Look, I'll see ya up Dunne's, hah?"

"Thanks."

Danny turned to leave, looking at the business card emblazoned with the official seal of NYPD. There was an office phone number, a pager number, and a cell phone number on the card under the cop's name: Detective Pat O'Rourke, Cold-Case Squad.

Danny placed his empty glass atop a ten-dollar tip, nodded to Houlie, and headed for the door. As he opened the door he heard Houlie whinny at Horsecock, who slammed his left hand into the crook of his right arm to give him the "up yours" salute.

"Hey, Danny," Houlie shouted above the roar.

Danny turned. Houlie gave him a dead-eyed nod of approval and said, "Welcome home."

six

Dunne's was near empty when Danny entered a little past one-thirty
P.M. The funeral director, a pleasant middle-aged woman named
Bridey McCann, greeted Danny at the door. He told her who he was
and she led him upstairs to the office to sign some formal papers, to
write checks, and to tell him how the wake and burial would pro-
ceed. They'd start the wake at 2 P.M. sharp for the afternoon session.

"They're usually fairly empty," she said, still blessed with the stubborn remnants of a Dublin brogue after years of life in Brooklyn.
"The older folks usually come by day so they won't have to venture
out after their tea. The wake will be today and tomorrow.
Unfortunately, as I might have mentioned, we'll be closed on
Sunday and on the Labor Day holiday come Monday. So your daddy
will be interred on the Tuesday. All right, then?"

"Sounds fine," Danny said.

"Father Finn in Blessed Virgin Mary will do the requiem mass,"
she said. "I've included the church fees, with tips for the priest and
altar boys in the package."

Danny nodded, remembering pocketing tips as an altar boy at
weddings, christenings, and funeral masses. The altar boys used to
battle to serve those special events. At requiems, Danny would stand
over the casket, swaying the incense urn, making sure the smoke
wafted into his eyes, so they would well with tears, which the
bereaved would assume were for the deceased, and that would
sometimes fatten the tip.

"You're all set then," Bridey McCann said, handing him her business card. "The less you have to worry about all this business, the
easier it will be for you to deal with your loss. If there's anything else
at all I can do for you, just call."

"Thanks," Danny said. "Can I go down now?"

"Sure," she said. "You might want a few wee minutes alone."

She led him down the dark carpeted stairs, across the hushed
lobby furnished with overstuffed armchairs and settees, every oaken
end table stocked with boxes of Kleenex. She stopped at the door of
chapel number one and made a small flourish with her hand. Danny

nodded to Bridey, who said, "God bless," turned on her heel, and hurried away.

Danny entered the chapel. It was the same one where his mother had been laid out thirty-two years before, after the pain caused by Brendan going to war and Danny leaving home at seventeen made her forty-three-year-old heart explode. The dead bastard in the front of this room was the cause of all that, Danny thought. It was hard to think of him as kin. And yet, he was his father. His DNA made up half of his life.

He scanned the room. Sixty chairs faced the mahogany casket. Five wreaths had already arrived, standing on pedestals on either side of the coffin. He paused as he breathed in the close flowery air of the windowless room. He looked up at his father, who lay still in the coffin, his face a miniaturized caricature of the old square-jawed hard-ass marine. Danny didn't walk to him, choosing instead to read the wreath cards.

The first one was from Houlie and the guys at Foley's, a green carnation shamrock, with the inscription "One for the road. RIP." The second wreath was from the local VFW post, poppies forming the insignia of the United States Marine Corps. The third wreath was smaller, traditional, and inscribed: "Give 'em hell in heaven, Mickey. RIP, Anthony Tufano."

*Ankles*, Danny thought. *Big flatfoot sends a wreath to my father while he's trying to put me in the can. Nice.*

The fourth was huge and ostentatious, red roses shaped as a heart, and the card was signed by Christopher Strong, "Peace, love, and eternal happiness." Like a recycled sixties farewell, Danny thought. One from the old cop. One from the old drug dealer. One from the Marines. Some send-off.

The fifth wreath was the classiest, fashioned of white roses, from a Manhattan florist. Danny examined the handwritten card and a tremor of excitement rocked him back on his heels: "Earth, receive another honored guest, Mickey Cassidy is laid to rest. . . ."

He knew the bastardized quote well, from the poem written by W. H. Auden on the death of William Butler Yeats. It was the same quote he'd used in his eulogy for his mother. But he'd never seen it written in such beautiful script before. He'd have recognized the handwriting anywhere, a Catholic schoolgirl's neatness, written in fountain pen, the penmanship of a strong-willed and confident woman. The card was signed with the initials E.M. Danny would recognize Erika Malone's handwriting if it were written in the summer sand of Coney Island.

*Everything is different,* he thought, *but nothing has changed. . . .*

Danny walked to the coffin, stood above his father. He did not kneel. He looked down at him in repose; his once big strong face now sharpened to an ax head of diminished bone and taut translucent skin, the mouth like an old jagged scar. The mortician's best efforts could not hide the nicotine stains on his right middle and index fingers from a lifetime of Camels. He looked like he had battled every day before he waved the white flag in the endless war he waged against himself. He didn't look so fucking tough, Danny thought. Didn't look at all like the son of a bitch who had tongue-lashed Brendan into going off to war. Or like the drunken foul-mouthed prick who'd driven his mother into despair and a wooden box in this same room, cheated of thirty or forty more good years.

He swore to himself that he would not speak to his father's corpse, like some mawkish scene out of a bad B movie. But when he looked down at his father, he sighed. Although he was a secular man who didn't believe in a spiritual afterlife, if anyone could hear him from beyond it would be his mother. And she'd had enough disappointment in this life, he thought. So in case she was listening Danny looked at his father and whispered, "You're gonna get yours from her now, asshole."

"Got a light?" asked the balding guy with the black shiny suit, black T-shirt, and black Nikes. He was standing with three other gray-haired guys dressed in sports jackets and dress slacks and polished shoes under the green canopy outside of Dunne's. Danny gave the bald guy a light. He puffed on his Marlboro and said, "Thanks, Danny."

Danny stepped back, smiled. "BW? That you, Walsh? Brian Walsh?"

BW was a Vietnam veteran who had come home from Nam with a Silver Star, a Bronze Star, two Purple Hearts, and hair to his shoulders. In the summer of 1969, he morphed from a killing machine of the First Air Cav into a flower-power hippie. BW was the first of the older Nam vets to blend into the counterculture of Hippie Hill, and who drove the local buzz-cut right-wingers of Foley's nuts by choosing to hang with the antiwar faction of the divided neighborhood. "After all the killing and dying all I want is to get high and get laid and not necessarily in that order," BW told the Foley's crowd. Danny remembered a day in 1969 when BW entered Foley's with his Silver Star pinned to his tie-dyed shirt, hair flowing, and ordered a beer. The whole place came to an ominous hush. Then Houlie pulled him a beer, knocked wood, and said it was on the house.

"Yeah, it's me, or what's left of me," BW said, with a throaty laugh. "Jesus Christ, Danny, you look . . . older . . . but the same. Sorry about the old man. Mine went twelve years ago. From these. . . ."

He held up his cigarette and coughed. And laughed. Then the other three guys gathered around and soon Danny was hugging and backslapping them. Kenny Byrne, now silver-haired and wearing thick-lensed glasses, was a year older than Danny and had been his best friend in Blessed Virgin Mary grammar school. Danny and Kenny had schemed together in the streets until he went off to Vietnam, even though three doctors had pronounced him legally blind in one eye and half blind in the other. Timmy O'Toole was now at least 300 pounds. He puffed a big cigar and smacked his big round belly. If he didn't know it, Danny would never have guessed that he'd almost lost his life to encephalitis in Nam, 117 pounds when he arrived home.

Eddie Fortune, kid brother of Wally Fortune, was still built like a Green Beret, his broad shoulders and big arms and hard trimmed waist filling up his suit like cement poured into a mold. He didn't smoke. He wore no glasses. His eyes were polar-blue and scary under a short crop of still-dark brown hair. Danny could detect a familiar haunted gleam of unfinished business in Eddie Fortune's frosty eyes. He'd seen that look before. In the mirror.

"Sorry about your loss," Eddie Fortune said. Danny nodded thanks.

"Errrr, Cassidy-ah, never thought you'd come back home-ah," Kenny Byrne said with the same peculiar speech pattern he'd had as a kid, a singsongy accent that was unique to just the Byrne family. The Byrnes started every sentence with the skeptical prefix "errr" and added the exasperated suffix "ah" to most proper nouns and the last word of every sentence.

"Death ends all contracts," Danny said.

"Errr," Byrne said. "Depends on who's dead-ah."

"Speaking of death," said BW. "I get this black suit dry-cleaned so often since I turned fifty that now I call it my gray suit. In case no one told you, everybody's dead almost."

"Who?" Danny asked.

BW counted fingers as he said, "Slappy, George, Bruno, Louie Arguento, Ocar, Tony Mauro, Tommy Ryan, Anthony, Richie, Mikey Hallahan, Lefty Mots, Harry Bowles. . . ."

"Jesus Christ," Danny said.

"Him too," O'Toole said and laughed at his own joke.

"What the fuck did they all die from?" Danny said.

"From being born in the same neighborhood as Christie Strong," Eddie Fortune said.

"Mots and Bowles snorted bad meth a few weeks after you left town," BW said.

"They were my roommates," Danny said.

"Funny how life is," O'Toole said. "If you didn't go on the lam over Boar's Head's murder, you might've snorted the same meth as your roommates."

Danny nodded and saw the green Crown Victoria slide past on Parkside West, pausing outside of Blessed Virgin Mary Church and then parking at a hydrant near the corner of Gorman Place. He remembered when he was a seventeen-year-old meth freak he used to think that every car that passed was filled with assassins—narcs, John Birchers, Black Muslims, FBI, his probation officer. Or Christie Strong's henchmen from the Village, dirty cops, Boar's Head's pals, people scheming to take his life as he raced through the streets.

Thirty years later he was sure the Crown Vic was no paranoid delusion. He was being tailed. By someone who thought he was a murderer. Looking to put him in a cage.

"Most of them died of drugs and AIDS," BW said. "But George blew his head off with a shotgun, while listening to the Mothers of Invention, in '93. That alone told you he needed serious fuckin' help but you gotta figure there was drugs in there somewhere, too. Slappy, he walked in front of a gypsy cab on the parkside smashed on goofballs in '86. Tony Mauro wound up with his throat cut on a parkside bench in '79, maybe '80. Turns out he was Ankles's son, with Marsha Mauro."

"No shit?" Danny said.

"Some people think Tommy Ryan had that crazy fuck Cisco ice him," O'Toole said. "But then they both got whacked in something to do with a bank heist. That kid Alley Boy, he got in the wind afterward. It was Ankles's case, but then what wasn't? Bruno and Mikey, they got the cancer in the last few years. Anthony and Ocar got the AIDS shootin' dope in the early nineties. You remember Ocar?"

Danny was distracted by the Crown Vic but decided not to remark on it. *BW and O'Toole mention Ankles,* Danny thought, *and there he is across the street watching me. Creepy. But Ankles is supposed to be watching me. He promised he would. Don't let him know he's bothering you. Laugh. . . .*

"Of course I remember Ocar," Danny said. "We called him Ocar because he spelled his name wrong giving himself a jailhouse tattoo, left out the letter *s*."

"When someone suggested he take the GED he thought it was a new drug," O'Toole said.

They all shared a laugh and the guys told Danny what they were doing these days. O'Toole was retired on a bad-back three-quarters medical pension from the Sanitation Department and collecting an army pension and SSI as well. Byrne was a successful real estate agent in Jersey. Eddie Fortune was a corrections officer in Rikers Island, getting ready to retire after putting in almost thirty years. BW was still working for the *New York Times* as a printer and had carved out a nice second career for himself as a photographer.

"Those're BW's wheels over there," said Timmy O'Toole, pointing to a Mercedes SL5000. "Fuckin' Benz. The fuckin old love-beads-and-balls-crabs hippie, the one who told us it was spring by being the first one to get naked on Hippie Hill, the first one to fuck Hippie Helen under the stars to kick off the season, the one with the fuckin' peace signs all over his cutoffs. This very same fuck-the-establishment anarchist is now a fuckin' Mercedes Benz yuppie."

"Bullshit," said BW, laughing. "I'm too old to be considered a young urban pig. I'm not a yuppie; I'm what you might call a successful hippie."

"Errr, Walsh-ah," said Byrne. "You believe in flower power, all right, F-L-O-U-R, the kind that makes the bread-ah."

The old friends exchanged some goofing and catch-up ball-busting for the next few minutes. No one mentioned Boar's Head or Erika or Christie Strong. There was too much time between them, too many kids, grandkids, divorces, new wives, second-marriage baby-boomer kids, and death for one sidewalk gabfest. They all promised they'd get together in Foley's as soon as Brendan came home.

"It's two now," said BW, checking his gold Tag Heuer watch. "I'm gonna go in and pay my respects to your pop and then I gotta go photograph a hot young dame I met in Williamsburg last week. I'm doing a series of nudes called 'Babes in a Benz.' "

"Williamsburg, the old Polack and Rican neighborhood, is the new yupp-a-hood," said O'Toole. "Filled with sculptors, artists, bull-shit artists, dot-comers, yups, and successful, aging hippies like BW. All pushing the native locals out with the sky-high rents like this neighborhood. The only one who can still afford to live in this neighborhood now is BW, because he inherited his parents rent-controlled apartment on the parkside for, like, three hundred and change a month, which is what parking spots go for around here now. Me, I bought in Staten Island."

"He complains, but he crashes at my pad every time he argues with his wife," said BW. "Which is every time he feels like going drinking."

O'Toole guffawed, jammed the cigar into his smiling face, flicked his white eyebrows, and smacked his big belly. "Once a month," he said. "Takes three weeks to recuperate from one three-six-pack night now."

"Err, I'll get you guys to buy out in Jersey, yet-ah," said Byrne. "I'll even take three percent instead of six-ah. Then I'll get you all into the rooms."

"You couldn't sell me a fuckin' headstone in Jersey," said BW, entering Dunne's.

"Only reason to ever go to Jersey is the Giants," said O'Toole, following BW.

"Better than Staten Island-ah," said Byrne, stepping into the lobby. "Which is a great place to live . . . if you're a fuckin' seagull-ah."

"I got no complaints," said O'Toole.

Danny was now standing outside alone with Eddie Fortune. He was silent for a long moment, staring off toward Prospect Park, where his brother had died in 1969.

"I been waiting a long time to see you," Eddie said.

"I think you know what I think I saw," Danny said. "I think I saw Boar's Head kill your brother but I was smashed. . . ."

"You protected that pig," Eddie said.

"I protected myself," he said. "We were kids. He was gonna kill me. No one would have believed me if I couldn't believe my own eyes. If he got off, I was next. Plus, I was in love with his daughter. I was in a box. I had every intention of . . . never mind. It was a crazy time. But Boar's Head is dead. So is Davis, his partner. Let it rest, Eddie."

Eddie was silent for a long, jaw-grinding moment. "For thirty years I been working in that fucking jailhouse," he said. "Breathing in the TB; listening to the mindless doped-out skells; watching people act like animals, slicing, dicing, and icing each other; watching a parade of neighborhood guys march in and out of the place. I always hoped and prayed that once, just one time, the guy I'm convinced was in cahoots with Boar's Head and Davis would strut in. The pusher who I'm convinced gave the orders to kill my big brother, Wally. I only wanted to have him for one fuckin' night. Put him in the bing. Slam the door. Just him and me. Alone. Nowhere to run. No lawyers. No flunkies. No witnesses. I'd get the fuckin' truth out of him. But no one ever laid a glove on Christie Strong."

"My advice, Eddie, leave it alone. No one's after you."

"What if it had been Brendan? Would you leave it alone?"

He looked Eddie in the cold blue eyes. They were like funhouse mirrors that showed a distorted reflection of Danny in the overcast afternoon. "No."

"I want you to help me put the pieces together," Eddie Fortune said. "I know you saw them kill him. I know you heard shit. I know you know things. I want this motherfucker Christie Strong in one of my cells before I put in my papers. The only reason I don't kill him is because I want him in jail. In a cage. Like a fucking trapped rat. Where he has to do what I say. Where I can watch him die a minute, an hour, and a day at a time. I've waited all my life. I never bothered you. Never tracked you down. Never badmouthed you because if you killed Boar's Head, like most people think, you deserve a fuckin' medal. If you helped make Davis eat his gun, I owe you a steak at Peter Luger's."

"Eddie, I'm not sure what happened. . . ."

"But here you are now," Eddie said. "And we both know those two dirty-cop mutts worked for Strong. Jesus Christ, Danny, this monster had my beautiful, sweet kid sister whacked. Wally knew that. But Strong found out he knew. And so Strong ordered Malone and Davis to ice Wally. They beat him like a fucking baby seal, Danny. I seen the murder-book pictures. Wally's happy, always-laughing face was gone, Danny. Gone."

Danny watched Eddie Fortune thumb away a single tear. He looked off toward Prospect Park, swallowed hard, his Adam's apple jumping in his neck. "Eddie, I'm so sorry, man. . . ."

"I need you to help me find out why I went away to war and lost my big brother and kid sister back home," Eddie said.

Danny was glad Eddie wasn't after him. He fell silent, took a last drag on a Vantage, and tossed it into the gutter. The Crown Vic pulled away and cruised down Gorman Place toward Eighth Avenue.

"You married, Eddie? Kids?"

"Divorced, two daughters. One's in college in Buffalo. The other married a lawyer, out in Long Island. I have a grandson. She named him Walter, after Wally."

Danny knew all this meant that 1969 had haunted Eddie Fortune's life, too. Eddie was ready to retire. His marriage was history. Kids grown and gone. He had nothing to lose. His single goal in life was to close a door left open in 1969. It made Eddie all the more dangerous, he thought.

"Eddie, I don't even know what happened the night Boar's Head was killed," Danny said. "I'm gonna try to find out. If I find the proof you're looking for, I'll let you know. As long as you promise me one thing."

"What?"

"You go with me to Ankles," he said. "You don't pop Christie yourself. Because if you do, then I become an accomplice, a coconspirator, whatever they can cook up. I want answers, you want answers. I'm too old for one of your fucking cells. OK?"

"Understood," he said, handing Danny a business card. "But if you need me, remember, I live in Marine Park and you can reach me twenty-four-seven on my cell phone. You call, I'm there. I have a legal gun. I gotta let my brother and sister rest in peace, Danny. I need peace, too."

"I know the feeling," Danny said and followed Eddie Fortune inside to look at the others pray over his dead father.

# *seven*

Danny spent two hours at the afternoon wake. After his pals signed the guest book, paid their respects, said their prayers, and stood in the back for ten minutes, they said good-bye. Then a few old-timers trickled in. They all signed the guest book, writing down their names and addresses so that thank-you cards could be mailed. Danny knew he would never send any. But it was part of the traditional ritual, a ghoulish ledger to let the bereaved know that they had come to pay their respects. In that neighborhood you signed the book maybe seventy-five to a hundred times, Danny thought, before people came and signed one for you. And that became the book of your life. And death.

He watched about twenty people sign in and after five o'clock, Danny drove downtown to the hotel, getting stuck in the rush-hour traffic for over forty minutes. He checked his rearview several times for the green Crown Victoria, but it was not there. Maybe Ankles went to eat, he thought.

In the hotel he saw the message light was blinking and he dialed up the voice mail. "Danny, this is Tammy. I just wanted you to know that I heard from Darlene. She lost her cell phone white-water rafting. A friend of hers almost drowned. She was very upset. She borrowed a friend's cell phone and asked me to send her condolences. But she said she didn't know if she could make it down for the wake or funeral because of bad weather but I sensed she really wanted to see you. I'm sorry about your father. Bye."

*Tammy probably added the part about Darlene really wanting to see me,* he thought. *How could I have blown my relationship with my own kid?* That was like another kind of murder.

He showered, had a shave, changed into a black Cerutti suit, fresh black socks, and black underwear, and put on a dressy black T-shirt and the same black loafers. He ate a turkey sandwich in the hotel restaurant, saw a black family eating dinner together in a booth, the father holding his daughter on his lap as he fed her mashed potatoes. He thought again of Darlene. A chord of self-pity twanged through him, making him feel maudlin and wispy. He ordered a beer, gulped it, and paid the bill in cash, overtipping the pretty waitress. She reminded him of a younger Tammy. Or Darlene right now.

He drove back to Parkside Gardens through light drizzle. He veered through Prospect Park into the fateful parking lot near Veteran's Mcmorial Square and nosed the Camry into the spot where Davis had killed himself. He sat for a long moment, looking up at Hippie Hill, watching the building rain nibble the yellowing lawn, remembering the horror on the faces of Davis's wife and kids as the awful splat hit the side window.

He gazed at the entrance to the park and tried to recall himself walking up there, gun in hand, on the night of Boar's Head's murder. Nothing came.

He exited the car and jogged through the slanting rain to Dunne's.

This time the room was packed. *How did this prick get so many mourners?* he wondered. Danny watched Horsecock sign in, the old-timer whose balls Houlie had busted like prison rocks. Horsecock was half in the bag and wobbled up to the coffin, knelt, blessed himself, and touched Mickey Cassidy's hand and prayed. Danny drifted over to the book and saw the old man's name—Henry Bush, 267-A Langston Place.

Most of the other guys had familiar, neighborhood faces that were like computer-aged renderings of themselves. He couldn't fit first names to most of the faces, but many of them were the older whiskey-crumpled versions of the hard-assed young buzz cuts who'd clashed with the long-haired hippies in the late sixties. The men were older and frailer now, most of them gray or bald, some using canes, others limping, one in a wheelchair. Clean-shaven and puffy-eyed, they all nodded and shook Danny's hand and said kind words about his father as they entered and left, heading for Foley's. The bizarre ritual of the Irish Catholic dead. There were only a few women, wearing Kmart raincoats, sitting in obligatory stoic silence with their men.

Horsecock approached Danny as he was leaving and gripped his hand so tight it felt like he'd caught his fingers in a steel door. His breath smelled like whiskey and denture plaque. "Me and your old man were as close as shit to a blanket," he said, his voice loud like a man too vain for hearing aids. "I lost my beautiful Eleanor six months ago, married sixty-one years. I thought I'd never come out of that depression. Now losing your old man is like losing my left nut. I'm gonna miss him. He loved the Mets. Me the Yanks. We busted each other's hump, drank, and cheered ourselves hoarse in Foley's during the subway series in 2000, just like we did in '56. That's how long we go back. You ever need anything, call me, Danny boy. 'Oh Danny boy. . . .' "

*Christ, how I hate that sappy fucking song,* Danny thought.

"You used to be Vito Malone's commanding officer on the cops?" Danny asked.

"Why would you bring up a shit bird like Vito Malone at a time like this?" asked Horsecock, in double-digit whiskey decibels.

Several hushed conversations paused as mourners turned to Horsecock.

"I need to know a few things about him," Danny whispered.

"Vito Malone would've needed a stepladder to sniff your father's ass."

"It's about his murder."

"I've spent over thirty years trying to forget him," Horsecock said. "Let it rest."

"I can't," Danny whispered.

"Why all this renewed interest in that mutt?" Horsecock asked, his voice lowering. "Oh, yeah, you're the young Cassidy kid who lammed west, huh? Well, I don't think of Vito Malone as a member of my PD. He lived like a skell. Died like a skell. Let sleeping skells lie."

"Can we talk soon, Henry? It's important."

"Well, for Mickey Cassidy's son, anything. I'm in the book."

Danny's eyes moved to the guest book pedestal where he saw Christie Strong singing in. Instead of the nondescript pen attached to the book on a small chain, Strong used his own gold Mont Blanc. A stunning Latina in her twenties, wearing a satin black pants suit stood by his side, clutching his arm. Her big dark eyes darted around the roomful of Irish mourners, a black velvet choker with one white pearl around her long elegant neck, accentuating the pronounced clavicle bone. *Sizzler,* Danny thought. *The kind of chick that made men knife each other in dance clubs.*

Christie Strong was at least thirty years older than she was, but she moved with a mature, world wise grace. Strong spotted Danny and nodded.

"I'll call you," Danny said to Horsecock.

"Get me in the mornings, before Foley's opens at eight,"

Horsecock said, crushing Danny's hand good-bye. "I do my morning constitutional."

Danny watched Christie Strong approach with the Latina, a resigned grin on his face. He and Horsecock exchanged a chilly look as the old man moved past him. Strong's eyes still had that eerie glint of foreboding Danny remembered as a kid. He extended his hand and Danny gave him a dead-fish shake.

"Sorry for your loss, Danny," Strong said. "Viviana, say hello to Danny Cassidy. He's the guy I told you about. A big-time reporter for the *L.A. Chronicle*. Viviana wants to be a reporter. I'm trying to help break her into the business. Maybe you can give her a few pointers sometime, Danny."

"Hi. Sorry about your poppi," Viviana said. "I lost mine when I was a kid. Nothing in life prepares you for it."

She had beautiful white teeth, and there wasn't a single wrinkle in her supple face.

"My first and last piece of advice is to try another business," Danny said. "Newspapering is a noble but dying business."

"Speaking of which," Strong said, "baby, would you please go say a prayer for me. In Spanish."

"I'll say two. One for each of us."

Danny watched Viviana stride up the side aisle of the chapel as the murmur of a dozen older men rustled the room like a small randy wind.

"You have a beautiful daughter."

Christie smiled. "Viv's the oldest of Team Strong," he said, grinning. "Twenty-four. The French say a trophy woman should be half your age plus seven. But I love America and I believe an American man's perfect mate should be half your age or less."

"The gospel according to Christie. Worship at the altar and all that."

"God, Danny, the sixties are so over they teach it in school now. Join the new century. It's cleaner, faster, and more lucrative. The minute you get nostalgic for the sixties I defy you to name one sixties chick you would sleep with now."

Erika Malone flashed into his mind's eye in a montage. But he realized that in every pose she was seventeen, in skintight bell-bottoms or a Catholic school uniform.

"With the exception of Erika Malone, of course," Strong said. Danny looked over Christie Strong's shoulder and saw Eddie

Fortune standing near the back wall, hands clasped in front of him, staring at the back of Strong's head like it had a bull's-eye on it.

Danny saw an obese sixtyish woman enter with a reed-thin man in a tan Armani suit that was spotted with rain. They took turns signing the book. Danny noticed the skinny man nod to Christie Strong while smoothing a desperate comb-over on an emaciated head that looked like the model for the Jolly Roger. He was so skinny that Danny could see his life ebbing and flowing through a network of blue veins beneath his taut translucent skin. The woman wore a black muumuu and flat sandals, and she walked like every step might be her thumping last, dabbing sweat with a damp hankie from her neck, upper lip, and familiar face. Her gray hair was long and straight and her horn-rimmed glasses were identical to the ones Hippie Helen had worn in 1969. . . .

*February 11, 1969*

*Danny saunters from the Grindbox, where he'd been interrupted dry-humping Erika by her mother clip-clopping down the hallway inside the house toward the front door, shouting, "Erika, that's you, love?" And a frustrated Danny had to make a run for it, Erika telling him to get some experience, hobbling with his boner up to the parkside.*

*He hurries along Parkside West, suffering from a case of blue balls. When he passes Eighth Street he sees Wally's infamous VW bus covered in Day-Glo-painted flowers parked at the curb. The door swings open, a cloud of marijuana wafting out. Wally invites Danny into the back of the bus. The seats have been removed to form a mini bedroom, big cushions tossed around, drapes over the windows. A beautiful, dreamy-eyed woman with straight blond hair and horn-rimmed glasses sucks weed from a bong as Bob Dylan sings "Sad-Eyed Lady of the Lowlands" on the car stereo. She wears a loose paisley peasant blouse and a short loose miniskirt and knee-length boots.*

*Danny and Wally gab for a few minutes about their brothers being away at war, comparing letters home as the beautiful blond woman, who is at least ten years older than Danny, sits bonging-up and singing along with Dylan in a gorgeous balladeer's voice, like Joan Baez or Judy Collins. She smiles at Danny and offers him some of the weed.*

*"That a microphone in your pants or you just excited to see me?" she says, laughing at the bulge in his dungarees.*

*Embarrassed, Danny tokes the bong. Coughs. Tokes again. Holds it in. Wally asks him if he'd like a cold beer. Danny nods as he holds in the weed smoke. Wally says he's gonna walk down to the bodega on Eighth Avenue to get a six-pack. "Helen, baby, by the time I come back I hope this boy has joined the sixties," he says.*

*"Far out," Helen says, smiling a mouthful of white teeth as Wally slams the door behind him. Helen locks it.*

*"Are you a virgin, baby?"*

*Danny coughs out the smoke and blurts, "No!"*

*"Let's find out," she says, reaching out and tracing one long psychedelic-painted fingernail along his erect penis.*

*"He was just seventeen, you know what I mean," Hippie Helen sings, pulling the peasant blouse down over her soft white shoulders and letting it fall over her breasts. "If the kids back home could see me now they'd shit. Bet they're all married to boring insurance guys. Everyone I knew was into insurance back home. My hometown was known for two things, insurance and Johnny Carson. God, I had to get out of there."*

*"Where you from?"*

*"America," she says. "And I'm twenty-seven. That scare you?"*

*It terrifies him but he shakes his head no.*

*"It scares the shit out of me," she says. "In three years I'll be thirty, too old to trust even myself."*

*Danny stares at Helen's beautiful breasts. He tries to swallow, but his mouth is too dry from fear and weed. Helen opens wide her legs to push herself to a crouching position, revealing that she's not wearing panties. She pauses long enough for him to gape. Then she gets up on her knees and takes his face in her hands and kisses his lips, pushing her wet tongue into his dry mouth. She unzips him and removes his dick. "Let me do all the work," she says, taking him in her mouth. He lasts less than thirty seconds. He watches her swallow him. "You're fucking beautiful," she says when he's done, kneading his big shoulders and his rippling arms. "You remind me of the farm boy who took my cherry and now I just took half of yours."*

*"I'm sorry," he says, blushing. "I just couldn't hold it."*

*"Don't you dare apologize, honey," she says, scribbling her phone number and her address on the back of a Bambu rolling-paper cover. She lives in a top-floor apartment on Parkside West, near Fifteenth Road, overlooking the park. "You have immortalized me. No matter what else happens in your life, you'll remember Hippie Helen. Because*

*no one ever forgets the first time. So thank you for making me memo-*
*rable. You come by my pad anytime and I'll take the rest of your cherry."*

*"I have a girlfriend. . . ."*

*"I hope so," she says. "And she's a virgin, too, right? I'll teach you all*
*you need to know and some you don't need to know to make her love*
*you forever. But for as long as you live, I'll own your cherry, baby, and*
*that gives me an earth mother's responsibility for you. If you're ever in*
*trouble, you come to Hippie Helen, day or night, and I'll make it better.*
*Promise?"*

*He stares at the phone number and address and promises himself*
*he will never, ever forget it, repeating it over and over in his mind.*

*He pulls on his pants and boots. She zips him up and gives him*
*another kiss on the lips. He looks once more at the address and phone*
*number, stares her in the star-burst eyes through the horn-rimmed*
*glasses, and says, "Promise."*

And here she was, wearing the same glasses, on a face that was
bitten by crow's-feet, sun gullies, and softer age wrinkles. Her
mouth was like an asterisk. Hippie Helen recognized Danny and
walked to him with her arms wide. *She's an old lady,* he thought.

"I'm so sorry about your dad," she said, then whispering in his
ear, "I bet you don't remember who I am."

"Seven-six-eight-oh-four-two-nine," Danny said. "Two forty-nine
Parkside West, Apartment Four B."

She looked at him in astonishment. "That's right," she said.
"Same Bat time, same Bat channel, after all these years."

"You said you'd be memorable, Helen."

"I'll always own your cherry," she said. "Anytime you want to
come visit it. . . ."

Danny saw the whippet-thin guy in the Armani suit who'd
nodded to Christie Strong standing several feet away waiting to be
introduced and playing with a set of keys with a Lexus emblem clat-
tering

"Who's your yuppie boyfriend?" Danny asked.

"That's James Dugan."

"Dirty Jim?"

"Only he's not dirty anymore. I do some work for him."

Danny was thunderstruck. Dirty Jim looked like Mr. Clean. Helen
signaled him over, and he moved across the floor, looking toward
Christie Strong. Eddie Fortune was still glaring at Christie.

"Yo, Danny," said Dirty Jim Dugan. "Sorry about the old man, and all that shit."

"Yeah, thanks," Danny said. "The hell happened to you? The lottery or you found the right keys to the kingdom."

"I unlock cyberdoors for people. Lucrative and legal. I have Helen to thank."

"When he went to prison I visited him," Helen said. "I wrote some letters for him. Got him into a high school diploma class, then a correspondence college in computer programming. The penal system put him to work. He helped computerize one whole prison upstate. He redesigned a local telephone company near Syracuse, using inmates as four-one-one operators. When he got out he opened his own consulting firm, staffed with ex-cons like him looking for a second chance in life. Took off."

"You were always earth mothering someone, Helen," Danny said.

"The Lord says you have to give something back in this life," she said.

*Uh-oh, born again,* Danny thought. "You always gave more than you took."

"You know the number," she said. "Don't be bashful."

Danny smiled. Christie called to Helen and she excused herself to go say hello.

"You need anything, come see me," Dirty Jim said to Danny. "My advice, bury your old man, hit the road back to L.A. There's trouble here, Danny."

"What are you talking about?"

"I did enough time," he said. "I'm not a well man. I don't want any more trouble. I know people're looking to dig up Boar's Head's murder again. And Wally's. Leave the past where it is, Danny. Buried."

"I need some answers, Jim," Danny said.

"I'm all aboveboard now," he said. "Legit. On parole. I pay taxes, I don't do scores. I'm asking you to just leave me out of anything you might be looking into."

"I might need your help," Danny said.

Dirty Jim noticed Christie looking over again, and it made him nervous. "Look, if I can help, I will," he said, his voice a nervous staccato. "But you can't let anyone know I'm helping you. I can't take a fall. Please understand. There are people in this room who can ruin me if they thought I was helping you. When I heard you were in town

I came here to put on a show to make them believe I'm not helping you. In fact, right now, I gotta let people think me and you, we got a long-standing beef. Call me at work when you wanna talk. From a hard line. And don't take what I'm about to say personal."

"Why," Danny asked. "What is all this shit, Jim?"

Danny watched Dirty Jim take two steps back, swing his arms wide, striking an antagonistic pose, staging a performance for an audience of one: Christie Strong.

"Hey, fuck you too, Danny," Dirty Jim said, loud enough to make it a commotion. "You gonna bring up old beefs, fine. You say I owe you money from the old days, fine. My accountant'll send you a check. I'm here to pay my respects, I don't need insults."

"Take a hike," Danny said, playing along, in case it paid off later.

"You got it," Dirty Jim said as he huffed toward the front door. All eyes were now on Danny, who shrugged.

Helen approached him and said, "What the hell was all that about?"

"Ask him."

"I intend to," she said. "Are you all right?"

"I gotta use the john," he said, feeling woozy and confused. He walked through the crowd to the men's room in the lobby. He splashed cold water on his face. He heard someone enter the men's room and close the door. When he turned from the sink to reach for the towel rack someone behind him handed him two paper towels. In the mirror he saw Ankles looming over him.

"Better not let anybody sneak up in the jailhouse shower on you like this," he said.

Danny gaped at Ankles, still an imposing six-four, two hundred and seventy pounds. Danny took the towels and dried his face. Ankles didn't look sixty-nine at first glance, but Danny could tell his age by the rings under his eyes and the white hair that sat on his head like snow on a statue. His trench coat was streaked with rain and he rotated a soggy fedora in his big hands, which always reminded Danny of a rack of prime ribs.

"Thanks for the wreath," Danny said. "Recycled?"

"Nice turnout," Ankles said.

"Till you showed on the set," Danny said.

"Hippie Helen, Dirty Jim, BW, O'Toole, Byrne, Fortune's kid brother," Ankles said. "And Strong, we don't wanna forget Christie Strong."

"No, we sure don't."

"Lot of the others are buried up at Evergreen."

"So I hear."

"OK, so you want answers," Ankles said. "Where you gonna start?"

"With you."

"Ask. Just remember, we ain't pals. To me you're a three-time loser—a reporter, a shit son, and a lam-mister. But that you came back for the old man's wake is like fouling off the third strike. So I'll humor you until you go down swinging. C'mon, ask."

"Where was Strong the night Boar's Head was killed?"

Ankles stared at him for a long moment, took a White Owl cigar still in a wrapper out of his coat pocket and waved it. "I've been off cigars five years," he said. "I still carry one to chew on when I'm in a bad mood. But you ask that question and it makes me wanna light up."

"Why?"

"He was with fuckin' me," Ankles said, groaning. "I got an anonymous tip he was buying weight that night with Tommy Ryan down on the waterfront, Java Street Pier. I nabbed them loading sacks into Christie's car trunk. Put them under the lamp while my guys took the car apart. All they found in the sacks was rock salt."

"But being with you gave him an all-night alibi?"

Ankles nodded.

"Convenient, no?"

"So convenient it still makes me want a cigar thirty-two years later."

"He used you as his alibi," Danny said. "So you figure he knew Boar's Head would get whacked that night."

"Possibility," Ankles said. "But it could also be a coincidence. Maybe you and him were in it together. Maybe he paid you to do it. You lived with two of his fucking two-bit dealers."

"And so you still think it comes back to me?"

"You also had all kinds of personal motive," Ankles said. "You saw him do Wally in. Plus he wanted to split up you and his daughter. There was a case recently where a black kid and a China doll deep-sixed the China doll's parents because they didn't want the two kids together. Found the mother and father floatin' in the East River. Do I believe young love is motive enough to kill, you bet your old Irish ass I do. 'Specially when it's mixed with ups, downs, and LSD or whatever the fuck else you were on back then."

Danny nodded.

"We have four days. I don't believe I did it. If I did, I want to know."

"If you're guilty I'll help swing you a deal with my boss. Man two."

"Get it straight, I'm not copping to anything I'm not certain I did."

"If I have to nail you on it, and the DA has to try you, we go for murder one."

Danny nodded. "Or maybe we find out it's somebody else."

"You ask her about it yet?"

"Who?"

"Malone's daughter. Erika, the one you used to wiggle."

"So how's Marsha?" Danny said. "You know, Mikey Mauro's wife?"

"Don't dare go there, Cassidy—"

"I hear her son Tony was murdered back in—"

Ankles grabbed him by the lapels and slammed him against the wall. He hoisted back his foot to kick him in the ankle, but he was too slow. Danny stomped on Ankles's foot, looked down, and saw that the old man's thick-soled cordovan's had been replaced by soft round orthopedic shoes.

"Yo, fuckhead," Danny said. "You're almost fucking seventy. Chill the fuck out. You kick me, I'll kick you back. You bring up my old girl, I'll bring up yours. . . ."

Ankles hobbled around the men's room, groaning, panting, walking off the sore toe. "Your tomata's part of an open murder investigation," Ankles said.

"OK, but I'm almost fuckin' fifty," Danny said. "Don't treat me like I'm seventeen, you old motherfucker."

Ankles sneered at him and said, "I'm gathering new evidence as we speak. You won't go more than a few hours without seeing or hearing from me. I'm gonna enjoy slamming the big door on you."

"We'll see."

"Remember, starting right now, I'll be watching you."

"So I've noticed. You've been on my ass all day."

"Not me."

"Nah, not you," Danny said. "You're about as subtle as a noose in a nuthouse. Following me since the goddamned airport—"

"The fuck you talking about?"

The door pushed open now before Danny could answer. Standing there was Christie Strong, smiling the confident smile.

"Gentlemen," Strong said, stepping into the toilet stall. "Like old times."

"It is old times," Danny said and left the men's room.

Danny walked back into the chapel, excusing himself as he brushed past a blond woman in her thirties, dressed in dungarees, sneakers, and a Mets jacket and Mets hat.

"Sorry," he said.

"Me too," she said.

Danny paused and smiled, a little puzzled. Then a pair of mourners buttonholed him to say good-bye. Soon he was standing by his father's coffin, saying good-bye to a parade of obligatory neighborhood mourners who all began to pull on coats and rain hats, clutching umbrellas, their death duty finished. Hippie Helen apologized for Dirty Jim's behavior and asked if Danny wanted to drop by later for coffee. He said he was tired but that maybe he would over the weekend. She looked disappointed and perhaps a little insulted. "There was a time," she said and shrugged.

Danny said good-bye to a respectful Viviana and a stoic Houlie. Eddie Fortune shook Danny's hand and said, "If he don't go to jail, the next wake I come to here might be Strong's."

"Who's his dame, Viviana? I know I can't know her. But she looks familiar."

"Remember Popcorn Gonzalez? His daughter."

"He was a cool guy. What happened to him?"

"They waked him here in '82, '83," Fortune said. "He was in and out of jail over the years. I always took care of him inside. Then I heard he muled for Strong and snorted the profits. Some cold-case squad detective exhumed Popcorn and my sister, Mary, last year. Never even asked permission. They don't need it on a murder investigation. They tested the remains. I got an official letter from some cop named Pat O'Rourke about my sister. Never interviewed me in person. I wasn't a suspect because I was in Nam when she died. I heard about Popcorn on the grapevine. Both of them died from strychnine poisoning from contaminated drugs. Both of them got their drugs from you-know-who. But try and prove it. He always comes up clean."

"Jesus . . . and now Popcorn's daughter is with Strong?"

"Yeah, like Mary," Eddie said.

"Does she know?"

"Doubt it."

"Some things never change. . . ."

Then as Danny stood at the head of his father's coffin he heard a hush in the commotion at the front door of the room. He looked up and saw the crowd parting as Erika Malone strode in, wearing a black Armani trench coat fastened at her wasp-thin waist, collar upturned, buttoned to the neck. Her maroon leather ankle boots matched her maroon beret, which was cocked left on a cascading mane of lustrous red hair. Rippling calf muscles strained her black stockings as she pranced with the long-legged confidence of a woman in charge of her self, her world, and every room she'd ever entered. *She carries herself like a woman who enjoys sleeping with herself at night,* Danny thought. Her makeup was so sparse and high quality that it looked like she wore none at all. Her skin was flawless and tight over her pronounced cheekbones and her big intelligent eyes stole most of the light in the room. If you had to bet, you might wager that her full-time job was taking exquisite care of herself. If he hadn't known her, Danny would have thought Erika Malone was at least a decade younger than her forty-nine years, which he calculated she'd turned on August 22.

*All her wrinkles are in her brain,* Danny thought.

She walked to Danny, as if no one else in the world had ever mattered, took both of his damp coarse hands in her strong angel-soft hands, and lifted herself on her tiptoes and kissed his cheek. Her perfume was familiar and rosy. Her breath warmed his left ear as she whispered into it, her lip touching his lobe, thrilling him. "I am so sorry, Danny," she said.

"So am I. And have been for thirty years."

He noticed Hippie Helen and Christie Strong glancing at him as they exited the chapel.

"Don't go anywhere," she said, "you're walking me home."

"My pleasure."

They embraced. She felt so good that it scared him. Over Erika's shoulder Danny spotted the blond woman in the Mets gear leaning on the door frame near the sign-in book pedestal. She cudded a piece of gum, hands in her back pockets, catching Danny's eye before turning and walking off in her tight jeans that showed off a perfect little body. She turned once, blew an obnoxious bubble. The bubble popped and she was gone.

Erika eased herself from Danny's embrace, stood at arm's length. Their eyes searched for answers to questions neither had yet asked.

She kneeled at his father's coffin, blessed herself, and bit the knuckle of her right hand. She closed her eyes, and Danny could see the silent prayers pulsating through the veins in her temples. When she was done she kissed Mickey Cassidy's cold dead hand, made the sign of the cross, and stood.

She walked to Danny and looked up at him, tilting her head back, her full lips glossed. The room was now almost empty of mourners. Ankles stood by the sign-in book pedestal, unwrapping the cellophane from a big fat cigar. He waved the cigar at Danny, jammed it in his mouth, and chewed it and wedged his fedora onto his head and left in a blocky lurch.

When he felt Erika Malone's small fingers intertwine with his, Danny Cassidy felt at long last like he was home.

# eight

As they stepped together onto the sidewalk Danny saw the headlights of the green Crown Victoria switch on across the street. It purred down the avenue, making a left onto Gorman Place. Danny watched the car go and took out his Vantages, bit one out of the pack, and fumbled for the lighter in his jacket pocket. Erika popped open an umbrella, reached up, and pulled the cigarette from his lips and flicked it into the gutter. She grabbed and crumpled the pack in her strong little fist, and as they began walking east along the avenue, she tossed the smokes into a box of trash piled outside of a Chinese takeout.

"You don't smoke anymore," she said, handing him the big expensive umbrella with a Gucci tab dangling from the Velcro buckle of the fastening belt.

"No shit?"

"Yeah," she said. "If you light another one, I'll kick you in the balls."

"We can't have that, can we?"

"It might make things difficult," she said. "Because if you're back for the reason I think you are, you're gonna need all the balls you have."

"Why do you think I'm back?"

"The mick in me wishes it was for your dead daddy," she said, eyes narrowing. "The guido in me, I guess she wishes it was for revenge." She cocked her head, looked him in the eyes. "And the little girl in me wishes it were for me." She took a deep breath, touched his face, and said, "But the woman in me tells me it's just to clear up some unfinished business."

"How about all of the above?"

"Then it's gonna take big balls," she said, crossing Gorman Place. He stared down and saw the Crown Vic turn right at Eighth Avenue.

"Why?"

"Because your unfinished business is my father's murder," she said. "That never blends too well with trying to score with me."

He nodded. "Who says I'm gonna try to score with you?"

"I might be long in the tooth but men still hit on me. Plus, I have a very successful Internet business. I own a factory and a loft in Soho, a condo in Bocca, a house in Positano, a brownstone in Park Slope. I'm still a vegetarian—"

"Did you say virgin?"

". . . I only drink champagne, I don't take drugs, I eat all my vitamins, I run four miles a day, I spend an hour a day in the gym with a trainer. I'm incapable of having children, so I have no stretch marks anywhere. But I'm so single there oughta be a fucking law. So, if you don't try to take advantage of this rapidly aging rich bitch who is starved for the companionship of a real man I'll assume you've come home to the new politically correct Brooklyn to come out of the closet."

The rain pattered on the umbrella as they passed a bagel shop, a new diner, and a pet-food supply store. He passed Balsam's Drugs, where an old pal named Stu "the Jew" Balsam, the son of the pharmacist, used to work. Danny remembered him as a great stickball player. He wondered if Stuey owned the place now, wearing his father's white Balsam's Rx tunic. He hadn't thought of him in thirty years, and now he popped out of memory like a little home movie, hitting home runs and stuffing basketballs.

Walking with Erika Malone on his arm was somehow surreal, one of those fantasies he thought would never again come true. If he was astounded at the fateful reunion, she was nonchalant.

"After I spill my guts you're supposed to tell me about you," Erika said. "That's what boys and girls still do in Brooklyn, Danny. They talk. The guy talks the most, trying to charm and lie his way into the chick's pants. C'mon, I'm all ears. And pants."

"I'm divorced," he said, crossing through Veteran's Memorial Square, littered and unkempt. "One kid, in college. I drink beer, I smoke, I write for a paper in L.A., I'm broke, and for the last thirty-two years I've been the prime suspect in your father's murder. And seeing you is a treat. But trying to score with you wasn't high on my list of expectations as I headed home to Brooklyn, which I had no idea was politically correct."

"I assume that by now you got the experience I told you to go get," she said with a sultry smile as they walked together past the Paragon movie house, which had been called the Sanders when they were teenagers.

"Some. I also hurt one very good woman along the way. I don't brag about it."

"Your daughter's mother?"

"Yeah. How'd you know my kid was a girl?"

"I know more about you than you probably do. I follow your work on-line. I traced your address and public records."

"Why?"

"Because you're a suspect in my father's murder."

"You believe I killed him?"

"What went wrong with the marriage?" she asked, pausing under the marquee.

"Me," he said. "My heart was never in it."

She looped her arm around his waist, bumped him with her hip, and his free arm wrapped around her shoulder. "Remember the time I gave you a butter-popcorn hand job in the balcony?"

"Of course. . . ."

"What was playing?"

"I remember the hand job. Not the movie."

"*Romeo and Juliet*, dummy," she said. "Directed by Franco Zeffirelli."

"He made a boxing movie once that was like watching cricket."

Arms wrapped around one another, they jaywalked across Parkside West, strolling under the umbrella. Danny glanced up at the window of apartment 4-B of 249 Parkside West where Hippie Helen used to watch all the goings-on on Hippie Hill through a telescope mounted on her windowsill. She would spot a police raid approaching five blocks away and be able to alert a freak on the bench across the street who would whistle to the hippies on the hill.

Helen said she still lived there and Danny noticed a light in her window. Through the rain he even thought he saw someone fiddle with the blinds. He kept walking with Erika in the direction of her mother's brownstone on Garvey Place.

"If it wasn't in the marriage, where was your heart?" Erika asked.

He felt uneasy. Was she grilling him? Was she trying to lull and disarm and seduce him into admitting he'd killed her father? He was wary of Erika. And magnetized. Like he'd never left.

"What about you?" he asked, changing the subject. "Where's your heart been?"

"You asking who I'm sleeping with these days? Or who I've slept with? Or who I want to go to bed with?"

"No, I'm asking where your heart's been for thirty years."

"Under my left tit. Excuse me for being crude, but there you have it. I don't loan my heart out. I learned my lesson. I did that once and I got it back broken. I lost my father, I lost the first boy I ever loved, I lost everything. No more. I promised myself after all of that that I would never again be a loser. My motto is: You want my heart, honey, come and rip it out of my chest."

"No wonder you're single."

She stopped him in the middle of Twelfth and Thirteenth Streets, in front of the Bench, led him by the hand to the granite park retaining wall. She clutched his right index finger and traced it over a wet heart that was long ago carved into the stone with a Rheingold beer can opener like ancient teenage Brooklyn hieroglyphics, bearing his and Erika's name and the lame pronouncement "4-Ever."

"I can't believe it's still here," he said, touching the letters in the stone.

"I can't believe you are," she said and kissed him on the lips. "C'mon, kiss me deeper. Deep as our fathers' graves."

"You're a morbid dame. . . ."

She kissed him again, making out with Danny like an adolescent. He opened one embarrassed eye as he heard tires whispering in the wet asphalt. The green Crown Victoria prowled past.

"Come on, I want to show you something," she said, grabbing his hand. "Forget the umbrella. Let's run."

They raced along the puddled parkside. By the time they hit Ninth Street, Danny was panting. She pushed him toward the statue of the Marquis de Lafayette. She yanked him to the shadowy rear, sat him down on the wet marble base, soaking his pants. She plopped on his lap and kissed him again in the pouring rain.

"This is the first place I ever kissed you," she said.

"I know but it's pouring for chrissakes. . . ."

She laughed and kissed him again, licking his neck and inserting her tongue in his ear. He shivered and she jumped up with athletic bounce and grabbed his hand and began to run again through the downpour.

By the time they reached Seventh Street he had to slow to a walk. She looked like she could run another five miles. She led him the rest of the way in a double-step until they got to Garvey Place.

She steered him down to her house, the gas lamp piercing the rainy haze. A mint-condition red '69 Cadillac El Dorado was parked at a hydrant outside of her house, two soggy parking tickets under a wiper. She grabbed the two tickets off the car, shoved them in her raincoat pocket. She clutched his hand and pulled him into the areaway where he'd gone a thousand times as a kid, like stepping through a portal into the past. Heavy drapes with a bald eagle pattern covered the windows. A bald eagle adorned the mailbox mounted on the brownstone wall. She grabbed the carved bald eagle doorknob and opened the heavy oak street door to the Grindbox. He followed her into the five-by-five cubicle. He mopped the rain from his face and raked his fingers through his wet hair. Nothing had changed except a fresh coat of paint. A big poster of a bald eagle hung on the brick wall. Both of them dripped with rain. Erika flattened herself against the wooden door to the storage space under the stoop where snow shovels, sleds, rakes, and rock salt were stored. She stared into Danny's eyes.

"What did you want to show me?" he asked.

Erika stepped toward him, unbuttoned the black trench coat, opened it, and let it fall to the floor. She was wearing her BVM Catholic high school uniform, the same maroon sweater with the raised letters, the same pleated skirt rolled up at the waist.

"Jesus—"

"No, Virgin Mary. . . ."

She grabbed two fists of his wet hair, kissed him, bit his lips, sucked his tongue until a small tear ripped in the soft undergully. Her tongue unfurled into his mouth as she ground herself against him as he stood against the wall where they used to dry-hump as kids, dreaming about a life that they never got to spend together.

She looped her arms around him, kissed him, big and wet and savage kisses, writhing in pelvic spasms. His hands went under her Catholic schoolgirl skirt, down the tight panty hose to where Alph the sacred river ran through caverns measureless to man down to a sunless sea. . . .

He became aroused. Erika's body felt the same to his touch as it had thirty-two years before. She hadn't gained an extra ounce, still as firm and toned as the sweet-sixteen swimmer-cheerleader. Her pelvic bone revolved harder on his stiff prick, and then she hopped up on him. Scissoring her legs around his hips, riding him through his pants.

"Jesus Christ," he said, his legs sagging, his lungs pumping. "I'm too fucking old for friction sores and coming in my pants."

But she rode him so hard and fast that he was about to come. Then he heard Erika's mother shuffling down the hallway inside the house.

"Erika, that's you, love?" the mother shouted. "Or Vito, that's you?"

"I don't fucking believe this!" he said and Erika started to laugh.

"You gotta go," she said, urgent and fitful with laughter.

"No! I have to come! You fucking kidding me? You can't do this to me—"

"Please," she said, laughing. "Before my mother opens the damned door. . . . "

"I'm almost fifty. You're forty-fucking-nine years old, Erika."

"Just turned forty-eight on August 22," she said, fine tuning her age. "But Mama still thinks I'm seventeen."

He adjusted himself and said, "Fifty-year-old blue balls could be fatal, ya know."

The inner door opened. Danny was startled. Angela Malone was in her seventies, her face still unlined, but in the half gloom her eyes looked like black holes in a skull.

"Vito, that's you? It's Thursday night, payday, we can go out. . . ."

"It's me, Erika, Mama. Daddy isn't coming home, Mama."

"He's working on a big case, getting the OT," the mother said and turned and walked back into the house, where he noticed bald eagle wallpaper.

Danny looked at Angela Malone, saw that she was clutching a rag doll by its stringy hair. He didn't know what to say. He felt like he was living a second or parallel life.

"I should go," he said. "She needs you."

"Meet me at Squared One for breakfast at ten," Erika said. "I'll wear something you'll like."

The way she cocked her head, the way she smiled and ran her tongue over her beautiful teeth, the way her nose crinkled and her eyes shone even in the muted light, in many ways Erika was still seventeen.

"Should I go get experience?" he asked, grinning.

"If you do I'll cut off your fucking blue balls."

The way she said it sent a shudder through him. There was a mad glint in her eye, a crush in her fist that was wrapped around his middle and index fingers, a risen pulsing vein in her neck that told him she half meant it. *Her father had been fucking crazy,* he thought. *Her mother is demented. After thirty years Erika runs through the rain with the guy who might have killed her father. Makes out with him like a teenager. Dresses in her high school uniform. Wants to dry-hump him like days of old. Why shouldn't I believe she's crazy enough to swipe off my nuts in my sleep?*

"Erika," the mother shouted. "You got homework to do. Come in, I'll heat your dinner and help you with your homework before your father gets home. He's on a big case. . . ."

"I'm sorry," he said, nodding toward the door.

"She never got over my father. Still thinks he's coming home. We still have his car, the '69 Caddy. I pay a guy to move it from one side of the street to the other for alternate side of the street parking. But he's away for the holiday weekend. So is my mother's nurse."

There was a sudden sadness in Erika's eyes. The laughter ended and the rain began to ebb.

"I have to find out what happened to him," Danny said.

"*We* have to," she said. "Me and you. Together. Again. We'll start with breakfast tomorrow, ten, Squared One, the old Parkhouse, next to the Paragon movie house."

"Erika, what if I find out it was me?"

She shrugged and said, "Then I'll have to kill you."

"I'm serious, Erika."

"So am I," she said, kissing him good night, and pushing him through the street door into the easing rain. She slammed the door. *Nuts,* he thought.

For the first time in thirty-two years, Danny Cassidy smiled when he thought of Erika Malone.

# nine

Danny walked out of the areaway, guiding the wrought-iron gate closed so that it wouldn't clang. He glanced up at the window that he remembered was Erika's bedroom, the one where she used to pull back the curtain when he left the Grindbox, waving good-bye, blowing him kisses. The window was now dark and the curtain was drawn.

He splashed through the rain toward the parkside, knowing he had a sixteen-block hike to his car. Bone-weary from travel and beer and jumbled emotions, he scrounged in his pocket for change for the B-69 bus that ran along the parkside. There was that number again: sixty-nine. It wouldn't go away. He didn't even know how much a bus or a subway token cost anymore. He guessed it was about a buck and a half, maybe two dollars. He stopped under a lamppost and shuffled the coins in the palm of his hand. He counted a dollar thirty-five. . . .

"Need a ride, Danny?" he heard a woman's voice ask.

Danny looked up, rain distorting his vision. The hazy blond woman with the Mets jacket and Mets hat stood leaning against the green Crown Victoria. He wiped his eyes to reveal a pearl white smile on a pretty face. Her hands were stuffed in her jacket pockets.

"Where's Ankles?"

"Not sure," she said. "Home, I expect. He's a little old for this kind of work these days. I haven't talked to him in a few weeks."

"Who the hell are you and why have you been following me all day?"

She stood up straight, took her hands out of her pocket. She opened a small wallet and showed him a gold badge and an ID card that said her name was Pat O'Rourke, detective first class.

"I work for the Cold-Case Squad," she said. "Vito Malone—"

"Vito Malone's been cold for thirty-two years."

She nodded. "Cold and dirty but he was still murdered. It's my job to bust whoever did it. When your father died I figured you'd come back."

"I understand."

O'Rourke glared at him and opened the passenger door for him. "Get in, I'll give you a lift up to your car."

"You know where it's parked?"

"I know a helluva lot more than that, Danny. But this isn't an official ride. Yet."

Danny climbed in and she slammed the door and walked around to the driver's door. As she did he saw the light switch on in Erika's bedroom. He saw the curtain flutter from the window, revealing a panel of amber light. *She's watching me get into a car with a younger chick,* he thought.

Pat O'Rourke climbed in and followed Danny's eyes to Erika's window.

"Me and her got something in common," she said, driving down past Erika's house as if trying to make trouble.

"What's that?"

"We both got an eye on you."

"I'm too old for flattery."

"My interest in you is purely a business one. And my business is *old* murder. Your *old* lady's *old* man's *old* murder."

He turned to her as she made a right onto Eighth Avenue and said, "She's not my old lady. She's—"

"I know who she is," Pat said. "She's beautiful. She's rich. She has a body like a prom queen. I even use her beauty aids. I know a lot about her. And you."

"I didn't keep tabs on her over the years," he said. "In fact, I tried hard to forget her and everything else that had to do with Brooklyn."

"Yeah," she said, ferrying through the puddles at the Third Street entrance to Prospect Park, blowing through a red light with the instinctive arrogance of a cop. "Her beauty products are all natural. Her vitamins are all organic. Her creams and shampoos and wrinkle creams are from secret formulas she collected all over Asia, the rain forests of South America, from natural herbs, roots, bark, plants. Erika's Earth products are one of the biggest movers on the Internet."

"She was always great at science," Danny said. "And a health nut."

Pat O'Rourke gnawed a Marlboro Light out of a pack and offered one to Danny.

"No, thanks," he said. "I'm trying to quit."

"You smoked thirteen cigarettes on my watch today," she said, lighting her butt with a disposable lighter, framing her pretty face against the coal black vastness of the park. "Since when did you quit?"

"I said I was trying."

"I'm trying, too. I'm trying to quit thinking of you as a cop killer."

She glanced at him, took a deep drag on the cigarette, the ember reflecting orange dots in her blue eyes. The wipers flapped and the smell of the cigarette was a slow striptease in the stuffy car.

"You working this case alone?" Danny asked. "Or with Ankles?"

"Detective Tufano works for the Brooklyn DA. I work for NYPD. Funny enough, your girlfriend's family has never raised much of a ruckus."

"Who wants to regurgitate that your father or husband was a dirty cop? And she *used* to be my girlfriend. . . ."

"Gee, you looked like a couple of puppy lovers tonight. Holding hands, laughing after your father's wake. Making out, tracing the old heart carved in the parkside wall."

"Christ," he said, sighing in an embarrassed way.

O'Rourke smirked, doing a cop's maddening five-mph prowl. "Kinda cute, except, ya know, there's a murder involved. Someone put six shots into her father. Smart money always said that someone was you. What girl swaps spits with her daddy's killer?"

"You think I did it?"

"Opinions are like spouses, Danny. Half the population has one that turns out to be wrong. So, instead of an opinion, I'll investigate and draw a conclusion."

"Thanks for the benefit of a doubt."

"I have doubts galore," she said, spiraling through the park, the wipers slapping on low speed. "About you. About her. About half the people at your father's wake. About Christie Strong. Helen Grabowski. Jim Dugan. Even about Detective Tufano."

"I understand you had doubts about the way a guy named Popcorn Gonzalez and Mary Fortune died. One in 1969 and one in 1982. Both from strychnine. That true?"

"Yeah, it's true. I've been trying to find patterns about people from Hippie Hill who died over the years. How and why. It might mean something. Maybe it doesn't. When I have doubts, I check 'em out."

She stopped the car for a green light this time. She put the car in park, shifted in her seat, turned on the overhead light, and searched Danny's eyes. "I even have doubts about myself," she said.

"What kind of doubts?"

"I've been a cop for almost fifteen years. I've put dozens of skells in the joint. Never once, not one time, did I ever feel anything good about any of them. But in the last few months I have spent almost every night home alone reading almost everything you have ever written. You're a talented writer. Used to be a pretty good investigative reporter until you switched to showbiz crap. Why'd you do that?"

"I like movies," he said.

"I read all your stuff from newspapers in Florida, Boston, Vegas, L.A. I read a couple of short stories you wrote under a pen name for *Playboy*, one about a guy running from his past, another about a guy who's still in love with his childhood sweetheart. . . ."

"How the hell. . . ."

"You included payment for them on your tax returns," she said. "I searched every return, every police database, to see if you ever so much as went through a red light. . . ."

The green light turned red and she drove through it. "You didn't," she said. "For thirty-two years you've lived a life so clean it sends up dirty red flags. You also lived a pretty sad life. According to your sealed divorce papers, you had a pretty, young wife who loved you. And a beautiful daughter. And you just up and walked away from both of them. Not even for another woman. How fucked-up is all that?"

Danny searched her lightly freckled face, so pretty she needed almost no makeup. She also didn't cover up her harsh words. "Is there a point to all this privacy invasion?"

"Yeah," she said, steering into the parking lot and easing into the spot alongside Danny's rented Camry. "Yeah, the point is that unlike most of the skells I've ever investigated, who killed for jealousy, greed, revenge, or blood lust, if you killed Vito Malone—and I'm not saying yet that you did—you did it for love. Which is the classiest of all motives. The romantic in me can almost understand it. But the cop in me says it's still murder. And I don't like murderers, especially ones who run like scared rats."

He stared into her eyes. Blinked. She didn't. She tossed the end of her smoke out into a puddle. "And maybe you also did it for self-protection," she said. "Which is a little different than self-defense. But not a murder-one rap."

"I still don't get the point."

She nodded toward Hippie Hill, which lay soggy and forlorn in front of them. "The point is you were a kid, seventeen, eighteen, and that monster Malone was trying to keep you from seeing his daughter, Erika, whom you adored. And maybe he knew that you'd witnessed him murder a guy named Wally Fortune. . . ."

"You've also been reading Ankles's dossier on me."

"It's the official one," she said, lifting a thin case file. "But incomplete. I will make it complete."

"Can I look through it?"

She removed printed material, handed him the case photos. He opened it.

"This the point?"

He looked at the crime-scene photos, black-and-white pictures of Vito "Boar's Head" Malone's corpse taken from every imaginable angle. Establishing shots. Close-ups of the wounds. Close-ups of the ground around him. Close-ups of his hands. The bag of drugs. The cash. Photos of Danny as a kid standing with Ankles at the crime scene. Danny's hair was to his shoulders and he wore a new leather jacket, new corduroys, and expensive leather boots. He looked drugged-over and pathetic. A little hippie asshole. If he represented the generation that was supposed to change history, it was understandable why it hadn't. The kid in that photo also looked scared. The picture renewed that fear in Danny. He flicked past it to some gruesome autopsy photos of Vito Malone.

"No, the point I was making was this," O'Rourke said. "I never investigated a suspect who looked less like a skell on paper than you do before. It's unsettling. If you ever were a killer, you're not one now. But that doesn't mean you shouldn't pay for your crime if you did it. You've led a good if sad life. If you don't know the truth, you deserve to know it. I promise you I will be straight with you. I will never manufacture evidence against you. I don't expect you to help me nail you, but if you cooperate I'll tell it to the DA and the judge. But if you did it and try to bullshit or mislead me, I won't lose one wink knowing you're sleeping in a five-by-eight cell for life."

"Jeez, you're too kind," he said, thumbing to the last series of photos. Taken inside and outside of Davis's BMW. Stomach-churning photos of the aftermath of Davis's suicide. Danny couldn't look at them. They were too awful. He snapped the file folder closed. He looked up at O'Rourke and saw that the photos had sent the muscles in her jaw into little spasms.

"Whenever I feel myself thinking you might be a good guy I'll look at these photos and remind myself you're still the prime suspect," she said.

"I guess you'll also show them to Erika. . . ."

"Are you still in love with her?"

"I don't even know who she is anymore," he said. "You told me more about her in the last fifteen minutes than I'd learned in thirty years. I've been busy trying to forget."

"Then I'll ask you to consider this," O'Rourke said. "After you left town Erika went to Columbia University, which isn't cheap. She studied chemistry, worked for some hippie organic beauty aids company that got into financial trouble. She bought them out, put in a bunch of money, renamed it Erika's Earth, and made a bundle."

"Yeah, so?"

"So where do you think the daughter of a housewife and a detective making $16,425 in 1969 got the dough to go to Columbia and buy a corporation?" she asked, lighting another cigarette. Which made Danny think she was nervous, a bit insecure. That was sexy in its own way, like the flip side of overconfident Erika.

"How should I know?" Danny said. "You're the cop."

"You used to be a pretty good reporter."

"You don't like Erika do you?"

"I haven't met her. Yet. I wanted to know all I could about this case before I went to the family. Work it from the outside in. And because—"

"Because I'm the prime suspect. . . ."

"Yup," she said, leaning closer to him, the cigarette bobbing in her mouth. Their noses were now inches apart, almost touching. She looked him in the eyes and blew the stream of smoke into his face. "Who knows. Maybe you and her were in on it together."

He glared at her, a confluence of fear and anger rising in him.

"Thanks for the ride," he said, yanking open the passenger door.

"The next one could be to central booking," she said. "But tell me something. Why'd you park here?"

Danny searched her face, pretty and strong, the eyes a little more fragile than her tough-broad performance.

"No spots near the funeral parlor," he said, shrugging. "And I guess to return to the scene of the proverbial crime."

She nodded, gripping the steering wheel, ringing it in her fists. "I hope you find what you're looking for," she said. "But don't worry. If you don't, I promise you I will."

Danny watched her window power up as she swished off into the Brooklyn rain.

# ten

When Danny entered his hotel room, Ankles stood by the window looking out at the downtown bridges spanning the rainy East River. He swiveled two fingers of whiskey in a hotel glass and ate from a can of cashews. The door to the mini bar was open. The contents of Danny's head bag had been dumped on his bed, the notebooks opened and scattered across the floral bedspread. Also sitting on the bed was an old-fashioned attaché case, the kind Danny figured a flatfoot gets from his cop pals when he first gets his gold shield.

"Was that wake we just came from for my father or the Fourth Amendment?" Danny asked, more annoyed than surprised.

Ankles grabbed a signed warrant from his attaché case and said, "I told you I was gonna be a rash on your balls. I work for the Brooklyn DA and I can get a judge who plays poker with my boss at the Brooklyn Club every Friday night to ante up one of these Pass Go cards anytime I feel like it. 'Specially for the prime suspect in a cop murder."

"You made your point," Danny said. "Find anything of value?"

Ankles pointed at Danny's journals and the letters to and from Brendan that he'd dumped on the bed. "You wrote good letters," Ankles said. "But good thing you didn't try making a living as a poet."

"We can agree on that."

"Most of the shit I read in there is gibberish," he said, putting the whiskey down on the dresser, pulling on a pair of bifocals. "Shorthand. Speed-freakese. I could take it to our decryption guys, find a coupla old gray-ponytail retired hippies to see if they could decode it. But I'm convinced they'd have to snort a few dimes of meth to crack it."

"I have a hard time making sense of a lot of it myself," Danny said. "I'm groovin' on it, pops. But my sixties references are all blowin' in the wind, man."

"It ain't Enigma, Danny," Ankles said, leafing through the journal for July 1969. "Some of it might be real evidence. In fact, while you were out today I had a couple of interns xerox all this shit. The DA's office is right next door in the Metro Tech center, too. And while they were out xeroxing, I read a bit before I went to the wake. The initial codes are pretty clear. E is Erika. B is Brendan, your brother. CS is either cocksucker or Christie Strong. . . ."

"Synonyms."

Ankles smiled and said, "You weren't in his fan club, were ya? Listen to yourself, 'CS is a capitalist pig. After the revolution he should be put up against a wall with BH. . . .' That would go over like a fart on a rush-hour IRT with a jury. And how about this entry, on July 23, 1969? Again, about BH, for Boar's Head, also known as Vito Malone. You scribbled, '. . . if BH is taken off the count me and E could be forever happy . . .' How fuckin' sweet. But, Danny boy, it also sounds like a kid who wanted to waste the father of his girl-friend for keeping him from dickin' her on a regular basis. . ."

" 'Off the count' didn't necessarily mean murder, Ankles," Danny said, walking to the mini bar. He grabbed a bottle of Heineken, popped the cap, and swigged. "Could mean if he went away. . . ."

"Went away how? Where? Vacation? To join the fuckin' circus? To jail, maybe? That's it. But for fuckin' what, Danny? Help me here. Help yourself."

"You're fishing in a bathtub, old man."

Ankles wet his finger and skipped backward in the journal and said, "OK, you said you and Erika could be happy if her old man went away. My guess is you mean if he went away for what hap-pened on July 20, 1969. Right, Danny? The night the astronauts first walked on the moon? The moon over Prospect Park? Where Wally Fortune was also taken 'off the count'? The murder you witnessed and lied to me about witnessing? That the thing you mean when you say BH could be taken off the count? You mean Boar's Head could have went away to the joint for murder, don't you, Danny? On your eyewitness testimony. But you couldn't do that, could you, Danny? Couldn't dime on your girlfriend's dad? Or you'd lose her forever. Talk to me Danny, we made a deal."

"There's nothing in any of those journals suggesting all that."

Ankles turned more pages, peering up over his bifocals at Danny, making his case. "Funny, the page for July 20 and July 21 are missing. How come, Danny? You needed paper to wipe your ass in the Hippie Hill bushes? After being scared shitless by what you saw? After seeing Vito Malone murder Wally Fortune?"

"I saw a lot of shit at night that summer, roaming the streets, the park, the rooftops, the hallways, the subways, smashed on speed and acid," Danny said. "I was a paranoid kid. I had a hard time distinguishing between reality and hallucinations. If you skip back to a page in February or March, you'll see that I thought I saw a big flat-foot with the initial A banging the buns off a married woman with the initials MM in a detective car near the Tennis House in Prospect Park. But I must have been wrong, because this MM I'm thinking about was married to Mikey Mauro, who came home a hero from Korea in a fucking wheelchair. And the cop with the initial A would never stoop so low as to dick a crippled war hero's bride."

"Watch your filthy mouth," Ankles said, his eyes more injured than angry.

Danny smirked. "You can throw, but you can't catch, old man."

Ankles strode back to the window, tossing Danny's journal onto the bed and picking up his whiskey, scooped a handful of nuts, popped them, and sipped.

"Mikey Mauro was no war hero," Ankles said. He fell silent for a long moment, staring out at the dark rain falling on the glittering city. "And Marsha's got maybe eighteen months left. So, please, leave her out of this."

Danny felt like a crumb. "Sorry. . . ."

"Me too. I guess you're still sweet on Erika, huh?"

"You can search through those old journals all you want," Danny said. "I already did. I doubt the thirty-two-year-old rantings of a seventeen-year-old druggie would ever make it to a jury. But if you think you can solve what happened on November 20 or 21 by reading them, be my guest."

"What about what happened on July 20?"

"Ask me after I have time to find out myself. I'm giving myself this time to find out what happened to Boar's Head first."

"Maybe I can at least put the Wally Fortune one to bed," Ankles said. "He still has family, a brother Eddie, who deserves some closure."

"I hate that word. There's no such thing. Nothing in my life ever feels like it's ever over. Murder has a life of its own. And when you're accused of it, murder never dies. Murder never closes."

Ankles reached in the attaché case again, pulling out a collection of old police logbooks. "I have my own blow by blow of that year. I also have Vito Malone's. I can't find Jack Davis's. You're all over my July log. So are all the other old dirtbags from Hippie Hill. Christie

Strong, JoJo Corcoran, Hippie Helen the Hole . . . if you did a blow by blow of her you'd get fuckin' lockjaw."

"She was our den mother."

"Of the Cock Scouts. She fucked everything that moved on Hippie Hill except the squirrels. Even fucked the fuckin' parkie. Didn't miss one dick. Now she's into Jesus. I figure it's the other way around. Jesus is into her—Jesus Garcia, Jesus Rodriguez, Jesus Perez. But I also got entries on Dirty Jim Dugan. He's all over the fucking map. He was a ghost, that little cock knocker, poppin' outta the night with that camera of his. And his keys. He even burgled the fucking precinct house once during a Christmas party. I can't believe that peckerhead is still alive. And legit. Some people are too slippery to kill. All your buddies you saw today are in here, too. Weedheads— Brian Walsh, Kenny Byrne, Timmy O'Toole, Eddie Fortune. Like a fuckin' IRA meeting."

"The Murphia," Danny said.

"Every one was spied in some kind of drug deal back then," Ankles said, tracing his finger down his logbook, cross-checking it with Boar's Head's. "All model citizens of Woodstock Nation."

"But I bet you don't have one entry on Christie Strong."

Ankles looked up at him, flicked through the pages of his book. He shook his head. He checked one of Boar's Head's 1969 logbooks and came up with another blank. He said, "Yeah, Strong's as clean as a bean. Which tells you he's dirty as old money. Anyone from that neighborhood in the sixties that didn't make bail at least once belongs in jail. Strong was never pinched."

"Except for the night of the Wally Fortune murder," Danny said. "When he was with you. Getting questioned for rock salt."

"But it wasn't an official arrest," Ankles said. "Just questioning."

"I always thought Wally had something on him," Danny said. "After Wally's kid sister, Mary, was found OD'd, he suspected she was one of Strong's little lambs. In this case, a lamb led to slaughter."

"You talking dosed? Poisoned?"

"That was the wire on the Hill at the time. But people 'woke up dead,' as the saying went, from ODs every other week back then. Mary was just another OD'd hippie chick. But I remember that she was more into weed, wine, sex, and hard rock and roll than hard drugs. Smart as hell and cute as an atomic button, too. But you didn't bang a friend's sisters for kicks. Unless you were Christie

Strong, who banged everything. My guess is that when Mary Fortune got involved with Strong, she dabbled in everything. Wound up in Strong's inner sanctum. And found out what Strong was up to. Then maybe she slipped and told Wally what she knew about his operation, about Vito Malone and Jack Davis being on his pad. Strong knew Wally was a motherfucker with a piece of valuable information. To shut Mary up and to show Wally what happens to people who blab about Christie Strong, Mary wound up OD'd in the bushes behind the horse corral. Pronounced dead in Methodist Hospital. But instead of dummying up, the usual nonconfrontational Wally vowed revenge. Told people he would bring Strong down. Next thing, before the end of the month, everybody's up at Dunne's at Wally's wake while his kid brother, Eddie, is off in the war. Eddie Fortune didn't come home for the wake because he was somewhere on a secret Special Forces mission in Cambodia, where no Americans were supposed to be, part of Nixon's great secret plan to end the war by spreading it into three countries."

"Fuck the world history, and your lefty theories are fine," Ankles said. "But you need evidence. Strong is now running for the fucking city council. Not that that scares me. This year you got bartenders, plumbers, and cab drivers running for the city council because term limits kicked all the regular mummies out. Besides, nothing I'd like better than taking down some cheap fuckin' politician."

"Strong's worth exploring."

"Sure," Ankles said, plopping Detective Vito Malone's NYPD logbook on the bed. "But where's the evidence? Still, I'd like to develop your theory a little further. Wally finds out from Mary Fortune that Strong is a big-time pusher. He has all his little neighborhood bims and mules pushing his shit for him. But when he wanted to move some weight, to the blacks on the other side of the park, to the Manhattan yippies in Alphabet City and the bohemians in the West Village, to the Ricans down Red Hook, to the blacks in Bed Stuy, he got someone who could move in all those circles with impunity. A dirty cop. One who could also provide Strong with protection. Then Mary Fortune tells Wally Fortune what she knows, who that cop was. Then Wally implies to Strong that he'd like a cut for his silence. Then Mary's dosed on what date . . ."

Danny thumbed through one of his old journals, tossed it aside. He picked up another, perused it, and grabbed a third. He turned pages, looking at his old chicken-scratch handwriting, much of it written when he was smashed. He located the Mary Fortune entry on July 8:

> MF OD's on GBs today. Good title for sad song. Same day as Marianne Faithful OD's on gorilla biscuits on foreign movie set. Funny both have same initials. MF . . . what a mother-fucker. But our Mary never took downs. Lotsa bad dope going around. Everybody on the Hill crying. Poor WF. He swears it's murder. Blames CS. Poor EF. Better write, tell B. . . .

"July eighth," Danny said.

Ankles rummaged in his portfolio bag, took out another one of Boar's Head's old logbooks. He turned to July 8. "Like flies on shit, Vito Malone and Jack Davis landed on that OD," Ankles said. "Odd that a pair of DTs would just stumble on that. They clerked it as a suicide. Found a bottle of Seconals in Mary Fortune's hand. The ME concurred. . . ."

Danny held out his hand for the logbook. "You mind?"

Ankles was reluctant. "This is evidence in a murder case," Ankles said.

"You looked through my dirty laundry," Danny said.

Ankles handed him the logbook. He paged through the meticulous, very detailed logbook in which Vito Malone registered the times, stage of the moon, weather, locations, people observed, witnesses interviewed, snitches questioned, suspects questioned. Danny knew from his crime reporting days that a cop's logbook was his diary, and also his alibi against charges of goldbricking or cooping. He looked at the entry for July 20, at 1130 hours: "Spoke with snitch nicknamed Linc about possible drug supplier, app. 45 min. DT car. Drive and talk along 4th Ave., Prospect Ave. to Union St. with partner Dt. Jack Davis."

"You ever ID this snitch named Linc, who Boar's Head said he was with at the time of Wally Fortune's murder on July 20?" Danny asked.

"Nope. He wouldn't divulge it in the few months when he was still alive. Then it was too late, 'specially since Davis was dead, too. But my guess is this snitch was gonna be his alibi if he ever was indicted or brought up on departmental charges. But since there was never any real evidence for either, he didn't give the name up. Maybe someone named Lincoln, first or last name. Maybe some guy from

Lincoln Place, in Park Slope or Bed Stuy. Maybe someboby from Lincoln High. Maybe somebody from Fifth Street, because Lincoln's on the five-dollar bill. Whoever the fuck he is, Linc's a missing link."

Danny closed the book, extended it toward Ankles, glanced at the cover, saw Detective Vito Malone's name printed with the date the logbook was officially signed by his supervising officer: Lieutenant Henry Bush.

Danny recognized Horsecock's real name but didn't comment.

"If you ask me," he said, handing the book back to Ankles, "Strong knows more about what happened on July 8, July 20, and November 20 of 1969 than anyone."

"I still think you know more than you're telling me," Ankles said.

"I don't even know yet what I do and don't remember."

Ankles dropped Boar's Head's logbook into the attaché case, landing next to the Xeroxed copies of Danny's journals. He tossed in the warrant, slammed it shut, and fastened the snaps. Only one snap worked. Danny thought Ankles was too old to invest in a new attaché case. As soon as he put this investigation to bed he wouldn't need one.

Ankles lifted the attaché case and moved toward the door with an aging stoop, limping from Danny's earlier toe stomp. He screwed on his fedora, which went out of fashion when JFK was elected president, and opened the door.

"For what it's worth, and it's worth everything to me," Ankles said, "the reason Marsha married Mikey Mauro in the first place was because he knocked her up when she was drunk. Abortions were illegal back then. Besides, she was a devout Catholic. Then Mikey beat that poor little baby out of her belly. Then he beat the rap by joining the fucking marines to go beat the commies in Korea. That's what the wonderful fucking courts did with wife beaters in those days. Marsha filed for an annulment while Mikey was away in Korea. Then the prick got blown up in a fucking whorehouse near Inchon. When he came home in a chair she withdrew the annulment papers. In Brooklyn in the fifties girls didn't cakewalk on crippled war vets. It just wasn't done. But she refused to stop living. I'd been sweet on Marsha Kelly since Blessed Virgin Mary grammar school. Before she ever got involved with that asshole Mikey Mauro. So, yeah, you saw us in my car in the park. That was no hallucination."

Danny felt embarrassed. He'd ripped an old scab off Ankles's personal history. But everyone's old wounds were being reopened. "No, I guess not," Danny said.

"Neither was what you saw the night Wally Fortune was murdered," Ankles said. "I've waited thirty-odd years for you to tell me the truth, on the record. I guess I can wait a few more days."

Ankles left without saying good-bye.

Danny walked to the bed and gathered the dumped contents of the head bag. He lifted one airmail envelope, Brendan's first letter home from Vietnam. He took it out, lay down on the bed, and read it.

Dec. 1, 1968
Yo, Bro:
   The flight over here was, like, 280 hours long. Nobody could sleep. Like the first line of Norman Mailer's *Naked and the Dead*. Well, so far, I've seen a lot of naked and dead people. My first job here was working in an army hospital in Saigon, sorting body parts with other medics. Lotta napalm victims, guys blown to bits by land mines and grenades, and our job is to try to match the arms and legs and other body parts. You measure the feet to see if they match. But after a while, in the humidity, with all the flies and the stench, some of the guys give up. They smoke a joint and start putting a black guy's leg in with a white guy's torso and a Puerto Rican guy's head. We call these bags "assorted nuts." What's the difference, anyway? They all died for nothing. But the thing I learned already that the freaks in the Movement don't understand is that the GIs aren't the bad guys here. They're just grunts. Just victims of the war, too. Even the gung-ho ones, because they've been fed the line of shit, about God, the flag, and country, like the old man.
   I joined as a medic because I thought I could do more over here to help save lives than I could with a protest sign back home. It's also a good place to get Maria out of my system. She's part of the World now. She can't break my heart over here. Besides, if I'm going to be a historian, if I am ever going to write history for a living, or maybe historical novels, I need to be here at the biggest historical event of our generation. Like Hemingway and Orwell, to write it right, sometimes you have to witness the history.
   I know you think this war and me being in it will break our

special brotherhood-friendship bond. But I hope it'll bring us to a new level, graduate us to manhood. You on the home front of America gone mad and me in Nam. It makes us cover both bases of our time, which is history in the making every single day. No decade of this century has been as electrifying as the sixties. You keep score at home and I'll do the same over here. Maybe someday we can write about it together. But you gotta keep straight and stay away from the druggies to do this fucking thing right, bro.

I'll be keeping a Nam journal and you keep your American journal. At the end of the year they might make the basis for a pretty good book. Never know. Mailer was twenty-five when he did *Naked and the Dead*. Hemingway was twenty-six when he wrote *The Sun Also Rises*. Maybe we can do it even younger than those guys.

I'm awaiting orders to be sent to the boonies. Don't know where yet but I hear it might be the Central Highlands. Write, you hard-on. Speaking of which, the hookers here are gorgeous I hear. As soon as I have details I'll fill you in.

Give Mom a hug for me, don't give her any fucking details.

Peace and love,
Brendan

P.S. I can't get the morning I left out of my mind, because I realized just how much I loved you and how much I was gonna miss you. Did you catch that pass? I'll know this war and the sixties will be over for us when you catch another one of my passes on Hippie Hill. Give my best to Erika. Did you cop her cherry yet? I want details, bro! Ha ha. Peace

Danny dropped the letter on the pile and stared at the ceiling, wondering if Brendan would bother coming home. He remembered that he'd left Brendan his E-mail address and walked to his laptop and turned it on and attached the telephone line to the computer jack. He logged on and checked his *L.A. Chronicle* E-mails. Most were from press agents pushing tintype profiles on actors and actresses. There were a few from readers who wanted to know how to get in touch with celebrities they'd read about in his stories. Then he saw one called stickballdays@earthlink.com. He knew that was Brendan's E-mail address. He hesitated a moment. Then clicked on to it.

Danny:

Got your message. Kinda surprised it took so long for the old man to go. Look, I'm mulling coming back to bury him with you for Mom's sake. But I'm too old now for nostalgia and sentimentality. So if I return, in her honor, let's shake hands, break bread, and maybe pop a brew. I'd like to meet your kid, if she's around. It would be good to see you, too, but if this is gonna be messy or if you expect me to get involved in that old "other business" let me know ASAP and I'll stay put.

Sorry if this all sounds a bit aloof. I don't mean it to be. Let's just bury the old man and catch up a little. Before I buy a ticket, let me know if this sounds cool.

Best,
Brendan

Danny reread the E-mail three times. It read like it had been chipped in ice. *But fuck it,* he thought. *If Brendan doesn't need me, I don't need him. Still, Mom would have wanted us to bury the old man together.* In the outside chance that Darlene showed up he'd also like her to meet Brendan, at least as a point of reference. Even if Brendan wasn't the same warm brother he remembered as a kid.

Danny hit the REPLY button and wrote what he thought was an appropriate one-word response to Brendan's icy E-mail.

Brendan:
Cool.
Danny

Danny hit the SEND button and plunged into bottomless sleep.

# eleven

*Saturday, September 1*

Danny knew that Foley's opened at 8 A.M. sharp and closed at 4 A.M., the legal limits. He checked his watch. It was only 6:13 A.M.

At the wake, after signing the death book, Henry Bush had told Danny that if he wanted to talk to him he should come by his home very early, before Foley's opened, when his mind was still clear. Foley's was just one block up Langston Place from the Cardinal Murphy Senior Apartments. They were new, too. Built sometime in the past three decades.

Danny hurried down Langston Place, passing a dozing security guard in the immaculate lobby and proceeded to apartment 1-C on the ground floor. The hallways smelled like life—home cooking, coffee, old ladies' perfume, the steam from clean laundry tumbling in a coin-operated dryer—unlike many of the warehouses for America's old that often reeked of decay, of once vital human beings left to ripen toward death.

Danny rang Horsecock's bell. He waited thirty seconds and rang it again. After another thirty seconds he rang it a third time. And Horsecock pulled open the door, angry.

"I'm having my morning dump, for chrissakes," he barked, tying the strings of his sweatpants, wearing a hooded NYPD sweatshirt and a pair of white polished Air Jordan sneakers. "Who the fuck are you?" He pulled on his glasses that hung on strings from his neck. "Oh, Mickey Cassidy's kid. Danny. Sorry. I thought you were Sister Michael, that old fuckin' hump buster. Come on in."

"I thought we could talk," Danny said, stepping into the immaculate apartment, the smell of bleach and ammonia and pine reeking from the bathroom. The kitchenette was spotless, not a potholder out of place.

"I hope those shitkickers are comfortable," Horsecock said, pointing to Danny's Timberland boots. "Because as soon as I feed the birds I'm outta here for my daily three-point-two constitutional."

"I could use some exercise," Danny said.

Horsecock crossed to the window that looked out onto a common backyard, where the walkways were lined with benches and shady maples and elms. An old woman watered flowers in a small garden, old men played chess at stone tables, and a workman hosed the blackened grill of a barbecue, scrubbing it with a steel brush. Beyond the yard was a parking lot filled with cars and small vans that Horsecock said were used to transport the seniors on day trips to places like Atlantic City and group-rate Broadway shows. All the seniors had their own one-bedroom apartments, with spacious living rooms, kitchenettes, and bathrooms equipped with emergency pull cords that activated emergency lights at the lobby security desk in case one of them fell. But with a dozing nine-dollars-an-hour square badge standing guard, it was a fifty-fifty toss of the coin that you'd get immediate help. Still, this was the most dignified living arrangement Danny had ever seen for seniors.

"The birds love fat from leftover steak," Horsecock said, tossing out scraps to the birds that flocked to the ground outside his window.

He slammed the window, locked it, and jammed a stick in the frame so no one could open it. "Some of these old fucks are kleptos, ya know," he said. "And the workers here get paid shit. It's human nature, if you make shit money, you supplement your income. Most cops I know did it. So I don't trust nobody. Plus, there's evil in the world."

"You look like you can still take care of yourself," Danny said.

"I'm eighty-fuckin'-two. But I eat me a moderate-size T-bone every night, drink my Four Roses whiskey every day, go for my three-point-two constitutional every morning, have my two over-easy afterward with rye toast and regular coffee, then a hot shower, a second dump, and a tight shave. I tried Viagra with Eleanor before she died. It works. But where am I gonna find a new hot broad at my age? Even cathouses won't take me. And I'm too old to pull my prick. Still, I bet I live to see you collect Social Security."

"I don't doubt it," Danny said, laughing as Horsecock pulled on a Foley's hat, a pair of sunglasses, and nudged Danny out the front door.

"I thought we were gonna walk," Danny said, gasping for breath as they jogged on Park Drive of Prospect Park, passing the zoo that was now called a nature preserve.

"Walkin's for pussies," Horsecock said, pushing his thin old body like a well-oiled bike. "My cholesterol is perfect. Believe it or not whiskey keeps your arteries and heart valves pristine. It burns away the plaque and cholesterol. I aced my stress test last month. Doc said I had a heart like a fifty-year-old man. Same with my PSA test. My last colonoscopy said my Hershey Highway's as clean as Pennsylvania Avenue on inauguration day. If you run, eat ice cream for calcium, steak for protein, greens for roughage, whiskey for clear veins, and take vitamins, you can maintain bone density. That way you don't fall and break a hip. As soon as an old cocksucker like me breaks a hip he's an official finished old fuck. Nursing home time, which if it ever comes to that, I eat my gun."

"Don't you have any kids who could take care of you?"

He fell silent for a long mournful moment. Other joggers passed them both ways in the humid morning, yuppies getting in their miles before climbing into business suits to sit at desks all day. One lone man passed them at a very quick pace, early fifties, trimmed blond-and-white beard and close-cropped hair, but in perfect shape, his body all hard sculpted muscles, his fair-skinned male-model-handsome face shiny with sweat. He wore a T-shirt with a legend: SLOPE SENTINEL. He looked very familiar to Danny, a face from the past but older now, like his own. The man's eyes caught Danny's and then shifted to Horsecock's. Danny thought there was a nod of recognition, an acknowledgment between them. Maybe they passed each other every morning, Danny thought. Like the familiar faces commuters see on the morning train. Horsecock looked back over his shoulder at the man. Danny turned and saw that the man turned to look at him.

"Friend?"

"Nah," Horsecock said, his pace quickening, throwing shadow punches. "To answer your other question, my Eleanor couldn't bear children. It broke her heart till the day she died. The idea that other dames—shit mothers, a lot of them—could bear children and she couldn't made Eleanor feel inadequate as a woman. I had to keep reassuring her that she was my honey. I was no angel, believe me. I fooled around a little bit, but I adored my Eleanor. For me the job became my family, ya know?"

"I need to talk to you about Vito Malone," Danny said.

"He was a dick," Horsecock said, flicking more shadow punches into the morning air as he bounced along. "I know Ankles Tufano is still chasing his murder. Some cold-case broad is also sniffing around. Me, I don't give a skell's shit about Malone. I'd piss on his grave for cheap laughs. He was not the kind of human being you mourn for. I don't like seeing anyone with a badge die like that. We all make mistakes. We all have our weaknesses, our flaws, and our human failings. We all have our moments of regret that sometimes last a lifetime."

"Yes, we all do," Danny said.

"But Malone went out every day and disgraced the badge. Under my watch. Which threw a monkey wrench into my life. I knew he wasn't kosher. But Malone was smart. He was slippery. But in the end, he got what was coming. Hey, make no mistake, considering how he lived, he died the way he was supposed to die."

Danny kept pace, feeling every day of his forty-nine years, paying for every cigarette he'd sucked into his lungs for the past thirty-five years, certain that he would turn sixty by the time he made a full 3.2 mile circle of the inner roadway of Prospect Park. "Me, if I was still working that case," Horsecock said. "I would concentrate less on Malone and more on the other poor fuck."

He stopped to do ten quick push-ups off a big boulder bearing a bronze plaque that claimed that a major piece of the Battle of Brooklyn had been fought right here on this spot. After the push-ups, Horsecock planted his feet and ripped off a pretty quick five-punch combination, throwing hooks and right uppercuts with his body instead of just his arms, as if he'd been trained right young and never forgotten. He grunted with each punch, ended with a short hook to an imaginary rib cage, did a pirouette, and started jogging again. Danny gasped, feeling ashamed of his physical inferiority to the old man.

"What other guy, Wally Fortune?" Danny asked.

"No," Horsecock said, grimacing. "Although that one was sad. I liked old Wally. He was a funny fuckin' kid. A few times we would bust him just to bring him into the station house to watch him do his floor show. He'd have us in stitches on a slow night, goofing on all the cops, like Don Rickles, ripping new assholes. Then he'd start on the other locked-up skells. He even busted my balls and I was wearing lieutenant stripes. I took it on the chin, because he was a pisser. Then we'd cut him loose. But, no, I'm not referring to Wally Fortune. I mean Davis. I think he's the key to all that 1969 shit."

Danny groaned, sniffled, pushed his legs, which were now scorching with shin splints. "Da . . . vis," Danny gasped. "Why . . . Da . . . vis? . . ."

"Davis was a sort of sad case," Horsecock said, his breathing as relaxed as someone collecting shells on the shore. "He was never at peace. Remember, it was '69, half the department was still on the pad. Cops tuned-up perps without getting indicted. They ate in diners for free. They went to ball games and the fights on the arm. They tinned their way into cathouses. The badge was like a line of credit. But still, nobody liked a cop on a drug dealer's pad. Gamblers, who gave a fuck? Madams, some of us even took some poony in trade when we were young. Instead of taking a pinch, losing a night's work, paying a lawyer, a bail bondsman, and a fine, a hooker was happy to toss your cookies in exchange for you to look the other way. It was just the way it was. Cigarette smugglers, or shylocks, or fences—you worked out a barter. I mean, are you gonna play poker all night, fly to Vegas with a dozen cop friends, and play the tables, bang legal whores, and then come home and collar guys for selling numbers and some poor broad from Nebraska or Minnesota for turning tricks? So you took a few skins, wiggled a few hookers, looked the other way as they made a living, made a token bust once or twice a year, for appearances. But drug dealers were out, forbidden."

"And you think Davis had reservations about taking drug money?" Danny asked, slowing Horsecock down with a grasp of the shoulder. Horsecock decelerated, jogged backward, facing Danny, who grunted to a power-walk, sucking and gulping air as they rounded Grand Army Plaza.

"Yeah, I do," Horsecock said. "I even talked to him about it one night. He was tortured after that Wally Fortune murder. He never looked like he slept. I thought he might even be popping a few of those uppies, those speed pills himself, those blackbirds or what-ever the fuck they called them."

"That's what they called them," Danny said. "Blackbirds and blue heavens. Amphetamines, Dexedrines, diet pills. In Brooklyn we called them uppies. Everywhere else they called them uppers. Same bad stuff."

"See, I think he was flying on them one night," Horsecock said, flicking jabs, rolling his head on his strong old neck, pounding his chest like Mighty Joe Young, doing a slow jog as Danny power-walked. "Those fuckin' uppies were like inoculating someone with a Victrola needle. I met him in George's all-night diner on Church Avenue one night after a four-to-twelve. As I remember, it was a few

days after the Wally Fortune thing. Davis was ranting, his mouth
foaming with that white shit that looks like Elmer's Glue, from the
dry mouth, bad breath, talking about God, man and creation, the
fuckin' big bang theory, Adam and Eve versus evolution, religion,
right and wrong, childhood and his future. One of those 'What does
it all fuckin' mean?' conversations. He talked about how much his
kids meant to him. How he hoped they'd be happier growing up
than he'd been. That he'd never let them join the cops, the way his
father pushed him. About how much he liked and cared about his
wife even though he didn't think he ever loved her as a wife. That he
loved her like a friend. You know, all kinds of weird shit like that."

Danny thought of Tammy. He liked her so much that he missed
her company every day. He also thought of Darlene, rafting on a
sparkling clean white-water river a galaxy away from Danny's
murky Brooklyn past.

"He blabbed about how unfair all that was to his wife,"
Horsecock said. "And his kids, who he adored. He just kept saying
that his wife deserved better than him. That his kids deserved better.
You know, nobody talked about that kinda personal stuff back then.
People go on TV today and talk about stuff like that. But I was
embarrassed, like. So, I told him he should get in touch with the
chaplain, Reverend Boyd. He said he thought that was a good idea.
That he had a load of shit to get off his chest. We tried to find Boyd
but we couldn't track him down. He was attending some Christians
and Jews powwow in Rome, or some shit, chasin' guinea butans
around the catacombs. Boyd was more of a swordsman than I was,
that Protestant fuck."

"What was the load Davis had on his chest?" Danny asked,
moving by the Third Street playground, where black nannies
minded white children.

"He wouldn't say," Horsecock said. "He was making me uncom-
fortable. His breath stunk like Jersey. His eyes looked like fuckin'
cracker balls. I thought smoke was gonna come outta his fuckin'
ears. Fuckin' guy was built like Steve Reeves in *Hercules*. I didn't
wanna havta wrestle with him if he threw a fuckin' convulsion on
me. I wanted to finish my steak and eggs and run to Foley's for four
good hours of Four Roses before closing. Before going home to
Eleanor. Anyway, a few days later, when Boyd the chaplain
returned, I called Davis into my office to meet with him. But Davis
was straight as an Arrow shirt this time. Back to his quiet, haunted,

shy self. Couldn't look either of us in the eye. He said he'd worked out all his personal problems. He looked scared, but you can't cite a guy for that."

They fell silent for several minutes as Danny tried to keep pace with Horsecock, huffing past the Tennis House, near where he'd spied Ankles humping Marsha. He looked left at the ball fields, gasping for breath and remembering the day in the spring of 1969 when he got thrown off the John Jay baseball and football teams by Coach Riley. . . .

*March 12, 1969*

*Danny's been up on speed and uppies for three days.*

*After getting busted for pot in February, Danny is on an eight-month Youthful Offender probation. Christie Strong sees that Danny is depressed. He likes Danny, who has turned him on to the paintings of Hieronymus Bosch and the poetry of Francois Villon, and William Blake and Samuel Taylor Coleridge. Strong tells his dealers Lefty Mots and Harry Bowles to turn Danny on to speed and uppies and let him crash in their pad. The euphoric "up" high chases away Danny's blues of missing Brendan and life with his mother. Strong calls speed lyric powder. Says Dylan uses it to write his songs. On speed Danny writes poetry all night long about the hidden meaning of life. For the 500-word English composition assignment Danny turns in 6,000 words on* Silas Marner. *He writes Brendan a sixteen-page letter about the glories of weed and ups and says he's gonna try acid.*

*But the drugs are causing problems with Erika, who notices that Danny starts acting strange. Gabbing a mile a minute. His mouth always dry, his breath bad, his lips cracked. He skin breaks out. He doesn't eat. He's losing weight. His muscles melt. He doesn't sleep. He imagines people are talking about him. Thinks people are following him. He writes Erika ten love poems a day, none of which she can understand.*

*Danny can't shut up in class at John Jay High. He raises his hand to answer every question every teacher asks. He gives ten-minute rambling answers, steering the topic to the existence of God, Albert Camus's existential meaning of life, and the need to listen to Dylan and Donovan, and to make love and not war. "This is algebra, Danny," says Mrs. Burke. "Not philosophy. . . ."*

*At the after-school baseball practice in Prospect Park, Coach Riley has the team jog around the diamonds. Danny sprints it. Twice. Riley has gotten reports from all of his teachers that Danny is stoned on something. In a practice game Riley signals for Danny to bunt. He swings away instead and stretches a single into a diving double when Riley tells him to hold up. Then Danny steals third without getting the sign. He gets thrown out stealing home without getting the go-ahead signal.*

*"What the hell are you hopped up on, Cassidy?"*

*"Did you know that 'Lucy in the Sky with Diamonds' is really John Lennon's code words for LSD? And here we are playing on a baseball diamond in the diamond dust and as Dylan says we should dance beneath a diamond sky with one hand waving free, and Sly Stone says everybody is a star and so if you can become a star on a diamond you can have heaven on earth and—"*

*"Get your fucking glove and take a hike," Coach Riley says. "You're off the fucking team, you pathetic little hophead. This team and the football team and any team in John Jay High. . . ."*

"So, you think Davis was haunted about taking drug money?" Danny asked Horsecock, breaking the silent, gasping flashback. "Or, worse, the Wally Fortune murder?"

"Maybe. My nickname's Horsecock, not Dr. Fuckin' Freud."

They were in the home stretch now, passing the Eleventh Street playground on his right, where Danny and Brendan had played almost every summer day of their childhood. Before graduating to the baseball diamonds to his left.

"Did you ever give Davis a drug test? A polygraph on the Wally Fortune case?"

"We were off duty. He was confiding in me. I kinda liked the poor kid. I wasn't gonna fuck with his job, fuck up his wife and kid's lives. Only a real prick plays with a guy's family. Davis lifted all those weights all the time. It never occurred to me back then that he was capable of killing someone. He was so withdrawn that he had a hard time making friends with the guys. He never once went out for a beer with the other cops. Always kept to himself. So nobody trusted him. And because no one else wanted to work with Malone, because he was a class-A prick, a dirt gatherer, poor Davis was paired with him. In fact, when Malone asked for him I paired them together because they were like a couple of odd socks. I gave them Hippie Hill, which was shit duty. You were always afraid if you rousted one of them hippies you'd catch crabs or cooties."

"But Malone struck fuckin' gold there," Danny said. "And manipulated Davis."

"Say what you want about Malone as a human being," Horsecock said, "but he was a very good fucking detective. Malone could crack a cold case like an egg and come up with two yolks. He used strong-arm, violated all ten of the Bill of Rights in one bust, but he could find out who did what and when and how and why to whom like nobody I ever seen. You just couldn't have a secret around Vito Malone. He was a control freak. A real bloodhound. A nosy fuck. He hadda know everything about you, wouldn't rest until he did. He kept a dossier on all of his commanding officers, including me. He used that information to keep himself from getting jammed up."

"He had dirt on you?"

"You see a fuckin' halo around my head?" Horsecock asked. "Bookies filled my Christmas stockings. I was married, I loved Eleanor, but I was human. I liked broads. Like I said, I accepted a little poony in trade here and there, when it was offered. I never took it. I also liked a good steak in a good restaurant but on a cop's salary you were lucky if you could afford Tad's dollar twenny-nine steaks. So when it was offered, you tied on the bib. But Malone kept count of every cup of coffee any commanding officer ever took. His fucking hero was J. Edgar Hoover. He kept files. He also loved his eagles."

"I know about the eagles," Danny said.

"But not because he was a great patriot," Horsecock said. "Because every night he went on duty he liked to say, 'The eagle's gonna shit tonight.' That was the expression for payday in the old days. Referring to the eagle on the back of the dollar bill. Every day was payday for Vito Malone."

"And you think he manipulated Davis because he had a file on him?"

"Put it this way," Horsecock said as they reached the Grecian columns at the mouth of the park. "When he ate his gun for breakfast I wasn't surprised. That whole ugly incident cost me big. I was on a fast track to be a captain, which would have meant a much bigger pension. And all captains got out on three-quarters tax-free medical retirement in those days. It was an unwritten perk. But the commissioner was humiliated by the headlines. He wanted to know how come I didn't know this Malone was dirty with drugs when he was murdered on my watch? And his partner, Davis, who had two homes, a boat and a BMW and who ate his gun. I was transferred to Staten Island. I was never getting another promotion in the PD. And so as soon as I had enough in my pension, I retired, half pay, which is taxable. I figure I won't get back what I lost unless I live to be a hundred and motherfuckin' twelve. And so, just to fuck the PD, I intend to live to a hundred and thirteen."

"Two more questions," Danny said, wiping his brow, still huffing. "Who do you think the drug dealer Malone and Davis were working for was?"

"That's fuckin' easy," Horsecock said. "Our next councilman, Christie Strong. But you'll never prove it. He washed every dime he ever made. Twice. Once off shore, in the islands, and once in legit cash businesses. Gotta go, what else?"

"Malone and Davis claim they were grilling a snitch named Linc the night Wally Fortune was murdered," Danny said. "You have any idea who Linc is?"

For the first time Horsecock looked a little hesitant, his old eyes looking around as if he were afraid he was being watched. "That came up back then," he said. "But my guess is he just made it up. Just a name he made up as an alibi. See ya."

Horsecock jogged across Veteran's Memorial Square, past the war memorial, and over to Langston Place toward the Cardinal Murphy Senior Apartments. Danny stood, watching him go, panting, glistening with morning sweat. Horsecock had been so forthcoming about everything else. But when it came to the Boar's Head's snitch named Linc the turbocharged geriatric shut down like an old jalopy that had run out of gas.

Danny turned, tingling with an eerie sense that someone was watching him. He did a slow 360 swivel and saw Pat O'Rourke's Crown Vic back up and slither from a space next to his Camry in the park lot.

Danny then noticed a dark Taurus with tinted windows wind around Veteran's Memorial Square. He suspected it was Ankles's car.

He kept turning and saw the handsome, muscular man with the *Slope Sentinel* T-shirt, blotted with sweat, completing his revolution of the park drive. The man seemed to stare at Danny, who watched him slow as the Crown Vic pulled alongside him. The man stopped, chatted with Pat O'Rourke, then circled the car, stared once in Danny's direction, and climbed into the passenger seat. Danny watched the Crown Vic whisk away, still trying to place the face of the fair-skinned man with the blond-and-white beard, when he heard his name being called. A woman's voice, coming from up high, the way his mother used to call him from their tenement window for his supper when he played stickball late in the Brooklyn street.

"Daaaaannnny," the female voice sang.

He looked up, scanning the rooftops and high windows of the tenements lining Parkside West. Then he spotted her. High above the parkside, above the top fire escape, in the same familiar window, in the big high-ceiling, rent-controlled tenement apartment.

"Daaaannnnny," Hippie Helen shouted again, waving her arm, signaling for him to come upstairs. He shuddered for a moment and waved back. Then Danny crossed the street to go see the generous lady who had relieved him of his virginity over three decades before.

# twelve

Hippie Helen opened the Medeco lock on her apartment door. She was wearing a pale blue cotton muumuu, red and yellow love beads and flat leather sandals with a toe loop, chewing a mouthful of what smelled like peanuts. A big beatific smile divided her soft pleasant face. Crow's-feet etched her eyes and when her smile faded her upper lip gathered into an accordion of cruel wrinkles. She looked like she'd aged under a sun lamp.

Danny cared for her too much to imagine what she looked like now under the muumuu, pushing sixty and maybe 200 pounds. A superheavyweight, he thought. He chose to remember her when she was twenty-seven, gorgeous, seventy-five to ninety pounds lighter, a dazzling featherweight who knocked you out with a wink of a baby blue eye. Danny was sure she'd prefer him to remember her that way, too.

"You look great," she said. He didn't know how to respond. She spread her arms, and he stepped into the fleshy embrace, her large swollen breasts pressing against him. She kneaded his muscled back. He patted her fat rolls.

"Bullshit, Helen. Like the rest of us I'm getting old. I'll be fifty in two weeks."

"You look early forties," she said, trying to extract a return compliment from him. He didn't give one. He was afraid she might try to build the compliment into a matinee. They broke the hug and he stepped past her into the big bright apartment. A time warp of rock posters—Dylan, Donovan, Cream, the Doors, and Hendrix. And other sixties rock posters from Woodstock, Powder Ridge, Altamont, and Peter Max paintings. Racks of old sixties albums were jammed into an overflowing ceiling-to-floor bookcase against a shellacked bare brick wall. A vinyl album crackled on an old-fashioned Garrard turntable, Bob Dylan singing "Mr. Tambourine Man."

"I always loved that song," Danny said.

"That's why I put it on."

"You always did have a great memory. I'm in need of one."

"I never did hard drugs," she said, shrugging. "While everyone else was dropping tabs, swallowing uppies and gorilla biscuits, or snorting crystal meth, I stuck with the weed and the wine. The way Wally preached."

"If I'd done the same thing, the last thirty years would have been a lot different."

"You're all sweaty," she said, waddling toward the kitchen. "I made ice tea."

Danny gazed around the spacious apartment. Billowed silk sheets with paisley designs hung like puffy clouds from the twelve-foot ceilings. His feet sunk into a deep ten-by-fourteen-foot Persian rug that sat on the gleaming parquet floor of the fifteen-by-thirty-foot living room. A startled white Persian cat hopped from one of two soft crushed velour couches to the top of a large old Con Edison cable spool that served as a coffee table. An antique now, Danny thought. Danny liked cats, but he was allergic to them. They made him sneeze and turned his eyes into itchy balls. Danny watched the cat prance across the spool table that bore the burn marks of a thousand sizzling pot seeds, and a zillion cigarettes and weed roaches. The cat padded across a leather-bound Bible lying next to polished brass incense burners that smoldered with a jasmine blend. Danny hated incense. It made him gag. He coughed from the incense. He sneezed from the cat. He pulled a tissue from a Waterford crystal tissue dispenser, wiped his eyes, and blew his nose.

There was also a crystal lazy Suzie on the tabletop, jammed with cheese and crackers, potato chips, M&M peanuts, Raisinettes, chocolate jellies, cheese doodles.

He stepped closer to some of the silk-screened posters and realized that they were signed and dated by the stars, made out to "Hippie" Helen Grabowski. These were now sixties original treasures that she could sell on E-bay for a nice price. The autographed Hendrix must be worth a fortune, he thought. So were the autographed Joplin, Brian Jones, and Jim Morrison posters. The *Sgt. Pepper*'s album cover signed by John Lennon was priceless. Helen had been a groupie-collector, and now the stuff could finance a decent retirement.

Scented candles flickered on a high mantel in front of a five-foot mirror that was covered in a collage of old laminated snapshots of the teenage male denizens of Hippie Hill, circa 1969. Every photo was taken here in Helen's pad, framed against the big window looking out onto Hippie Hill. Each snapped after a fucking tsunami on her legendary water bed, Danny thought. Bet she de-cherried every kid here.

He spotted a photo of himself, shirtless and wearing cutoff jeans, stoned, a just-fucked smirk on his face, a beer in one hand, a joint in the other. His long hair was wet like he'd just showered after sex. Danny couldn't remember the day the photo was taken. He'd have to check his journals. But he guessed that he would have blow-dried his hair, kissed Helen good-bye, and left to meet Erika. Hoping that that would be the night Erika would surrender her cherry. So that he could teach her all that Helen had taught him. . . .

*March 17, 1969*

*Hippie Helen answers the door with a smile, wearing a green muumuu, thinner and younger, her braless nipples erupting through the sheer cotton. She grabs Danny by the hands. "Happy St. Patrick's Day, my Danny boy," she says. "Why're your palms so damp? The luck of the Irish is with you today, lad."*

*She leads him into the apartment. Danny is nervous. His dick is feeling like a cold useless stub in his dirty jeans. It's the first time he's ever been alone in an apartment with a grown woman. Never mind one who'd already sucked him off in Wally Fortune's VW bus a month before. Incense and candles burn. Marvin Gaye is on the stereo, singing "I Heard It Through the Grapevine."*

*Hippie Helen sticks a lit joint in Danny's dry mouth. Puts her mouth over the lit end and blows through the joint until a thick heavy stream of cannabis smoke rushes down into Danny's lungs. Her big wet lips touch his, thrilling him. He holds it as long as he can. Then he explodes the smoke out of his lungs in a coughing fit. She gives him a sip of wine, but he keeps coughing and coughing and coughing as the pot makes him lightheaded and stoned and parched.*

*"Only one cure for that," Helen says, pulling the straps of her muumuu off her shoulders and letting it fall to the floor in a slow-motion soft blue pile. She stands naked before Danny, thin and firm and big-breasted, her thick blond bush like a live sparkling fantasy. She nudges him to the couch as he continues to cough. She dangles her large swaying breasts over his face, dunking one nipple at a time into her glass of freezing cold white wine and then—icy firm and bittersweet—she dips each dripping erect nipple into Danny's dry mouth.*

*In seconds the coughing ceases and the stub between his legs springs to a full erection. Judy Collins belts out "Both Sides Now" as Danny grabs handfuls of Helen's tight bare behind.*

*He's afraid he's going to come in his pants before he can get it in her.*

*Helen slides down him, rubbing her breasts across his groin, kneels, pulls off his boots, opens his buckle and zipper. "Give me that big bad boy," she whispers. And in one practiced flourish she depants Danny, coins rattling from his pockets onto the floor. She yanks off his sweatshirt, suckles his nipples.*

*Then she leads Danny across the living room into her big bedroom, with the ornate mahogany dressers and matching armoire she says her parents had shipped to her across the country. She rolls off his Jockey underpants. She kneads him, scratching his scrotum and inner thighs with her long sharp nails. Kisses and licks and sucks him. Then pushes him onto his back on her king-size water bed, where he sinks and rolls in a boneless lightheaded wave. "Let Mama Helen do all the work," she says. . . .*

"At least your dad's at peace," Helen said, walking back into the room, handing him a frosted mug of ice tea and popping another handful of M&M peanuts.

"I'm glad someone is," Danny said, walking to the window that looked out over the parkside, adjusting his half-aroused penis in his pants. It was a catbird seat on the part of the world that in 1969 had been the center of Danny's universe. Hippie Helen still had a telescope mounted on a tripod at the window. Aside from the early-warning system, Danny knew Helen had also used the telescope to stake out hot new young hippie dudes that she could bring back to the water bed, give them a crash course in deflower power, and later pose them for pictures.

Danny cupped his eye around the telescope eyepiece, adjusted the focus dial, and racked a clear plain view of Hippie Hill, where Boar's Head was murdered. Then he panned to the bridle path where Mary Fortune was found OD'd. He widened the view to include the parking lot where Davis blew out his brains. And then he opened up the scope further to include the serpentine path that twisted toward the Elephant Steps, where Wally was murdered.

Helen could have witnessed all of those events sitting right here, Danny thought.

He turned and faced her, gulping some ice tea. She smiled and said, "Bring back memories?"

"Some," he said. "Some good. Some not so good. But not the ones I need."

"Maybe I can help," she said, walking to him, taking him by the hands and leading him to the couch.

"Helen, I don't—"

"Relax," she said. Her hands were soft and thick, their backs wrinkled and freckled. He felt like a coldhearted prick reacting to her unappealing appearance. *She's aged like a fucking ham,* he thought, and knew he'd go to hell, if there was one, for thinking like that. He sat a couple of feet away from her, the incense triggering the rest of the memory of the first time he came here, memories of March 1969. . . .

*Helen lubricates him with her mouth and then she mounts him, her steaming vagina sinking onto him. He comes in three glorious humps, unable to hold it, bucking and writhing on the roiled bed. Once again, he feels ashamed. Helen smiles. "I'm sorry," he says.*

*"We'll smoke another joint, sip some wine, and then I'm gonna teach you how to drive a woman mad," she says. "I'll make your girlfriend love you forever."*

*A half hour later Helen brings Danny back to full erection. And then she gives him his first real lesson in how to make love to a woman.*

*"Here's what I want you to do to your girlfriend," she whispers, showing him where and how to kiss her, changing his speeds, showing him how to flick his fingers, exploring her body, making her feel beautiful, sexy, unique, and adored. She demonstrates all the assorted positions, until he erupts again inside her with what Helen calls the "ink of the poets." And since he is only seventeen, "young, dumb, and full of cum," she makes him do it a third time. This time he lasts longer and learns more about how to derive pleasure out of giving it. . . .*

Danny became aroused thinking of the twenty-seven-year-old Helen while sitting here across from the present-day Helen, who was pushing sixty and 200 pounds. He was afraid she'd notice the bulge in his pants. He crossed his legs.

"What do you need help with?" she said, probing his eyes.

"I'm trying to make sense of November 20 and 21, 1969."

"Boar's Head's murder?"

"Yeah."

"You don't know if you did it or not, huh?"

"Right."

"Not surprised."

"Why?" Danny asked.

"Because I saw you earlier that night," Helen said. "Don't you remember?"

Danny searched her jowl-jiggled face, trying to fit it into that dark hole that was November 20 and 21, 1969. "No," he said. "I don't remember being here that night."

"You came in around, oh, I dunno, nine. You were smashed. You said you were just drinking. But you were flying on something else. Some kind of hallucinogen. Acid, THC, maybe even STP. I don't think you even remembered what you were on. You insisted we smoke a joint. And then, you know, I went down on you."

Danny looked at her, flicked a dark abashed smile, and drew a deep breath.

"Sorry," he said. "That's blank, too. . . ."

"Not surprised because I couldn't make you come," Helen said. "When Hippie Helen can't make a horny seventeen-year-old pop his jollies, he's gotta be wasted. The trip was bad. So you scored some gorilla biscuits to come down. No one can make a guy on acid, goofballs, weed, and booze ejaculate. Nobody."

"The only time I ever took barbiturates was when I wanted to come down from acid," Danny said. "But I don't remember taking acid. If I was gonna . . . if I was on a mission I would have drank. For balls. I remember drinking. Not dropping acid."

"Maybe you didn't. Maybe somebody did it for you. Or to you."

"Dosed me?"

"You were hallucinating when you came here. You thought I was your chick, what was her name?" She snapped her fingers, trying to pop the name into her brain.

"Erika."

"Right," she said. "I've never met her."

"She was at the wake last night."

"Yeah, I know, someone pointed her out. Attractive woman. 'Course, I was better-looking at her age before . . . never mind. Anyway, that night you thought I was her and you were telling me you were gonna take my cherry and then you were gonna meet my father. And you were gonna tell him. I started to laugh. But you got pissed. You stumbled all around the apartment. You babbled about your brother's gun."

Danny looked at her. He remembered that fuzzy part of the early night. . . .

*November 20, 1969*

*Danny hasn't been back to the Cassidy family apartment on Prospect Road since his mother died. But he stumbles in on November 20, 1969, after gulping some Hennessey cognac and six beers. His father shaves in the bathroom, getting ready for Foley's. The TV in the living room broadcasts Apollo 12's second moon landing. Merle Haggard sings, "We don't burn no draft cards in Muskogee" on a small transistor sitting on the bathroom sink.*

*"Good old USA, first and second on the moon," Mickey Foley says, shaving.*

*"Good old Mickey Foley," Danny says. "Drove my mother into a grave."*

*"Say that to my face sober and I'll knock your fuckin' teeth down your throat."*

*"Do it now, you cocksucker."*

*"I don't beat up drunk faggots," Mickey says, smacking on Old Spice and leaving.*

*Danny staggers into Brendan's old room, reaches onto the high shelf, pulls down Brendan's army footlocker, grabs the medic's .45. Jams it in his army coat pocket. And lurches out, gunning for Boar's Head. . . .*

Then the night went black.

He looked at Helen sitting a few feet away on the couch. "What happened next?"

She took him by the hand, led him across the living room to the bedroom. He felt his body stiffen as she led him through the door.

"Relax," she said, letting go of his hand. "I'm older, not contagious."

Guilt rose in him. This woman had been so generous to him when he was a scared and ignorant little shitbird and he was treating her like a used-up hag.

She pointed at the big bed. It wasn't a water bed anymore. "I had to get rid of the water bed," she said. "Doctor said my back needed firmer, orthopedic support. As you get older, you need all the support you can't get, ya know?"

"Yeah. I know."

"Anyway, I threw you in there. You collapsed. But your head was exploding with acid, gorilla biscuits, alcohol, THC, God knows what else you had. You were awake again in a couple of hours. I tried to stop you from leaving. I tried *everything*. But you wouldn't hear it. I had tickets to see the Doors at the Fillmore. That pissed you off, too. . . ."

"Who'd you go with?"

"What difference does that make," she said, laughing. "You're jealous thirty-two years later? I was with two, three guys a night sometimes back then."

"Not jealous, Hel. Just curious."

She shrugged, rummaged in a top junk drawer of her bureau. She found a wooden box with Celtic designs containing stacks of old concert ticket stubs bound with rubber bands, like the ones Danny had saved in his head bag. Hippie Helen sorted through them, valuable sixties mementos.

She took out a pair of stubs. "November 20, '69, here we go," she said. "JD. Jim Dugan. I went with Dirty Jim."

He laughed. "Dirty Jim? You were doing Dirty Jim back then, too?"

"He always had good tickets," she said, shrugging. "What? I always made him take a shower. He had a good heart. He's part of my cherry blossom garden outside. I took the cherry off every kid on that mirror over the mantel."

"But Dirty Jim was a fucking Peeping Tom and a blackmailer," Danny said. "Not that anyone had any money. But I know he got dirty pictures of a few married women and used them to make them do the dirty with him. That's why we called him Dirty Jim."

"So he cheated a few cheats. We all did stuff we lived to regret in those days."

"So the last you saw of me was when I stumbled out of here?"

"Babbling about a gun," she said.

"How come you never told this to Ankles?"

"I never have and never will talk to the cops," she said. "I found Jesus, not Judas. Besides, I don't think you killed Boar's Head."

Danny knew that she'd had at least one relationship with a cop. He once walked in on her on a Thursday night, using the key to her apartment she'd given him. She'd told him Thursday night was the only night he wasn't allowed to visit. But when Danny stayed up three and four nights without sleep, all the days became jumbled into one. And Danny had walked in on a Thursday night in June 1969 and saw a cop degrading Helen in a sexual ritual that was even risqué for the sixties. That cop was Boar's Head. Hippie Helen had fucked Boar's Head, but Danny never mentioned that he knew. He hadn't back then and he wasn't going to now. Not yet, anyway.

"Why don't you think I killed Boar's Head?"

"You were too smashed," she said, laughing. "You couldn't fire your dick, never mind a gun. And Boar's Head was smart and fast and ruthless. How the hell could you have pulled it off? He would have had you in handcuffs. He would have killed you."

*I could have waited in the bushes and ambushed him, even stoned,* Danny thought. But he didn't say it because he didn't want to create the possibility in Helen's mind in case she was ever called as a witness against him.

"So you were in Manhattan around two A.M. when Boar's Head was killed?"

"You know the Fillmore East," she said. "The shows were always late. Poco opened for the Doors and they didn't go on until almost midnight. Then Jim Morrison came on, grabbed on to the curtain, and rode it all the way to the top of the stage. Dropped down, grabbed the mike and broke into 'People Are Strange.' He had that gorgeous bulge in his skintight leather pants. God, I wish I would have sinned with him before I found the Lord."

"You and every other chick," Danny said. "Can I use the bathroom?"

"It's where it's always been," she said.

Danny walked to the bathroom, passing the kitchen that had been ripped out and replaced with oak cabinets and terra-cotta tiles, the walls all bared to the brick and hung with gleaming copper pots. High-backed oak stools surrounded a big butcher-block island. New ebony enamel appliances gleamed under track spotlights. *Must've sold a few posters,* he thought.

He entered the bathroom, now modernized with an eight-foot oval Jacuzzi tub and large Italian marble tiles on the floors, walls, and ceiling. Gleaming brass faucets complemented the deep, spotless delft sink. Danny closed the heavy oak door, since stripped to the original wood and lacquered. As he relieved himself he glanced at the row of shampoos and beauty products on the deep windowsill above the tub. Everything was Erika's Earth brand—shampoo, conditioner, body scrub, moisturizer. At first he thought it odd, because Helen said she'd never met Erika, even though they had lived together in the same neighborhood for over forty years. But Pat O'Rourke had said Erika's stuff was the hottest line on the Internet. *Just because you use Revlon products doesn't mean you know Ron Perleman,* Danny thought.

But the coincidence made him just curious enough to repeat a sneaky sixties habit of rooting in other people's medicine cabinets. In '69, whenever Danny went into anyone's home, particularly the homes of fat women, he would always ask to use the toilet and then rifle the medicine chest in search of diet pills, which were often amphetamines or Dexedrines. Sometimes he got lucky. Other times he would find tranquilizers or barbiturates. He'd swipe anything for the "head." And now he found himself rummaging Helen's medicine cabinet. He found some Erika's Earth creams and lotions and vitamins. He ignored those and picked up the assorted prescription pill bottles from Balsam's Pharmacy.

The pills were made out to Helen Grabowski. He had no idea what any of the prescriptions were for, but they all said she needed to take them three times daily. He dashed down the names of the medicines and also wrote down the name of the doctor.

He closed the cabinet, flushed the silent toilet, washed his hands, dried them on a fancy show towel, and stepped back outside. He walked into the living room, where Helen was placing a needle on an old album. The Beatles came on, singing "When I'm 64."

"I used to play this for you when we made love," Helen said.

"That I remember."

"I asked you if you would still make love to me when I was sixty-four," she said, walking to him, her eyes a little dreamy.

"Those were some days. . . ."

"Just because I found spiritual salvation doesn't mean I lost my human needs."

Uh-oh, he thought as the white cat rubbed against his legs. "Jesus, Helen, there's nothing I'd love better," Danny said, scrounging for a graceful dodge. "But I've been under such stress that I had a few arrhythmia attacks. And I'm on this heart medicine, a beta-blocker called Lopressor that causes temporary impotence in the first few weeks."

Helen looked at him, smiled in a sad way, staring him deep in the eyes. "I wasn't asking you, numb nuts," she said, fumbling for dignity. "I have human needs and I satisfy them with a monogamous partner now."

"Who's the lucky guy?"

"Wouldn't you like to know."

Danny felt an enormous wave of sadness move over him. Helen reminded him of just how old he'd gotten himself, how many haunted years had vanished. Gone in a clap of the hands. And yet, at the same time, the Beatles song sounded like something from another century. Christ, it was from another century, he thought. Seemed so long, long ago. In four years, the once gorgeous Helen who had taken his seventeen-year-old cherry would be sixty-fucking-four. Holy shit, he thought. How the fuck did that happen?

"You OK, Danny?"

"Did you ever know anyone named Linc? Linc with a *c*?"

Danny saw a tiny scribble of fear in Helen's eyes. Her soft smile drooped and she shrugged. "Doesn't ring a bell," she said.

Danny waved at the mirror over the mantel, at the hundreds of photos of Helen's old bedmates. "None of them could have been nicknamed Linc?"

"No," she said, a little too certain for Danny's liking. "Why? Who is he?"

"Not sure. Maybe he doesn't even exist."

"Another hallucination?"

"Never know," Danny said. "Oh, I know what else I wanted to ask you. Do you remember what I was wearing that night, November 20, when I came up here?"

"Sure," she said. "Same clothes you wore the day before. And the day before that. And before that. Blue bell-bottom jeans. The gray hooded John Jay sweatshirt. The clothes I always washed for you every Saturday while you lay in my water bed with your ball bag emptied, watching cartoons and *Honeymooners* reruns on channel 11. You also wore your brown Frye boots and the army jacket."

He remembered that he didn't awaken in those clothes. Somewhere that night he'd changed into brand-new clothes. But he didn't mention it. He checked his watch. It was almost nine-thirty. He had to meet Erika in a few minutes. He walked to the window and took one last reconnoiter of the world outside, a tableau of personal history, death, first love, sex, drugs, rock and roll, and murder. He panned the park.

He spotted the green Crown Victoria parked next to his car. Pat O'Rourke leaned against her fender, sporting her Mets hat, wearing black jeans this time and black sneakers with kelly green laces and a loose Mets jersey to hide her gun. She was wearing shades, so he couldn't tell if she was staring straight up at him. All doubt faded when he saw her wave in his direction. It unnerved him. Made him squirm.

"I gotta go, babe," he said, turning to Hippie Helen. She spread her arms. He wished he had it in him to give Helen a good, riotous charity fuck. But in some ways that would be more insulting than abstinence. He was afraid he would suffer erectile dysfunction, or dead dick, as they used to call it in Brooklyn, if he saw her naked. Not out of meanness. But a dick was a fickle creature and had a fussy mind of its own. He embraced Hippie Helen with affection. In her arms all suspicions disappeared about this kind sixties earth mother. She'd taught him some of life's fundamentals and had grown a bit tragic as she approached sixty. It was as if Michelle Phillips had morphed into Mama Cass.

"Can I buy you lunch while you're in town, Danny?" she asked.

"I'll call you."

Before he descended the stairs, she said, "Do I look that bad?"

"C'mon, you'll always be beautiful, Helen," Danny said and hurried down the stairs.

# *thirteen*

Danny left Hippie Helen's vestibule, stood on the high stoop, took out a Kleenex, and blew the cat dander out of his nose. He cleared his throat and spat, vanquishing the incense. He was fidgety for a cigarette, wrestling an octopus of mixed emotions about his old sex-ed teacher. He couldn't sort out everything in his brain. His craving for nicotine was so strong he didn't think he could endure it much longer.

He looked across to the park lot where he'd seen Pat O'Rourke staring up at him. She was gone. *Broad's like a fucking ghost,* he thought.

He took one step down the stoop and looked right toward Veteran's Memorial Square, one short city block away. Erika Malone stood in front of the Squared One restaurant, located next to the Paragon movie theater, standing in a provocative pose like a model on a photo shoot. Danny felt all the old lustful desires he'd ever felt for Erika rise in him. *This is fucking crazy,* he thought. *I'm a tired old hound chasing puppy love.*

Erika paced, her perfect bubble ass bunching in skintight hiphugger bell-bottom jeans, moving lightly in her thick cork-soled leather sandals. She wore a peasant blouse that revealed her bare muscle-ripped midriff. A diamond piercing her belly button blazed in the sun like a third eye. Holy shit, he thought. Where'd she get those clothes?

Erika ran her fingers through her thick red hair, which cascaded in natural curls to her bare tanned shoulders. She adjusted her large sunglasses and switched a picnic basket, covered with a blue-and-white checkerboard cloth that made Danny think of Yogi and Boo Boo from one hand to the other. She checked her thin platinum watch, the toned muscles in her right arm rippling. The girl worked out, he thought. Worked out hard.

Erika hopped on the hood of her illegally parked red '69 El Dorado, hoisting up one foot.

Danny trotted down Hippie Helen's stoop, marching to Erika, who watched him approach, a big sexy smile spreading on her youthful face.

"Good morning," he said. She hopped down, grabbed him by the chin, and kissed him, her glossy lips warm and soft. Unlike Hippie Helen, Erika looked like she'd been preserved in a time capsule. He stepped back, eyed her, focused on the red and yellow drawstrings that climbed from her crotch, crisscrossing her flat belly, and fell in a big dazzling loose bow from her tiny waist. All the seams of her jeans were embroidered with matching red and yellow thread in an American Indian pattern.

"Where the hell did you find a pair of jeans identical to the ones you wore in '69?" he asked. "Trying to untie those goddamned laces was like cracking a frigging safe."

"They're the same ones," she said. "I put 'em away. In plastic. Just in case. . . ."

"Get outta here! In case what?"

"In case you came back." She shrugged and smiled.

"OK."

"I knew you would someday," she said, wiggling her hips like Goldie Hawn in *Laugh In*. "And you always wanted to get in my pants. *These* pants. So I saved 'em. Because if at first you don't succeed . . ."

"I'll give it my best shot."

"First prove to me you didn't kill my father," she said.

"Aw, Erika, man . . . listen, I'll give that my best shot, too."

"Some people think you gave him six shots."

He rolled his eyes and nodded. She bit the tip of her wet tongue. He felt like grabbing her and screwing her on the hood of her red '69 El Dorado. He didn't think about a cigarette.

He searched for Pat O'Rourke's Crown Vic or Ankles's Taurus. He didn't see them. His rented Camry was the only car parked in the park lot across the street.

He nodded at the picnic basket. "I thought we were eating breakfast in this Squared One joint."

"I made brunch instead. C'mon. . . ."

She twined her small fingers between his big thick ones and yanked him into oncoming traffic, jaywalking toward Prospect Park. A B-69 bus screeched to a halt, the angry black driver slamming his hand onto the horn. Two cars braked and skidded, avoiding the bus.

"Assholes," the bus driver shouted.

Erika blew him a kiss and smacked her ass. The disarmed bus

driver smiled and shook his head and drove on, checking out Erika as he looped the traffic circle.

"Your car's gonna get a ticket," Danny said.

"Who cares?" she said. "I'm rich."

"I always knew you would be."

"Here, you carry this," she said, handing him the basket. "You're the guy."

He grabbed the basket. "Nah, makes you look gay as Par-ee," she said, grabbing it back. He crossed the parking lot, unlocked the trunk of his Camry, and took out one of his 1969 journals. He jammed it into his left back pocket as they left the lot, passing Hippie Hill and the bridle path. His other back pocket bulged with his wallet and a reporter's notebook. Danny gaped at the spot where Mary Fortune had OD'd, as if expecting an apparition to materialize naming names. Erika gripped his hand harder, trotting him across Park Drive toward the baseball diamonds.

Running hand in hand with gorgeous Erika, Danny feared that he was in the crosshairs of Hippie Helen's telescope. Once upon a younger time it wouldn't have fazed beautiful Helen, when Danny was just one of a long list of her hippie boy toys. But today the sight of Danny with the youthful and beautiful Erika Malone could drive the haggish Helen to distraction. He didn't want to make an esteem-defeated Helen any sadder. Or angrier. Helen could make his life difficult if she got too chatty with Ankles or Pat O'Rourke about November 21, 1969.

As soon as they were on the other side of Park Drive, Erika broke into a mock bump-and-grind dance step, backing Danny to the bough of a maple. She dropped the basket on the grass, looped her arms around his neck, kissed him deep and wet, her tongue roaming his mouth, gliding across his teeth, sucking on his lips. She pressed herself against him, the laces at the front of her hip-huggers rippling against his buckle.

His dick grew down his leg, her pelvic bone pressing against it, her perfectly firm, pear-shaped breasts crushed against him. He broke away, testosterone bubbling. "You can't do this to me, Erika," he said. "For chrissakes, I'm forty-fucking-nine. You keep cock-teasing me I won't be able to think straight. I need very important information."

"What's more important than us?"

"Us? We don't know if there is an *us*, do we? If I don't learn some hard facts, Ankles and another cop on this case are gonna come at me from different angles."

"What other cop?" she said, lifting the basket, taking his arm, and leading him across the ball fields toward the Long Meadow. Ball players from Cardinal Murphy High shagged flies in fielding practice. A middle-aged couple flung a Frisbee into the breezy morning. Unleashed dogs chased each other in mad circles as three other yuppie couples strolled toward Swan Lake.

"Her name is Pat O'Rourke," Danny said.

"She the bitch that followed us home last night in the Crown Victoria? The one you got into the car with in the rain after dry-humping me?"

"You saw her?"

"I see everything. Did you fuck her?"

"Of course not."

"She follows me sometimes, too. But she never stops to talk. How old is she?"

"I didn't ask," he said.

"Why the fuck not?"

"I have a hard and fast rule of not asking cops who wanna bust me for murder how old they are. Female cops top the list."

"Same old sarcastic Danny," she said, taking his right hand and jamming it into her back pocket as she looped her left arm around his waist, their hips rubbing, the way he'd always loved walking with her, showing off his hot chick like a prize.

"Sorry."

"It's OK. It's you. Is she pretty up close?"

"I don't find cops who wanna jail me pretty."

"Guys are dogs. . . ."

"Women are bitches."

"You'd fuck her."

He couldn't find much of an argument with that. "Maybe once, but just for experience," he said. "For you, my darling."

"Fuck you," she said, tilting her head, smiling.

"I'd fuck you right here, right now, in front of everyone."

"Let's."

"You serious?"

"Sure," she said. "But it takes balls. You have big enough ones?"

"There's kids. . . ."

"They'd love it, too. Especially Catholic schoolboys. Come on, take off your clothes, take off mine, and fuck me right here, right now, in the grass. In front of everyone. This is the field where we both first laid eyes on each other. I was the cheerleader for the other team. You were the halfback for John Jay. C'mon. Fuck me like you would have that day, right here on the field where we met. Right now, right here."

He called her bluff, yanked on his belt. She dropped the basket, lay down on the grass, opened her arms and legs in surrender, the crotch seam of her skintight pants splitting her vagina. He stopped. Rebuckled his belt.

"You don't have the balls," she said.

"I guess not."

"That's why we will fuck soon," she said and snapped to her feet like an acrobat, without the help of her hands.

"I'm not following."

"If you don't have the balls to whip it out and fuck me right here and now in Prospect Park, no way did you ever have the balls to whip out a gun and murder my father in the same park. Which means you didn't do it. Which also means that before you go back to California—if I ever let you—I'm gonna fuck your brains out."

He blinked a few times, trying to follow her logic. She grabbed the picnic basket and pranced across the meadow. As if she'd just solved a major piece of an old puzzle. *What an ass*, he thought. Danny noticed that the high school outfielders were also watching her, peeking through the webbing of their baseball gloves.

He caught up with her. "You figured it all out, just then and there, huh?

"Sure," she said.

"That's it?"

"I think the big picture's pretty clear. You didn't do it."

They strolled hand in hand past the Tennis House, the big granite and marble rest station where lawn tennis players in the nineteenth century used to change clothes, use the rest rooms, and have tea after games in the cool shade of the center pavilion. Erika stopped, pointed. "Remember the time we saw Ankles and Marsha fucking in his detective car right behind there?"

"You weren't with me," Danny said, pulling out his journal, paging through it, finding the entry he was looking for.

"Yes, I was," she said.

"No, you were with that son of a bitch Lars Andersen," he said, the old jealousy rising, embarrassing him, as he traced his finger across the old entry. "I told you about Ankles and Marsha. I know what I saw. I was alone."

"I thought you couldn't remember things?"

"It's in my journal, right here," he said. "It was the same month you broke my fucking heart. That's why I was alone. Aimless. Smashed on uppies. Roaming the night. Listen: 'A boffing MM near Tennis House. While L takes E's cherry in Bay Ridge. Everybody in love and making love but me.' I was feeling sorry for myself. But you ripped my heart out of my goddamned chest and you jumped up and down on it by being with Lars. Lars who took your fucking virginity. . . .'"

"Stop!"

"You went out with me for nineteen months and I never got more than a BJ—and that was for my birthday—and that German fuck got your cherry in less than a month."

"He was Norwegian," she said, her voice dropping to a whisper. "And I didn't *give* my virginity to anyone."

He flipped through more pages of the old journal. "Look, this is ancient history and shouldn't matter, but I need to get the facts straight in order to make sense of what happened. It says here that you came to my door, bleeding, and said Lars forced himself on you. Raped you. You bled like a stuck pig. I gave you a Valium. You passed out. I went looking for Lars. It's all here in my journal—"

"I don't want to hear this," Erika said, waving her hand.

Danny flipped to the next page. "What I never told you was that I tracked Lars down that night," Danny said. "And I beat that son of a bitch to within an inch of his life for what he did to you."

Which was another reason Danny'd always feared that he might have killed Boar's Head, because a monster stepped out of him that night, the night he beat Lars. A killer that he knew lived inside him. He gave Lars a beating that was almost as savage as the one Vito Malone gave Wally Fortune. It scared him then. More now.

"Please, don't tell me this," Erika whispered, her eyes glittering in the sun.

"But part of me blamed you, too," Danny said, reading from his September 15, 1969, journal entry again: 'If E hadn't been with L, cockteasing him, the way she drives me nuts, it would never have happened.' What can I say now? I was seventeen. I blamed the victim. I'm sorry. But I'm not sagging with guilt about avenging your honor."

Erika stared at him for a long astonished moment, blinking, absorbing what he was saying. "You're saying that you're the one who gave Lars that beating? My God, he was in the hospital for two months, broken cheekbones, missing teeth, stitches under both eyes, broken nose, broken elbow, severe concussion, crushed pelvis, ruptured testicles."

"I'm not bragging about it," Danny said. "I was young, it was a different Brooklyn. Before they even coined a phrase for it, Lars date-raped you. To be honest I'd do it again, if some prick forced himself on my daughter. Or you."

Her eyes did a skittery little dance in the sun, as if events didn't fit into her memory and therefore left her confused. Out of control.

"I thought it was my father who beat Lars. When he found out I was dating him he went insane. Like I was dating Abbie Hoffman. Or H. Rap Brown."

"I have a lot of regrets from those days," Danny said. "Giving Lars that beating isn't on top of the list. But I'll never forget him crying, swearing he didn't do anything wrong. I remember feeling sorry for him after a while. I beat him for a good three straight minutes. I'm lucky I didn't kill him."

He wished he hadn't said that. But Erika seemed lost in thought, staring at middle space, her long neck craned as if reeling backward in time.

"He wasn't gonna use his dick or his balls again for a long, long time. I just left him in a pile and I ran. I ran all night, flying on the uppies. Hoping you would take me back, be my girl again but you—"

"Stop!" Erika shouted, holding up a hand like a crossing guard. "Drop it! Now!"

Danny saw two yuppie couples near Swan Lake turn toward the lovers' quarrel. He felt foolish. Erika turned away from him, quickening her pace across the sweeping meadow, mounting the hillock that led to the Picnic House.

He followed her to a picnic table overlooking the Sugar Bowl, where Danny used to sleigh ride as a kid. Erika dropped the basket down on the table, removed the checkerboard tablecloth, snapped it outward, and spread it out on the table. She plunked two over-stuffed sandwiches on a pair of paper plates. She clunked down a bottle of champagne and a wicker bowl of homemade potato chips.

"Eat, you fucking son of a bitch," she said, ripping the metal seal off the Roederer Cristal champagne, wrestling the wire fastener loose, and strangling the cork out of the bottle with her powerful little hands. Beautiful hands. Flawless hands. Sexy hands. *The hands I dreamed about having wrapped around my dick,* he thought.

"Fuck's the matter with you?"

"The goat cheese with garlic and basil is homemade," she said, shoving a sandwich toward him. "With avocado, lettuce, and organic tomatoes that I grow in my backyard. The sprouts, olives, roasted peppers, and stone-ground mustard are all health-food-store-bought. The chips I made, sprayed with olive oil, coated with sea salt, and baked. I showered first and I was naked when I prepared the food to make sure no mites get in it. I always stay naked after a shower when I'm going to cook or pre-pare food."

"You should do a cooking show like that."

He took a big giant bite of the sandwich. It was delicious. "Food that's good for you is not supposed to taste this good," he said.

"Oh, shut the fuck up," she said, pouring the champagne into two real glasses and taking a sensible bite of her sandwich. She nibbled a chip, sipped her champagne.

"I'm sorry."

"Eat the goddamned sandwich," she said.

"I shouldn't have brought all that up," Danny said. "I just need to put things in perspective, in some kind of chronology. I need to reestablish my mind-set. I was a crazy fucking kid."

"Can we not talk about this anymore. Christ, I thought I had a problem with growing up. But you have a father lying in a box, we both want to know who killed my father, and you're still obsessed with how I lost my virginity thirty-two years ago?"

"If you were raped, yeah," he said.

"Why?"

"Because . . . because, it sort of ties into things. My mind-set. My motives, if I had any. Because you were seventeen and still my girl.

And I was eighteen. And because shit like that matters a whole bunch at that age."

"I was not still your girl. We'd broken up. You just said so. Which I will cross-check in my diary when we get to my house later."

"Together or broken up, I still loved you when it happened, so. . . ."

She looked at him, sipped some more champagne.

"Do you still love me now?"

"How the fuck do I know?"

She looked offended. He paused for a long moment, trying to figure out how to explain it without sounding like an asshole. "I guess I've always *thought* I loved you, as ridiculous as that sounds," he said. "First love is like a teenage tattoo. It follows you through life. Sometimes you can't get rid of it. You hide it, but it's still there. Like I said, ridiculous but—"

"What's ridiculous about loving someone, Danny?"

"Nothing," he said. "Except it's been over thirty years. Since then I got married, had a kid, and got divorced. . . ."

A squirrel and a seagull from Swan Lake came mooching for grub. Danny tossed each a piece of bread from his sandwich. This brought pigeons, sparrows, and starlings.

"Did you get married to try to fall out of love with me? Then get divorced because you still weren't sure?"

"Maybe," he said.

"Bullshit! If you're not sure, then it was true. Love is never a maybe, baby. Me, I never denied for a minute that I loved you. There were other men, of course, but they were just company. Rainy-night booty calls. You were why I never married. You, and because I never wanted a rich man who thought his money could control or intimidate me. And because I didn't want some poor lazy asshole getting half the money I worked my ass off for. I never found anyone in between. Except you."

"I don't have a spare dime," he said. "I get pissed off paying traffic tickets. But I don't want a dime from you either. Money doesn't mean that much to me."

"I know," she said. "It never did. That's sexy to me."

He stared at her, nodded his head, and tore into another giant bite. He jammed chips into his mouth. They were the best potato chips he'd ever tasted. "Christ Almighty," she said. "Leave some room for your taste buds. You eat like a convict."

"That might come in handy," he said, washing down the food with some Cristal. "At every meal I'd think about you cooking me meals naked."

She stared at him, as if he were a portrait in a gallery, searching for flaws or signature brush strokes. He stared her right back, dead into the beautiful crazy eyes. Behind her, on Park Drive, he saw a creeping black car. He broke his stare with Erika to focus on the black car that moved behind a tapestry of leaves. He thought it was a Taurus.

"If we don't figure it all out first, I'll hire the best lawyers in New York to prove you didn't kill my father. But I think we can figure it out."

"What's this 'we' shit? Whoever did it—and I think I know who's at least behind it—could be a mass murderer. Killed more than once. I'm not gonna expose you to that."

"Get off the happy horseshit about protecting your defenseless little damsel," she said. "Pound for pound I'm tougher than you. And I think I might even have more balls. Do you doubt for one minute that I am capable of killing someone?"

"No."

"I'm not afraid to take on anybody to protect what's mine."

"Like who?"

"Like you."

"I'm *yours*, all of a sudden? Since when?"

"Since you came back to me."

He studied her this time, perused this crazy beautiful rich bitch that he was afraid he'd loved—even when he'd tried his hardest not to—for thirty-two years. She ate her health food. She dressed in the same clothes she wore the summer they fell in love. She dared him to push his own envelope. She was as unpredictable as hurricane weather, leaping from emotion to emotion like a frog with a chemical imbalance. Or was it some kind of performance, some elaborate cocktease, he wondered. Erika's way of lulling him into confessing that he'd killed her father?

He wasn't sure.

She had come out of the sweaty past, into his midlife, as timeless as her old clothes that were back in chic fashion now. Like Bob Dylan, who'd just won an Oscar. And Santana, who'd won a bunch of Grammys and was playing to soldout crowds of kids his daughter's age. And Clapton, who still packed the Garden. Erika sucked him deep into the sixties—that dirty, bloody, diabolical decade—that just wouldn't die. *It's the vampire decade,* Danny thought. *And she's pulling me back to first love.*

"I was gonna talk to a guy named Jim Dugan next," he said. "Dirty Jim."

"I know who he is. Little anorexic weirdo. Who else?

"Christie Strong."

She fell silent for a long moment, chewing in long slow bites, her jaw muscles bunching under her taut tanned skin, filaments of platinum down highlighted in the morning sun. "He's a wicked prick," she said. "He's been trying to bed me since I was a kid. He started writing me love letters when I was going out with you."

"I knew he hit on you; the letters you never told me about," he said.

"You would have gone after him. And you would've gotten hurt. But he's written me all these handwritten letters all through the years. He wanted to make me one of his trophy girls. The thought of it makes me want to vomit. Never happened, never will."

"Even as an adult he's written you these letters?"

"Yeah, and sends cards and flowers. I throw them all away. Unread. Unopened. But tell me why you think he's involved in my father's murder."

Danny told her some of what he knew. He didn't tell her he'd witnessed Boar's Head kill Wally Fortune. But he did tell her he thought her father and Jack Davis were on Strong's payroll. "Your father wasn't Officer Joe Bolton. He didn't get killed because he was an angel."

"You think I didn't figure out he was on the take? I knew. My mother knew. But all the cops were on the pad back then. That's just how it was, an unofficial cop benny."

"For a lot of cops, but not all of them."

"OK, so there were a few Serpicos."

"And look what happened to him," Danny said. "Serpico put them in danger. Cut off their money. Threatened their jobs and pensions. Some guys were even gonna go to jail. So they set him up. Tried to kill him. Maybe that's what happened to your father."

"You hesitate because you're still not sure if you didn't kill him, huh?"

He didn't answer that. He took a final bite of the sandwich, broke up the last crusty corner and scattered it to the birds. He watched them flap and peck each other for the crumbs. It made him feel like Christie Strong.

"I'm not sure about anything."

"Including me?"

He didn't answer.

"Good," she said, sipping her champagne. "That'll make it more interesting. We're going to find out who killed my father . . . and along the way I'm gonna make you say you love me."

# fourteen

Dirty Jim Dugan peered out through the dusty blinds of Clubweb.com Inc., his computer graphics firm located in a small, dusty two-room storefront on Eleventh Avenue, between Terrace Avenue and Langston Place, a block and a half from Prospect Park. He turned back to Danny and Erika, leaned on his big metal desk, even more emaciated than in the old days, built like a human praying mantis, his bones coming to sharpened points at the elbows, shoulders, and knees. Most of his hair was gone now.

"I wish you didn't come here," Dirty Jim said, fidgeting a set of keys, maybe twenty of them, on a big ring that was attached to a retractable holder on the belt of his jeans.

"I didn't want to talk on the phone," Danny said.

"Why'd you bring the broad?" He slugged from a bottle of Pepto Bismol and grimaced, baring chalky-pink horse teeth.

"He talks behind my back in front of me, this little protein molecule."

"It's her father who was killed," Danny said. "She'd sort of like to know who did it as much as I would. Daughters are funny like that."

Danny sat in a swivel chair as Erika paced the cramped office, which was clogged with banks of computer terminals, file cabinets, ringing phones, and the big metal desk. Danny watched Erika trace a finger across the top of the metal filing cabinets, relics that were being made obsolete by computer files. She lifted a black finger and ran it under the red-hot water spigot of the watercooler, wringing it dry on a paper napkin.

"You live up to your nickname," Erika said. "Dirty fuck."

"I gotta listen to this?" Dirty Jim said. "From a broad? Fuck you both."

He took another slug of the pink stomach medicine.

"You said you'd help me," Danny said.

"Why should I trust this nasty broad?"

"Because I'm rich," she said. "Maybe I can make it worth your while."

Dirty Jim smiled at her, his eyes focusing on her crotch, as if he were having a conversation with her vagina.

"Everybody's afraid of somebody, honey," Dirty Jim said, still staring at her crotch, the way audiences paid more attention to the dummy than the ventriloquist. "I'm afraid of Ankles, cold-case cops, my PO. I'm afraid of the NASDAQ taking another nosedive, baby. And I'm afraid of nosy insulting broads like you, lady. Once upon a time I put hot stuck-up broads like you in their place. On their knees. Copping my joint so their husbands wouldn't get pictures in the mail of them copping his best friend's mahoska. You know how far and fast one of those pictures can travel today by E-mail? So that everyone in the world can see it? But since I'm on parole and there's laws against that sort of thing, I'm afraid to do it. But we all have our breaking point, puss 'n boots."

"You should be afraid of me breaking your fucking nose if you keep talking to her like that," Danny said.

"I don't need you to do it," Erika said.

"You think I'm a little skinny fuck you can strong-arm?" Dirty Jim said. "Fine. Go ahead, kick my ass. I did time and lived. Because I make alliances. I'm a politician, not a fighter. I got people. I got better than people. I got fucking *keys*."

He rattled his key ring the way Danny used to rattle the magical altar bells as the priest transformed cheap Gallo port into the blood of Christ.

"And I got three days to get answers," Danny said.

"I got information. Believe me, you don't want me as an enemy. I'll come through every keyhole in your life, past and present. You don't want me outside your door with the keys to get in. You wanna be afraid of that. You want me inside with you, helping to keep all the doors locked and bolted from the inside."

Danny knew Dirty Jim was right. The meeting had jumped off ugly from the start. He needed to dial back the approach, tone it down. Lull in Dirty Jim.

"You're right," Danny said. "We apologize."

"Speak for yourself," Erika said. "He needs a good kick up his ass."

"That's it," Dirty Jim said. "This is a wrap."

Danny turned to Erika, asked her to wait in the car. She shot him a furious look.

"It smells like death waiting to happen in here, anyway," she said and strutted out.

"Man, she's got a twat like a pair of balls in them pants," he said, grinning pink Pepto Bismol–coated teeth.

"The apology wasn't a license to talk dirty about my . . . about Erika."

"You didn't waste no time hooking up with her again, huh?" Dirty Jim said. "I used to hit the wood over her. I used to follow her around with the camera. But she was faithful to ya, Danny baby. Except for that pretty boy Lars Andersen. But all she ever did was kiss him good night. Him I caught in the act, all right, but never with Erika."

Danny leaned back in the chair, curious. He had imagined seedy, almost pornographic images of Erika and Lars together. What Dirty Jim was saying didn't jibe with those images.

"You telling me you followed Lars and Erika and never caught them getting it on?"

"I always wanted to catch her coppin' somebody's joint. But she didn't. And she stayed vacuum-packed in them hot dungarees. I never even seen the pretty boy cop a little of her tittie or heinie. Nothin'. So tell me, c'mon, is the bush just as red as her head? I always imagined it was. . . ."

"You keep talking like that and I'm gonna bring her back to kick the shit out of you. Now talk to me about her father. Boar's Head."

"Sure," he said. "But listen to me, and listen good. I survived two years in the joint on the hacking bit. I survived on favors. Paying for protection. Teaching cons how to work computers. Showing them how to download porn. How to communicate with friends and family. How to plan scores and do scams, from inside, on handheld Palm Pilots. But I ain't built for major jail time, Danny. I'm a skinny little fuck. I got Crohn's disease. You ever hear of it?"

"Yeah, but I'm not familiar with the details and I don't give a sh—"

"Crohn's causes partial obstruction of the intestine, gives you pain like appendicitis, and bad diarrhea. Any fuckin' time it feels stress. Stress triggers it. Jail causes stress. And that don't go over big inside, moaning in pain and shittin' like an Uzi all night in the one toilet in a four-man cell like the one I did federal time in Otisville, where you're the only white guy, weighing a wet 129—"

"Jim, Christ Almighty, I don't need a medical history, here. . . ."

". . . Crohn's can also can cause fistulas in the anus. But, you think that stops some cracked-out horny yom from trying to pork me in the shower? I'm built like a bulimic junkie fashion model, chrissakes. I got an ass like a fuckin' soup chicken. But I turn certain weird fucks on inside. They called me Ally McBeal on my cell-block. I escaped gangbangs by doing favors and spending my nest egg on protection and because I was a short timer. If I go back for a long stretch in a state pen with city crackhead yoms it's in the actuary charts that I get bungholed. Which is a death sentence for a guy with Crohn's. It'll cause fistulas. Feces'll escape into my bloodstream and—"

"Whoa, Jim," Danny said, holding up his hand. "Stop! I don't wanna hear any more—"

"In order to live I need rest, corticosteroids, immunosuppressive drugs, antibiotics, a sensible modified diet," he said, picking up a prescription bottle from the desktop, emptying several pills into his hand, washing them down with a slug of Pepto Bismol. "You think I get rest and a sensible diet livin' with the yomskies in Sing Sing? I already had two pieces of my intestine removed. If it's necessary again, you think I'm gonna let them do that to me in a prison hospital? I'd rather go to the fuckin' ASPCA. So do I make myself clear? I ain't risking jail for nobody. One violation, my PO can send me right back to Cornhole University with the yoms."

"I don't wanna go to the joint either, Jim."

"You at least have a fightin' chance."

"I need to know about Boar's Head," Danny said. "I need to know about that night, November 20, 1969."

"I was with Hippie Helen seeing the Doors," he said. "Fillmore East."

"You lie to me, Jim, I'll do whatever I can to see you back in the joint."

"Helen has the ticket stubs. I don't remember everything from those days. A lot of dead bodies under the bridge since then. But people from this neighborhood remember the night Boar's Head was whacked the way they remember what they were doing when JFK bought it. I was with Helen at the Fillmore."

"Did you see me that night?"

"Earlier. You were fuckin' whacked. Walkin' like Gumby. Talkin' like JoJo Corcoran. Nonsense. Psychadelerium. Acid rap. Mix whiskey with LSD, a little Tuinal and Dexedrine and we're talkin' zombieonics."

"Where'd you see me?"

"On Eighth and Fifteenth, first," Dirty Jim said. "I was scoring some uppies for the show offa Lefty Mots. So were you."

"What was I wearing?"

"The fuck do I know? Your regular hippie shit, the outfit Helen washed all the time for you. You weren't exactly Cary fuckin' Grant in them days. Matter fact, you looked better under a black light than daylight."

"Was I scoring pills off Mots, too?"

"You were always scorin' pills. You wanted uppies because you said you had an appointment at two in the mornin' you hadda keep and you needed to stay awake."

"You sure it was Mots? My own roommate?"

"Yeah. But he's dead now."

"I heard," Danny said. "So's Bowles. I heard they both died a few weeks after Boar's Head."

"They got strychnined meth," Jim said, twirling his key ring on the thin wire cable. "Mots died at home. But fuckin' Harry snorted his bad speed in McCaulie's men's room, Christmas week. He busted through the fuckin' door into the barroom, his back arching like a fuckin' Halloween cat, gasping like he was havin' a fuckin' exorcism conniption, suckin' for air, clutchin' his neck, lurchin' all over the fuckin' place like a hoople in a rodeo. He did a death rattle on the fuckin' pool table, his left foot rattlin' back and forth like Ingemar Johansen after Floyd Patterson hit him with the leapin' left hook. Then he flipped onto the floor, dead as mackerel."

"Where was Christie Strong?"

"The Bahamas," he said. "He went every Christmas. Still does."

Danny sat and nodded, looked at the bony little man who sat on the edge of his desk, jiggling his keys as he talked, his bug eyes wide in reflection.

"Both Mots and Bowles worked for Christie," Danny said. "I go on the lam, half framed for murder. Boar's Head is dead. Davis kills himself. Then Mots and Bowles get bad meth. Sound like Christie did a little housecleaning to you?"

Dirty Jim hopped off the desk and peered out through the blinds again, his heavy gold Rolex weighing down his wrist, which was no thicker than the handle of a baseball bat. "I don't want any trouble from that crazy fuck," he said.

"What are you afraid of, Jim? He's legit now, isn't he? A businessman, restaurateur, real estate baron, politician. His ruthless dope-dealing days are over."

"You been away too long," Dirty Jim said. "One thing that illness, time itself and doing time, and success teaches you is that people— the great fuckin' majority anyways—never change. They are what they are. Once an ass man, always an ass man. Once a tit man, always a tit man. Once a who-wa, always a who-wa. Once a cutthroat, always a cutthroat."

"Even, say, when they find Jesus?"

Dirty Jim looked at Danny and smirked. "If you're talking Helen, the answer's yeah, even her," said Jim. "I love Helen. She's a good egg. But see, she's a cockaholic. A recovering cockaholic but still a cockaholic. She didn't change."

"Did she have any kind of a fling with Christie Strong?"

Dirty Jim squinted, as if trying to figure out if Danny knew something he wasn't supposed to know. "No, he might be one of the few she didn't bang."

"Why?"

"They were like the flipside of a coin. The chemistry was all wrong. Besides, Strong liked his little flock to be monogamous to him. Helen was too good, too beautiful inside for him. Helen was always a saint inside. She was always a bit of a Mother Teresa. The one person she was never good to was Helen. She never put anything away for her old age. For when her looks left. I help her out because she helped me when I was inside. She visited. Got me on my feet. Wrote me letters. Sent me care packages. Money for commissary. So I throw her a wiggle once in a while. No one else will. I turn out the light because the sight of me banging her is like somethin' outta an R. Crumb cartoon. We might look like Laurel and Hardy, but we don't laugh about gettin' old. It sucks a big one. Helen didn't change. If anything she's just learning now to be as good to herself as she always was to everyone else. I had to convince her that it ain't selfish to take care of number one. That's generous because the longer she lives the longer she'll be around to be kind to other people. She's so fuckin' sweet that she even humped me when she was gorgeous and I looked like I do now back then."

"How's Helen's health now?" he asked, thinking of all her prescriptions.

"Helen's good. Fine. I wish she'd drop a fast fifty so she could get on top, but other than that, she's OK. Why, what'd she tell you?"

"Nothing. I didn't ask. But, changing the subject, you ever hear of someone named Linc? Maybe Boar's Head and Davis knew him? A snitch, maybe?"

Dirty Jim peered through the blinds again. "Maybe by sight, not by name."

Danny thought his movements were a little too quick, as if deflecting the question, turning his head so that Danny couldn't see his eyes as he answered. He seemed to get a lot of fidgety answers to the name Linc.

"What's your relationship to Christie Strong now?"

"I try to avoid him like the bubonic plague."

"What was that charade at the wake last night all about? Pretending we were having static, nasty words?"

"Ankles was there and—"

"Bullshit," Danny said. "C'mon, Jim. That was for Christie Strong's edification. You didn't want him to think me and you might exchange any information. I want to know what information that is. Don't bullshit me, Jim. I don't have time to waste."

He paced the floor, walked to a computer, taped a few keys; images appeared and disappeared on the screen. He rattled his keys, he smoothed the comb-over on his transparent scalp, and he looked out through the blinds. He turned. He leaned on the desk and faced Danny, his shoulders folding inward like a man you could collapse and fit into a suitcase.

"You want to know if you killed Boar's Head," he said. "I can tell you that you didn't, Danny. I can't tell you how I know. Or else I'll wind up back inside."

Danny rose from his chair for the first time, walked around the desk. Dirty Jim backed up against the wall beside the street window. "I don't wanna hurt you, little guy," Danny said. "But you better tell me what you know. Now. Or I'll shove a mop up your ass and break a few hundred fistulas, or whatever the fuck you call them."

"OK, OK," he said. "When I came home from the Doors concert, I was crashing from the uppies. I needed more. I had my camera with me. I went up to Hippie Hill, looking for Mots or Bowles, to see if I could score some more uppies."

"What time?"

"Two-thirty, maybe."

"And?"

"And Boar's Head was on the ground," Dirty Jim said. "I thought he was sleeping. The bums slept there all the time, even in the cold. So I didn't even know it was him. Until I got close. Then I saw it was Boar's Head. Dead. Shot. Bloody. I ran. I was crashing. I needed uppies. Or downs, to crash. I needed to find Mots or Bowles. I couldn't find them. So I ran down Fifteenth Place to the pad you shared with them. I rang the bell. No one answered. I rang again. No answer. So I used my key—"

"You had a fucking key? To our pad?"

"I had a key to every crash pad in the neighborhood. In fact, I got it off you when you were crashed out in Hippie Helen's one night. I made a duplicate and returned it to your ring before you even woke up. I knew it'd come in handy one day. Because I knew it would open the door to your roommates' stash. I had keys to all the small-time dealers' pads. I always just took enough for my own head, and maybe to get a little hippie chick high enough to give me a stand-up blow job. The shit I took was never missed."

"You slithering weasel."

"Fuck're you upset about? You never had nothin' worth stealing. You were a hippie skell. In fact, you got so bad there on the speed that I think I might have even held my own in a fair one with you."

"You might be right. But how do you know I didn't kill Boar's Head?"

"Because when I broke into the apartment I was crashing and I was so shaken up by seeing Boar's Head shot to death, that I knocked over one of them fuckin' mayonnaise jars filled with change," Dirty Jim said.

"I remember it. My roommates used to throw their spare change in there. I used to hit it up all the time because those guys had money from dealing. I never did."

"Anyways, it smashed onto the fucking floor like an F train just roared into the living room. A real loud fuckin' smash. Coins rattlin' and rollin' all over the floor. I froze. But no one stirred. I was certain no one was home. I took out my penlight flashlight I had on my key ring. Like this one here but an old model. I fumbled in the dark for the stash, which I knew they kept on the dumbwaiter in the kitchen, hoisted up between floors. It wasn't until after I snatched ten uppies and six downs from Mott's stash and I was using my flashlight to make it back to the front door when my beam caught your face in the dark. I almost broke a fistula right then and there. I realized you were out fuckin' cold on the mattress on the floor. And you hadda be one fuckin' breath away from rigor mortis not to have heard me. I checked to make sure you were breathing, that you weren't OD'd."

"Jesus, that's fuckin' big of you," Danny said.

"Hey, I had nothing against you," Dirty Jim said, shrugging. "You were Helen's friend. She talked about you a lot. Thought you were a special kid. Smart, talented, a writer or some shit. She loved your body before you went from jock to joke."

"So you think I was too stoned to have shot Boar's Head and then staggered home and fell onto the mattress?"

"Without a doubt. They said Boar's Head probably got shot around two A.M. He was dead when I saw him at two-thirty. You were out cold by like two-forty when I let myself into your pad. And the funny thing is, your hair was still wet. And you had on new clothes. I remember that. Because you almost always wore the same shit. No way you killed Boar's Head in the park, stumbled home, took a shower, changed your clothes, got rid of the old clothes and the gun, and lay down for a nap. Nah."

"And no one else was there?"

"Nope," he said. "But this is between you and me and the prison wall because even all these years later if Christie knew I robbed his dealers' stash all the way back then, he'd still get even."

"There's gotta be other reasons you're still afraid of him," Danny said.

"Sure," Dirty Jim said. "Like I said, people don't change. He's as ruthless and treacherous as he was thirty years ago. Except now Christie is legit. He belongs to civic and political clubs. He has friends on Court Street. In Borough Hall. In city hall. Judges, DAs, police captains, and politicians eat in his restaurant. They buy and rent property from him. He donates to their campaigns. If he wanted to he could have my parole violated with one phone call. Him I do not fuck with. And I know he is not thrilled that you are back in town. So I made like you and me had a beef."

"How do you know he's not thrilled I'm back in town?"

"Because he called me and told me he thought it would be a good idea if me and you didn't talk," Dirty Jim said.

Danny nodded and looked at the file cabinets. "Whadda you keep in here?"

"Old photos. I scan them into the computer for people. A lot of photographers ask me to create and design Web sites for them. Then I scan their photos into the computer and if someone wants to buy a print, they call. I keep the negatives here."

"You still have a lot of the old photos from back then, back in the sixties?"

"Some. Stashed in my house somewhere. They aren't worth a dime now."

"Any of that night? The night Boar's Head was whacked? You said you had your camera with you. Did you take pictures of the dead body?"

"No," he said, too fast for Danny's liking.

"I hope you're not holding out on me."

"I'm not. But my advice, leave it alone. Ankles don't have enough to convict you even if he does bust you for a cheap headline for his boss's reelection campaign."

"I can't take that chance," Danny said. "There's a dead cop involved. And his partner, who killed himself. Which reminds me. Davis, Boar's Head's partner, Jack Davis. Someone told me Davis might be the key to this whole thing."

"Who?" Dirty Jim said, rattling his keys, pulling them out on his metal cord and letting them retract, over and over. "Who told you that? Who talked to you about Davis?"

Dirty Jim grabbed the Pepto Bismol, took a slug. Danny sensed he'd touched a frayed nerve. "What difference does it make?" Danny said. "I'm asking you what you know about Jack Davis."

"Nothing. Now you better go. Please. I told you everything I know."

He hadn't but Danny knew he wasn't going to get any more out of him right now.

"I'm leaving," Danny said. "But I'm not going far. I will see you around, Jim. Don't hold out on me. This is my life here."

"It's my fucking life, too," Dirty Jim said, clutching his belly, lurching toward the men's room. "I'm supposed to get rest, but instead you give me the gallopin' stress. If I eat two french fries, I'll shit six. Please, get the fuck out. . . ."

Dirty Jim rushed into the men's room, slammed the door. Danny left.

"What did he say?" Erika asked when Danny climbed into her '69 Caddy.

"He said I didn't do it," Danny said.

Erika raced from the curb. "Did he say who he thought did?"

"No," Danny said as they passed Langston Place, where he glanced right and saw a green Crown Victoria parked near the corner. Detective Pat O'Rourke sat on the front fender, facing him, talking to a man in the passenger seat of a double-parked silver Jaguar that bore the bumper sticker: BE STRONG, VOTE STRONG. Erika didn't seem to notice. But as Erika raced her red '69 El Dorado past Langston Place, heading for Parkside South, Danny saw Pat O'Rourke give a little wave.

fifteen

Everywhere Danny turned in Erika's house, he saw bald eagles. Light-switch plates, cushion covers, wallpaper patterns, lamp figurines, handles of the fireplace set, knobs of the oaken dining room chairs, place settings, china-set motif, paintings on the walls, living room curtains, patterns of the living room rug—all bald eagles.

Horsecock had told Danny about why Boar's Head loved Eagles so much. Because every day was payday, the eagle shit for Vito Malone every night.

Danny had been inside Erika's house just once before. Back on August 22, 1969, on Erika's seventeenth birthday, wearing long hair under a short-hair wig and a tight shave. He also wore a new suit. Boar's Head didn't even recognize him as one of the little hippie mutts from Hippie Hill, never mind the one who'd witnessed him murdering Wally Fortune.

"Erika, that's you?" an old woman's voice asked. Danny turned from the foyer into the large living room, where Angela Malone sat in a recliner chair covered with a quilt with a bald eagle print, watching *Barney and Friends*. "Or is that Vito?"

"It's me, Mama, Erika."

"Where's your father?"

"He's not here, Mama."

"It's Friday so he must be working late on a big case. For the OT."

"He won't be home, Mama."

Erika walked to her mother and kissed her. In her seventies, Angela Malone had a strong face that was still wrinkle-free and attractive. But her bitter chocolate eyes were as deep set as the finger holes in a bowling ball. When she glared at you it was like she was peering through knotholes from the dark side of a private dimension. A place where you needed a secret password that only she knew.

Angela removed her Adidas tennis shoes, placed them on the end table, and rubbed her small slender feet. Erika clicked the remote to CNN. Danny watched the mother sit and stare at the TV, where the latest carnage from the Middle East played in dumbshow as she stroked the red hair of a rag doll.

"Mama, this is Danny," she said. "Do you remember Danny?"

"Vaffanculo," Angela said, stroking the nails of her right hand across the underside of her chin. "Vito's working on a big case. A huge case. He's gonna find you."

"Mama, behave—"

"He's gonna cut off your fuckin' balls," she said, glaring at Danny.

"I'm sorry," Erika said, fetching some pills from an Erika's Earth supplement jar and pouring a glass of swampy-looking ice tea, adding lemon and a sprig of fresh mint.

"Don't be silly," Danny said.

"My daughter is not silly, you little cocksucker," said Angela Malone.

"Here, Mama, take this," Erika said, feeding her the pills and ice tea. "I'd offer you some tea, Danny, but it's a special blend for Mama. Made from crushed Amazon rain forest leaves—Arronceae, Lundia eriomena, Tabernaemontana heterophyllia mixed with the oil of the Jessemia palm. It's what they give to what they call 'the old people who forgot how to talk' or those who 'speak crazily and without making sense.' From the research of a Harvard professor named Richard Evans Schultes. I'm going to market holistic treatment for Alzheimer's and Pick's disease."

"She gonna be all right?"

"Oh, yeah," Erika said. "She's harmless, in stage four of the seven stages. I'll go get my old diaries in the attic."

The phone rang and Angela Malone leaned forward and lifted her left sneaker from the end table and held it to her ear. "Hello, Erika, is this you. . . ."

The phone kept ringing. Erika picked it up and said hello in the dining room.

"Vaffanculo," Angela shouted into her Adidas, then tossed it at the TV. She pushed herself up from the recliner, jogged to an upright Steinway piano, and plopped down. "You like Chopin, asshole?" she asked Danny.

"Love him," Danny said, watching Erika pace toward the bright country kitchen with the phone, speaking in hushed tones, yanking open and closing the fridge, closing all the doors of the cherry-wood cabinets, adjusting the vertical cherry-wood blinds on the sliding doors. The doors looked out onto a backyard that resembled a mini Eden. Erika's mood dissolved from her cocksure rich-bitch swagger to one of quiet trepidation.

"I understand," Erika said. "It'll be taken care of."

"Vito loves Chopin when he comes home after a bad night of rousting skells," Angela said, playing the keys with gusto. "He likes pasta, some wine, Chopin, and nasty sex. He likes being in charge. He's a real man. Are you a real man?"

"I hope so," Danny said as Angela played a piano piece he knew he'd heard somewhere before. After several bars it registered. He'd heard it that night in Hippie Helen's pad, the night he walked in on Helen and Boar's Head having nasty sex. But Danny didn't follow the music to the flashback. He half listened, more concerned with eavesdropping on Erika's hushed phone conversation from the kitchen.

"Not now," Erika said into the phone, her back to him. "Please . . . it's nothing I can't handle myself . . . OK, OK. No! Don't do that. Please. Hold on. . . ."

Erika pressed the phone transmitter against her breasts to mute the sound and turned to Danny. "I'm sorry, but I better take this upstairs. There's a complication at work. Make yourself comfortable. Raid the fridge if you want, put on whatever you like on the TV. I'll get the diaries while I'm upstairs. It might take a little while."

Danny nodded. Erika hurried up the stairs, carpeted with a bald eagle runner. He turned to Angela. She played with her eyes closed, tears coursing down her cheeks.

Danny was troubled by the snippets he'd heard of Erika's conversation. She sure didn't sound like a boss settling a dispute. But she might have been talking to a disgruntled client. Gone was the arrogance of the woman who collected parking tickets like baseball cards.

Danny prowled the house like a predator, searching for information, any kind of data. He'd learned a lot about police work from covering cops in L.A. Heaven and hell were in the details. He checked the supplement bottle from which Erika had given her mother the pills—a St. John's Wort and kava blend that the pitch line on the bottle said was a mild natural tranquilizer. As Angela Malone played on in the background, switching to a different piano concerto now, Danny rooted in kitchen cabinets and opened kitchen drawers. He found nothing useful.

He slid open a rolltop desk in the dining room, sorting through bound stacks of old mail jammed into various cubbyholes. Most were ordinary bills from Verizon telephone, Con Ed, Brooklyn

Union Gas, the cable company. He grabbed the stack of AT&T long-distance bills, dating back to January. He checked the numbers dialed. A lot of the calls were to the same number in area code 631, South Hampton. On the January bill there were a bunch of very expensive calls to the same number in area code 814, Paradise Island. He wrote these numbers. There were others, made in clusters, to different regions of the country—Oklahoma, Utah, Illinois, Nebraska, Kansas, Idaho.

"Danny, you OK down there?" he heard Erika shout down the stairs.

"Fine," he shouted back. "Your mother is great on the piano."

"Just a few more minutes," she shouted.

Danny opened a few American Express bills, saw that in Brooklyn she ate almost exclusively in a place called the Strong Arms and Pasta Bello. He took out a stack of unopened envelopes, all bearing the same return address logo that sent a shiver up his spine: Clubweb.com Inc. With the address on Eleventh Avenue.

Dirty Jim's company, he thought. What the hell does she have to do with him?

The envelopes had clear cellophane windows that indicated they were invoices. He was unwinding the rubber band when he realized that Angela had stopped playing. He turned to glance at her. And peered into her bitter chocolate eyes. Angela stood next to him as silent as smoke. He jerked, heart leaping. Angela Malone grabbed his face, kissed Danny on the lips, a lingering wet kiss, her lipstick smearing his cheek and upper lip.

"You're not my Vito," she said, her voice a primordial growl, her eyes raw from tears, wild and angry. She looked at once dangerous and vulnerable, a cornered raccoon.

"No, I'm not," he said.

"Then what are you doing in my Vito's desk?"

"I was looking for a pen."

"You have a pen in your hand. You think I'm stupid because I'm nuts? That makes you dumb. I know the score. You're trying to steal Vito's cases, all the glory."

She slammed the rolltop closed and locked it with a key she wore around her neck, along with a house key and an Alzheimer's medical-alert tag.

"No, Angela, I was just looking for a pen."

"You're trying to steal his cases, like Davis. Like Bush. Well, I have news for you, buddy boy, no one can top-cop my Vito. When he gets home I'm gonna tell on you."

She stormed away from him, into the kitchen, snatched up a flower watering can, and stepped through the sliding glass door into the lush backyard, amid tomato bushes and grapevines and assorted patches of eggplants, cucumbers, lettuce, peppers, and herbs.

Danny watched Angela water the plants, babbling to herself, to the plants, stifling a yawn as the pills took effect. She climbed into a low-slung hammock. Danny knew there was a small toilet off the kitchen. But he thought he could play dumb and pretend to be searching for a toilet in the basement. He wanted to see the place where Boar's Head had once taken him as a kid.

He walked down the basement stairs. The bald eagle carpet had not been replaced all these years later. He crossed the floor and knelt by the water heater. He probed the cracks of the ceramic tile floor, pressing individual tiles. One tile depressed, popping up a small handgrip. He lifted it, looked under the four-by-four section of flooring that swung open on invisible interior hinges, and saw the old combination dial on the steel plate. . . . .

*August 22, 1969*

*A little more than a month after witnessing the Wally Fortune murder, Danny's scared. Erika wants him to meet her parents on her birthday. He has no idea what her parents even look like. Danny refuses to meet them.*

*But Erika had promised that if he got a shave, a haircut, wore a suit, and picked her up on her seventeenth birthday from her house, where he'd meet her parents, she'd go to his pad and go all the way with him. Give him her cherry.*

*Danny had caved. Got the shave and suit. And borrowed his friend Gordon's short-hair wig that he used for weekends in the National Guard, which he'd joined to evade the draft.*

*Danny, his long hair tucked under the Clark Kent hairdo wig, appears at the door on Garvey Place looking like a model for a Marine recruitment poster. He has three condoms in his wallet. Erika answers the door, grabs his dick in the Grindbox.*

*"You ready?"*

*"You bet."*

*"You better have experience. Because I don't know what to do."*

*"Leave it all up to me." Hippie Helen has taught him everything.*

*Erika leads Danny inside to meet her parents. He meets the mother first. A sweet, skeptical Italian woman. She's polite, reserved, cautious. Then Erica yanks Danny into the kitchen to meet her father, who's bent halfway into the fridge. "Daddy meet Danny," Erika says. Danny extends his hand. The big man emerges from the fridge, switching a beer from one hand to the other, wiping his right hand on his pants. He crushes Danny's hand in his big hand. And Danny freezes. He looks in Erika's father's face.*

*Jesus Christ, he thinks. Vito Malone is Boar's Head.*

*The cop who killed Wally. The same cop he'd seen violating Hippie Helen.*

*Boar's Head doesn't recognize Danny with his crew cut and tight shave, pressed suit, white shirt, and tie. "At least he's white, Angela," Vito says.*

*Danny trembles, a nervous wreck when Boar's Head ushers Danny down the basement for a man-to-man talk, his feet thudding on the bald eagle carpet runner. Boar's Head leads him across the unfinished basement, staring him dead in the eye like a man leading a prisoner to a dungeon cell.*

*Boar's Head bends, pushes a tile, and an invisible handle appears from a crack in the floor. He lifts a removable three-by-four section of the ceramic tile flooring next to the hot water heater, revealing a thick steel-plate door with a combination dial like that on the face of a safe. Danny watches Boar's Head dial the month, day, and year of Erika's birth. Then he turns a handle. The steel door opens. Vito Malone pushes in the plate on two heavy metal hinges, revealing a ladder leading into a subbasement. Malone flicks a wall switch and motions for Danny to climb down the steel ladder into the hidden room. Danny descends to the loud whir of underground exhaust fans. Boar's Head follows him halfway down, closing the ceramic trapdoor. Then slams the four-inch-thick steel-plate door, locking it from the inside. Danny is trapped. Sealed into the twelve-by-twelve-foot steel cube.*

*With a killer.*

*He's never felt this kind of claustrophobia before. Locked in a bomb shelter with the man he'd watched beat Wally Fortune to death.*

*A bunk bed, a Castro convertible, a table, and chairs crowd the wood-paneled room. A sink, stove, and fridge jam the kitchen alcove, next to a small utilitarian bathroom. Boxes of canned food climb to the ceiling.*

*Danny gapes at one wall that is stocked with rifles, pistols, knives, bayonets, sabers, rapiers, and other weapons.*

"I had this bomb shelter put in for good reason," Malone says, taking down a .45, ejecting the clip, and ramming it back in, working the slide. "In the fifties everybody worried about the A-bomb and the red chinks and the Rooskies. That hasn't happened. Yet. But I think it might come in handy in the sixties and seventies as a sanctuary from the jigaboo invasion. The Black Panthers and the Young Lords or the Black Muslims. I call this the niggerproof room. They just collared that Bobby Seale yom a couple of days ago for murdering one of his own. But that means the other natives'll be on the warpath—your Eldridge Cleaver, your H. Rap Brown, your Stokely Carmichael. The yoms ever get through my front door upstairs, the way those people were slaughtered out in Sharon Tate's house a few weeks ago out in L.A., we can all retreat here to the niggerproof room. The people who did that were white hippies, which are nothing but yoms turned inside out. They'll never get through these four-inch-thick steel walls. Thicker than a yom's head. Fireproof. Got running water, piped-in air, autonomous generator, gasoline, canned goods to last three weeks. Guns, ammo, and other provisions in case of bombs, fallout, or yoms. There's a special phone line and a ham radio hooked up to the outside world."

"Wow." *Danny's heart thumps. His mouth is too dry to say more. He's terrified Boar's Head will recognize him, or that the wig will shift, come loose, and his long hair will spill out.*

"If these Black yombo Panthers ever invade Brooklyn the same way, they ain't getting near me or my wife or daughter," he says, cleaning the .45 with special cheesecloth. "I'll just lock 'em both in here and I'll fight the yomos to the last breath."

*Danny nods, doesn't respond.*

*Boar's Head sits on a stool in front of the weapons wall, motions for Danny to sit on another. For the first time in his life Danny looks dead in the eyes of a murderer.*

"OK, asshole," *Boar's Head says.* "Here's the fuckin' things you can never do with my little girl. You don't ever let her listen to yom music. You don't take her to yom movies. No yom concerts, no yom dances, no yom neighborhoods. No fuckin' yoms, period, end of fuckin' yom story. And no dirty fuckin' hippies, either. No Hippie Hill, no Greenwich Village, no Woodstocks, no Alice's Restaurant movies, no antiwar protests or draft-card burnings. No nudie movies. And you *don't even look at Erika's tits through a winter coat. You never, ever touch her tits, ever. Or her ass, hear me?"*

*Danny nods. Says nothing. Watches Boar's Head take down a Japanese sword, sharpening it with a gray stone.*

*"And you don't even think about her other fuckin' thing between her legs, which we won't even mention because as far as you're concerned, she ain't got one. If I find a hickey on her neck, I'll cut your fuckin' neck open with this here Jap bayonet that I took out of a nip's lung in Bataan, OK?"*

*Danny nods again, swallowing hard.*

*"God forbid you ever take out your dick near my little girl, I'll cut it off, slap it on the barbecue, and make you fuckin' eat your own dick on a roll while you're bleeding to death. Keep your fuckin' hair short and your dick shorter around Erika. And watch your fuckin' mouth around my little girl and have her home by eleven on weekends and we got no fuckin' problems, asshole. Capisce?"*

*Danny nods.*

*"You violate one of my fucking orders and I'll drag you down here in handcuffs in the middle of the night and you can scream until your tongue falls out and no one will ever hear you," Boar's Head says. "Then I'll just kill you and mummify you with arsenic and get rid of you one limb at a time. No one will ever find you. Not even my wife or daughter knows about this room. Another thing, if they ever find out, it's because you told them. And that means you'll die here, understand?"*

*"Understood."*

*"Good. You look like a nice kid. Keep it that way."*

*He shakes Danny's hand, squeezing until he thinks his fingers will break.*

*Later, when Erika leaves with a shaken Danny to go to his crash pad to do it, he's confused, distracted, and panicked.*

*Erika gets naked. Just like that. Takes off all her clothes. Flawless. Gorgeous. Perfect. But Danny is shaking. Boar's Head's left him trembling.*

*As Erika falls spread-eagle naked on the bed, waiting for Danny to lead her into womanhood, Danny cannot perform. Everything Hippie Helen has taught him is for naught. His mouth's so dry he can't even summon the saliva necessary to make out with Erika, never mind moisten her between her legs. He fumbles. He shivers. He breaks into a sweat. His dick's a useless nub.*

*Erika explodes into tears. Humiliated. Insulted. Then angry. She storms off as Danny sits flaccid, speechless. As if mummified with arsenic.*

*Danny learns that Erika spent the rest of her birthday with Lars Andersen.*

"What the hell are you doing down here," Erika asked, halfway down the stairs.

"Looking for the bathroom," he said.

"There's one upstairs," she said, holding a diary.

"Nothing's changed since your father took me down here for a man-to-man."

"I keep it the way he left it."

"As a kind of shrine?"

She hesitated and said, "Something like that."

"He scared me so bad that night that I couldn't even get it up to take your cherry. And then you dumped me for Lars."

"Think how that changed everything."

"Yeah, I'm sorry I keep bringing up what he did to you. . . ."

"Forget him. But who knows, maybe if we'd done it that night, you would have knocked me up. Had a baby. We could've had a shotgun wedding. Divorced. We'd have a kid thirty-one years old."

"I thought you couldn't have children."

She bit her lower lip and said, "When I was seventeen, who knows?"

He nodded, didn't pursue it.

"One event in one night can change everything," she said.

"Tell me about it."

"Be honest, what are you looking for, Danny?"

"What do you mean?"

"My mother said you were looking in my desk."

Danny was shocked. "You believe her? No offense, but she's sort of scattered."

"She has her moments. She's still at stage four, which I'm not so sure they can really gauge. . . . Were you in my desk, Danny?"

"I was looking for a pen. I wanted to jot down a few things Dirty Jim had told me before I forgot them. As I get older I forget stuff."

"Most times I remember everything," she said, waving her diary. "But you were right about being alone when you saw Ankles with Marsha. I was with Lars Andersen."

Danny followed her upstairs. They sat at the kitchen table, where Erika opened the blue-backed diary. "There's some horny stuff in here about you," she said. "I can't let you read it. It'll go to your head."

"Look up July 20," he said. She flipped through her book, came to the page, traced her finger down. "You met me after work at the library, we had pizza down in Smiling Pizzeria, you walked me home. We made out and did our thing in the Grindbox. I accused you of being on drugs. I hated you when you were high."

"I was on mescaline. I confess."

"My mother was home, my father was working late," she said.

"How late?"

"The four to twelve plus OT."

"He worked a lot of OT?"

"Oh, yeah. He brought home good money. I guess not all of it was clean money. Who knows where he was, who he was with."

Danny thought of a particular late Thursday night. . . .

*June 12, 1969*

*He lets himself into Hippie Helen's apartment. Classical music blares from the speakers of her stereo, which Danny finds strange. Then he sees them. Helen and Boar's Head. Fucking like savages. A different kind of sex than Danny has ever had with Helen. Boar's Head calls her nasty names—cunt, whore, pig—as he humps her with a ferocious, almost vengeful frenzy. He manhandles her. Spins Helen on her belly. Smacks her hard on the ass. She submits to him as he handcuffs her hands behind her back. He loops his belt around her neck, like a leash, grabs and twists her hair, and rams her from behind. "When I fuck you in the ass," he says. "I'm fucking him in the ass. Who do you want me to fuck?"*

*"Fuck me," Helen shouts. "Fuck him. Fuck me. Fuck him. . . ."*

*At seventeen, Danny doesn't understand the turn-on, some deviant cop-prisoner S&M ritual. But Helen is Helen. She redefines different strokes for different folks. Danny sneaks out, afraid of being caught. He never mentions it to Helen. A month later he will witness the same cop kill Wally Fortune. And soon after that he will discover that that same cop is Erika's father. Fuck me, fuck him. . . .*

Pieces of 1969 started to coalesce, converge, and fit themselves together.

"What's your diary say about November 20 and 21?" Danny asked.

"Blank," she said without looking. "I know that."

He looked over her shoulder at the diary as she turned to the jagged edges of several torn out pages.

"My mother tore them out right after I wrote them," she said. "She thought I was too traumatized to ever revisit those two days. The day he died and the day after, which is the same you left me. She tore them out of the book. She was always overprotective."

"You always adored your mom," Danny said.

"I miss her so much," she said. "She became my best buddy. And then this happened. It's like someone killed her, too."

She pointed to her mother, who now watched the Teletubbies on satellite TV, the ugly little creatures talking in nonsense syllables, asking for "biiiig huuugs."

"Almost noon and I have to make Mama her lunch," she said. "Fresh eggplants from the garden, sliced thick and sautéed in olive oil, fresh mozzarella and topped with wheels of fresh tomatoes. Then baked until the fresh mozzarella melts them together. With whole wheat linguini and diced tomato, minced garlic, fresh basil, and shaved Romano. I have to shower and get naked first. You're welcome to stay for a bite."

"Stay and watch you cook naked?"

"Sure," she said. "If you want."

He smiled. "I'm still full from the sandwich. Besides, I don't wanna torture myself, watching you bend over the oven naked, if we're not gonna—"

"Like I said, we will, but not yet. There's too much to do. . . ."

Danny thought about how weird it would be to sit and watch Erika cook naked, in front of her mother, who was suffering from advanced dementia. Her father was a sociopath, borderline psychotic. Why shouldn't she be a wack-job, too?

"I think I'll pass. Have to change for the wake. Can I use your phone?"

"I thought you were looking for a toilet," Erika said, her eyes suspicions.

"I am."

She handed him the phone, nodded toward the bathroom, and then she walked into the living room and changed the TV to the Bloomberg financial channel. Danny walked into the bathroom, pressed star-six-nine. *There's that fucking number again,* he thought.

He wrote down the number of the last person who called Erika. The caller who'd caused Erika such concern. It was a 718 area code number with a local 788 exchange. As he relieved himself Danny dialed his hotel and asked if there were any messages. There were no messages from his brother, Brendan, or his daughter, Darlene, just two voice mail messages. One was from his old pal Kenny Byrne, who said it was great seeing Danny again after all these years. He hoped he'd see him tonight and grab a coffee.

The second message was from Horsecock.

"Hey, kid, Danny boy, this is Henry, Henry Horsecock Bush," he said, loud and excited with whiskey. Foley's loud din echoed in the background, drunks bouncing large "fuck yous" and "ass-holes" off the tin ceilings, followed by boisterous boozy laughter, and two blaring TVs and people shouting for Houlie to bring them beers.

"Listen to me, I been thinkin,' " Horsecock said. "I wasn't square with you this morning. About this Linc character. I know all too well about Linc—"

Someone banged on the phone booth door, shouting to use the phone, saying, "C'mon, off the fuckin' phone and go sleep it off, old man."

"Fuck you and your mother's horse she rode you in on," Horsecock said. Then Danny heard Horsecock close the folding door on the old-fashioned phone booth. Horsecock spoke faster, more frantic, his breathing wheezy. "I should throw caution to the fuckin' wind and tell you the truth. Why the fuck should you take the fall? I owe it to your old man, who was a good guy to do right by you. I'm gonna go have a nap. Then I'm gonna go see someone about this Linc vis-à-vis Vito Malone. I owe that hump at least a fair and square warnin'. Meet me in the mornin', we'll run again. I'll fill you in. Wear fuckin' sneakers this time, kid. Oh, shit. Can't breath. Outta breath. Need a nap. My God! What the fuck. Who am I talkin' too, anyway? Don't anyone touch me. Gimme air. Air."

Danny heard the phone booth door squeal open on unoiled hinges, banging, and an impatient Foley's customer with a foreign accent grope for the phone. "Gimme the focking phone, olt man."

Horsecock cursed whoever it was. "Fucking asshole," Horsecock said. "Owww. Don't touch—"

"Calm down, olt man," the foreigner said, and then Danny heard another scuffle over the receiver, a series of clicks as the guy tried to hang up on Horsecock. Then he heard the quarter drop with a loud clunk and then a snap and then the line went dead.

As he listened to that voice message, two drunks fighting over Foley's single pay phone, Danny half listened to a recorded voice announce he could save it by hitting the number one, or erase it by hitting number two. Danny hit two and smiled, and rummaged in Erika's medicine chest. *Fucking place hasn't changed one bit*, he thought. Still, he was eager to hear what Horsecock was going to tell him about this missing link named Linc.

There were no prescription bottles in Erika's medicine chest. He washed his hands, stepped back out of the bathroom, and handed Erika her phone.

"Hey, what was your father's relationship with Jack Davis?" Danny asked. "They were partners, but how did he feel about him?"

"I don't think he was my father's kind of guy. He was all muscles but a bit of a wimp in my father's eyes. He was always calling him a pussy. He never had him over for dinner. Never spent time with him after work. His wife and kids were nice, but we only saw them at big cop barbecues or weddings they were both invited to."

"Did you ever think your father had something on him?"

"Like what?"

"Like something to coerce him to join him in some dirty business."

"Nobody is a better cop than Vito," Angela screamed. "Vaffanculo on you."

She spit at Danny, her body quivering, her eyes wild and astonished.

The doorbell rang, an elaborate set of chimes. "Vito, my Vito is home. Lost his keys again. This is Friday—"

"Relax, Mama, relax. . . ."

"You can walk me out," Danny said, as Erika draped her arm around his waist and walked him down the hallway to the door.

"Might be Federal Express," Erika said. "I'll catch up to you later."

"Where?"

"Don't worry. I'll find you. All your answers are within twenty square blocks, where they have been for thirty long years. You won't be hard to find."

They kissed in the Grindbox, his hands drifting to her butt, her hands on his.

"Keep that thing in your pants," she said.

"I'd rather keep it in yours," he said and grabbed the bald eagle doorknob and opened the door. Ankles stood on the other side.

# sixteen

Ankles tipped his hat to Erika, told her it was official business, and led Danny to his double-parked black Taurus and said, "Get in."

"I'd rather walk."

"No, you wouldn't. We need to talk. You need to see something."

Danny climbed into the front seat. He looked at Erika standing in the areaway, watching him drive off. She looked concerned. The same trapped look she'd had on her face when she spoke earlier on the cell phone.

Ankles drove toward the parkside. "She's one steamy tomata."

"What do you want now?"

"First you tell me something," Ankles said. "You've been all over the neighborhood, talking to all the fucking gentry from yesteryear. What'd you learn before I show you what I wanna show you?"

"Everybody I meet says I didn't kill Vito Malone."

"Like who?"

"Dirty Jim Dugan? Hippie Helen Grabowski? Even Erika."

"C'mon," Ankles said. "The town pump, a fuckin' emaciated predicate felon, and your girlfriend? They have any evidence?"

"Not hard evidence yet. But it's helping me lift the fog. You have no idea how hard it is to piece together a single thirty-two-year-old night. Because that night is connected to a whole series of other nights, nights that fade into weeks, weeks that blur into months, and months that add up to one big fuzzy fucking year. Most of it stoned. So, I'm making some progress. Not much. But enough to make me feel like I'm off the treadmill and on the track."

Ankles turned off Parkside West into the park at the Third Street entrance, cruised along the park drive that was now closed to automobile traffic, reserved for joggers, walkers, in-line skaters, bicyclists, and pram pushers. The same place where he'd run with Horsecock about six hours earlier.

"You forgettin' one name?"

"Who?"

"Henry Bush. Horsecock. You ran with him this morning, didn't you?"

"If you already know, why do you ask?"

"To see if you'd lie."

"No, I bullshitted with him. He was Boar's Head's CO back then."

"Mine too."

"He didn't mention that, but I guess there was no need. Nice old guy."

"Depends on who you talk to."

"Who feuds with an eighty-two-year-old man?"

"Hate builds with age," Ankles said. "And the older you get, the older your enemies get, and the older they get, the more frightened they become of things like death. And jail—in what little time's left. Sometimes the fear can turn violent if you know things about them that they don't want anyone else to know."

"Like what?"

"That's what I want to know," Ankles said as they passed the Tennis House. He glanced over at the old granite and marble building and then at Danny. Neither said a word, but each knew what the other was thinking. "What did you talk to Horsecock about this morning?"

"Boar's Head, Davis, Wally Fortune. What you'd expect I'd talk to him about if you were trying to learn why all three wound up dead."

"You talk about Christie Strong?"

"Of course," Danny said.

"What'd he say about him?"

They passed the Eleventh Street playground, winding toward Veteran's Memorial Square. "Like everyone else from back then, Horsecock thinks he's a prick. Said that Strong was one of those guys who parlayed his sixties dope-pushing racket into a successful real estate and restaurant business, helped reinvent the new Prospect Gardens. This Strong has delusions, thinks of himself as a pioneer, Daniel Boone inventing Boonesboro. Levit of Levittown."

"What else did Horsecock say?"

"I think he knows who Linc is."

"Oh, yeah?" Ankles turned to him, his eyes widening.

"I think so."

"He don't know anymore," Ankles said as they passed Hippie Hill, twisting toward the Elephant Steps on the park drive.

"What do you mean?"

Then Danny saw the police activity up ahead, saw parked cop cars and detective cars and an ambulance, lights twirling. There was a black van bearing a simple legend: MEDICAL EXAMINER. Yellow crime-scene tape billowed in the afternoon breeze, framing a forty-square-foot piece of the park, fastened to trees, a lamppost, and a few parked cop cars. A small crowd milled behind the tape, a multi-ethnic crowd of park users—kids and old people, yuppies and natives, immigrants and homegrowns.

"No. . . ."

"Yeah," Ankles said. "They were ready to declare it a heart attack and box Horsecock up, tag his toe, and send him straight to Dunne's for embalming. But I seen this old man running with you this morning. He looked to me like he coulda run for fuckin' president. And they're sayin' he was out joggin' again this afternoon. . . ."

"Bullshit, he only runs in the morning," Danny said. "Before Foley's opens. We ran, we talked, he went home. Later, around eleven and change, he left me a message on my hotel voice mail. From Foley's. He was shit-faced on Four Roses. He wasn't out fucking jogging, Ankles. He didn't have a heart attack. He bragged about passing his stress test, his PSA tests, his colonoscopy. This guy was fitter than Nero's fiddle."

"Lucky I heard the call. I'd just followed you and your tomata to her house when I heard the radio dispatch. I flew up here. Saw who it was. Told the uniforms to please ask for a crime-scene unit. They bitched and balked. Said it was an old man. I called my boss, convinced him to call NYPD and to insist. I preserved the area. Then I went and got you."

"Ah, Jesus Christ. . . ."

Ankles parked the car near the scene, and he and Danny walked to the corpse. A criminalist was picking hairs off Henry Bush's clothes with a tweezers, placing them in small manila envelopes.

Danny thought of Mary Fortune, Popcorn Gonzalez, Lefty Mots, and Harry Bowles, all of whom had been poisoned with strychnine a long time ago. Dirty Jim had described how Mots had spun into a seizure, grasping his heart, before he died. Who knew how many others who crossed Christie Strong's path had been poisoned?

"What poisons can make it look like you had a heart attack?" Danny asked.

"The oldest one is arsenic," Ankles said. "Or strychnine. But they're as easy to detect as pimples these days. A simple overnight liver toxin test. You think?"

"I think they'd think no one would think to check for strychnine in an eighty-two-year-old man," Danny said.

"They being who?"

"They being whoever didn't like that he was talking to me," Danny said. "And planned to talk some more. He was gonna tell me who Linc was."

"I'm gonna need that voice mail," Ankles said.

"I erased it."

"Fucking marvelous."

Pat O'Rourke's Crown Vic pulled up to the scene, her cherry light flashing. She got out and walked toward the corpse. "This broad's a pain in the ass," Ankles said. "I can't tell you not to talk to her, but I don't have to share anything with her. Yet."

She lifted the sheet, stared at Horsecock, lit a cigarette, and approached Danny and Ankles. Ankles twirled his unlit cigar. Danny liked the smell of her cigarette better than the scent of her soft rosy perfume.

"Hi, guys," she said, tightening her lips to blow out a long stream of smoke.

Ankles nodded.

"I can vouch for both of you," she said.

"Say what?" Ankles said, twiddling the cigar.

"In case anyone tries to ever pin this on either of you," she said with a smile. "I was tailing you, Detective Tufano, as you tailed him."

She nodded to Danny.

"You were tailing me?" Ankles said. "*Me?* Like I was a skell?"

"I didn't think of it that way," O'Rourke said. "What I meant was I couldn't help tagging you. If there were ten brand-new black Tauruses I couldn't miss the one with the driver wearing a sixties fedora. In August."

"You have some nerve, lady," Ankles said. "My office already flagged this one."

"Relax, Detective," O'Rourke said. "We aren't even calling this a homicide yet, are we? Henry Bush was eighty-two. People his age, sometimes, ya know, they die. Of natural causes."

"Let me tell you something, sister," Ankles said. "That poor old fella is still warm. So he's not a cold case. Which means you're walking on thin ice. And since you guys have a hard enough time selling old crimes that stick to my boss, I wouldn't go out of my way if I was you to break balls on this one."

"If you were still in the PD, I could cite you for sexual harassment," she said.

"I ain't PD," he said. "I'm DA."

Danny was getting a mild kick out of the jurisdictional turf war between the two cops. He liked the way O'Rourke handled herself—confident, smart, energetic. It made her sexy. The cigarette made her even more desirable.

"I've heard some people say that DA stands for Dumb Asshole," O'Rourke said. "And as for making old cases stick, you've been on the Vito Malone case for thirty-two years, Sherlock. One reason Cold Case gets involved is because the original DTs bollixed up the case in the first seventy-two hours. And you were in charge of the Malone case from hour and day one. And the other one, Wally Fortune. And I know that Bush was Malone's and your CO back then. So this involves me, and official PD business. So don't try belittling me, my gender, or my squad, Detective Tufano, for rolling up my sleeves and trying to wash some dirty dishes that you left in the fucking sink in 1969."

Ankles twiddled his unlit cigar, stared at her with a quiet rattle that Danny feared was a mild palsy setting in.

O'Rourke clicked a disposable lighter in front of Ankles. "Light?"

Ankles hesitated, stared at her, rolled the cigar between his fingers. He was about to accept the light when a crime-scene cop walked over to Ankles, holding another hair in his tweezers. "Hey, Tufano, this old geezer got a cat?"

"I dunno," Ankles said, turning his back to O'Rourke. "I know he loved pussy, but cats. . . ."

"I didn't see one when I was in his place this morning," Danny said. "Didn't smell one. Didn't sneeze at one either."

"Well, this would be one of them fancy cats," the criminalist said. "A long-haired cat. Like a Persian. Solid white."

Danny looked at him as he thought of the white cat that had sent him into a fit of sneezing that very morning after his run with Horsecock. It made the hairs on his neck rise as he did a slow turn and peered down toward the parkside, tilting his gaze up at the tenement condos that loomed above the park, and focused on a certain window. He guessed that right then, as they stood over the body of old Henry Horsecock Bush, that Hippie Helen was standing at the telescope, stroking her white cat. Staring down at the scene. He wondered who was standing with her.

He realized that O'Rourke had followed his line of vision. Danny looked away.

"You wanna tell me what you and the old man talked about when you jogged this morning?" O'Rourke said.

"I already told Ankles," Danny said.

"I could buy you lunch. Or dinner."

"I don't think so," Danny said.

"Afraid Erika will get jealous?"

He looked at her, all blue eyes, smart, pretty, and tough. And yet there was a part of her that was a crafty, cunning little seductress trying to tantalize him.

"I don't have the time," he said.

"I always liked a guy who played hard to get. It tests your imagination."

He didn't know what she meant by that, as she strolled away, extinguishing her smoke on the sole of her sneaker. She looked good in snug jeans. Tight, strong, sexy.

"Hey, Scanlon," Ankles said to the criminalist. "Do me a favor. I know this is the twenty-first century. But do a strychnine test on him for cheap laughs, will ya?"

"Strychnine? The old hump do X?"

"Try arsenic, too. How long will that take?"

"Overnight," Scanlon said. "We're gonna ask for a complete autopsy now anyway, since you butted your big nose in. But if you're looking for specifics, we'll ask them to test the liver and kidneys for strychnine and arsenic. We're treating it as a possible homicide instead of an old fuck who blew a gasket, which is what I say it is."

As Ankles and Scanlon yakked, Danny took out his cell phone, drifted a few steps, and dialed the number he'd gotten by hitting star-six-nine on Erika's phone.

"Strong for City Council, may I help you?" the woman on the other end asked.

Danny looked at the phone at arm's length. Amazed that he was amazed. Then disconnected. He scanned the faces of the ghoulish crowd of onlookers. He didn't recognize anyone. But then out of the collage of faces he saw JoJo Corcoran, the babbling village idiot who was working the crowd, panhandling change at the scene of a dead body. Maybe a homicide. JoJo had always popped up out of the neighborhood crevices, an astounding survivor, and a guy whose lunacy seemed to fuel his longevity. Danny thought of asking JoJo if he'd seen anything. But he didn't want to shake him down for information in front of Ankles and O'Rourke, both of whom had a stake in putting Danny in a cage.

"Did Bush say anything about Malone's partner?" O'Rourke whispered in his ear, her breath moist and warm. He shivered. Turned to her, her blue eyes inches from his.

"Is this an official debriefing?"

She looked at him and smiled. "If I wanted to debrief you, Danny," she said, her voice a soft purr, "I wouldn't do it here."

"Call me in an hour on my cell phone," he said, hoping that her call would come at a strategic time and place. "I'll give you the number. . . ."

"I have it," she said, grasping his bicep as she passed him. He flexed, an adolescent macho reflex. She strode toward her car, passing Ankles. "Detective Tufano," she said, "I'm requesting a copy of the full report on this incident ASAP, is that OK?"

"Fax it through channels, toots," he said. "You know the drill."

Danny stood on a spot halfway between where Wally Fortune and Vito Malone had been murdered thirty-two years before and stared up at Hippie Helen's window. He checked his watch. It was 12:35. He searched the crowd again for JoJo Corcoran. But he was gone.

# seventeen

Christie Strong breezed out of his storefront campaign headquarters on Parkside West near Seventeenth Road, flanked by two campaign workers. He was dressed in a dark suit, white shirt, and a blue tie with red stripes. His polished loafers gleamed in the afternoon sun. A slogan in the storefront window read: BE STRONG, VOTE STRONG. Another read: FAIR MARKET, FAIR RENTS.

His two aides looked more like advance men for Crunch Fitness. One was a big square-shouldered blond with a lantern jaw that hung as if on a clothesline, like a Russian heavyweight's. The other was a smaller, black man, a middleweight with tiny oval shades, who kept shooting his cuffs to show off emerald cufflinks. Danny shadowed them for a block as Strong stopped to talk to a pair of old ladies, and then an inquisitive yuppie couple. The big blond flashed a goofy smile and handed out campaign palm cards. The small emotionless black guy just observed Strong, his face like a No Trespassing signpost.

Danny had been sitting in his parked car across the street from Strong's campaign office for almost a half hour, trying to figure out how to approach this guy. Should he come on tough and strong? Accusatorial? Or should he play it by Christie's rules, smooth and polished, a chess game of quiet, refined, and unpredictable moves?

Danny wanted answers, not a confrontation. Besides, when you reach fifty, even the fights you win you lose. You hurt your hands, you throw out your fucking back, he thought. Cracked ribs take months to heal. Knees don't go back in place the same way they did when you were a kid. Plus, he'd been away from Brooklyn so long he didn't know if he could even win a fair one with Hippie Helen if it went more than a full minute. He'd be out of breath. By the time Horsecock had finished running the ass off him around the park in the morning, Danny was in need of an ambulette.

So Danny figured the best way to approach Christie Strong was chummy. Two old Hippie Hill survivors. Play it by ear from there.

"Why don't you wear the old caftan and sandals on the campaign trail?" Danny asked, smiling as he approached Strong after crossing from his rented car. "Get the gray ponytail, Volkswagen-bus vote."

The black guy took one step toward Danny, like a fighter stepping into his jab, shooting his cuffs. Strong grinned, flicking the bodyguard an almost imperceptible shake of his head. The black guy stepped back, clasping his hands in front of his snakeskin belt.

"Danny baby," Strong said, draping an arm over Danny's shoulder. "I hope you've decided you're back for good. Come inside, I'll get my people to find you an apartment and register you to vote, and I'll buy you a drink at my place before my lunch date. I'm running on the Independent line so you don't have to vote in the primary, just the general election. I could sure use your vote. Right now, I'm just a spoiler. But, because the incumbent is getting the boot under the new term-limits law, the seat's up for grabs. I'm building momentum, could snag a plurality come November."

Danny stopped, turning, Strong's arm gliding off his shoulder. Danny looked at Strong and said, "John Lindsay won reelection as mayor as a third-party candidate that way, splitting the Democratic and Republican vote, didn't he, back in—"

"Sixty-nine," Strong said, nodding, smiling.

"Funny how that number keeps popping up like a bad penny."

"You should play it," Strong said. "Play it straight, oh-six-nine. Or box it."

"I never had any luck in lotteries. I pulled a 137 in the draft lottery. I remember you pulled a 361, you lucky bastard."

"Yeah," Strong said. "But some service time and a tour of Nam might have helped me in this campaign. But then again, I might've come home in a body bag."

"For some people it was more dangerous back here than over there."

"How do you mean?"

"Eddie Fortune came home from a Special Forces tour of Nam to visit the graves of his brother and sister, who died at home," said Danny. "He was off on some godforsaken clandestine mission in the mountains of Laos, counting trucks on the Ho Chi Minh Trail, calling in illegal air strikes, while his sister OD'd and his brother was murdered in Prospect Park. Poor Eddie couldn't even get a compassionate leave to come home for the funerals. He came home to find he'd lost a second war back here."

"That was a terrible shame," Strong said. "They were awful times."

The big blond guy handed Danny a palm card. Danny looked at it. There was a photo of Christie Strong accepting an award from the Brooklyn Realtors Association. And a deep italicized caption under the photo, quoted candidate Strong: "Rent control is a holdover from the last century. It's time for a fair deal for all New Yorkers in a fair market in the new century. I'll shake loose the millionaire rent-control abusers, the hand-me-down-apartment scammers who claim their one-bedroom apartments are their primary residences and not the five-bedroom beach houses in the Hamptons."

Under the caption was the familiar campaign slogan: BE STRONG, VOTE STRONG.

"I'm registered in L.A., but I'll take you up on the drink."

"Good, we'll walk to my place," Strong said. "I have to meet some backers at the restaurant anyway. I have a half hour to kill."

They strolled along Parkside West to the corner of Gorman Street, where the ebony-and-gold-trimmed façade of the Strong Arms gleamed in the baking sun. Heavy red-gold drapes obscured the lower half of the sparkling windows.

"Did you hear about Henry Bush?" Danny asked as they neared the front doors.

"Old Horsecock? What'd he do now? Win the marathon?"

"They just found him dead in Prospect Park," Danny said.

"Christ, that's a shame," Strong said. "Still, he had one helluva run."

The big blond pulled open the heavy front door of the Strong Arms, held it for Danny and Strong, who entered. Danny shivered in the powerful air-conditioning, glancing around at the bare brick walls that were covered with custom-framed modern art and large black-and-white photos of the "new" Brooklyn, pictures of gentrified Prospect Gardens, Lower Park Slope, Windsor Terrace, Williamsburg, and Red Hook. There was another wall covered with framed three- and four-star reviews from the *New York Times*, *Zagat*, *Gourmet*, the *Daily News*, *New York* magazine, and other periodicals. Framed eight-by-ten-inch photos also adorned the walls, posed shots of Christopher Strong with celebrities who'd eaten in his restaurant, sports stars, politicians, Tony Sirico from *The Sopranos*, Danny Aiello, Woody Allen, actors from *Law & Order*, and a few others who had stopped in for lunch when filming in Brooklyn.

Etched mirrors gave the already spacious barroom an even

greater sense of breadth. Twenty gold-cushioned high-backed black stools were positioned in front of a teak-topped thirty-foot bar. Customers gabbed and smoked while awaiting their names to be called for lunch tables. The back bar was an iceberg of gleaming mirrors, polished bottles, sparkling glasses, and ever gurgling silver cash registers.

"Good afternoon, Monsieur Strong," said the maître d'. "Your table is set."

Strong nodded and the big blond guy and the compact black man took seats at the end of the busy bar. Danny and Strong followed the maître d' past five very pretty waitresses, none of them more than twenty-five or carrying an extra pinch of fat, all dressed in tight white blouses, black bow ties, and tight black pants. The maître d' pulled out Strong's chair, which faced the front door, at a large round table in a private corner of the rear dining room. A beautiful brunet waitress pulled out Danny's chair.

"Thanks," Danny said. She beamed as he sat down, nervous in front of the boss.

"Please bring us some water, Liz," Strong said. "Effervescent, Italian." He looked at Danny. "Unless you want something stronger?"

"Water's great," Danny said, and the waitress hurried off.

"I love my one container of Foley's beer every day at noon," Strong said. "It's more habit than anything. Gives me a psychological turbocharge that gets me through the day. Levels out the serotonin in my brain. But it also reminds me of when I was young, of where I come from. I've traveled just two blocks but a million miles. And I've carried this entire neighborhood on my shoulders with me into the new century. But other than the daily Foley's beer, I stick to water, good food, and home by twelve-thirty A.M. every night, bed by one, up at seven. Life is good to those who are good to life."

Strong's megalomania, bordering on messianic delusion, had not diminished much since the days when he dressed as Jesus and led a flock. But he dressed better and he'd found a new barber. Still, Danny found it maddening. But he didn't react to it. It was like listening to certain actors tick off their credits and quoting from their good reviews.

"Were you there at Foley's today at noon?"

"Of course," Strong said. "Clockwork."

"Did you see Horsecock?"

"Ya know," he said, casting his eyes toward the copper ceiling. "I might've. Place was packed. People buttonholing me for apartments for their newlywed daughters. One guy had a problem with the school board. Someone else's kid needed a reference letter. The usual contracts. My constituents. My customers. My people. Whenever any of them are ready to sell their homes, they know who to come to. When they want a four-star meal without having to travel to Manhattan, they come here and ask for me on a first-name basis. So . . . what was I saying? Oh, old Henry might've been there in the Foley's crowd today, but I can't say for sure. Terrible that he went like that. Was he jogging?"

The waitress came back with the water, poured it into two spotless glasses.

"I would say he would've had a hard time walking by the time he died," Danny said. "He was at least three sheets of Four Roses to the wind."

"More than his heart could bear at his age."

Danny hadn't mentioned that the paramedics and cops suspected a heart attack. But he didn't point it out to Strong. He just let it sit there, like an uncashed chit.

"Yeah."

Strong reached across the table, clinked his glass against Danny's. "We're both busy gents," Strong said. "I have businesses to run and a campaign to orchestrate, endorsements to secure, and funds to raise. You have a father to bury and some old unpleasant business to clear up. So what do you want to talk to me about, Danny?"

"Vito Malone," Danny said, taking a sip of the sparkling water.

Strong broke off the end of a bread stick and munched it. "What about him?"

"There's no delicate way to say this, so I'll just say it plainly," Danny said, leaning over the table, closer to Strong, so he could talk low and still be heard. "A lot of people thought he was on your pad back then."

Strong broke off the other end of the bread stick, nibbled it, staring into Danny's eyes. "Pad? Heating pad? Notepad? Landing pad? Kotex pad? The pad where I lived? What pad are you talking about, Danny?"

"Don't worry, I'm not wired."

"You must be wired on something if you think I had any kind of illegal relationship with Vito Malone. He was a cop. I was a—"

"You were a drug dealer," Danny said. "I don't mean to disparage you about the sins of the sixties. We all lived outside the law. That's why they have this thing called maturity and statutes of limitation. Some crimes are committed when you're young and foolish and crazy. They're better buried by time, because people mature, they become upstanding citizens. Like you did."

Strong looked at him with a bemused grin, not a hair out of place, not a shadow of beard visible, the tie perfect, the teeth all capped and symmetrical.

"I was a member of the counterculture," Strong said. "But I never sold an illegal substance in my life."

"C'mon, Christie, I lived with Lefty Mots and Harry Bowles," Danny said. "They worked for you. They dealt everything for the head for every kind of head on the street for you. Ups, downs, beepers, acid, THC, coke, speed, tranqs."

"They were your roommates, Danny," Strong said. "Not mine."

"I lived with them because I was seventeen and had nowhere else to go," Danny said. "I looked after the crash pad, cleaned up, shopped, cooked, and they gave me a place to crash and enough drugs for my speed jones. I was a dumb-ass kid user. I was never a dealer. But you wanted me to be. You told them to recruit me."

"This conversation going somewhere?" Strong asked, picking up another bread stick, nipping off another end, crunching it with his back molars. "Besides down the toilet? As I recall, you were arrested for marijuana. I was never arrested."

"Where'd you get the money for all of this?" Danny asked, sweeping his hand across the restaurant. "You hit another lottery after the draft? Your parents leave you some money—"

"I didn't have any parents," he said. "I'm a self-made man, Danny. When other people fled this neighborhood, the way you did, after the sixties were over, I stayed. I bought condemned tenements at city auctions. I had them rehabbed. I bought empty lots. I converted prime old buildings into luxury co-ops and condos. I built new homes. I helped raise money and break ground for the Cardinal Murphy Senior Citizens Apartments. When I bought out some of those old-timers who were taking up three- and four-bedroom rent-controlled apartments, I didn't let them go into the street. I put them in Cardinal Murphy, where they would be cared for, with dignity. When they abandoned the old Mayflower Laundry factory, I tore that dump down and erected classy condos. All mine. Whenever I saw an empty storefront, I turned it into a successful business and put local people and their kids to work. I have a pet-food supplier, a Java Jones coffee boutique, I opened the first video store in the neighborhood, a piece of a pharmacy. I own a piece of the movie house. I have the biggest and busiest real estate business in the neighborhood. And I'm single. No kids. No gold-digging wife to take half when she hits the road. I get all the women I want by making them want me. I don't pick up chicks in single bars. I own the singles bars and chicks pick up me. I own businesses and real estate all over this neighborhood. Every one of them legitimate."

"I didn't ask you what you had. I asked you where it all came from."

Strong picked up another bread stick and pointed to his right temple. "From in there," he said and bit off the end. He pointed the stem at his crotch and said, "And from those."

"C'mon, man, it came from drugs, Christie," Danny said. "From Hippie Hill. From 1969. And the money has blood all over it."

Strong laughed and sipped his water. He checked his gold Rolex. "I've been under the interrogation lamp, Danny," he said. "The IRS has sniffed every one of my dollars. I've been audited and reviewed and questioned and examined. They can stick lights down my throat and scopes up my anus, but they won't find one dirty dime. Because it's all legitimate. The main reason people like you question my integrity is because of envy. You all thought it was hip, cool, politically correct to stumble out of the sixties like dirty, penniless homeless slobs. 'Power to the people, right on, man, by the way got any spare change?' The sixties weren't about love, peace, and happiness, Danny. Not about sex, drugs, and rock and roll. The sixties were about *freedom*. Like Kristofferson's song, 'Freedom's just another word for nothing left to lose.' When you have nothing to lose you have the *cojones* to roll the dice. Some of us came up winners. Some crapped out. Others, like you, Danny, aspired to mediocrity, to a newspaper byline, writing about rich and famous people, your nose pressed to the glass. Well, I became one of the people on the other side of the window, Danny. And I don't apologize for it. No mea culpas. I'm tired of people haunting me about being successful. Trying to make me feel guilty because I didn't wind up OD'd, brain dead, or penniless, with no teeth and a Medicaid card. By 1969, I discovered the freedom to succeed. I refused to leave the sixties broke. I made a few investments, they paid off. You followed the sun, Danny, and got burnt. I reached for the moon. And got it."

"We landed on the moon that year," Danny said. "On the night Wally Fortune was murdered. That when you got your inspiration?"

"I was inspired by coming from nothing. I came here as an orphan and slept under the moon and promised myself one day I would own it. Ask anyone in this neighborhood about Christie Strong—"

"I have."

"Ask any of them if this isn't a better place because of me? A family's greatest asset is their home, and I increased the property value of every homeowner in this neighborhood. I improved the quality of life. I even formed a civic and merchants association, and we brought pressure on the police to crack down on street crime. Prospect Gardens is a better place now, Danny. I'm not afraid to take credit when credit is due. I'm not waiting for the statue to go up after I'm dead and gone. I'll take my bows now, that's why I will win this campaign."

"You're talking in campaign circles, Christie. Where'd you get the fucking seed money? To make those first 'few investments.' To build your empire?"

Christie Strong smiled again, sipped his water.

"Check the public records. But I'm interested in how you think I got it, Danny."

"I think you got it selling narcotics. I'm not saying you still push nickel bags. That would be risky. And dumb, which you're not. But I think you did it in the late sixties from your pad in the apartment overlooking Hippie Hill. I think you paid Vito 'Boar's Head' Malone to run interference and supply protection. He even moved major weight for you to other neighborhoods as you expanded. I think he got his partner, Jack Davis, to go along because he had something on him, the way he had a secret dossier on everyone. But you made a few stupid mistakes. Mostly with your dick. You let Wally Fortune's sister, Mary, into your loyal flock of hippie bimbo chicks. She was a cutie, a stunner, and she resisted you. And your ego couldn't accept that. And so you wanted her even more. You chased her. And then when you spent enough money, gave her enough drugs, took her to enough concerts, she joined your inner circle. But Mary was different than the other chicks. Mary was smarter than the rest of them. She didn't miss a trick. You thought you were using her, but she was

using you. And she found out about you and Boar's Head. She told
Wally about it. And Wally was a con man, an opportunist, a world-
class scammer. He wanted a taste, sure. But first he wanted you to
leave his sister alone. You obliged, by having Mary hot-shotted for
daring to expose your secrets, your relationship with Boar's Head.
After you killed his sister, Wally didn't want just money anymore. He
also wanted revenge. He wasn't a violent guy, couldn't break an egg.
But you were terrified he was gonna cash in and then expose all of
you. So, on your order, Vito Malone killed him on July 20, on the
night when Neil Armstrong walked on that moon of yours."

Christie Strong stared at Danny for a long moment, his always
half-dreamy eyes not blinking. He sipped some of the sparkling
water, kept staring, a small smile curling the edge of his lip.

"Ya know something, maybe Art Linkletter was right," Strong
said. "Everybody laughed when he said his daughter committed suicide when she took a swan dive off a rooftop during an LSD flashback. Not when she was high on acid, but years later, in a flashback.
It was a regular joke on the Hill. But now I'm starting to think there
might be something to this flashback theory. You're hallucinating,
Danny. Delirious. Lost in an acid flashback. I've seen old ladies with
Alzheimer's who make more sense. . . ."

He took a drink of water, checked his watch again.

"Which old lady with Alzheimer's would that be, Christie?" Danny
asked, thinking of the phone call Erika had received earlier from
Strong's campaign headquarters. He felt the first flare of heartburn
ignite in his esophagus, as if some lost trapped soul had lit a match
as he searched to find his way out of Danny's dark life.

"Figure of speech," Strong said, regaining his composure and his
insincere smile. "Look, Danny, I know you're under a lot of stress.
Ankles has dogged you for thirty-two years about Vito Malone's
murder. You lost contact with your family, the old one and the new
one. Your life's been, for lack of a better word, a bit of a flop. Please
don't take it out on me because mine hasn't been. If you need a little
help, just ask. Maybe I can help you get a line of credit for a lawyer,
or to try your hand at a new venture, maybe. I could use a man with
a command of the language on my staff. Someone who knows both
the voice of the common man and the world of success. For campaign speeches, testimonial dinners, press releases. A guy to work
the press. I could pay much better than the eighty-two thousand
they're paying you on the *L.A. Chronicle.*"

"How do you know so much about my personal life, Christie?"

"This is my neighborhood," Strong said. "I know everything that goes on with the people here. And the people who come from here. The people who come back. I knew your dad. I know your old friends. I know how to use a computer. Information is my business. I know that knowing stuff, lots of stuff about lots of people, is power. Power is success. And it all comes from knowledge."

Danny wondered how well he knew his old girlfriend, Erika Malone. He felt jealousy slither through him. *Is he fucking her,* he wondered, the heartburn spreading. *Has Erika just been picking my brain for Christie Strong?*

"Just like you knew Horsecock had a heart attack this afternoon, huh?"

Strong paused, took a sip of mineral water, and pursed his lips. "An educated guess, Danny. Christ, he was eighty-two."

"All of this is going to come out about you, Christie," Danny said. "I'm a newspaperman. Like you said, I know how to work the press, to leak stuff to the right people. The past never goes away, never for people in politics."

Strong looked at him and said, "Don't embarrass yourself, Danny. You don't have a single supportable fact. It's all conjecture. I'll sue the ass off you and any paper that even suggests these mad ravings of an old speed freak who is the prime suspect in an old cop killing. Come off it, man. The one thing I learned the hard way about Brooklyn as soon I arrived here is that you can't shit a shitter, Danny."

Danny knew Strong was right. "But the damage will already be done," he said.

Strong laughed and said, "OK, let's say you do it. Say you get some reckless hack columnist to print this crap. So it causes a ripple. Maybe it even keeps me from getting a seventy-thousand-dollar-a-year city council seat. So what? I make that in rent every month from just one building on the parkside, Danny. So you slander me, I lose the seat, I go back to being rich. And then I sue you and I win and you never work in journalism again. Which means you never work again, period, because you're too fucking old now to do anything else. Without some help from a benefactor. Like me. And then how would you pay your daughter Darlene's Harvard tuition? She doesn't talk to you now. Imagine how she'd feel about you if you let her down on that one? How would you make your child-support payments? Health insurance? How could you pay your rent on Sweetzer Avenue in West Hollywood? How could a homeless man pushing a shopping cart, collecting cans on Santa Monica pier, afford to make a long-distance phone call to talk to his estranged brother, Brendan, in Vietnam, who so far hasn't even showed up to say good-bye to your poor old man? How could you ever afford to take Erika Malone to dinner here in my restaurant? Try a bread stick, Danny, they're great."

"I'll find more information," said Danny, belching into his fist, the heartburn like a trash fire in his chest now. "I'll find evidence."

Danny's cell phone rang. He answered it. It was Pat O'Rourke. "Hi, you told me to call you in an hour," she said. "It's an hour."

"You're kidding me," Danny said, sitting up straight, checking his watch, putting on a performance for Strong.

"Why would I kid you?"

"Where are we supposed to meet?"

Strong snapped another end of the bread stick and waved to three men in their sixties dressed in dark expensive business attire who entered the restaurant.

"Sorry, Danny, but my lunch guests are here and—"

Danny held up a finger to his lips for him to shush. It unnerved Strong, who stood up. Motioning for his guests to come and sit.

"You should go now—"

"No, not in an hour!" Danny said into his cell phone, still sitting. "Now! Just tell this . . . *Linc* that I'm on my way. . . ."

Danny saw Strong stop chewing. Strong brushed some crumbs from his suit jacket, looking from his arriving guests to Danny, a long stare as his face darkened. He took a small sip of water.

"What the hell are you talking about?" Pat O'Rourke asked from the other end of Danny's cell phone. "Are you in some sort of trouble?"

Danny hit the disconnect button. "Sorry, Christie, I was gonna tell you all about how I thought you had the motive to also kill Vito Malone, but that'll have to wait until I have more time. Right now I have to go see someone about, well, about a dog."

Danny stood and smiled as the businessmen reached the table. One of them Danny recognized as the face from the campaign poster for Marvin Levy Jr., Supreme Court judge. Danny didn't recognize the other two, but they glowed with summer tans.

"I'd be careful around this guy," Danny said. "He's a real killer."

The men looked at Danny and then at a smiling Christie Strong.

"Just kidding," Danny said. "He has other people do it for him. But that's off the record. *Bon appétit.*"

And then he strolled out of the dining room, passing the big blond man and the short silent black man, and left the Strong Arms, his chest in flames.

# eighteen

Danny was hurting. Strong had wounded him, deep in the soul. In a few deft strokes, the son of a bitch had dissected and belittled his life in such a vicious, ruthless way that Danny was feeling every bit the failure that Strong had described.

As he passed Dunne's funeral parlor, where the wake was scheduled to start again in twenty minutes, Danny faced some home truths that Strong had ground in his face. Danny'd wasted so much of his life running from 1969 that he did feel like a flop. He'd frittered away a vast treasure of precious, irretrievable time. Never pushed himself to excel in journalism, to a column, or an editor's job. Had never written a book or a movie or a play. He'd blown a good marriage to a fine woman. Cakewalked on his kid, a beautiful loving daughter. Lost contact with his lone sibling.

He pined for his long-dead mother and had never made peace with his father before his death.

He'd also carried an irrational fixation with Erika Malone, which if it wasn't love was enough of an emotional distraction to keep him from ever loving anyone else. And now, after that lifelong emotional investment, he wondered if Erika was fucking Christie Strong. Was Erika's whole song and dance about not sleeping with Danny until after he'd proved he didn't kill her father some charade because she was sharing Christie Strong's bed? *Is she just cockteasing me for information?* he wondered.

The whole twisted affair had him nauseated. He felt hot bile rise in him, like human lava. Felt the dirty acid swell in his breastplate, his esophagus sizzling with heartburn. He needed Maalox or Rolaids. Something chalky and white, like a physical absolution, to make the pain go away, the way Father McBride, stewed to the balls, used to absolve him of youthful mortal sins: missing mass, jerking off, and eating meat on Fridays.

He entered Balsam's Pharmacy, where he'd gone as a kid to get prescriptions filled for his parents. The drugstore was still open on the corner of Gorman Place and Parkside West, a block from Dunne's funeral parlor.

Danny grabbed a bottle of springwater from the soft-drink cooler and searched the heartburn shelf when he heard the familiar voice. "Danny? Danny Cassidy? Hey, buddy, long, long time, huh." Danny turned and saw Stuey Balsam, son of Sy Balsam, who used to own the store. He was still skinny but bald with glasses now, a wedding ring on his left finger. The Balsam family had lived above the store, one of the few Jewish families in Prospect Gardens in the fifties and sixties. While most local Catholic kids went to Blessed Virgin Mary across the street, Stuey went to some private Jewish school in Flatbush. The kids in the neighborhood always called him Stu the Jew. But the ribbing stopped there because Stuey could hit a Spaldeen three sewers in a game of stickball and was the best basketball player in Blessed Virgin Mary schoolyard, so he was always picked first when the guys chose up sides for street and schoolyard games.

Stuey knew when he was ten that when he grew up he would be a pharmacist like his dad and take over the family business. And here he was, in the same store, all these years later, wearing the white Balsam's Rx tunic. The two old friends exchanged pleasantries, talked a little about their own kids. Danny lied, said he saw his daughter all the time, expected her to come down for the funeral. Stuey expressed condolences about his dad, and because he'd been his pharmacist, he knew he'd been sick for years.

"Cirrhosis," Danny said. "The Irish virus. Call it what it was."

"More than the Irish, I can tell ya. But the only way to stop the alcoholic cirrhosis like your pop had is with total abstinence, which can cause convulsions and DTs, so he needed Dilantin and tranquilizers, Xanax or Valium, to stop the shakes, and to sleep. And Theragram vitamins to help regenerate the liver. But your pop, sorry, Danny, he tried a few times. But after two refills, or two months, he stopped coming for the Dilantin. Which I knew meant he went back to Foley's for the Dewers. Which leads to Dunne's. Sad."

"Yeah," Danny said, although he still couldn't feel any sadness.

"But you look good. So, how you feeling?"

"Right now I have heartburn, like I just swallowed Liquid Plumber," Danny said.

"So take the Zantac," Stuey said. "It's the fire department in a pill."

Danny grabbed a box of Zantac and followed Stuey to the register at the rear of the store, where the pharmacy section was located. He reached in his back pocket to pull out his wallet and removed his reporter's notebook. He gave Stuey a ten-dollar bill and he rang up the pills, a bottle of water, and two packs of Rolaids.

Danny flipped through the pages of his notebook until he came to the names of the drugs he'd seen on the Balsam's Pharmacy bottles in Hippie Helen's medicine chest.

"Hey, Stuey," Danny said, opening the Zantac, popping two, swallowing them with a gulp of water. "I'm working on a story out in L.A. and there was this autopsy report that said they found these drugs in someone's body. You know what they are?"

Stuey looked at the names on the notebook, his eyes widening. "The first three include two nucleoside analog reverse transcriptease inhibitors best known as AZT and 3TC and a protease inhibitor called nelfinavir. An AIDS cocktail."

"But this person was obese. I thought AIDS victims suffered from weight loss."

"Yeah, but the fourth drug you have listed there is something called clozapine," Stuey said. "It's a psychotropic or an antipsychotic drug. For people with schizophrenia, or for people suffering from severe depression. Having AIDS isn't a beach party. People with predisposed mental problems get suicidal. But one of the side effects of clozapine is that it throws the body chemistry for a loop, makes you eat like a racehorse. People on clozapine crave cheese, butter, bacon, potato chips, sugar, salt, hungry for fatty, salty foods. They're always thirsty, looking for sweet drinks. They munch candy and cookies. They also get lethargic, so they don't exercise enough. If they're older, with slower metabolisms, they pack on the poundage. So you could wind up with an obese AIDS patient, sure. I wouldn't have many clients on a combo like that. In fact, I think I have just . . . well, never mind."

"Thanks," Danny said. "Oh, another thing. Are there any real drugs for Alzheimer's?"

"A few but between me and you I'd forget them," Stuey said, laughing at his own joke. "People say there's been some mild success with ginko biloba in clinical trials, but I think it's bullshit. I do think the research is getting closer to preventing it. Preventing the plaque from setting in the crevices of the brain to begin with. But what do I know. I sell cough drops in Brooklyn."

"How difficult do you think it would be to fake?"

"I don't think you can verify it with a blood or urine test," he said. "It's behavioral. I guess you could fake it. If you could remember to pretend to forget every day. But why the hell would anyone do that? Maybe, if you're like that gangster Vincent Gigante, you do it to stay out of jail. But he walked around in a bathrobe for ten years in public and he couldn't convince a jury he had it. Because people testified he was lucid behind closed doors. Depends on monitoring. I know there's seven stages. Once you hit four and five you're deep space nine. You can put food in their mouth and they won't even know they're supposed to chew. They forget how to eat. The food goes down the wrong pipe when they swallow. . . ."

"Thanks, Stuey."

"My condolences about your pop. Me and my wife live on the two floors above the store now. As soon as Brooklyn became chic my wife wanted to move back from Westchester. We made it a duplex. So I'll go to the church for the funeral. Wakes I don't do. That's at least one thing my tribe does better than yours. In the ground the same day, and get on with the healing."

"I agree."

Danny left the store, walked to his car, grabbed his dress clothes out of the trunk, and changed in the bathroom at Dunne's Funeral Home.

He didn't walk up to the front of the viewing room to look at his father in the coffin this time. He stood in the lobby and waited to greet the visitors. For the first half hour no one came. Danny kept glancing at his father, a lump in a box, all alone in the big flowery room, which he would have thought was faggy. Danny craved a cigarette.

Three old guys from the Fort Hamilton Veterans hospital arrived in a hospital van. They signed the book, saluted Mickey Cassidy in his coffin, said a prayer.

"Your old man had some pair," said one guy, three nicotine-stained lower teeth in front, none up top. He smelled like an ashtray. Smelled wonderful to Danny.

And then they were gone. No one else came to the afternoon wake. Except Ankles, who walked in carrying his fedora and his unlit cigar at a little after four.

"I must be gettin' fuckin' soft," he said.

"I wish I could find a soft place to fall," Danny said.

"I'm going down to Horsecock's apartment, to sniff around. I thought I'd make you a gesture, hoping maybe you'll reciprocate. You wanna come between the five and seven break here, I'll let you take a look around his place. You were the last one besides whoever mighta killed him to talk to him about Vito Malone and Wally Fortune and all that '69 business. I figure you're not telling me everything he told you. So maybe you'll spot something I'd miss. If Horsecock comes up with strychnine in him, NYPD will be all over this in the morning. 'Specially that fresh-mouthed O'Rourke broad."

"I'll come now."

After Ankles flashed his gold shield, the square badge security guard opened Horsecock's door with a master key. Ankles handed Danny a pair of latex gloves and said, "Put these on."

As Danny pulled on the gloves he noticed that the ground-floor window was open and that the place looked like a gang of teenagers had partied here all day long.

"Looks like the skanky crash pad where I rousted you thirty-two years ago," Ankles said. "Was Horsecock a nasty-ass?"

"No, when I was here this morning the place was impeccable. He also made a point of locking the window after he fed the birds the leftover fat from his daily medium T-bone. He said he didn't trust anyone. Guards, workers, the other old-timers."

"So you figure the place's been tossed?"

"I'd say so," Danny said.

"Let's toss it again," Ankles said. "You start out here in the living room, I'll try the bedroom. We'll meet in the kitchen. At least the place is small."

After twenty minutes of searching through drawers, under seat cushions, in an old secretary and closets, Danny opened Horsecock's bathroom medicine chest, where he found a Balsam's prescription jar for clozapine, the same psychotropic drug as Hippie Helen used. *Fucking nut jobs everywhere I turn*, Danny thought.

But Horsecock sure hadn't blown up from the side effects of the drug. Danny wasn't surprised. The date on the pill jar said they were six months old. Danny guessed they were prescribed for the depression that set in right after old Henry Bush's beloved but barren wife of sixty years died. But when Danny shook out the pills he did a quick eyeball count and was sure the thirty pills that had been prescribed were still in the jar. Meaning he'd never taken a single one of them. Danny pocketed the pill jar without telling

Ankles. He appreciated Ankles's gesture, but Danny was still the one facing time.

Ankles shouted that he'd found two boxes stuffed with Horsecock's old NYPD memorabilia. Guns, shield, medals, plaques, uniform, photos, framed newspaper stories. "Plus, all his old log-books," Ankles said from the other room. "Holy shit! Here's the 1969 one."

"Try the July 20 page," Danny shouted over his shoulder, as he dug around in the bottom of a big cardboard box in the rear of a hall closet, pulling out old IRS forms, canceled checks, and old bills. Danny shuffled through stacks of old NYPD paycheck stubs, some dating back to the forties, fifties, to the sixties. He flipped through them, amazed at how little a cop made back then. In 1969 a lieu-tenant made just shy of $18,000. Back in the forties and fifties when Henry Bush—he felt bad thinking of him in death as Horsecock—was making a lot less. In 1942, when WWII was raging, Henry Bush was a young patrolman making $2,300 a year. His take-home pay was $86 every two weeks. *No wonder they all went on the fucking pad*, Danny thought.

In 1944, Danny noticed, an eighteen-dollar garnishee appeared on every check. Danny figured it was an IRS attachment but the initials on the check stub read NYCDSS. He had no idea what it meant. Maybe he owed the city money in back taxes. Maybe he'd been sued, and they were garnisheeing him. There was a claim number next to it and rather than try to write it down and have Ankles stumble in from the bedroom and catch him, Danny swiped one old pay stub and stuffed it into his inside jacket pocket. He flicked forward several months and the garnishee stopped appearing on Henry Bush's pay stubs. As if he'd satisfied it. A blip from the past.

Then Danny found a collection of U.S. post office money order receipts in the same exact amount, eighteen dollars every two weeks, with the same NYCDSS account number on it.

And made out to an attorney named Marvin Levy, 32 Court Street, Brooklyn.

Marvin Levy got around. Today his son was a judge, affiliated with Christie Strong. *What the fuck?* Danny thought, stuffing the receipt in his inside jacket pocket with the garnishee stub. Baffled.

"He look like he owed anybody any money?" Ankles said.

"Not enough to kill the poor son of a bitch over. He saved every check he ever wrote. But there's nothing here that links him to Vito Malone. Or anyone named Linc."

"Speaking of Vito Malone and Linc, listen to this from July 20," Ankles said, then read aloud: " 'Wally Fortune murdered at app. 0200 hours. On my watch. VM says he was with CI "Linc" at TOD. JD concurs. Impossible. Linc was with me at TOD.' "

"You lost me."

"In other words Malone says he was with this confidential informant named Linc at the time of Wally Fortune's death. Jack Davis corroborated it. But Horsecock says no way this is possible because Linc was with *him* at the same time Wally Fortune died."

Danny walked to Ankles, took the logbook, and read it himself. "This must be what he wanted to tell me. How come this was never subpoenaed, Ankles?"

"Because Vito Malone was never an official suspect in Wally Fortune's killing," Ankles said. "I thought he did it because I thought he was dirty all along. I thought he was on Christie Strong's pad. But Henry Bush was our CO and whenever I mentioned this he told me to lay off. That I was paranoid. You better have hard evidence to buck your commanding officer."

"Think he was covering it up?"

"He wasn't interested in uncovering anything, that's for sure," Ankles said. "Fact, after Wally got killed, Horsecock vouched for Vito Malone and Jack Davis. When your CO vouches for another detective's whereabouts at the time of an incident, it ends there. I was a young DT. I couldn't go over my CO's head over the murder of some local pot-smoking hippie con artist like Wally Fortune. There was never an indictment so no DA ever subpoenaed his logbook. I had no idea what was in it. This was 1969, Danny. Besides, if it was subpoenaed, he'd woulda destroyed it and said it was boosted from his work locker."

"When Malone was killed, couldn't you tie the two murders together somehow?"

Ankles looked at him, took the unlit cigar out of his mouth, stuck his face in front of Danny's, and smirked. "The only one who could've done that, shit-for-brains, was fuckin' you," Ankles said. "Without your eyewitness account of the Wally Fortune murder, I couldn't make that sale to police brass, never mind to the DA. They wanted the Vito Malone murder swept off the front page and under the rug as fast as they could make it happen. It was an embarrassment. It was a highly anticop climate under Lindsay, a politically charged time after the cops and the hippies swung it out in Chicago. Besides Abbie Hoffman, Jerry Rubin, and the other yippies, eight cops got indicted, too. Plus, there were riots out in Berkley, and the civil rights riots down south. And we had our own homegrown problems with the SDS ass wipes up in Columbia University and police brutality charges in the ghetto and the TPF cops fighting with hippies in Greenwich Village and I think maybe even the Weathermen radicals, white kids with chemistry sets makin' bombs, were forming—"

"Did you know the Weathermen got their name from a Bob Dylan song called 'Subterranean Homesick Blues'?" Danny asked, then sang a line. " 'You don't need a weatherman to know which way the wind blows.' "

Ankles stared at him, blinking, chewing the unlit cigar. "This is supposed to mean fuckin' *what* to me?"

"I was just trying to broaden your cultural horizons."

"Broaden this," Ankles said, pointing the cigar at his crotch. "Anyways, with dickheads like Bob Dylan singing trouble-makin' protest songs, Lindsay the liberal had senatorial and presidential plans. And his whiz kids wanted to keep this dirty drug-dealing cop murder low-key. So all they did was transfer Horsecock to Staten Island. Put him out to pasture. He never cooperated with me. He wasn't hostile, but he wasn't helpful, either."

"Didn't you at least ask him about it off the record?"

"Jesus, I didn't know this about Malone's alibi being bad. Besides, Bush would never even talk about it. I don't know why I'm even telling you this, but all he ever said to me was, 'Leave Mickey Cassidy's kid out of it. He had nothing to do with it.' Which told me he knew more than he was saying, but he never elaborated. Why the hell do you think you were allowed to walk away back then? If I'd had enough to hold you, I would have."

"Then why are you busting my fucking stones now?"

"Because I have built enough circumstantial evidence over the years to convince the guy I work for to put you in the defendant's chair," Ankles said. "I have motive. Now that I have copies of your journals, I have intent."

"But you don't think I did it, do you?"

"Hey, asshole, if you don't know for sure, why the fuck should I say so? One thing's for sure, I'm not lettin' this O'Rourke broad make the collar before I do."

"Tell the truth, Ankles. You don't think I killed Vito Malone, do you?"

"Put it this way. If it turns out Horsecock was murdered, I know you didn't have anything to do with that one."

"And you know that if he was murdered it has something to do with Vito Malone's murder," Danny said. "And maybe both the Fortunes."

"I don't know what the fuck to think," Ankles said. "Yet."

"What's Horsecock's logbook for November 20 and 21 say?"

Ankles flipped to it and grimaced. "This one doesn't go up that far," he said, reaching for the next one. He opened it, turned the page. "Here it is," he said and rolled his eyes. "RNO. But I already knew that."

"What's that?"

"Regular night off," Ankles said. "He didn't work that night."

"I wonder where he was. You don't think he might have killed Malone, do you?"

Ankles bit the unlit cigar, looked at Danny. "You got a match?"

"Not yet."

# nineteen

Danny got back in time for the last fifteen minutes of the afternoon wake. The lone mourner was JoJo Corcoran. He was dressed in his dirty street clothes, blackened sneakers, shiny jeans, and Cardinal Murphy High sweatshirt. His pinprick pupils told Danny he was high on something derived from the poppy plant, but Danny didn't ask him to leave. There was no one else there. Besides, JoJo had known Danny's father. He couldn't refuse someone paying his respects.

JoJo knelt over his father's coffin. Danny heard him praying in the Latin he'd learned as a Blessed Virgin Mary altar boy. Danny glanced at the name and address JoJo had put in the sign-in book. The handwriting was parochial-school elegant, as beautiful a script as he'd ever seen: Joseph John Corcoran. Sewer Seven, Pipe Eleven, Brooklyn, New York.

Danny grinned and shook his head.

After getting out of the army, JoJo lived in Sewer 7. Danny suspected he still did.

Before the army JoJo'd been a brilliant guy, an A-student at Blessed Virgin Mary and Cardinal Murphy High, where he dazzled everyone on the debating team and even played some football. Then JoJo discovered Tester's airplane glue. And sniffed his way into truancy, petty robbery busts, and dropping out of high school. When he was drafted, he continued sniffing, getting stoned in boot camp on shoe polish and Carbona fumes and the amphetamine-soaked cotton from Dristan inhalers. When his drill instructor busted him, a zonked JoJo hit him with a lock on a chain and wound up in the brig. Instead of a dishonorable discharge, the army put JoJo to use in the most appropriate way they saw fit. As a human guinea pig, performing medical tests on him, dousing him with LSD and placing him in sensory deprivation tanks to see how POWs might deal with similar conditions in places like the Hanoi Hilton. They brought JoJo out of his mad ravings with massive volts of electroshock, did a few more fried-brains experiments, and later gave him a psychological discharge with after-care that included

Thorazine, Stelazine, and other psychotropic drugs of the sixties. And a permanent residence in Sewer 7, Pipe 11, of his old Brooklyn stomping ground.

"I got the bread I owed your pop," JoJo said. "Did good at Horsecock's last rites."

"Forget it, JoJo," Danny said. "Death ends all contracts."

"That's very humanitarian of you. Red-letter day for me. I owed Horsecock eighteen rubles, five from April thirteenth. It was raining, and I caught him while he was runnin' in the park in the ay em. He said he didn't carry money with him when he ran but that if I caught up to him outside Foley's at eight he'd loan me ten till my psycho pension arrived. He did. Then on June sixteenth, sunny, 73 degrees, he lent me the other eight outside of the Strong Arms, after he had a steak and cursed out Christie Strong, who wouldn't serve him any more booze. He left with Helen."

Danny half listened. But when JoJo mentioned Christie and Helen he furrowed his brow. "He left with which Helen?"

"Hippie Helen Grabowski. She walked him home because he had his lump on. But she didn't sing. She sang like an earth angel back in the Hippie Hill days. Then everyone seemed to stop singing and the sixties were over. I think she stopped singing around the time Joan Baez disappeared off the face of the planet. Speaking of which, do you subscribe to the theory that Bob Dylan hung Phil Ochs? Or was it suicide? I've been trying to find out the whereabouts of A. J. Webberman, the Dylanologist who used to go through Dylan's garbage. He would have had a theory on whether Dylan strung up Ochs because I was never positively Fourth Street about it myself. . . ."

"JoJo, you're leaving orbit. Tell me about Helen and Horsecock."

"One thing I learned in Pilgrim State was that nut jobs don't always commit suicide all at once, ya know. You can do it on the lay-away plan. You got a voice like Helen's, and you stop singing, and you spend June sixteenth with Horsecock, well, any fool can see there's a reason for it, and it might be that when you're not busy being born, you're busy dying. Thanks for letting me say an Our Father for your old man. Peace. . . ."

JoJo lurched for the door. Danny grabbed his arm, looked in his vapid eyes, the inky black pupils the size of caviar. "Did you see what happened to Horsecock today?"

"My life might not look like it's worth living to you," he said. "But

I'm a survivor, Danny. Most people bet I wouldn't make it out of the sixties and here I am in the new century. I'm a Vietnam veteran without my body ever going there. They sent my fucking mind into combat instead. Most of it never came back, still MIA. No one ever searches for it either. I deserve a Purple Heart for what they did to my mind. I'm still sane enough to know they made me a bedbug. But what's left of whatever the fuck I am saw Horsecock in the park today. I surfaced from Sewer 7 at 12:08 P.M. 'Bout half an hour before Horsecock was found dead. When I saw him later, he was deader than Abraham, Martin, John, and Tim Hardin. I phoned it in from the cop box on the Elephant Steps path. But anyone who would believe me as a witness is fucking crazier than I am. But you know and I know that a certain guy in this neighborhood makes his own laws, and one of them is that there's no statute of limitations on ratting. But between you, me, and who I used to be, a guy who looked a lot like I do now saw Horsecock with another guy from a long time ago, before he wound up dead today."

Danny was trying to follow JoJo's zigzag of gibberish. It worried Danny again that he could decipher most of it.

"Who?" Danny asked.

"You must think I'm crazier than I am if you think I'm gonna admit this to the cops or the MPs or the shrinks," JoJo said and hurried toward the front door of the funeral home. "But the guy that the guy who used to be me saw talking to Horsecock just before he died in the park today was a guy you should remember well."

"Who, JoJo?"

"Lars Andersen," JoJo said, bolting out of the funeral parlor. "He's the publisher of the *Slope Sentinel* now."

Now Danny placed the face of the fair-skinned man who'd nodded to Horsecock that morning. The same Lars Andersen who raped Erika Malone in 1969.

# twenty

Danny parked his car at a meter on Seventh Avenue in Park Slope in front of an outdoor café called Pasta Bello. He put three quarters in the meter, walked a block along Seventh Avenue that was now like a strip of Greenwich Village cut and pasted into his old Brooklyn neighborhood. All the old saloons were gone—Ryan's, the Coach Inn, Minsky's, the Gaslight—all replaced by designer-coffee joints, boutiques, crafts stores, frame shops, computer stores, and chic restaurants. *It's about as Brooklyn as the Yankees,* Danny thought.

But it was the new Brooklyn, here to stay, whether any of the old cranky natives liked it or not. The Brooklyn Danny remembered was now being sold in nostalgia and history books in the Neighborhood Bookstore a few doors away from the *Slope Sentinel*.

The other place to find the old Brooklyn, he reminded himself, was in an old NYPD "murder book" from 1969. His name was in it as a prime suspect. He wanted to get it out.

One of the people he remembered from 1969 was Lars Andersen. He hadn't seen him since the night of September 24, 1969. As he looked in the bookstore window, sorting out what he'd say to Lars, he remembered the date because it was the night Gary Gentry pitched a four-hit 6–0 victory over the St. Louis Cardinals to clinch the National League East. It was also the night Erika lost her virginity. And the night Danny donned a ski mask and went looking for Lars Andersen. . . .

*September 24, 1969*

*Danny is giddy with the Mets' victory, when he hears a girl whimpering outside his crash pad door. Her knock is so weak it's almost a tap. He tiptoes to the door. Paranoid of cops. Of Boar's Head. Of Ankles. Of narcos. Of life. Of death. Of a soldier with a telegram telling him that Brendan is dead. He turns off all the lights. He peers through the peephole. Sees Erika. He opens the door. Danny's bug-eyed and wired on blackbirds, from being up for four straight days. His mouth is a pot of Elmer's Glue. Erika stands there. Mascara tears zigzagging her cheeks. Clutching herself, her legs crossed, wearing a dark dress, a bloody towel dangling from one hand. Her face is bruised. Her wrists are looped with friction burns.*

*He yanks her inside, double-locks the door.*

*"What the fuck happened?"*

*"I couldn't stop him. . . ."*

*"He raped you?"*

*She buries her head in his shoulder. His girl is back. But she is no longer a virgin. Someone stole her cherry. Raped it from her. And him. From them. He takes the bloody towel from her. Pulls her into the bathroom. He washes her face with cool water. He gives her clean towels. She presses the towels up between her blood-runny legs.*

*"Wanna go the hospital?"*

*"No! I can't let my mother know."*

*Danny dips into his Valium stash, the ones he was saving for the crash. He takes one himself, to level out. Then he makes Erika take one. She refuses at first. She's never taken drugs. He tells her she's never been raped before. She takes it. He puts her in a back bedroom, in Bowles's bed. He's away for a week, on a weed run from Florida for Christie Strong.*

*"I'm so, so sorry, Danny," she says as the Valium soon makes her droopy-eyed, holding the towels between her bloodied legs. "I never meant to hurt you. . . ."*

*In another twenty minutes, she's fast asleep.*

*Danny roots in the closet, pulls on a pair of Frye boots with solid square toes and two-inch leather heels. He pockets a ski mask and a pair of leather gloves. He finds his two-pound, twelve-inch blackjack that he carries on paranoid night crawls. A vicious little weapon that can break bones and inflict a concussion. Danny needs a weapon. He's no jock anymore. All his muscle mass has been eaten away by amphetamines, his body devouring itself in place of food. But even in his light-in-the-ass speed-freak condition Danny still has enough Brooklyn street rage in him to go and deliver a little street justice.*

*He remembers tailing Erika one night to a Bay Ridge bar called Eric the Red's, where she met Lars. It was Lars's hangout. Danny'd stood in the shadows of a pissy doorway across the street from Eric the Red's, watching in a twisted jealous sweat as Erika and Lars bumped and grinded to "Honky Tonk Woman" by the Stones inside the bar, all the other guys gaping at Erika scorching the dance floor. Then later Danny'd followed them at a one-block distance as Erika and Lars*

*walked hand in hand down Fifth Avenue in a crowd of Lars's square-
head pals.*

*Now, as Erika sank deeper into post-rape sleep, Danny steals some
change from his roommate's change jar and goes straight to Bay Ridge
on the Fifth Avenue bus, carrying the blackjack, the gloves, and ski
mask in his pockets. He spots Lars with some pals in Eric the Red's.
He waits in the same doorway across the street until Lars leaves after
last call, horsing around with drunken pals. He follows. The guys dis-
perse up different Bay Ridge streets. Danny follows Lars home, pulling
on his gloves and ski mask. He tails him into the vestibule of Lars's
apartment building. Danny taps him on the shoulder. A startled Lars
turns. Terrified. Danny raps the blackjack across the bridge of his
nose. Then he backhands it across Lars's teeth, knocking out several,
blood lashing. Danny buries a left hook into Lars's rib cage. Lars
squats in pain and Danny rams his knee between his legs.*

*The pretty boy sinks, covering his face with his hands. Danny beats
his fingers with the blackjack until he's certain every one is broken at
every joint, mashing the tips that'd fondled and violated Erika's body
until the nails break and split and bleed. He pounds the thumbs and
wrists and elbows until the arms drop. Then Danny beats his face,
crushing the high, proud cheekbones, the pronounced jawbone, beats
him around the blue eyes and full mouth, beating the lips that kissed
and suckled his girl.*

*Danny spreads Lars out on the tile floor, crushing his ribs with the
blackjack. Danny smashes Lars's kneecaps and his ankles, beating
him at every joint and bone he can locate. Danny kicks Lars a dozen
times—clear, straight punts in the balls—feeling the soft tissue crush
against the hard square toe of his scuffy boot, hoping to mash his testicles into jelly. He makes sure that the dick that broke Erika's cherry
wouldn't be used again anytime soon. Lars's whimpers are muffled by
gurgling blood as Danny beats him for almost three straight minutes,
almost one full round of professional boxing. He beats Lars Andersen,
who'd raped his girl, until Danny can swing the blackjack and kick no
more. When he looks down at pretty boy Lars he doesn't look so pretty
anymore. "If you ever lay a finger on Erika Malone again I'll kill you,"
Danny whispers in Lars's blood-pooled ear. And leaves. When he gets
back to his apartment Erika is gone.*

As Danny scanned the bookstore window, his eyes gliding over
books on Brooklyn neighborhoods, Prospect Park, the Brooklyn

Bridge, the Brooklyn Dodgers, Coney Island, and the Battle of Brooklyn, he remembered he hadn't seen Erika for over a month after she was raped.

She called once to say she didn't want to see him or anyone else for a while. Danny also went into hiding, afraid of getting caught for the Lars beating. Afraid of running into Ankles or Boar's Head. He went with Hippie Helen to a commune in Upstate New York called Mallard Ridge for two weeks. Speeding and tripping and ingesting any other intoxicant he could get his hands on.

He got kicked out of the commune for almost OD'ing on after-shave and Dramamine motion-sickness pills and sniffing Carbona cleaning fluid and for being "generally too uncool Brooklyn." Before he left, Danny pissed in the pacifists' well, shit in their lettuce patch, and hitchhiked like a homing pigeon back to Brooklyn. He slithered through the neighborhood, crashing in Hippie Helen's, in doorways, on rooftops, in the cellar of his parent's house, and in Sewer 7, Pipe 11, with JoJo Corcoran. He catnapped by day, speeding and tripping by night, roaming the netherworld of the neighborhood, avoiding Ankles and Boar's Head.

Danny saw a book in the window about Murder Incorporated and remembered that his own encounter with murder neared when Ankles finally caught up with him on a brisk fall day in November.

*November 10, 1969*

*The run ends when Ankles lays for him outside of the Municipal Building in Downtown Brooklyn after Danny makes his next-to-last visit to his probation officer for the pot bust in February.*

*"I'm gonna have you violated," Ankles says. "Skinny speed freak like you doing three to five upstate, you'll be a cover boy for 'Modern Jailhouse Bride.' Unless you give me Vito Malone for Wally Fortune."*

*"I can't give you Vito Malone," Danny says.*

*"Yes, you can. You got a week till your last PO visit. If you don't give me him by then, I'll have you violated and the wedding bells will start chiming in Rikers."*

*Ankles kicked Danny in the ankles. "By the way, that kid Lars Andersen is still in the hospital," Ankles said. "He thinks Malone had him beaten because he went out with your girl. Malone might try doing that to you next. . . ."*

\*     \*     \*

Now Lars Andersen was the publisher of the *Slope Sentinel*, the headquarters of which was next door, a few blocks from Erika Malone's brownstone. It was inconceivable to Danny that those two had not crossed paths in the years since, many times. The way Danny had crossed his path this morning, running with Horsecock in Prospect Park. The way that Pat O'Rourke had crossed his path and given him a lift in her Crown Victoria.

When he stepped inside he saw two tired, eager-to-leave reporters shutting down computer terminals and closing notebooks and phone books at their desks in a newsroom with six desks. A woman receptionist with a great figure was half turned away from Danny on her swivel chair, pushing files into a rack behind her.

"I'm looking for Lars Andersen," Danny said.

"I'm sorry but we're about to close for the holiday weekend and if you don't have an appointment— Oh, hi."

The receptionist was Viviana Gonzalez, the beautiful Latina who had been Christie Strong's arm candy at Danny's father's wake the night before. She was even more beautiful in the magic-hour light of evening that spilled through the front doors from the big Brooklyn sky.

"Hi," Danny said. "I was with your boyfriend a little earlier."

"Christie wouldn't like you to say that," Viviana said. "We just, ya know, talk. He's a very smart, very important man. He likes to say I'm part of Team Strong, but I'm very much my own person. He's trying to help me out, that's all. I'll see if I can get Mr. Andersen to see you."

Viviana pushed a few buttons and got through to Lars Andersen. She told him that Danny Cassidy was here to see him. Viviana listened and turned to Danny. "He wants to know what it's about."

"Tell him it's about Christie Strong and Vito Malone."

Viviana relayed the message. She listened, shook her head and hung up. "He'll be right out," she said. "Said he only has a minute to chat."

"Great," Danny said.

Viviana said good-bye to the two reporters, who left for the long weekend. Danny and Viviana were now alone, waiting for Andersen.

"Is this Vito Malone one of Christie's campaign supporters?" she asked.

"He used to be," Danny said. "He was murdered. So, Christie Strong got you this job, huh?"

"Yeah," she said. "He's a big advertiser so Mr. Andersen hired me. He lets me do the community happenings page and the calendar of events page. But I'm dying to get a byline. I minored in journalism in the College of Staten Island. I worked for the school paper. But it's so hard to break in. You can't get a job anywhere in America without clips. Everyone wants to see clips, but I can't get a reporter's job to build clips. You have any advice on how to get past the catch-22?"

"Are you serious about newspapering?"

"Yes! I read three newspapers a day, all the newsweeklies, and a few monthlies. I read six books a month, three novels and three nonfiction books. I love to write. I get the feeling that sometimes people look at me and think I'm a bimbo, because I'm young and, you know. . . ."

"Hot," Danny said.

"Oh, Jesus, I get that all the time. 'You have a face like an angel. A J Lo butt.' But I want them to know I have a B.A. in English. I love journalism. I'm just looking for a break. It's just so hard. No one will give me an assignment, even here. All I want is to see my byline, 'by Viviana Gonzalez,' in a legit newspaper."

"It would have made your father proud."

She cocked her head, looked up at him sideways. "You knew my poppi?"

"I hung out with him a little bit," Danny said. "He was older than me, but he was a nice guy. If he had five bucks he'd borrow five to lend you ten. He'd often spend his whole paycheck in one night on everybody else."

"Yeah. On drugs. That's why I grew up without him."

"It was the sixties, Viviana. Everybody did drugs. But Popcorn Gonzalez didn't have a mean bone in his body. Good-hearted. Humane. Funny. He was the best of the sixties. The ultimate hippie, believed in sharing and nonviolence. He gave you the gift of life, girl. Don't look that gift horse too deep in the mouth."

"He died from drugs."

"I think it was from strychnine poisoning," Danny said.

"I got some kind of letter about that last year from some homicide cop," she said. "They exhumed his body and tested the remains and said it was strychnine poisoning. But it didn't matter much to me. Way I look at it, if he never took the drugs he never would have gotten poisoned. Drugs are poison, whatever way you look at them. But I never heard anything about it since."

"If he was given poisoned cocaine on purpose, it makes it a homicide instead of an accident or an overdose. Someone cut his coke with strychnine."

"That's the same stuff they lace some of the ecstasy with these days," she said. "I've read about it in the papers. You saying all those people are murder victims?"

"Maybe not all of them. But some, maybe."

"Tell you the truth I never looked into it because I was too angry at my father. It's too painful. But maybe someday I'll research his death, and I'll write about him. If anyone ever gives me my first byline first."

"Viviana, let me be honest with you. You're what, twenty-four? If you want to be a reporter, you gotta get out on the street with a notebook and a pen, covering fires and homicides, community-board meetings. Don't wait for assignments. Find news. You should be making contacts, talking to local mobsters and yuppie landlords and tenants' right associations leaders."

"Hold on," she said, grabbing a notebook and a pen, scribbling notes. "Go ahead."

"Park Slope has a big lesbian community, so you should be covering issues important to those readers—health, culture, discrimination, same-sex insurance policies, same-sex marriages, gay politicians, gays and the church, gay teachers, lesbian soccer moms. Viviana, believe me, you won't learn to be a reporter sitting on your behind. You have to take off your high heels, put on a pair of sneakers, climb some stairs, look people in the eye, smell them, ask them questions, listen to them, write down what they say. Come back, assemble it into a story using action verbs and specific concrete nouns, stingy on the adverbs, and paint a you-are-there picture for the reader. If Mr. Andersen doesn't give you the time to do this during work hours, do it after hours and on weekends and I bet that when you turn in good, well-written stories you will see your byline in the paper on more than community happenings and calendar of events."

Viviana scribbled the notes, flicking pages, excited, her eyes widening and brow furrowing. Danny knew right away this kid was eager and ready for the trade.

"Which one should I start with first?"

"Listen, instead of just listing those community events, you have prior knowledge of them, so call some people up, go to a murder

victim's grief session. Profile the loved ones. Same with West Nile
virus victims. Attend a crimes-against-the-elderly seminar. Write
about the real people living those lives. And starting tonight, call the
morgue, check on an old ex-cop named Henry Bush, who was found
dead today in Prospect Park. It might turn out he was murdered.
Poisoned with the same stuff that killed your father twenty years
ago—strychnine."

Viviana leaned backward, her face twisting in disbelief. "You
jiving me? What a coincidence."

"I'm not so sure it's a coincidence," Danny said. "This neighborhood is like a small town in the big city. A Peyton Place. Some of the
same players that were around in your dad's and my time are still
around. They'd like to keep a lot of old secrets buried. If the morgue
confirms that Henry Bush was poisoned with strychnine, check with
a cop named Anthony Tufano at the Brooklyn District Attorney's
office and a cop named Pat O'Rourke at the Cold-Case Squad."

"That's the one who sent me the letter about my father."

"Right. Ask them what they know about Bush. Ask O'Rourke if
she thinks it's connected to your father's death. Or to the death of a
girl named Mary Fortune in 1969. It could be an exclusive. You're a
weekly so you'll have time to work this story so well you might be
able to sell it to the *Village Voice* or the *New York Press*. Get *details*,
Viviana, not just names and ages, but notice everything, what
people wear, the smell of the morgue."

"You just gave me fifteen story ideas," she said. "You make it
sound so easy."

"No, it's hard work," he said. "But it's doable. It gets easier as you
go along, with confidence. If you want you can bounce ideas off me,
show me your work, E-mail me or fax me. While I'm in town, call
me on the phone, and I'll shoot the breeze with you. Everyone in
this business needs a rabbi. I will be that rabbi for you if you want.
But remember, even the Talmud can be edited."

"Wow," she said, then grew skeptical, giving him one of those
another-asshole-trying-to-get-in-my-pants looks. "On what condition?"

"On two conditions. One, an understanding that we never sleep
together."

"Huh? You gay, too?"

"No, but you're gorgeous, and I'm too old for you and you don't
need my baggage." She laughed and shook her head.

"I never had a straight guy make me promise not to try to get in *his* pants before," she said. "Kinda sexy. I'll think that one over. What's the second condition, poppi?"

"Two, that you don't tell Christie Strong anything about our arrangement or what you're working on. He's the jealous type. So I have to ask for your strictest journalistic confidence on the second one. Don't even tell Andersen. Spring it on him when you have the story done."

"You have a deal on that one," she said.

"Remember, you just made me a confidential source," Danny said. "You give me up, and you have violated the first tenet of journalism. You give your word to a source, you keep it. Understand?"

"Yes, of course," she said.

He gave her his *L.A. Chronicle* card and jotted his cell phone number. "Any questions, on any story, call me, OK?"

"That's it? No more strings attached?"

"No," Danny said. "Except the unwritten rule that when a reporter helps you, you reciprocate when he needs help. It's quid pro quo."

"You have no idea how excited you just made me," she said.

"One other thing," he said. "It's your call, but as your rabbi I have to say Christie Strong is older than me. You deserve better."

She looked flattered and abashed as she stacked a bunch of invoices and mail. Danny spotted one envelope that had a familiar return address: Clubweb.com Inc.

"Andersen a steady customer of Clubweb.com?" Danny asked.

"They do all the computer—"

Viviana stopped talking when Lars Andersen walked out of the rear office of the *Slope Sentinel*, clutching a gym bag with a protruding racquet, dressed in a blue blazer, designer white T-shirt, pressed blue jeans, and oxblood penny loafers with no socks. He carried himself with a powerful roll of the shoulders and confident stride. *If he'd been built like that when I caught him in the Bay Ridge vestibule thirty-two years ago,* Danny thought, *I would have spent the two months in Methodist Hospital.*

"Dan Cassidy?" Andersen said, initiating a firm handshake. "I only have a minute. Walk me to my car, I'm late for my racquetball game."

"Fine," Danny said, following him to the door.

"Lock up, Viv, have a good one."

"Bye," she said and waved. Danny gave her a thumbs-up and left with Andersen.

"What can I do you for, guy?" Andersen asked, double-timing toward Union Street, carrying his gym bag.

"I saw you jogging in the park today, didn't I?"

"I run every morning," he said. "If I saw you, I don't remember, sorry."

"I was with an old-timer. Henry Bush. Ring a bell?"

"No."

"They found him dead in the park a little past noon."

"Not a relative, I hope."

"No."

"My receptionist said you wanted to talk about Christie Strong and Vito Malone."

"Do you remember Vito Malone?"

"Why don't we knock off the charade, Danny," Andersen said, stopping and staring Danny in the eyes. "We both used to date his daughter. Deep in another century. The man didn't like me. I'm sure he wasn't fond of you, either."

"You remember when he died?"

"I was in Methodist Hospital," Andersen said, continuing his fast pace. "He had me put there. So I'll never forget him. Forgive me, but I didn't send flowers to his wake."

"You still see Erika around?"

"Sure. But we don't talk. I hear she spends a lot of her time in her Soho place. Takes care of her mother here in the Slope brownstone. Look, I'm running late. Is there something specific you want to talk to me about?"

"Do you remember Christie Strong?"

"He's one of my biggest advertisers. I didn't know him all that well back then. Met him once or twice. He was always after Erika, too. Who wasn't?"

And you raped her, Danny thought, itching to say it aloud. But he held back. Hoping to get more information.

"Your paper supporting Strong in the election?"

"Yeah, but not just because he's an advertiser," Andersen said, entering a parking garage on Union Street. "He's a doer. Take a walk through Prospect Gardens today. The reason it's the hot new Brooklyn neighborhood is Christie Strong. Period. If he says he's going to do something, he does it. He's right on all the issues. What's not to support?"

"Did you ever have much to do with Vito Malone's partner, Jack Davis?"

They walked up the shadowy ramp, the garage reeking of spilled oil and gasoline. Andersen clicked open his canary-yellow Explorer at the top of the first ramp and tossed in his gym bag. "Who remembers obscure details like that?" Andersen said, climbing in and starting the car. "Look, all of this is a million years ago and I'm ten minutes late for my game. The guys'll be furious. I'm sorry, Dan, but I better go."

"You didn't see Henry Bush in Prospect Park today just past noon, huh?"

"Not me. Enjoy your holiday weekend, Dan."

Danny watched Lars glide out of the shadowy garage.

# twenty-one

When he got back to his car he had just five minutes left on the meter.

"Hey, Danny," a woman called from behind him. He turned and Pat O'Rourke flipped him a quarter from her sidewalk table outside Pasta Bello. Danny caught the quarter, jammed it in the computerized meter, realized there was no dial, and joined her at the table. This time she was wearing tight white jeans, a tight white top with a low scooped neck, white sneakers, and a white denim jacket contrasting against her glowing summer tan.

"You look like a vanilla egg cream," Danny said.

"I wear white off duty."

Another crackpot, Danny thought.

"I ordered fried calamari for two and the black linguini pescatori for you," she said. "And an arugula salad."

She poured Danny a glass of cold white pinot grigio and returned the bottle to a silver ice bucket.

"Jesus, this is thoughtful of you," Danny said.

"Your credit card receipts tell me that you order arugula salad and pescatori in the Café Med on Sunset Plaza in L.A. twice a week. Must be hot waitresses there."

"There are. All of them my daughter's age. But I go for the side-walk parade. It's one of the few places in L.A. where you can watch people walk."

"What did Andersen say?" she asked as the waiter brought Danny his black pasta with red sauce, covered with shrimp, clams, calamari, and mussels. He also placed an arugula salad with shaved parmesan cheese on the table at the same time. Danny sipped the wine. It was delicious. He ignored the salad and dug into and twirled the pasta, taking a big mouthful. It was good, but not as good as Café Med's.

"I was going to ask you the same question."

"Huh?"

"Andersen got in your car this morning."

"I wondered if you'd noticed," she said. "I asked him questions but I didn't learn much. I don't think he was involved in all that stuff back in 1969. Although he did say he dated the same girl as you for a short while."

"Erika is and was Vito Malone's daughter. That makes Andersen part of 'all that stuff back in 1969.' Like the beating that put him in Methodist Hospital for two months?"

Stunned, she said, "Beating? Lars looks like he could deliver a good whupping."

"Now. He was a wimp back then. When he came up against a guy, anyway."

"Who gave him this beating?"

"Ask him," he said, digging a mussel out of a shell, dipping bread in red sauce. "He was there. Maybe you should talk to some of his other old girlfriends from back then, see what kind of a guy Andersen was."

"What are you implying?"

"I'm not implying anything," he said. "I'm suggesting."

"So what did he tell you?"

"He told me he didn't know Henry Bush," Danny said. "Which is bullshit. He and Horsecock nodded to each other on the park drive this morning."

"Horsecock? Is that what they called that poor old gent?"

"They say he was hung like Mister Ed," Danny said.

"Guys like that always end up tripping over it," she said. "The way rich guys always trip over their money. Don't get me wrong, size might count, but too much of a good thing can screw up your thinking. But anyway, just because two joggers nod to each other, doesn't mean they know each other. Maybe Lars was just being polite. He's a well-mannered, well-groomed, good-looking man."

"Maybe that's why you 'picked' Lars up this morning," Danny said. "Maybe you were picking him up *up*."

"Never."

"You single?" he asked, looking at her naked wedding finger.

"Yes, I am."

"You ever get involved with people you meet on cases?"

"Not yet." She took a sip of her wine, ate some calamari, avoided the bread. "But 60 percent of all marriages start in the workplace."

"Maybe you should ask good-looking, well-groomed, well-mannered Lars Andersen what he talked to Henry Bush about less than an hour before he was discovered dead in Prospect Park,"

Danny said, shoveling a wad of black linguini into his mouth, reaching for the wine bottle, pouring himself another two inches.

"Who told you that?"

"Plus this morning, Horsec—old Henry told me the key to this case might be Vito Malone's partner, Jack Davis," Danny said. "The narc we used to call Apeshape. Brooklyn has more lame nicknames than street names."

"What else did he say?"

Danny was interrupted by a loud screech. Danny turned and saw Erika Malone's red El Dorado lurch into the bus stop outside the restaurant. Erika hopped out of the car, slammed the door, and strutted straight to the table where Danny and Pat O'Rourke sat. She wore a tie-dyed shirt knotted at the sternum, no bra, and a pair of tight cutoff jeans and sandals. She had the kind of legs that make some men act like fools. She pulled off her big sunglasses as she moved from sun to shade and dragged a chair from another table and sat at their table.

"Yuck," she said, looking at the calamari and the pescatori. "Flesh."

"What good is an unholy trinity without a few sins of the flesh?" O'Rourke said. "Hi, I'm Pat O'Rourke. Don't be bashful, why don't you join us?"

Erika appropriated Danny's salad, pored on some olive oil, scooped a piece of lemon out of his glass of water, squeezed it on the arugula, and dug in.

"How come you're investigating my father's murder without interviewing me, police lady?"

"Should I?" O'Rourke asked, spearing a wheel of calamari, dipping it in red sauce, placing it in her mouth.

"I would if I was you. I'm smart. I know the language. I have an emotional connection. I knew the deceased quite well, thank you. . . ."

"You were a seventeen-year-old girl," O'Rourke said. "You were a wreck. You were home with your mother. Why would I bother dredging up all the old pain?"

"Why are you dredging up all this time with my old boyfriend?"

O'Rourke pointed with her fork to a meter maid who was writing a ticket for the red El Dorado. "You're getting a new summons on your old car," O'Rourke said.

"At least the law is paying *some* attention to me."

"Feeling left out, are we?"

Danny sipped his wine, ate his pescatori, looked from one beautiful woman to the other. He didn't say a word. Guys strolling by, even the gay ones, gazed at Danny sandwiched between the two attractive women. He was the prime suspect in the murder of one woman's father. The second woman's job was to nail him for it. And they went at each other as if he weren't there. *Life is a visitor's pass to a nuthouse,* he thought.

"The man who was killed was only my father."

O'Rourke looked her in the eyes, nodded. There was a lull in the bitching as Danny watched the passing human parade of harried shoppers, yuppies eating Häagen Dazs ice cream, dog walkers, mothers pushing strollers, hand-holding couples, straight and gay and lesbian. Thirty-two years ago a gay or lesbian couple strolling hand in hand in Park Slope would've been tormented, Danny thought. Maybe even assaulted by nasty drunks rolling out of the saloons. Maybe a lot of the changes were for the better. . . .

"I can imagine how that must feel," O'Rourke said.

"Can you?"

O'Rourke looked Erika in the eyes, her stare braver than most people's. Prolonged eye contact was one of the more uneasy human interactions.

"I come across the human grief caused by murder all the time in my job," O'Rourke said. "There's an element of survivor's guilt involved. A frustrated impotence in not being able to find revenge or justice. It's the reason I kept you at arm's length, Erika. So you wouldn't have to relive all that. Until it's unavoidable."

"I don't need to be mollycoddled," Erika said. "I was seventeen when this happened. My guess is you were a baby. I can handle it, police lady."

O'Rourke ate a few more calamari rings, took a deep breath, wiped her hands, and took a sip of wine. She slid a cigarette out of a pack, lit it, the smoke enticing Danny.

"Easy on the fried food, the nicotine, and all the time in the sun, girl," Erika said, fanning away the smoke. "Use olive oil, and try my self-tan lotion, all natural. For the cigarettes try a shrink, because that's connect-the-dots suicide. A little advice, change your lifestyle or you'll look like an old lady by the time you're my age."

"If you want I can come around and pester you," O'Rourke said, whatever compassion she might have had now vanished with a long stream of smoke. "But you already have a full dance card, what with your company, your ailing mother, Danny back in town, Christie Strong. . . ."

Danny looked from O'Rourke to Erika, his chewing slowing. He swallowed a half-chewed lump of mixed shellfish, washing it down with the freezing wine. He watched the meter maid tuck the orange parking ticket under the wiper of the El Dorado. He guessed that Vito Malone had paid cash for the Caddy when it was new. Cash made from renting his badge to Christie Strong. Whom he'd just learned from O'Rourke was somehow connected to Erika. As he'd already suspected.

"If there's as much shit flying in the kitchen as there is at this table we're all gonna catch shigellosis," Erika said, pantomiming the busboy over to crack some pepper into her salad and thanking him with a big smile. Then she asked O'Rourke, "Where did you ever get the idea that Christie Strong is part of my life?"

"Your company donated five thousand dollars to his campaign," O'Rourke said.

"That's why you worry about parking tickets and I don't, police lady. A campaign contribution is a surcharge for doing business in New York. If you'd dug deeper you'd have learned I gave the same amount to both of Strong's rivals for the city council. It's called hedging your bets. All tax deductible. All legal. All part of doing business in New York, Detective O'Rourke."

O'Rourke seemed one-upped. She sipped her wine, waved for the waiter to bring a check. "For the daughter of a cop, I detect a disdain for people who do the same job. Especially for someone who wants to find out who murdered your father. I thought of trying another line of work, but when I read the Vito Malone file I thought I should stay in this line of work. Maybe if I played my cards right I too could buy a Park Slope brownstone, a brand-new Cadillac, and send my daughter through Columbia."

"Pass the salt," Danny said, pointing past Erika.

"You don't need salt," Erika said and Danny tilted his head, as if he'd just been enlightened, and kept eating. He reached for the grated cheese and O'Rourke touched his hand. "Never put cheese on fish, Danny."

"OK," Danny said, shrugging.

The waiter brought the check, placing it near Danny. He reached for it but O'Rourke hit his hand with the prongs of her fork. He withdrew his hand, shook it.

Erika smiled at O'Rourke and said, "In 1956, when my father bought the brownstone, he paid sixteen thousand dollars. The Caddy he bought at a police auction, after it was seized from a heroin pusher he'd busted. And I won a scholarship to Columbia. See, these are things you could have learned if you had come around and interviewed me, police lady."

"I stand corrected," O'Rourke said, standing from her chair and placing a hundred-dollar bill on top of the check. She reached past Erika and lifted the salt shaker, placed it on top of the bill so it wouldn't waft away in the thin summer breeze. Danny felt sort of sorry for O'Rourke, the way he sometimes did for the fighter who goes home a loser after fighting his best fight.

"Maybe I will take you up on that," O'Rourke said to Erika. "But it's my night off and I have someone to meet. But maybe I will come around one of these days to ask where you got the money to start a multimillion-dollar international company at the age of twenty-two."

"Drop by the house," Erika said. "Better, drop by the company. I'm in Soho. You can't miss it. It's on Greene Street, I own the whole building. It has my name on it. My condo is on the top floor."

"Erika's Earth," O'Rourke said. "I never use anything else."

"I'll give you some free samples."

"How kind. Sorry, but I have to run. See you around, Danny."

"Thanks for dinner," Danny said. "I owe you one."

"I'll take you up on that," O'Rourke said and hurried off down the busy avenue, weaving through the sidewalk scrimmage of Park Slope, a very attractive lady in white. Then as she turned to walk up Carroll Street to her parked car, O'Rourke looked back once. Then she was gone. Something told Danny that her date would be with a well-mannered, well-groomed, good-looking man.

"You have the hots for her," Erika said.

"Hey, she paid."

"Don't trust her, Danny."

He looked at Erika, trying to penetrate her deep dark eyes. He couldn't. She just looked back at him, her stare as wide and confident as a big cat's.

"I don't trust anybody," Danny said.

"Except me, I hope."

Danny's silence lay on the table with the dirty dishes. Erika glared at him, stood up, slid on her dark shades. She peered down at him, strolled to her El Dorado, grabbed the ticket off the windscreen, got in, and without even looking in her mirrors, Erika swung a squealing U-turn, causing motorists to brake, pedestrians to backpedal, and people to stare as she roared through a red light and off down Seventh Avenue. Danny smiled.

Balls, he thought.

# twenty-two

Danny had greeted about a dozen old men who'd missed the first night's wake. Now the mourners had dwindled to three dapper, elderly gents in the rear, whispering in a gnarled knot. Old-timers at wakes always reminded him of actors at dress rehearsals. By that standard Danny was auditioning. He was also exhausted. It had been a long day of reacquainting himself with the changed neighborhood and the players of the events of 1969.

He'd learned a lot. Not all of it made sense. But what he now knew told him there was something bigger he hadn't yet learned. As if a giant lid had been kept on this big old long-simmering soup pot of a neighborhood. It was a small town in a big city, filled with old, dangerous, and lousy family secrets. *The interlocking of people's lives in this neighborhood is so close, guarded, and sweaty that it borders on incest,* he thought.

Twenty minutes before closing, Eddie Fortune, BW, O'Toole, and Kenny Byrne drifted over from Foley's. They'd come to see if Brendan had made it back from Asia for the wake. Danny said he heard from Brendan and that he would be home for the funeral. They nodded and drifted up to the coffin to take turns making signs of the cross and saying silent prayers over Mickey Cassidy's body.

Eddie Fortune stood in the lobby with Danny, fresh beer on his breath, fire in his eyes. "Whadda you hear?"

"Nothing that adds up yet. I promise I'll let you know when I know."

"Thanks," Eddie Fortune said as he hurried from the funeral home.

BW, O'Toole, and Kenny Byrne walked to the lobby, fidgety with the absurd protocol of the ritual of the wake.

"I better get back to Jersey-ah, before my wife thinks I abandoned the family-ah," Byrne said. "She always feared that I'd stray back to the old neighborhood. But it just isn't what it used to be. Foley's is still the same, but everything else is gone-ah."

"Yeah," BW said. "If I didn't have a rent-controlled apartment I'd leave. I love the neighborhood, don't get me wrong, but I don't have anything in common with the new people moving in. My building is one of the last holdouts on the parkside."

"I left when mine went co-op," O'Toole said. "No way I was gonna stay and pay four hundred large for an apartment where I was paying $450 a month. I took the Christie Strong buyout, bought a whole house with a yard in Staten Island."

"But not all the other apartment buildings on Parkside West have gone condo, have they?" Danny asked.

"Every one except mine," BW said.

"Not the one Hippie Helen lives in," Danny said.

"Shit, that turned ten years ago," BW said.

"Who converted it?"

"Who else," said O'Toole. "Christie Strong. He owns most of them."

"Errr, if I had stayed-ah, I could've been Strong's main competition-ah," Kenny Byrne said. "But of course my wife thought I'd still be drinkin' every night-ah. I would have, too. I've been a friend of Bill's for thirteen years now-ah."

"Who the fuck is Bill?" O'Toole asked.

Danny knew he meant he was in Alcoholics Anonymous for thirteen years. Danny let this sink in with the other information he'd just learned. Christie Strong was Hippie Helen's landlord. She'd never mentioned it to Danny. Either that or she'd bought the condo herself. She's never mentioned that, either. But then again Danny hadn't asked. He'd just assumed her apartment was still rent-controlled.

"I know this is a shot in the deep dark past," Danny said, "but do any of you guys remember seeing me the night Boar's Head was murdered? November 20, 1969?"

"I was in the Fort Hamilton veteran's hospital," O'Toole said. "With encephalitis from a fucking mosquito bite I got in Nam."

"I was working that night," BW said. "I heard all about it in the morning. I remember seeing the aftermath of the other cop, Apeshape Davis, who killed himself when I got off the train. You were in Ankles's car."

"I was at a Doors concert at the Fillmore," Kenny Byrne said. "Smashed on uppies. I remember the whole neighborhood was talking about Boar's Head's murder when I got back around four-thirty in the morning."

"You were at the Doors concert, too, huh?" Danny said.

"Why, you were there?"

"No, I don't think so," Danny said. "That's the problem. I don't know where I was. Hippie Helen and Dirty Jim went, but they were back by like two-thirty, not four—"

"How the fuck could that be?" Kenny Byrne said.

"Whadda you mean?"

"I bought Hippie Helen's Doors tickets from her-ah," Byrne said. "Twenty fuckin' dollars she charged me, too-ah. Which was fuckin' highway robbery in those days-ah. But Bridget loved Jim Morrison. It was soldout. I thought if I bought Helen's tickets and brought Bridget she might drop her drawers and give me her cherry after staring at Jim Morrison's mahoska in those leather pants all night. But all I got was a dry-hump and a handsky in the vestibule. You know I never did get Bridget's cherry. She gave it to some 4-F Bath Beach ginzo when I was getting jungle rot in Da Nang. Cunt."

"You sure Hippie Helen and Dirty Jim didn't use those tickets?" Danny asked. "She still has the stubs?"

"Yeah, she made me promise to bring her back the stubs-ah," Byrne said. "She said she was a collector. That someday they'd be worth money-ah. Which they are. You could sell Jim Morrison's shit-stained Fruit of the Looms on E-bay."

The funeral director approached Danny, telling him it was nine P.M., closing time. She reminded him that there would be no wake on Sunday.

"I'm going back to Foley's," BW said.

"Me too," said O'Toole.

"Err, I'm headin' back to Jersey-ah," Byrne said. "I already spent two days in Brooklyn. I'll tell ya what, though. I might come back again tomorrow-ah. Bring my camera and some business cards. I'd like to cash in on this yuppie stampede myself-ah. I could give this Christie Strong a run for his moola. I know this neighborhood and I can sell. I'll undersell him, take five points from the sellers instead of six in the first year. These days you don't even need a storefront. All I need to do is advertise in the local papers and the *Times*, and have a phone, fax, and E-mail address."

BW and O'Toole shook Danny's hand, told him to let them know as soon as Brendan arrived. Danny promised and they headed off for Foley's.

"What time you coming in the morning?"

"Err, early," Byrne said. "Figure nine. I'll scope the whole neighborhood. Get a lay of the land. This is primo real estate now-ah. I can hand out my cards after mass. Leave some in all the candy stores, delis, and Foley's. Snap some pictures of some homes, write some letters asking people to call me if they ever want to sell."

"Can we meet at nine?" Danny asked. "I'd sort of like to confront Hippie Helen about those tickets you said you bought off her that night."

"No problem," Byrne said. "I remember that night like it was yesterday. Because I almost fuckin' died-ah."

"Really? How? Tell me about when you got back from the concert."

"I'll never forget," he said. "I was crashing on the uppies, and I went straight from the subway to walk Bridget home. We made out and dry-humped in her vestibule, she gave me the quick handsky. On the way back to Helen's pad I passed all the activity on Hippie Hill. Cop cars, crime-scene tape, and ambulances. Cops stood at the entrance to the park keeping everyone out. I went straight up to Helen's pad, to give her the ticket stubs. When I went up Dirty Jim was with her, and a few of Strong's dealers."

"Lefty Mots and Harry Bowles."

"Right-ah," Byrne said. "How'd you know? Anyway, she picked my brain about the concert, what time it started, what time it finished, what Morrison wore, what songs he did, whether or not he whipped out his mahoska and beat off, who sat next to us, the whole deal. I gave her the ticket stubs-ah. Mots and Bowles were staring out the window at the scene on the Hill, where Boar's Head was lying on the grass, cop cars everywhere. Dirty Jim had his camera with the big long fucking lens on this tripod by the window. Snapping pictures-ah. I had the uppie-crash jimjams. Helen told Lefty Mots to give me some Seconals to help me with the crash, zonk me to sleep. I swallowed three. I left. And on the way home they almost fucking killed me-ah. I wound up in Methodist Hospital. They were from a bad batch. Doctors said they were cut with fucking strychnine-ah. They pumped my stomach. My parents came. A month later I was in boot camp in Fort Benning, getting ready for Nam."

Danny stared at him, a cluster bomb of information exploding in his brain.

"Helen was with Dirty Jim in the neighborhood all night? And Dirty was taking pictures?"

"Yeah, wasn't he always-ah," Byrne said. "He sent me one in Nam of Bridget getting dicked by the guido from Bath Beach in his Lincoln in Prospect Park. Taken with infrared film. He robbed the film and the cameras from the police surveillance team with his keys. Dirty Jim has more keys than Rikers Island. Dirty Jim was a fucking ghoul-ah. Gave me the willies. When I was crashing on uppies I used to get paranoid and think he was gonna come into my house with his fucking keys-ah. There I am nine thousand miles away in Nam and Dirty Fuckin' Jim crawls out of an envelope with a photo of my girl who I never banged getting humped by a gindaloon with a Caesar haircut."

"Come with me right now and repeat this story to Helen and Dirty?"

"My fuckin' pleasure. But I don't have much time-ah. Take my car."

Danny hurried to Byrne's royal blue Lincoln Navigator and climbed into the soft leather bucket seat. He asked Byrne to drive straight to Hippie Helen's pad on Parkside West where Byrne double-parked. Danny rang Helen's bell. He hadn't called Helen first because he wanted to exploit the element of surprise. He rang again but there was no answer. He dialed her number on his cell phone. A machine answered. He hung up.

Byrne drove down to the Clubweb.com Inc. storefront on Eleventh Avenue but it was dark. He rang the bell, knocked on the window. No answer.

"The idea of Dirty Jim with a computer company is fucking terrifying-ah. He could transfer all my money into his off-shore account with one click of a mouse-ah."

"Can we meet 9 A.M. sharp?" Danny asked. "Right outside Helen's house?"

"Sure. But I gotta get going now before they shut down all but one lane on the Verrazano at ten, which could cost me an hour."

"Thanks for the info," Danny said.

"I'm looking forward to confronting Helen-ah. And I'd love to give Dirty Jim one good smack on general principle. By all rights, I should get half of whatever she sells those Doors stubs for. And I wanna check out the neighborhood some more, because I would take personal satisfaction out of outselling Christie Strong the old dope dealer whose strychnine Seconals almost killed me-ah."

He dropped Danny off near the Prospect Park parking lot. When

Danny hopped out he noticed that a silver Jaguar stopped a few car lengths away in a pool of wet shadow cast by a big elm. After saying good-bye, Danny slammed the Navigator door and Byrne sped away. The silver Jaguar with the tinted windows followed. Danny watched both cars loop around the traffic circle and then head down Fifteenth Road toward the Gowanus Expressway, which Byrne would take to the Verrazano Bridge and out to the outer-bridge crossing to New Jersey.

Danny walked to his rented Camry and climbed in. He looked up at Hippie Helen's window. A light went on. But it was too late. He wanted to confront her with Kenny Byrne.

*Lies,* he thought, yawning as he pulled out of the lot. *All I get are old lies.*

# twenty-three

A few minutes before ten P.M. Danny walked down the fifth-floor corridor of the Brooklyn Marriott, reviewing the day's events, passing a room-service waiter who waited for a door to be opened. During the morning run in Prospect Park, Horsecock had said to concentrate more on Jack Davis than Boar's Head, Danny thought, as he fished in his pockets for his computer key card. In a drunken afterthought Horsecock called to say he was ready to reveal Linc's identity. Then he wound up dead. Then Hippie Helen claimed she was at a Doors concert with Dirty Jim in Manhattan at the time of Boar's Head's murder. Which Kenny Byrne says was horseshit.

He stopped, patted all his pockets, located the key card in his back pants pocket, and walked toward the end of the corridor, where a hotel worker stood on a stepladder, changing a fluorescent light rod. *Erika, the woman I think I've loved all my life, has some kind of creepy relationship with Christie Strong,* Danny thought. *Dirty Jim Dugan talked about living in fear of going back to jail and how Christie Strong could have him sent there with a single phone call. Then Strong threatens me if I dare interfere with his life. I find out Hippie Helen has AIDS and might be a schizo. And according to Kenny Byrne she's also a fucking liar.*

The big hotel worker up on the stepladder removed the bulb, casting the end of the corridor into half gloom. Even in the low light Danny now noticed something wrong with the picture. *Wait a minute, what custodian wears silver-toed cowboy boots with coveralls?*

He paused, squinted for a better look, was about to turn to the smaller room-service waiter when the first blow landed square in the middle of Danny's back, a thundering punch that blew all the air out of his lungs. It buckled his knees, made him think of his mother singing "The Blue Danube" as she ironed. He turned toward the attacker and the big guy on the stepladder smashed the fluorescent bulb across Danny's face, the popping glass and the gas in the tube blurring his vision. Danny swung a right hand, but it hit the stepladder and he caught a right hand square in the jaw from the big guy. Danny was slammed against his hotel-room door. He fell to all fours. Danny started to rise when the big guy grabbed his arms from behind. Through the blood and the haze he noticed the small room-service waiter approaching, brandishing something.

"Stick the fucking needle in and let's go," said the big guy, his Russian accent almost as strong as his grip. Danny took a deep breath. Concentrated. Then rammed the big guy against the door. He heard an *ughnn*. He braced himself for leverage, thrust his legs outward, trying to kick the syringe out of the smaller black man's hands.

He missed.

Danny kept kicking, the only thing he could do to keep from getting jabbed with the needle. The big guy let loose one of his arms, chopped Danny in the throat. Danny gagged but used the opportunity to wriggle his mouth onto the big guy's other hand. He bit down so hard on the big guy's thumb knuckle Danny thought his teeth would meet. The big man screamed. Doors opened. Then he heard a woman's voice.

"Freeze!"

Pat O'Rourke training her 9-mm NYPD-issue automatic. Danny stopped biting. The big guy stood shaking his hand. O'Rourke walked closer.

"Watch it," Danny screamed.

But the little black guy spun from his room-service cart like a fighter coming off the ropes, hurling a plate of steaming linguini with red clam sauce into O'Rourke's face. She screamed as the big guy backhanded her across the side of her head with his bleeding hand. Danny heard the thud. O'Rourke dropped straight down, the gun plopping from her small hand. Unfired. The big man yanked the stepladder down on top of her. Danny managed to land one good right hand onto the big man's cheek. The big Russian countered with a hook to Danny's belly, then lurched across the corridor, banged the panic bar of the exit door, and raced down the stairs. The small guy followed him.

O'Rourke pushed off the stepladder, got to her feet, and did a little crazy dance as she tried to get the clam sauce out of her eyes. Danny grabbed a bucket of ice from the room-service tray, and dashed it into O'Rourke face. She snatched up her gun.

"Holy shit," she said, holding the side of her wet skull. "I never got hit by a man in my life. When I do I pick a fucking monster."

Danny panted, blood trickling from a small cut over his left eye. His body aching. He wrapped some of the ice in a linen napkin and handed it to her. He made a second press for himself.

"Who were those guys?" she asked, wiping red clam sauce off her white jacket and white pants, pulling linguini out of her hair.

"Keep the ice on your skin so you won't blister," he said.

"Nothing from room service is ever as hot as it should be. Thank God."

He knew who the attackers were. He thought she should have, too.

"You didn't recognize them?" Danny asked.

"It was dark."

"Yeah."

"They had this thought out," she said. "They came with coveralls and a room-service uniform. Probably checked into a room under some bullshit name, ordered room service, then used it as a prop. It's an old hotel burglar's gimmick. You can go in and out of rooms unsuspected."

"Who knew where I was staying? Besides you? Ankles and—"

"Your girlfriend."

"You don't like Erika much, do you?"

"She likes herself so much I wouldn't want to get in her way."

Danny saw her wobble a few steps, grabbing her head. "I'll call the cops."

"No!" she said. "I am the cops. No shots fired, no incident. Unless you insist on reporting it. But I better go."

"You can't drive," he said. "Come on into my room. Wash up."

She looked at him, smiled, and cocked her head. "I need clean clothes," she said. "I better go. If someone else called the cops and they come, I'll have too much embarrassing explaining to do. You have me in a compromising position here."

She took a step toward the fire exit, wobbled again.

"I'll drive you home," he said.

"I'd like that."

Danny drove her green Crown Vic along the Gowanus Expressway until they hit a snarl of traffic near Thirty-sixth Street, red brake lights backed up for miles. The police radio crackled, saying there was a major accident up ahead. "We got a DWI DOA ready for KCH here," Danny heard a highway cop tell a dispatcher, which O'Rourke told him meant a drunk driver ready for the Kings County Hospital morgue.

"This is an hour jam, at least," O'Rourke said, slamming her cherry light on the roof and beeping her siren, making cars inch out of their way. Danny never enjoyed that kind of power in a car before, watching traffic part just for him. O'Rourke told him to make a U-turn at a break in the divider up ahead. Danny made the turn, O'Rourke put on the siren again, and traffic in the other lane slowed to a stop as Danny sped for the Thirty-sixth Street exit. He took Third Avenue out to Bay Ridge. He slowed down when he passed the vestibule on Third Avenue where he'd beaten Lars Andersen all those years ago. O'Rourke saw him staring at the building. The Andersen deli was now a tanning parlor.

"What are you gaping at?" she asked.

"Nothing," Danny said.

"Before your bashful girlfriend dive-bombed into our table this evening, you were going to tell me about Henry Bush and Lars Andersen," she said.

*Eerie*, he thought. *How'd she know I was thinking of Andersen?* Did she know Andersen used to live there? Maybe he told her. "Did you ask him about it on your date?"

She looked at him, pulled away. He glanced over at her. Even stained with red clam sauce, linguini threading in her hair, she was stunning. She laughed.

"You think I'm dating Lars Andersen?"

"You mean good-looking, well-groomed, well-mannered Lars?"

"Believe me, even if . . . he's not my type."

"What's your type?"

She just looked at him, said nothing, let the silence answer for her. The smell of fresh red clam sauce filled the air as she said, "Make the next right to Shore Road."

"Shore Road was expensive when I was a kid," he said. "Today—"

"Rent-stabilized. But it has a garage."

She directed him to her underground garage, clicked the remote control, and they parked. They rode the elevator up together in silence. It stopped in the lobby and two couples got on together. They looked at Danny with the cuts on his face and at O'Rourke covered in linguini with red clam sauce.

"We have to try that restaurant again," Danny said, picking a piece of linguini from her hair and nibbling it.

The couples looked at each other, an awkward silence bubbling in the small lift.

"Maybe next time we won't have to fight for a table," O'Rourke said as Danny finger-fed her some of the linguini.

The two couples exited on the fifth floor, buzzing and murmuring as the elevator doors closed. Danny and O'Rourke laughed. Then they looked into each other's eyes.

"My 'type' is a good-looking mature man with a surreal sense of humor," she said, leading him off the elevator on the ninth floor. She opened the Medeco lock.

They entered the studio apartment, and Danny could smell the cat right away, a long-haired black-and-white ball of fur that looked like a muff with paws. The cat meowed until O'Rourke picked her up, snuggled her, kissed her. "How's my Zsa Zsa?" she said. The cat licked the clam bits in her hair.

"Want a beer?"

"Why not?"

She walked to the kitchenette while he glanced around the studio apartment. The walls were covered with framed impressionist prints—Matisse, Pissarro, Monet. An oval rug lay in the center of a parquet floor, with an elaborate stainless-steel and glass entertainment center stacked with big-screen TV, stereo, DVDs, CDs, and videos and a collection of books. A lot of the books were true-crime paperbacks, stories about serial killers, kidnappers, sexual predators, and swindlers. And a bunch of books on the sixties like Abbie Hoffman's *Steal This Book, Soul on Ice,* by Eldridge Cleaver, *Seize the Time,* by Bobby Seale, *Miami and the Siege of Chicago,* by Norman Mailer. It looked like she'd taken a college course on the sixties. Danny lifted Mailer's book off the shelf and saw a bookmark from the College of Staten Island.

He placed the book back on the shelf, turned, saw Zsa Zsa the cat parade from the expensive futon shoved against a long flat wall to an end table with drawers and a plain white lamp. An old leather steamer trunk served as a coffee table. The Roman numerals on the brass clock with rotating globes said it was 10:45. Blue drapes were tied back to reveal a big bay window that looked out on the dark glistening Narrows, and the brilliant Verrazano Bridge and the sleepy dark mass that was Staten Island. When Danny looked right the Manhattan skyline glowed like a constellation of human hope.

O'Rourke lived the way she dressed—comfortable, Spartan, spotless. She carried in two bottles of Beck's, handed one to Danny, clinked her bottle against his, and washed down three Tylenol with a big gulp of beer. She walked to the stereo, put on Jimmy Buffet's greatest hits CD, and switched on the Mets game with the sound turned down. They were losing to the Dodgers 4 to 3 in the top of the second inning from the left coast.

"Goddamned Mets're the same as most men. They steal your heart and strike out in the clutch. You'll have to excuse me while I take a fast shower."

"Take your time."

"You can take one after me unless. . . ."

"Unless what?" He smiled.

"Unless you want to take one . . . first."

"It's OK."

"Make yourself at home," she said.

She walked to a hall closet that had been subdivided with neat wire racks, utilizing every inch of space in the most economical fashion. She snatched a pair of panties and a few clothes and disappeared into the bathroom.

As soon as he heard the hiss of the shower Danny began to search the apartment. He pulled open the drawers of the end table. They were filled with takeout menus from local restaurants, TV and video remotes, matches and disposable lighters. He opened up the steamer trunk that was filled with old magazines, photo albums, and a high school yearbook. He didn't know what he was looking for but nothing there caught his attention yet. He peered into her hall closet but it was filled with clothes, most of it off-the-rack stuff within a single cop's budget.

The kitchen was sparse. The fridge contained a few beers, three Diet Cokes, and a container of Skim Plus. Not even mustard or mayonnaise. The fruit and vegetable drawers were empty, the warrantee and instruction booklet for the fridge still in one drawer. He looked in the freezer and saw three plastic ice trays, all full. The silverware drawer had three knives, forks, and spoons. Three mugs, three plates, three bowls, and six glasses sat in a cabinet, the kind of stuff you win at a church bazaar. The junk drawer consisted of matches from every bar in Bay Ridge and some more takeout menus. The food cabinet had a dozen cans of cat food, a box of Equal, a jar of Folgers instant coffee, and a box of Red Rose tea. Nothing else. He'd seen better-stocked motel rooms.

The stove was spotless, as if O'Rourke had never cooked here. He leaned closer, sniffing for signs of garlic or roasts. Nothing. He opened the oven door, looked in. Spotless, never used. He was about to walk out of the kitchen when he pulled out the broiler drawer and was about to close it when he saw the corner of brown cardboard peeking out from under the broiler pan. He reached under the broiler pan and in the space between the pan and the bottom of the drawer he discovered a brown cardboard portfolio.

He slid it out, listened to O'Rourke sing "Margaritaville," imagining the suds drooling down over her plump breasts, over the wet round pink behind, and converging into the girlie-soap-scented bush. *Concentrate, asshole,* he thought.

He rummaged through the portfolio. He found a fax copy of an NYPD file on Anthony Tufano, with a "do not copy" stamped right across page one. The phone number of origin was listed as Internal Affairs Bureau with a 212 area code. O'Rourke had pulled Ankles's file and faxed it to herself at home, a clever way of smuggling it out of the IAB office. There was another file folder all about Danny, filled with tax records, credit card information, his daughter's grades from Harvard, a copy of his divorce papers, old telephone bills with circled phone numbers of women he'd forgotten he'd ever dated. There was also a file with medical records on his father and information on his brother, Brendan.

O'Rourke didn't miss a trick, he thought.

Danny wasn't surprised so much as he was unnerved. The stuff about his daughter infuriated him. The old girlfriend stuff was just invasive and lame, because she wouldn't learn anything from any of them.

He found a third file on Erika Malone and one on Vito Malone and another on Jack Davis. The Davis file was the thickest, and he remembered that Horsecock had said that Davis might be the answer to this whole mess.

He also found Jack Davis's logbook from 1969, the one everybody said had disappeared. Danny heard O'Rourke sing, "But it's a real beauty, a Mexican cutie . . ." as the water hissed and gurgled in the drain. He leafed through the logbook. The July 20 entry said he had picked up "CI LA for questioning, while VM was with CI LINC." Danny flicked ahead to November 20 and 21. It showed that "VM went to meet CI LINC" while Davis again "picked up CI LA for questioning."

Danny wondered about the identity of this confidential informant named LA. Could it have been Lars Andersen? People on the Hill used to think Lars was a snitch. A few people said they'd seen Lars get into Boar's Head and Apeshape's green Plymouth Fury narc car a few times. When challenged about it, Lars always told everyone that the narcs would take him for rides, trying to get him to talk about who was dealing or getting high. But Lars always said he didn't know because he didn't use drugs. Which was true. Which was also why no one ever trusted him. He wasn't a "head." Which is why Erika said she went out with him when Danny became strung out.

Danny flipped through the pages. He realized that this CI LA was all over Davis's book. He seemed to meet him every Thursday night at eight P.M. Davis and CI LA would rendezvous in Evergreen Cemetery. "While VM on meal, I gleaned drug traffic info from CI LA," or "while VM meeting with CI LINC, I gleaned drug traffic info from CI LA" was how Davis always accounted for that hour every Thursday.

*Always while VM was on meal,* Danny thought. *Or with CI Linc.*

The final logbook entry was on November 21. "Ankles calls. Says VM murdered. On Hippie Hill. Wants to know my whereabouts on 11/21/69 at 200 hrs. I'm in box between kid and Ankles. Maybe no way out. . . ."

Jammed after the final entry of the logbook Danny found a sheet of yellow legal-pad paper with a woman's handwriting. It looked like a note to herself, a hypothesis to work on. It wasn't meant for anyone else's eyes but her own. "Tufano and Cassidy conspired to frame Davis for Wally Fortune murder? Cassidy kid afraid to implicate Vito Malone for Wally Fortune murder out of fear of losing his girlfriend, Erika Malone? Tufano afraid of losing gold shield going over head of Henry Bush to go after Vito Malone? All of them terrified of Christie Strong for some reason? So they all conspired to make Jack Davis take fall? Once set up, Davis saw no way out except suicide? Maybe time to put Tufano and Cassidy in same squeeze as Davis. Work one against the other?"

Danny heard the shower turn off. He took the information on his daughter, folded it, and stuck it into his back pocket. He put everything else back under the never-used broiler pan. He now knew where it was when he wanted it.

He walked back into the living room. The cat hopped up on his lap. He petted it and sneezed, which startled the cat, making it run away. Danny knew O'Rourke was drying herself now, rubbing silky scented lotions all over her body, towel-drying and wrapping her hair, doing all the girlie things that always took so fucking long when he lived with his wife and daughter but now that he was single he missed so much.

He opened the steamer trunk again and took out a photo album. He leafed through it. There were pictures of O'Rourke with friends. One with a guy who looked like a brother. Another with a guy with his arm around her shoulder, and in which she wore a wedding ring. There were photos of O'Rourke from the police academy, young and gorgeous. Some high school shots with girlfriends. And then at the back of the album he saw a photo that made his heart jump and the hair on his neck rise.

It was a photo of a young couple with their two kids, a boy and a girl. The girl seemed to be about five. The boy about four. The second Danny looked at them he knew they were the same kids that he saw in the powder blue station wagon back on the morning of November 21, 1969, when the man in the picture blew out his brains. The mother looked a lot like what Pat O'Rourke looked like now. This was why she had looked familiar to Danny when he first laid eyes on her in the funeral parlor the night before.

Danny stuffed the photo album back in the steamer trunk, closed it, and took a long drink of the bitter beer. His hands trembled.

*Pat O'Rourke is Jack Davis's daughter,* he thought. *Holy shit. . . .*

He lifted the phone, called information, asked for the number of the Bay Ridge car service, ordered a car. Three minutes later the bathroom door opened and O'Rourke stepped out in a swirl of steam, her hair wet and wild, her hot pink skin scrubbed clean. She wore a pair of skintight white shorts, red clogs, and a small white blouse. She wore no bra, her nipples almost visible through her damp sheer blouse.

"Want another beer?" she asked.

"I'm fine," he said, looking at her with a brand-new lens, a woman also haunted by that very same day in 1969, now investigating it as a thirty-seven-year-old cold-case cop.

"What's up with the Mets?"

"I wasn't paying attention."

"You want to have your shower?"

She walked to him, shaking her hair, her breasts swaying under the blouse, her shorts clinging to all the indentations of her tight body. She looked him in the eye, grabbed a Kleenex from a box on an end table, dabbing the small cut above his eye.

"I'm allergic to cats," he said, sneezing. "I should probably go."

She seemed disappointed. "I thought I could order some Chinese," she said. "We could, ya know, talk. Or whatever."

"I think I should go. I'm exhausted. I have a ton to do tomorrow."

He walked toward the door. She stepped in front of him. She shifted her weight on one foot in a submissive kind of way, like an invitation.

"I didn't say I had a date tonight," she said. "I said I had to see somebody. I did. Then I came looking for you. On my night off."

"Why?"

"I think you know why."

She dabbed his eye again. He also knew she was trying to put him in a squeeze, the same one she thought Danny had put her father in. Treacherous chick, he thought. Be careful. . . .

"I think you're on a mission," he said. "So am I. Both of us would do almost anything to get the answers we want. But let's not do something we'll regret."

She nodded, unlocked and opened the door. "You love her, don't you?"

"I don't know," he said. "That's another thing I'm trying to find out."

# twenty-four

Danny sat in the back of the Shore Road car service station wagon on the Gowanus Expressway as traffic slowed to rubberneck the accident on the other side of the traffic divider. It was the same accident that Danny had avoided on the way out. He checked his watch: 11:16. He was exhausted.

"Focking roober knockers," the Russian driver complained, gaping at the accident. It took Danny a few seconds to realize he was complaining about rubberneckers. As they approached the twirling lights of the police, ambulances, and tow trucks, Danny glanced over with ghoulish curiosity. And his heart leaped. He saw two things that made the bile start to rise. He reached for the Rolaids when he saw a royal blue Lincoln Navigator with Jersey plates crunched up like a big metal fist. He searched for the Zantac when he saw the big cop with the fedora gaping at the face of a corpse under a gurney sheet.

"Stop!" Danny said, spearing a twenty-dollar bill over the backseat to the Russian driver.

"Focking crazy?"

The car kept moving in a stop-and-go stagger. Danny pulled up the door handle. The driver slammed the brakes. "Focking scrowball!"

Danny exited the car and climbed over the steel divider and walked toward the accident scene, past the red flares and the orange traffic cones. A uniformed cop rushed to him.

"Hey, asshole, where the fuck you think you're going?"

"I think I know the driver of that car. . . ."

Ankles looked over at Danny and signaled for the uniformed cop to let Danny through. Danny walked to Ankles, who grabbed his arm and led him to the gurney and lifted the sheet. Kenny Byrne's face was almost unrecognizable. Rubies of bloody glass encrusted his forehead, the bridge of his nose, and his chin, shimmering in the swirling emergency lights. His cheekbones had vanished beneath piles of exposed bloody flesh where the epidermis was sheered off. The smell of excrement, urine, vomit, and whiskey reeked from his flesh and his clothes.

"Your friend Kenny Byrne, ain't it? Least that's what his license says."

Danny nodded, taking short breaths to fight back the nausea as the EMS crew loaded Kenny Byrne into the back of their ambulance. Behind them a tow truck hoisted the blue Navigator onto a flat bed truck as frustrated drivers stood outside of their cars for as far as Danny could see.

"I was with Kenny Byrne until about nine-fifteen," Danny said, his guts churning and his mouth watery. He gripped his chest.

"Then you must have seen him piss-the-pants drunk."

"He didn't drink."

"Well he musta chugalugged a fifth of Dewar's after he left you."

"Kenny Byrne was in AA. Sober for thirteen years."

"An unlucky number," Ankles said. "I know guys sober twenty years who get four flats on their milk wagon over a broad. Or a pink slip."

"He was on his way home to his family in Ramsey, New Jersey. Byrne raved about his wife and kids. He had a successful business. I left him sober just before this happened. But I did see a silver Jaguar following him."

"Did you get a plate number?"

"I couldn't find my glasses in time," Danny said. "It was dark."

Danny raked his fingers through his salt-and-pepper hair, walked in a tight little circle. He chewed three Rolaids and swallowed a Zantac. The pill lodged halfway down. He felt sweat burst through his skin like a lawn sprinkler set on a stress-triggered timer. His shirt clung to his back and chest. He was certain that poor Kenny Byrne had been killed because he screwed up Hippie Helen's and Dirty Jim's alibi for the night Vito Malone was murdered.

As he watched the ambulance containing Kenny Byrne's dead body whisk away, lights flashing but no siren, Danny decided to level with Ankles about a few things.

"Get in my car and I'll take you to your hotel," Ankles said.

They climbed in the black Taurus and Ankles put the bubble flasher on the roof, drove down to the break in the divider, and crossed over into downtown traffic. He took the bubble flasher off the roof and eased into the ballet of traffic.

"OK, what about this attack?" Ankles said.

Danny told him about the big Russian and the small black guy. Even in the darkened hotel corridor, he was sure they were the guys who worked for Christie Strong.

"But because you're too fucking cheap or lazy or conceited to get a pair of prescription cheaters," Ankles said, "you can't say what the fuck you saw, never mind who the fuck you saw."

"It was them. The silver-toed boots. Plus, I bit the guy."

"The bite mark is a possibility, if we can find this pirogi. My guess he's on his way to Leningrad to heal with straight vodka and blond pussy. And fuck the boots, will ya? That's a worthless ID. 'I got a suspect in a cop murder, boss, who wants to ID a pair of muggers by one skell's boots. And he has a corroborating witness who saw everything, through a plate of linguini with red clam sauce. Oh, and she's a cop but she didn't think it was important enough to report it at the time of occurrence.' I couldn't sell that to my boss if I had it delivered on a silver platter by Sharon Stone. Naked. Tell me again what you saw in this smart mouth O'Rourke's place."

He told him about the files on Ankles and himself, on his father, his kid, his ex-wife, and Erika and Vito Malone.

He also told him about the discovery of and entries in Jack Davis's logbook. And about the photo in the album and his suspicions that O'Rourke was Davis's daughter.

"Jesus, Joseph, and Mary, the plot sickens," Ankles said. "If she is Davis's daughter, she shouldn't be working this fuckin' case. Conflict of interest. I have to look into all this shit. That logbook is evidence in a murder investigation. I never laid eyes on this fucking logbook. I've been looking for it since the day Davis shot himself. If she's his daughter it would make sense that she found it."

Ankles veered toward the ramp to the Brooklyn Queens Expressway, getting clogged in downtown bridge and tunnel traffic.

"There was also a note that looks like she made to herself jammed into the logbook," Danny said. "It suggested that she thinks me, you, and Horsecock conspired to make Davis take a fall for Wally Fortune. And then for Vito Malone's murder. She more or less holds us responsible for making her father eat his gun. She wants to set us up, the way she thinks we set up her father."

"She might think I was strong-arming you into perjuring yourself against Davis," Ankles said. "She knows how some cops operate."

"I don't think she's looking to solve the murders for the sake of the murders," Danny said. "I think Patricia O'Rourke is on a mission to clear her father's name. To free the ghost that's been haunting her all this time. I know that ghost. I bet she relives the horror. And the shame. Has recurring nightmares. A life without anyone to draw a card for on Father's Day and watching her mother scrounge to make ends meet after Davis died. Counseling, therapy, a very sad fucking life. And now she's decided to get even with the people who she thinks framed him. She has a personal agenda."

"Don't we all," Ankles said. "That neighborhood has more strange bedfellows than the mountains of Appalachia. You wouldn't believe the family secrets I've uncovered over the years. A lot of them led to murder. Every family in Parkside Gardens has its twisted little secrets."

"You had one of your own," Danny said. "How is Marsha anyway?"

Ankles stared at him for a long moment, trying to see if Danny was being disrespectful. He wasn't. "Good and bad days," he said. "Yesterday was bad. Today's better, knock wood. But every day she's still here is a good day for me."

"You gonna be able to get a warrant on a holiday weekend?"

"Sure, half the judges live down Breezy Point. They'll all be at the Mardi Gras, getting stewed, playing judicial ass grab. The reason they wear robes is so they can stroke their hard dicks as they play God. But before we do anything else I need to check out a few things in the PD. First, I gotta make sure O'Rourke is Jack Davis's kid."

"I don't want to get her in trouble."

"No, you wanna get in her fuckin' pants."

"Who wouldn't? But if she's Davis's kid, remember she witnessed her father blowing his brains out that morning. It was awful enough for you and me. Imagine what it was like for a five-year-old daughter. I'd go easy on her. She's a victim here, too."

Ankles glanced over at him as they hit a pocket of traffic. Danny studied him, the old cop's eyes weary from a lifetime of dead bodies, one of them his own murdered son.

"Yeah," Ankles said. "I'll never forget that kid. She was hysterical. The mother was worse. Her brother was cold, like in shock."

"Maybe we should talk to them," Danny said.

"I'll find out where they are," Ankles said. "They have this computer now, it's called a Carr's computer. It can pinpoint the last place you stepped in dog shit."

"While you're at it, can you check out a few other things on other people?"

"Sure. Who?"

"Do you know where Christie Strong comes from?"

"Hell's subbasement," Ankles said. "Other than that, no. I don't know where he came from. In the sixties so many people came from all over the place to hang out on Hippie Hill you didn't question it. If I had Social Security numbers I could find their life history in five minutes. But I never actually arrested him."

"Find out everything you can," Danny said. "Same with Helen Grabowski. They had to come from somewhere. She always said she came from 'America.' Whatever that meant. Said her hometown was famous for insurance and Johnny Carson."

"Carson's from Nebraska, I think," Ankles said.

"I did a long piece on him when he left the *Tonight Show*," Danny said. "Actually he was born in Iowa, raised in Nebraska, got his showbiz start in Lincoln."

They looked at each other. "The missing *Linc,*" Ankles said. "Nah. Ya think?"

"Possibility. Are we gonna work this together?"

"I made you a gesture this afternoon, and you made one back tonight. I'll never be your partner. But we've been in this together since we stood on that dirty fucking mud pile called Hippie Hill thirty-two years ago."

Danny sighed and said, "So much wasted time."

"Know what I hate most about getting old?"

"Pissing every five minutes?"

"No, not being able to kick fuckin' ass like I used to. Nowadays I lose my breath after thirty seconds. I throw my knee out kicking. My big toe swells. My joints get stiff when I smack someone too hard."

"Yeah, having to use your brain must be a real pain in the colostomy bag, huh?"

"Your shit for brains sure helped out your friend Kenny Byrne."

"The way you helped Horsecock?"

Ankles nodded and sighed. "Speaking of which," Ankles said. "I found out about Byrne when I got a call from pathology at KCH on Horsecock. Poor old fuck did die from strychnine poisoning. They found a needle hole in Horsecock's upper thigh. He had over two hundred milligrams in him. Enough to kill a horse, excuse the pun. They say it looks like some of it was ingested, like someone spiked his whiskey in Foley's. He woulda gone through a period of restlessness, apprehension, exaggerated reflexes."

"He was all souped up when he called my voice mail from Foley's," Danny said. "Yammering a mile a minute about Linc, how he had to see me. But someone was trying to get him out of the damned phone booth. JoJo Corcoran told me old Henry was all agitated when he saw him talking to Andersen in the park earlier, too, and—"

"I'm gonna pretend I didn't hear that. I'm talking serious business here—M-U-R-D-E-R—and you're talking JoJo Corcoran?" Ankles said, as he exited at Cadman Plaza into Downtown Brooklyn. "Please, if not for me, have some respect for the dead. JoJo Corcoran, boots, broad cops who don't report attacks—no wonder you're as poor as me."

"Finish what you were saying," Danny said.

"The ME says the killer underestimated just how strong this old guy was. Had a heart like a thoroughbred. The dose they gave him in his drink wasn't enough to kill him. So they jabbed him with a needle. About a half hour after that they figured he woulda thrown his first conniption. Then a coupla convulsions, real shit fits with his eyes bulgin,' his back archin,' turnin' blue, and then the poor old bastard suffocated to death, his jaws clenched with that big twat-eatin' grin on his face."

Danny reminded Ankles that the two attackers earlier in the night had also tried to inject him with a needle. He shivered. Ankles took Tillary Street up to Adams Streets and made a right toward Danny's hotel.

"Do you have any doubts about who was behind all this?"

"I have doubts about everybody," Ankles said. "I don't need a cane, a shepherd, and a tin cup. But I don't want anyone else to know what we know. Not yet."

Danny repeated that JoJo Corcoran had seen Andersen with Horsecock before he died.

"How can you offer me JoJo Corcoran as a witness?" Ankles said. "His fucking brains belong under glass in the Museum of Natural History. The Feds send him a wacko pension every month. You put a guy nuts on paper on a fuckin' witness stand, you need more help than him."

"JoJo's got a photographic memory. He sees things. He remembers things."

"Sure he does. Problem is most of them never happened. Except inside his fuckin' head, which looks like Woodstock the day after everyone went home."

"I believe he saw Andersen and Horsecock. I also think the confidential informant Jack Davis met every Thursday night in Evergreen Cemetery was Lars Andersen."

"It could also be Lonnie Andersen with the cement tits. Or Lick-Ass McNamara. Or Luke Asteroid from your *Star Wars* show, or Lou Abbot or anyone else with the initials L.A. Maybe it's a center from the Los Angeles Lakers or a dwarf from Louisiana. CI's have initials for a reason. So only you know who they are."

"I think LA was Lars Andersen. And I think Linc might be Helen Grabowski from Lincoln, Nebraska. The same way you were sure who the initials in my journal belonged to. And didn't you tell me that commanding officers often demanded to know who the CI's were? The way editors often ask you who your secret sources are? The way the editor of the *Washington Post* knew all along who Deep Throat was?"

"Yeah, a lot of times they did ask who the CI's are before they sign the logbook. So?"

"So, if he was trying to account for Davis's time, wouldn't old Henry Bush have demanded to know the identity of this CI initialed LA that Jack Davis saw every Thursday like clockwork?" Danny asked. "And maybe he would have mentioned who it was in his own logs."

"Maybe. OK, so I'll check Horsecock's logs. But don't get your hopes up because he never says who Linc is, just that he knows who he is."

"But Horsecock told me that Davis was the key to the whole thing."

"I get your point," he said, doing an illegal U-turn on Adams and pulling up in front of the hotel. "You don't have to sell me a half-good idea twice just to prove you're a fuckin' genius."

Ankles parked in the traffic circle in front of the Marriott. Danny reached in his pocket and pulled out Horsecock's old check stubs with the garnishees and the other checks written and mailed to the Court Street lawyer named Marvin Levy.

"You were holding out on me, you prick," Ankles said, snatching the check stubs and the canceled checks. "These have court docket numbers on them. I can open any file on anyone in a murder investigation, day, night, holiday weekend. Why the fuck are you holding out on me? I took you into Horsecock's pad. I trusted you. You don't trust me?"

"I needed time to think," Danny said. "My ass is on the line here.

You're the cop who's haunted me for thirty years, trying to put me in a cage. Now I know there's another cop trying to make us fucking roommates. That makes me trust you a little more. So I'm giving you what I got."

He fell silent for a moment, as Ankles studied the check stubs and the court docket numbers. The first drops of rain began to speckle the part of the sidewalk not shielded by the hotel marquee.

"This is not just about thirty-two years ago anymore, Ankles," Danny said. "This fucking monster Christie Strong is killing people again, in the here and now. Still getting away with murder."

Ankles said nothing, just stared ahead at the rain as it fell on the Brooklyn Bridge.

"Not for long," Ankles said, nodding toward the building next to Danny's hotel where the Brooklyn DA's office was located. "I got an all-night shitload of computer searching to do. Meet me at noon tomorrow. I'll be in Evergreen, just south of the Twentieth Place gates, on the little hill overlooking the neighborhood."

"I know where it is," Danny said.

# twenty-five

He waited until Ankles left and then Danny got his car out of the garage. He had little time to waste. He called the Strong Arms and asked if Christy Strong was there. The French maître d' said he was but couldn't come to the phone at the moment. Danny disconnected and ramped onto the Gowanus Expressway at Atlantic Avenue and drove toward the Prospect Expressway as rain pelted the city, lightning cracking over the roiled harbor, thunder bellowing across the borough of Brooklyn.

He thought of poor old Henry Bush, locked in a cold morgue drawer in KCH, his life breath sucked from him after talking to Danny. And Kenny Byrne, whose wife and kids at that moment would be drowning in anguish, also after speaking to Danny.

*I'm the kiss of death,* he thought. *Wherever I turn people die. I hurt good people. If I had not come back, these people might be alive.*

He turned on 88 WCBS, the all-news station, and with a confident voice, a newscaster named Debbie Rodriguez said the big storm was the top story. There was no mention of Henry Bush, an eighty-one-year-old man who had been poisoned. Kenny Byrne was just another drunk driver who wasn't worth a mention. But the newscaster said the storm would last through the night and all the next day, dropping some four inches of rain on the metropolitan area.

Danny peered through the slurping wipers, his blood wailing for a cigarette, or sweets to replace the craving. He had wanted to quit for twenty-five years and now Erika Malone had started him on a painful cold-turkey withdrawal just as he was doing a reentry into his old life on his old turf about an old murder that had shadowed him through his forties. He thought for a moment that it might not be a good time to quit. But it served as a perfect reminder that he was here to save his own life. He couldn't even waste the minutes between cravings. Every time he yearned for a smoke, he should be learning something new. Every minute counted. He had things to learn, people to see, lies to uncover, secrets to expose, wrongs to right.

He ate two Certs breath mints, the sweetness distracting him from tobacco.

He was still smarting over Brendan's arctic E-mail. Danny wondered if the coldness and the decades-long silence was his big brother's way of severing ties with a cheap killer who just happened to be kin. Did Brendan know something he'd never said about that night? After seeing all the death in Nam, did it sicken Brendan to return home to find out that his kid brother had become a two-bit speed-freak murderer? Is that why Brendan had not answered so many letters over the years? Why he hadn't returned phone calls and E-mails? Keeping continents, cultures, and oceans between them? Christ, the Unabomber's brother had turned him in, Danny thought. And there was a story on the AP wire not long ago about a bank robber in Queens who had recognized a photo of his brother in a bank surveillance photo that had been published in the New York *Daily News* and dimed on him for the $10,000 reward. Down in Delaware a local assistant district attorney who'd killed his wife was convicted without a body on the testimony of his brother.

So after learning that his brother was a common killer, why wouldn't Brendan just decide that Danny didn't exist? Edit him out of his life? And maybe Brendan's silence was more of a blessing for Danny than a curse. If Brendan ever really broke his silence maybe it would put Danny in a cage. Every time he began to believe he was innocent, doubt and dread rose in him. He needed proof of his innocence. For himself as much as for Ankles or O'Rourke. He needed a real answer.

Danny passed the Red Hook piers, most abandoned but some being converted into harborside plazas with new bistros and cafés that had replaced the bucket-of-blood longshoreman's saloons.

He veered onto the Prospect Expressway and exited at the first exit and made a pair of rights toward the Strong Arms as his mind drifted to Darlene. *Jesus Christ,* he thought. *What if Pat O'Rourke or Ankles decide they have enough to make a sale to the DA to have me indicted? Will Darlene take my phone call? Will she come to the trial? Will she support me? Believe in my innocence? Or will she look at me as if I have abandoned her again? A final disappointment in a long line of let downs and dropped balls as a failed father?* He wondered if she would return his mail from prison. *Would she visit me? Maybe it's better that she doesn't see me in jail. . . .*

He wondered what Tammy was doing at that moment, who she

was with, whether or not she was laughing and happy. He hoped she was. He envied the guy—whoever he was—who'd won her heart. Tammy was better off with anyone but Danny. *I wish I'd never left her*, he thought.

Instead he was here, in Brooklyn, three decades back in time, turning old stones and finding fresh bodies.

He dialed his hotel from his cell phone and was connected to his voice messages. There was only one and he hoped it was from Darlene. "Danny, Brendan here. I got your E-mail. I'll see you at the funeral. Bye."

Danny shivered as if a north wind had blown through the car. *Brendan is coming home from Nam*, he thought. *Again. . . .*

*My life is a fucking swamp*, he thought, as the rain lashed and the thunder clapped. He parked in a bus stop across the street from the Strong Arms, convinced no New York City cop was going to step out of a patrol car in the middle of the storm to give him a summons. He wished he had an umbrella as he rushed for the shelter of the canopy of the Strong Arms.

He entered the handsome restaurant, which was still crowded with a midnight crowd, one of the few places in Brooklyn to get a meal until one A.M. The smiling maître d' asked Danny if he had a reservation. Danny shook his head and spotted Christy Strong leaning over a table where two couples in casual but expensive summer clothes watched a busboy clear dinner plates as a platinum-blond waitress padded away with her order book. The maître d' hurried to Strong, whispered in his ear, and Strong glanced toward Danny, a smile on his face. He nodded to Danny, held up his right index finger to indicate he'd be with him in a minute, and kept chatting and laughing with the couples at the table.

Danny drifted to the crowded bar, where a twenty-something brunet barmaid—dressed in tight black jeans and tight ruffled blouse with black bow tie—served the upscale midnight crowd. She approached Danny, dropped a cocktail napkin on the bar, and said, "Hi, what can I get you?"

"A bottle of Amstel, no glass," Danny said, as he watched the platinum-blond waitress remove three bowls of sherbet from the brightly lit dessert cabinet stocked with almost obscenely rich cakes and puddings and pies.

Danny was parched and craving sugar to substitute for nicotine.

He licked his lips and pointed at the sherbets. "Make it one of those instead," Danny said.

"Homemade, and great," the smiling barmaid said, calling to the platinum blonde to bring a sherbet to the bar.

Danny searched the faces at the crowded bar and dining area, hoping to locate some old familiar neighborhood bloodlines, some kind of psychological backup. He didn't recognize anyone. These were new faces, he thought, imported faces, faces from other places, faces that shined like new coins. Racially mixed couples, lesbian couples, gay couples. It was a Manhattan crowd cut and pasted into the new Brooklyn, and Danny felt oddly out of place as the barmaid put the sherbet in front of him while murmuring on a cell phone.

Strong strode to Danny, hand out and smile beaming, a polished candidate working his own room. "Danny, good to see ya."

"I just saw a friend of mine dead."

"God . . . so sorry."

"On the Gowanus Expressway," Danny said.

Danny watched the platinum waitress deliver the other sherbets to the table where Strong had chatted. Danny ate some of his sherbet, cold and sweet and delicious, a riot of fresh fruity flavors washing the taste of death from his mouth.

"Terrible," Strong said. "Was there booze involved? Our policy is to refuse to give back the valet car keys to anyone we think is over-served. We gladly pay the cab-fare home and back rather than see someone get hurt. Besides, the law says a bar is responsible for damage done by a drunk served past sobriety in your establishment. Actually when I'm elected I intend to make the laws even tougher with mandatory—"

"Stop the bullshit," Danny said. "I can't vote in your district. And if I could I wouldn't vote for you for rat catcher."

Danny ate more of the sherbet as Strong looked him deep in the eyes, his smile never fading but a two-inch vein rising at his left temple like a bolt of blue lightning. "I understand you might be upset about your friend, but you demean yourself when you—"

The maître d' approached Strong and said, "Pardon, Monsieur Strong, but the international call you've been expecting is waiting for you in the office."

Strong nodded, kept his eyes on Danny, and said, "Excuse me, Danny."

"I'll wait."

Strong hurried toward the rear of the Strong Arms as Danny ate some more of the sherbet. After checking his watch three times in ten minutes Danny was getting impatient. He walked to the men's room, relieved himself at the modern black marble urinal, washed his hands and face, and combed his hair. As he dried his face, with a cloth towel, he glanced at himself in the mirror and momentarily saw the whiskey-grizzled, gray-haired face of his father. He shook his head and wiped his eyes. He studied himself and sighed and wondered: *Christ, now that my fifties are almost here, will I look like him?*

He stepped back out to the bar, looked both ways for Strong, and checked his watch again. He approached the maître d' and asked how long Strong would be. "Pardon, but I thought you knew. Monsieur Strong left through the back carport immediately after his call and—"

Danny raced through the storm to his car and drove directly toward Christy Strong's house. The windshield wipers peeled away the relentless rain as Danny stopped for a red light at War Memorial Square. He looked deep into the crimson beacon and flashed on Kenny Byrne's bloodied face as one large silver dollar of rain spiraled through the red hue and exploded on the windscreen like a splotch of blood. The wipers smeared the scarlet splatter. Danny shut the wipers and his eyes. When he opened them the window was pebbled with clear rain. He switched back on the wipers and drove faster to Christy Strong's, a nauseating tingle consuming him like a roachy molting of his very skin.

Danny parked on another bus stop and entered the lobby, where a doorman wearing a maroon cap with gold braids and a Park Palace Condos shirt rose from a chair, putting down a copy of the *Daily News*. The Mets game broadcast from L.A. over a twelve-inch TV, tied 4 to 4, with the Dodgers in the top of the tenth inning.

"Help ya?"

"I wanna see Christie Strong."

"Name?"

"Danny Cassidy."

The doorman lifted an intercom phone, pressed a code, and waited.

"Danny Cassidy here to see you."

Danny waited, impatient, speeches forming in his head. He didn't know what he was going to say to Christie Strong. He just wanted to let him know he was in his face, day and night. That he knew he'd killed Kenny Byrne and that he was going to dog him.

"Mmmm hmmmmm," the doorman said into the house phone. The doorman led Danny to a private elevator on the left alcove of the marble lobby, pressed open the door, and turned a key in the penthouse floor. "Only goes one place," he said.

Danny thanked him, stepped onto the private smoke-mirrored elevator with scrolled gold leaf trim, and rode it upstairs to the penthouse. When the door opened Strong stood waiting, wearing a silk Hawaiian shirt, shorts, and slippers. Two of his hard-bodied Strong Arms waitresses—including the platinum blonde who'd fetched him the sherbet—wore large men's Hawaiian shirts and nothing else, sitting on a white leather sectional watching a goofball comedy on a sixty-inch TV.

"Sorry I had to leave so abruptly but this was a very important call and all the paperwork I needed was here," Strong said, turning to one of the young women. "Liz, bring me and my old friend a couple of drinks. And excuse me if I get interrupted again, I'm waiting for the same call again any minute now."

Liz sprung to her feet, putting the movie on pause, as Strong turned to Danny. "I'm going to have the ice tea, with fresh mint I grow on the terrace," he said to Danny. "But if you want something stronger. . . ."

He pointed across the forty-by-sixty-foot living room to a full-service bar with six stools surrounding it. "Nothing for me," Danny said, wary of strychnine. Strong held up one finger to Liz, who ambled off into the kitchen. Danny took a step onto the immense three-inch deep Persian rug, peering at the expensive art on the walls. Most were originals, including a Jasper Johns, a Warhol, and a Pollock. A twenty-foot oil-on-wood replica of Bosch's *Garden of Earthly Delights* stood as a triptych altarpiece in one big empty corner.

"That the altar where the flock worships?" Danny said.

"You mind wiping your shoes? I handpicked the carpets in Kuwait."

Danny wiped his feet on a woolen mat near the door.

"You always liked Bosch, didn't you?" Strong said, as Danny followed him across the rug so deep it made him wobble. "In fact, it was you who turned me on to Bosch. You used to carry around a book of his paintings in that dirty old head bag of yours. Back in the eighties when I was in the Prado I commissioned a replica, on wood, like the original altarpiece, by a copy artist. It's a three-act play, a symphony, a novel, and an opera all in one painting. A masterpiece. If he were alive today instead of during the fifteenth century, Bosch would be a great epic filmmaker. All of life is right there in that corner—creation, man's sins, and punishment in three panels, like the three dramatic movements of life itself."

"Your whole life has been spent sending people to the third panel of hell."

Strong smiled, looking from the naked copulating bodies in the center panel to the two young women who were his company for the night. "I'm still in the middle, earthly pleasures panel, Danny. And let's not start with name-calling again. You do yourself a disservice. You're smarter than this."

Danny walked to a white grand Steinway, the gleaming top of which was crowded with a glistening spectacle of crystal figurines—dancers, warriors, lovers, bullfighters, animals, bells, stars, birds, fish, Celtic crosses, mythological figures.

Danny followed Strong through the big room, passing fresh flowers stuffed into expensive Chinese vases that stood on either side of the marble and oak fireplace and on six different end tables. He heard the ticking of a row of synchronized antique cuckoo clocks lining the mantelpiece that said it was 12:35 A.M. He circled a dozen antique Tiffany lamps that bathed the room in muted amber light, creating a celestial hue in Strong's vantage high above the Brooklyn streets on which he'd made his fortune.

A glass cabinet of fine china rattled like wind chimes with each step Danny made across the floor toward a teak dining table gleaming under the soft glow of a priceless Waterford crystal chandelier.

Danny trailed Strong toward the big bay windows and sliding glass doors leading to the wraparound terrace overlooking Prospect Park. Lightning forked in the sky, illuminating the soggy meadows, dimpled ponds, serpentine paths, and lush forest. Strong and Danny stepped onto the terrace, which was a jungle of potted trees, flowers, herbs, bushes, and exotic plants. Crayon-colored birds squawked in large ornate cages. Custom-made rattan patio furniture lined the walkways of the twenty-foot-wide terrace, like the decks of a luxury ocean liner, replete with shuffleboard court and a glass-framed one-on-one basketball court on one section of the terrace.

"We eat breakfast here on the southern exposure facing the park in the morning," Strong said as Liz stepped out onto the terrace, handing Strong his ice tea. She smiled at Danny. He said thanks. Liz turned to walk back inside, when Strong dropped his cocktail napkin. On purpose.

"Take the film into the bedroom, Liz," Strong said. "I'll be with you both in a jiff."

Liz smiled, bent to pick up the cocktail napkin, revealing the bottoms of her bare butt, and then skipped barefoot into the penthouse, removed the disc from the DVD player, and she and the other girl hurried for the bedroom. Danny watched Liz open the door to a bedroom dominated by a massive four-poster water bed stationed between big cathedral windows facing north toward the Manhattan skyline. Liz closed the bedroom door as Strong snipped fresh mint from an herb garden.

"I take dinner on the northeast side, watching the sun go down behind Lady Liberty. Life is good here. Very good, Danny. I knew when I first moved here forty years ago that Brooklyn would one day be the sane alternative for sensible people of means, for those who wanted to raise safe families. I made sure I got the best penthouse in the Slope when it was still affordable. And I invested in Prospect Gardens, which I knew would one day be a diamond mine."

"My friend who was killed tonight was Kenny Byrne," Danny said. The rain pelted down on the rolled-out awning, rushing in long streams over the roof edge.

"Jeez, I thought he was already dead," Strong said. "I thought Kenny'd died in Nam, or from an OD, or something a long, long time ago."

"I know you thought that," Danny said. "Until yesterday. When he turned up alive at my old man's wake. It fucked up your alibi."

"Alibi?" Strong said, laughing. "What alibi?"

"For the night Vito Malone was murdered."

"I was in a police precinct all night. I didn't need an alibi."

Danny heard a phone ring and Strong excused himself and sauntered through his living room to another door. "Excuse me, Danny, but I've been expecting my call from Tokyo. Make yourself comfortable. I'll be out in a few." Strong opened the heavy wood door, revealing a wood-burnished study covered in bookcases and furnished with reclining chairs and a big cherry-wood desk and conference table. Strong answered the phone and closed the door as lightning flashed through wooden blinds covering the windows looking east over Downtown Brooklyn.

Danny stood by the terrace door in the living room, staring out at the endless rain. *Just as I started getting on a roll the son of bitch gets a phone call,* he thought. As if it were planned. One of those rich-cocksucker tactics that they teach in Millionaire Scumbag School in dealing with working people. Sit on a raised platform so you can look down at them. Interrupt them. Get buzzed by secretaries. Be reminded of pressing lunch or dinner appointments at impossible-to-get-into restaurants. Get phone calls from overseas. All to make you appear more important than the turd you're meeting with.

*Strong lives like city royalty,* he thought, a dagger of jealousy twisting in him. Broads, money, luxury, power. But it was all dirty. Like the heathen behavior in Bosch's middle panel. But someday Strong would pay for his sins. Someday soon.

He circled the awning-sheltered terrace, checking out the exotic plants, his custom furniture, and his Olympus views. Fresh tomatoes and peppers flourished from big ceramic planters. A dozen wooden deck chairs with thick cushions surrounded a twelve-foot-square plunge pool and smaller Jacuzzi hot tub. Danny imagined twelve naked women, all spending the day here, guzzling tropical drinks, and then romping the night away here with Strong and his political pals, the judges, the congressmen and senators, and the brownstone-belt real estate barons. He envisioned Erika spending time here. Naked.

A bird cawed and Danny turned and looked into its orange-rimmed eye. "Who's the fucking boss, bitch?" the bird said. The bird lifted one talon to its beak. Danny thought he saw the bird puff a cigarette.

He shook his head and took three quick breaths.

After almost fifteen minutes, Strong returned, smiling and apologetic.

"Sorry, Dan, business, international time zones, ya know. Where were we?"

"We were talking about how Kenny Byrne showed up out of the

past," Danny said, stepping back into the apartment, walking to the delicate crystal collection on the piano, lifting a carved crystal globe of the planet Earth, tossing it in the air and catching it. "Which upsets the apple cart, because—"

"Please! Don't touch any of those. They're irreplaceable. It's taken me a lifetime to collect them all."

"One for every corpse you've left," Danny said, tossing the globe to a startled Strong. Danny finger-walked over several of the other figurines. "Kids dead from ODs, hot shots, acid-dosed suicides, and plain old-fashioned poisonings. . . ."

Danny wobbled a figurine of a violinist, who he could have sworn moved his bow. He lifted it and stared at it with dread, then heard the whispers of men coming from the office. He suspected it was the bodyguards, the ones who'd attacked him in the hotel.

"There you go again," Strong said, placing the globe on the piano top. "With the wild accusations, the innuendoes, the irresponsible rantings. You have to learn to relax, man. Get into the groove again. Turn on, tune in, drop out all over again. You're spending so much time with your head up the ass of 1969 that you might as well be there. You're chasing an old girlfriend. Garbage picking in people's old, private lives. Your life has an oldies soundtrack, Danny. Learn some new tunes. You're disconnected from the new century, man. Like I said before, see a shrink; I think you might be experiencing an Art Linkletter flashback."

"I just want you to know that what Kenny Byrne knew didn't die with him," Danny said, glancing at the office.

Strong looked at him, his smile cemented in place, but Danny noticed a loose pebble of dread in the corner of one eye.

"What's that piece of cryptic nonsense supposed to mean?"

"I'm a reporter. My source material would convince the toughest city editor in my guild. Or a jury."

"I understand your job out there on the *Chronicle* is a little shaky as it is," Strong said. "Newspapers are downsizing, Danny. Don't blow your job, your career, on a wild-goose chase. Forget me. Bury your father. Go home. Go to work. Stay under the radar. Call your daughter. Take your brother to lunch, my place. On me. Enjoy the rest of this wonderful thing called life."

*Fucking O'Rourke must've told him all about my personal life,* he thought.

"I know you had Kenny Byrne killed, Christie. I know you were behind Henry Bush and Mary and Wally Fortune dying. And Vito Malone's murder. . . ."

"I think it's time you said good night, Danny. I have some very pressing business."

Danny felt thirsty, his skin a touchpad of tics, tingles, and vibrations. Strong pulled the glass figurine from him, and Danny's cold fingers seemed to stick to the glass, stretching like hot bubble gum. Strong swung away the figurine in a spectrum of light that plumed like a brief mini explosion. Danny closed his eyes and rotated his head, cricks snapping in his spinal stem. The walk across the Persian rug seemed endless, as if he were wearing leg irons and platform shoes. The cuckoo clocks chirped one A.M. in unison, a loud cacophonous outburst, launching a rocket of adrenaline through him. Danny jumped, turned to the cuckoos, stumbled sideways.

"You OK?" Strong asked.

"Who's the fucking boss, bitch?" asked the mynah bird from the terrace.

"I'm fine," Danny said, eyes jerking from the bird to Strong, who was backlit, resembling Alfred Hitchcock's silhouette on the old TV show. Danny spun away from him and the blood-red liquid light reflecting off the crystal figurines streaked across the room like a shower of comets. Danny whipped his gaze to the *Garden of Earthly Delights*, where the naked people in the center panel were engaged in an undulating live-action orgy. One woman was handcuffed behind her back, being sodomized by a man wearing a policeman's hat backward on his head. The four-legged man with the body of a rotting tree, whose face, Danny knew, was a self-portrait of Bosch, was now the face of Mickey Cassidy, covered in shaving cream, singing, "We don't burn our draft cards in Muskogee," above the roar of the cuckoos.

Danny closed his eyes, rubbed them. *Did they dose the fucking sherbet?* he wondered.

When he opened his eyes he was fine. He gazed at the office door that was ajar and bobbing with shadows and murmurs. Christie Strong's face was smiling, big and tanned and happy as the elevator door opened.

"Thanks for stopping by," Strong said, nudging Danny into the elevator that was a vertical coffin. "I'll try to make the funeral, but if I don't see you before you go back to L.A., have a nice trip."

The elevator door snapped shut. As it descended Danny felt a rumble in his head, a slow building wave that kept rising, foam bubbling, crest clawing. He gripped the hand railings as the bottom fell out of his life.

"What the fuck," he said aloud, putting his hands over his ears. He shook his head and opened his eyes as the elevator dived through time and space, into a bottomless void, crashing through the lobby and the sidewalk and the cellar and the sewer system, picking up speed until it fell off the edge of the planet into bottomless space. Danny felt weightless, his bladder swelling, ears popping, eyes bugging until he came to a slamming stop. He stood in a corner of the elevator, like a fighter, grasping two ropes as the elevator door ground open, revealing the blinding lobby light and the roar of a crowd.

"You all right, buddy?" asked the doorman, who was now Johnnie Cochran, the famous criminal lawyer.

"I might be charged with murder," Danny said. The doorman backed away. The roar of the crowd rose as Danny lurched toward the exit, passing the tiny TV, where an announcer with a chipmunk's voice said that a Dodger had just hit a three-run homer in the bottom of the twelfth inning.

Danny saw Johnnie Cochran eye him with mild terror and pick up the house phone. "Mr. Strong, you OK?" he said into the house phone, snatching up a baseball bat he kept behind the door. Danny wrestled the bat from the older, cowering man. Danny ran to the middle of the lobby, took his place at the plate, wiggled his ass, scratched his balls, spit twice, waited for the right pitch, and took a mighty swing. He heard the crack of the lumber on the ball, felt it sail out the door of the building and arc toward the upper decks as the fans on the TV roared.

Danny dropped the bat on the marble floor in a rattling echo and hurried into the dizzying rain to run the bases after hitting the winning home run.

Danny raced across the street to Prospect Park, a small sports car skidding around him, hydroplaning in a 360-degree carousel of head- and brake and taillights. He bounded up and over a park bench, hopped across the retaining wall, and into the darkened teeming park.

He stopped to wave, glancing around, but the roar of the fans fell silent. He whipped his head back and forth, looking for the fans, for the other players, for the umpire's home-run call. But all he saw were the streaks of the sodium lampposts and the steady silver daggers of the rain.

Jesus Christ, he thought in a moment of blurred lucidity. *I'm not seventeen. I'm not playing for John Jay High. I'm an almost-fifty-year-old murder suspect. Alone in Prospect Park. Smashed on LS-fucking-D. I've been dosed! Fucking Christie Strong had me dosed . . . Jesus Christ . . . oh, mother of Jesus Christ. Get a grip. Get to a hospital. No! If there's a medical record of me on acid at fifty, it'll come out in court. I'll be discredited. I'll be marked as a retro-sixties crazy man. What fucking jury will believe me? I'll lose my job.* "Grown man on acid! Newspaper reporter on acid!" *Holy fuck. Disaster. I can't control this. I'm not young and strong enough to handle this. The thing about acid is that it controls you. It takes you out of your senses. Seizes the mind. How much did this sick fuck give me? Does it have strychnine in it? Jesus Christ, Jesus Christ, Jesus Christ . . . motherfucker. . . .*

And then he felt the rumble again, like rolling, building waves of volcanic ash carrying him into an out-of-body dimension. He was now floating on the rain. Lightning crackled in the sky, and he saw the smiling face of his mother stenciled in the afterglow. "Daaaaaannnnneeeeeeyyyyy, come home for diiiiiiiinnnnnnneeeeeer!" He stared at his mother's happy smiling face. And then she popped into the vapors, into the rain, into eternity, back into the sixties.

"Mom!" Danny shouted, sprinting toward the face in the sky, slushing along the muddied footpath until he came to the clump of trees where he had always stood to spy on Erika Malone's house. He glared down Garvey Place, rain soaking him, the street opening wider than he'd ever seen it before, like facades on wheels on a Hollywood movie set. The gas lamp hissed in Erika's front yard and Erika's bedroom curtain fluttered, sending out a secret come-fuck-me code of amber light to Christie Strong. *Strong will get himself aroused with the two bimbos, like fluff girls, and then run around the corner to drop his load in Erika,* he thought.

"You lost, yo?" asked a homeless man, who appeared behind him wearing a hooded poncho, his cartoon-distorted face reflecting so much time on the street that his eyes were the color of glittered sidewalks, his face the texture of wet cement, his rotted teeth like a rusting fence.

"Who knows where the time goes," Danny said and bolted

through the park, splattering along the Park Drive. Jim Morrison's voice echoed from the Tennis House, where he'd once spied Ankles with Marsha Mauro: "*. . . faces come out of the rain, when you're strange. . . .*" He ran faster, faster than he did when he ran with Horsecock. He heard his heart do a full rendition of "Wipeout" in his chest, could hear the voice screaming the title in an echo chamber, as if he were wearing invisible headphones. Lightning short-circuited the heavens. Ghosts sizzled like moths in a zap lamp.

"You're off the fucking team, you pathetic little hophead," he heard Coach Riley scream as he passed the ball fields where he once ran for glory and where he now ran for his life. Searching for his sanity as the suffocating waves of LSD ash climbed toward a harrowing crest. He saw the taillights and red traffic lights on the parkside. The part of him that was real knew they were taillights and traffic signals. But the other half of him, the part of him lost in the ash, knew they were the red eyes of cleft-footed goats with the sharpened stainless-steel teeth, all clambering out of the backs of milk trucks driven by eyeless farmers. The goats would soon be climbing the metal-edged steps of Danny's tenement hallway to take him out of his bed for a human sacrifice.

Somewhere between the ball fields and playground his head tore upward out of his neck, like a cork yanked from a bottle, and every one of his footfalls sent jackhammer shocks up his legs, electrifying his balls and his arms and fingers. As he raced through the park, he kept looking over his shoulder, searching for his head. Making sure that it was following him, sailing like a kite with an entrails tail, trying to get back on his own bloody neck like a ball-on-string toy that he'd tried to sail into a catch cup as a kid.

"Take my fucking head back," his head screamed as his body ran past the Eleventh Street playground, chasing his headless body, wondering how he was moving forward if his feet were pointed backward. He increased his speed as he passed Hippie Helen's house, aware that his body was moving faster than a man his age was ever supposed to travel with an aging heart. Danny was desperate to get his head back on his shoulders before his heart exploded like a cherry bomb in his chest.

He barreled for Blessed Virgin Mary Church, streaking past Fort Foley's, which was under mortar attack, and heard someone shouting his name. He quickened his pace. Sprinted for the church where he'd been an altar boy as a kid, banged on the rectory door.

It opened.

"Help me get my head on my neck," Danny shouted.

"I'll call the police," the young Filipino priest said, his face the size of a hand puppet's on a pair of massive shoulders. Danny crossed Parkside West, still looking over his shoulder for his head, which was panting, his tongue parched white with fatigue. He burst through the door of Foley's and stopped, panting, searching all the faces of friends he knew were already dead. Slappy, Gordon, Ocar, Wally and Mary Fortune, Horsecock, Kenny Byrne were all standing at the bar, glasses half full, waving for him to have a drink. His father was behind the bar, pulling draft beers. "You got a fucking draft card?" his father asked.

*Am I dead?* Danny wondered. *Did I die of strychnine and go to fucking Foley's! For eternity?*

Danny zoomed past them all, bumping into Eddie Fortune, and burst out the back door, his head sailing after him in a bloody lash. He sprinted to Prospect Park, ran toward Hippie Hill, where he saw the brilliant shimmering light illuminating four figures in the rain, all of them holding pistols in their hands. Creedence Clearwater was singing "Bad Moon Rising," which cross-faded into Dylan's "Mr. Tambourine Man," as the white light shone on Erika Malone's seventeen-year-old face, so gorgeous that she needed a halo. Everyone else was dripping wet but she was as dry as the dust of the dead.

"*. . . in the jingle jangle mornin', I'll come followin' you. . . .*"

And there was Boar's Head pointing his gun at Danny, eighteen-year-old Danny, who pointed a .45 that was too heavy for his speed-freak arm. "Go ahead and shoot me, you little fucking faggot!" Boar's Head screamed. And then the fourth figure walked out of the storm into the blinding light, which was shining from the direction of Sewer 7, Pipe 11, like Hieronymus Bosch's other painting, *The Blessed and the Damned,* a wondrous white cone of light spiraling from purgatory toward the gates of heaven. Danny ran faster to see the face of the fourth figure in the rain. His heart was a propeller ready to burst from his chest.

Then he felt himself tackled. From behind. Slammed to the wet ground. The last gasp of air on the entire planet exploded from his heaving lungs.

"Danny, you OK?" Eddie Fortune screamed, pinning Danny's flailing arms to the wet ground of Hippie Hill. "It's me, Eddie, Eddie Fortune. You were running faster than anyone I ever saw before. Calm the fuck down. Is someone chasing you?"

"My head is after me."

"Your what? Your fucking head is after . . . hey, your eyes look like fucking Dondi's. In the comic strip. You stoned? What're you on, man?"

"Give me back my fucking head!"

"Holy shit."

Now Danny heard the voice of JoJo Corcoran coming from over Eddie Fortune's shoulder. "He's jimjammed on acid, man," JoJo said. "Bad trippin'. Musta got dosed."

JoJo held up what Danny thought was his own head, shaking it, his brains rattling like dice in a croupier's cup. Danny stared down at his headless body, belly laughing as JoJo held his head by the hair, shaking.

"Give me back my fucking head, JoJo! Please!" Danny exploded into a conniption of laughter, uncontrollable laughter, an epileptic fit of laughter that contracted his stomach muscles, robbed him again of all his breath, a big Day-Glo purple, orange, and pink-striped circus tent of billowing laughter.

"I gotta get him down to Methodist Hospital, man," said Eddie Fortune, lifting Danny. "Help me get him to the my car."

Danny writhed and wrestled, flailing his arms. "I ain't going nowhere without my fucking head. No hospitals!"

JoJo rattled the pill jar in his hand and said, "Take it from a guy with experience. They ain't gonna give him anything different in the ER than what I got right here except a bill. Chlorpromazine, the generic for Thorazine because the Medicaid don't let you get brand names. Three of these and he'll crash like a fuckin' Osprey."

"I think I better get him to the hospital," Eddie shouted.

"No hospital!" Danny screamed in a lucid moment, a blue patch in a stormy sky. "Too many questions. I can't have it on my medical record. JoJo, give, give me, give me my head, and give us the fucking Thorazine. Get Stuey Balsam. Get Stu the Jew. Get Stuey."

JoJo shoved the Thorazine pills into Danny's mouth, which Danny thought was his open neck wound because they got stuck in his throat. Eddie gave JoJo his keys, made him run to his car to retrieve a bottle of water. After he returned Eddie made Danny drink big long gulps, washing down the Thorazines. Danny wondered how his mouth reattached itself to his neck.

Eddie looped his big strong arms around Danny, pulled him to his car, and buckled him in. "Put on the classical station for him," JoJo said. "It'll relax him. That's what they do in the G building at KCH." Then JoJo ran to awaken Stuey Balsam from his sleep.

Danny and Eddie sat there in the Jeep Cherokee, Brahms lofting from the radio. And less than fifteen minutes later Danny's head floated through the window and docked into his open neck, as the rain drummed on the roof of the car.

As the horrors left him, draining like dirty bath water, the afterbuzz of the LSD and the rain on Hippie Hill made Danny cock his head. A deep, rich, color-saturated clarity precision-focused his brain. As if some magical key had just unlocked a long-sealed door. The hallucination he'd just witnessed about the night of November 20, 1969, seemed more real than the others did. More like revealed memory than fantasy.

Stu Balsam arrived, angry, astonished, sleep-tousled, wearing a hooded jacket and pajama bottoms. He climbed into the backseat of Eddie Fortune's Cherokee, slamming the door after him.

"Do you have any fucking idea what my wife's reaction to being woken up by JoJo-fucking-Corcoran knocking on my bedroom window from the fire escape at two A.M. was like? I bet she's on the phone with her Uncle Meyer, a divorce attorney, right now! Maybe your tribe is used to this behavior, Danny. But Jews don't appreciate psychos with no teeth at the bedroom window in the middle of the fucking night talking about bad trips and Thorazine!"

"He got dosed," Eddie Fortune said.

"It's the new century, for chrissakes! The Electric Circus is closed! Who doses fifty-year-old men?"

"Christie."

"Oy. Say no more. I didn't believe JoJo at first. But then he told me he gave you three of his Thorazines. That should do it. There's nothing else. Why'd you ask for me?"

"Stuey, let me ask you a question, you read the literature on all this stuff, no?"

"I try to keep up. Like I try to stay married."

"I covered a child molestation trial once, where the prosecution put a woman on the stand who said she'd been tested in a process called state-dependent memory. She remembered twenty years later that her father forced himself on her as a seven-year-old girl."

"Sure, I know all about that stuff," Stu Balsam said. "Because there's a lot of new pharmacological experimentation going on with it. First of all, there's mood-related state-dependent memory. Putting someone in the same room with the same smells and music, and certain memories can be triggered. Then there's the drug-related variety, a much narrower version but well documented and researched. A lot of the experimentation has been done with LSD, as a matter of fact. They even teach psych courses in it."

"What if you are high on the same stuff—acid—as you were in a similar rainstorm years ago?"

"That could trigger a repressed memory," Stu said. "Same location, same drug, same environmental conditions. The actual phenomenological state of being high gets associated with the cognitive data locked in your memory. See, memories are laid down on a material substrate. Neurons and neuronal complexes in the brain. But certain groups of neurons may sit mute for decades, neither used nor stimulated, or otherwise fired into activity. Like the ones I try to reserve for whack-jobs like JoJo Corcoran."

"I just forgot every fucking thing you just said," Eddie Fortune said, staring at Stu in the rearview mirror, rain dancing on the fogging windows.

"But if acid was used in a similar environment it could activate those memories?" Danny said.

"Then you could see a case for concealed memories getting activated when that certain unique complex of neurons is again brought into associative-combinatorial life."

"In other words, it's plausible that the presence of a drug like LSD could unlock otherwise hidden or buried original memories that were laid down under its influence?"

"You got it."

"I fucking don't," Eddie said.

"The over-the-counter version is that acid can trigger a flashback to an old acid trip," Stu said. "The way a song triggers memories."

"OK," Eddie said.

"But it isn't always reliable," Stu said. "There is such a thing as false memory. There's a whole organization dedicated to this because some people have convicted people on testimony of reactivated repressed memories, only to be proved wrong by DNA and other evidence. So memory is never infallible. Alcohol is a huge factor. Alcohol is a drug that kills memory."

"Thanks, Stu," Danny said.

"That's it? You have JoJo fucking Corcoran climb up my fire escape at two in the morning, have my wife screaming and looking to call 911 and her sleazeball uncle the matrimonial attorney, all so I can give you a rundown on state-dependent memory? We aren't fucking kids anymore, Danny! I don't live like this. Go get some sleep. You're still tripping."

Stu Balsam hurried out into the rain.

Danny sat in the parking lot, staring up at Hippie Hill, where he had just seen the apparitions, hallucinations of the past. "I saw a light," Danny said.

"People always say that about near-death experiences," Eddie Fortune said.

"But this wasn't a light from heaven. This was a light from purgatory. This was a light from that night, from November 20, 1969."

"Like Stu the Jew said, you need some sleep," Eddie said. "I'm gonna take you to your hotel. OK?"

Danny nodded. JoJo appeared, knocking at the passenger window. Danny rolled it down.

"I still owe you fourteen bucks," JoJo said. "I owed you thirteen, plus a single so I wouldn't owe you a bad-luck number. No charge for the Thorazines. I get them on prescription on the Medicaid for free. I can't charge a fellow traveler. Like George W. Bush said, 'A mind is a terrible thing to lose.' I lost mine on April 12, 1966, in Fort Benning, when they put me in the sensory-deprivation box on ten tabs of what you just had and then turned on the electroshock. You ain't heard rock and roll until you heard it with my ears. I know what you were talking about when you said you wanted your head back on your neck. I'm still searching for mine. If you find my mind in your travels, hold on to it for me, will ya?"

"JoJo, I owe you one," Danny said.

Eddie backed out of the park drive, as Danny started to yawn. Danny looked out at the night, the colors like a Disney cartoon, the rain a shower of diamonds and rubies, a tranquil, mellow sensation he thought he would never experience again melting through him like orange sunshine.

"Christie Strong did this to you?"

"He did something to all of us," Danny said.

"You have to make me one promise. You have to promise that when this all comes to a head, I'm there."

Danny nodded, unable to get any more words out of his mouth as the LSD was diminished in his mind and body and the Thorazine mummified him in steel bandages.

# twenty-six

Danny slept for seven hours. A little after nine the ringing phone
awakened him in his hotel bed, his head clanging with drug residue.
His chest was tight and sore. His legs ached with shin splints and
strained muscles. His pasty mouth tasted like dirty fingers. The
phone rang a fifth time.

He answered.

"Hello."

"Brother Brendan here."

"Hey. . . ."

"What're you doing?"

"Talking to you."

"You on glue?"

Danny laughed and said, "No, acid."

"You OK?"

"I guess."

"I'm calling from the plane."

"Great."

"You sure you're OK?"

"Yeah," Danny said.

"Your E-mail was, well, a little abrupt."

"Sorry . . . you OK?"

"Yeah, sure . . . fine. OK, then I'll see you when I get there, huh?"

"Great."

"All right, then, bye."

"Safe home."

Danny hung up and wished he'd said a million other words.

He hobbled to the bathroom, every joint and bone ablaze. He
showered, dressed in jeans, rainproof Timberland boots, a zipper
jacket with hood. He swallowed a multivitamin, four Tylenol, and a
Zantac. He dug his voice-activated tape recorder and two fresh
ninety-minute tapes from his suitcase and rode the elevator to the
lobby.

He bought a large Brooklyn Cyclones umbrella, a pair of flexible batting gloves, and a steel baseball bat from the gift shop, which was chockablock full of Brooklyn memorabilia. He asked the concierge to get him a car service. He had to collect his car near Christie Strong's house.

Danny overtipped the driver, uncertain if he'd ever get to tip again, tossed the bat and gloves in the Camry trunk, and pulled two parking tickets off the windshield. He gazed up into the rain, trying to see Strong's terrace. *I will get even with this motherfucker,* he promised himself, climbing into his rental car.

He had come back to his old neighborhood after three decades away to bury his father and to learn if he was a killer. And now people were being killed because he'd returned. Christie Strong ridiculed him the night before, dosed him with acid the way he had thirty-two years ago. Sent a grown man rampaging through the streets. It was all making him sick, an empty gaping feeling that made his bones feel hollow. He pined for his daughter, missed her once-unconditional love that he had betrayed by walking out on her and her mother. Because of an old murder and a woman from the past whom he did not even know if he loved. He'd made so many bad choices. Ran for too long. And now almost fifty years had piled on top of each other like a mountain of cosmic debris. Guilt stained his days. Fear tossed his nights. When this was all over, if he was still a free man, he would find his daughter. He'd sit her down. He'd look into her fractured eyes. And he would apologize to her, try to repair the pain and the hurt, try to salvage what was left of his life. *Maybe I still have twenty-five good years left,* he thought. *If I do, I want to spend as many as possible near her, in her presence, in earshot of Darlene's laughter. I want to embrace her on holidays, dance with her at her wedding, and change a grandchild's diaper on an anonymous Tuesday afternoon. I want to live a normal life, enjoy whatever is left. . . .*

He parked across from Erika's brownstone. He took the small Panasonic voice-activated tape recorder he always used on interview assignments and clicked a fresh ninety-minute microcassette into the wheelhouse. He set the Vox voice-activating mechanism and placed the tape recorder into the folds of the umbrella. He then fastened the umbrella with the Velcro strap. It would pick up all conversations in the house as soon as anyone began speaking. It was an old fly-on-the-wall trick a savvy police reporter had taught him in Florida. The gimmick was to carry the umbrella into an interview with the tape recorder hidden in the umbrella. Place the umbrella in an umbrella rack or as close to the telephone as possible. You started the interview with gentle softball questions. After the subject knocked a few of them out of the park you started throwing heat. When the tough questions pissed off the subject enough, you were often asked to leave. You left.

Then fifteen minutes later, after he made calls to his lawyer and his accomplices or discussed you and your questions with his pals, you'd return. Knock on the door. Apologize for interrupting again. And say you forgot your umbrella.

After retrieving your umbrella you took out your tape recorder and played back everything that was said in your absence.

Danny ran from his car through the rain with his folded umbrella in his hand. He rang Erika's bell. She stepped into the Grindbox vestibule dressed in a smart, dark blue business suit.

"Hi," she said. She was subdued and looked happy to see him.

"Can I—"

"Of course," she said, pulling open the gate, reaching out, and grabbing his hand.

He stopped in the vestibule. He looked at her. Something disarming happened every time Danny looked at Erika. His defenses collapsed. She touched his face and kissed him, her lips gluing to his. She surrendered a little sigh.

"I'm sorry I've acted like such a self-absorbed idiot," she said.

"It's an awkward thing. After all this time. It's like trying to start an old motor. It kicks, grinds, sputters, and whines. Misbehaves. I'm no bargain."

"My mother is asleep," she said. "I was just about to run down to the health-food store to get some more St. John's Wort and kava. It's the only thing that calms her down. I have to take her to an Alzheimer's group therapy session in Manhattan in about an hour and I'm afraid they'll ask her to leave if she's too agitated."

"Should I come back another time?"

"No," she said. "I'll go to the health-food store later. Enough with the fooling around. Come inside and make love to me, Danny. Now. Please. I need you."

He'd been waiting all his life for this moment and when she grabbed his hand he followed. They reached the entrance to the living room, where Erika nodded toward her mother, who was sleeping on her recliner. Erika took the umbrella from his hand and placed it in an umbrella stand in the hallway just outside the living room. She put her finger to her lips as she led Danny up the stairs.

On the second-floor landing Danny saw that one room on the right facing the yard was furnished as a home office—desk, file cabinets, computer, printer, scanner, shredder, fax and Xerox machines. Bulletin boards lined the walls. Erika turned left, leading Danny to her bedroom that he'd imagined in erotic fantasies. He entered the big oak-trimmed room, dim with stormy morning light that seeped through sheer lace curtains. Rain pecked the windows. A lance of lightning pierced the steel sky, illuminating a dozen of Erika's childhood antique dolls piled on the puffy pillows of her queen-size canopy bed.

Erika let go of Danny's hand, turned to him and with uninhibited grace she undressed as she stared into his eyes. Danny pulled off his shirt, unbuckled his pants. Erika took off everything but her high heels and white thong panties. Her thin toned body belonged to a woman half her age. Healthful food, miles of swimming, gym sweat, and plenty of money were her fountain of youth. She let him ogle, walking to the bed to lift the chintz canopy, strutting back, then rolling off and tossing her thong panties at Danny. He caught them, buried his face in them as she knelt on the shag rug and untied his boots, removing each one. She pulled down his pants, making him step out of them. She licked the inside of his thighs as she slid her hands under the back of his underwear, scratching his behind. And then in a half-violent motion she yanked them down, inside out. Danny's penis sprung out like a freed animal. She caught it in her mouth, her low moan turning to a growl as she dug her nails into his butt, pulling him deeper into her.

"Oh . . . my . . . God," Danny said, knowing he was no longer capable of any rational thought about Erika Malone. She fellated him for over a minute, until his knees buckled; then she stood and she led him by the dick to the bed, where she collapsed onto her back, scattering the antique dolls as rain pelted the windows. She lifted her legs high in the air and then parted them, revealing the four square inches under the sun that he had chased for most of his adult life. It was more beautiful than he imagined, every firm and soft contour, every hair and follicle. She smelled as clean as spring and tasted even better and her small low moans made him feel for that moment like a virile young man all over again. Made him feel seventeen.

"Do anything you want," she said.

Danny pushed himself up above her, staring into her eyes. She held out one hand and grabbed him by the hair on the back of his head, reached down with her other hand to guide him into her when Danny heard the creak of the bedroom door.

"Vito, that's you?" said Angela Malone.

Danny turned, his boner melting, his mouth parching. Erika's mother stood naked in the doorway, her breasts like wrinkled yams, a thick gray V between her skinny legs. Angela held a black telephone in her right hand. *But maybe it's her fucking sneaker,* Danny thought as Erika flung him off her with the strength of a man.

Erika ran to Angela, wrapping her arms around her, like the bands on a stack of newspapers, leading her into the hallway as Angela ranted in Italian, spitting in Danny's direction. "It's OK, Mama," Erika said, soothing her mother. "Pop isn't here. Time for you to take a bath. Then we're going to meet your friends. I'm here, Mama."

Danny yanked on his clothes, leaving his laces untied as he rushed out of the room. As he passed the bathroom Danny heard Angela ranting in Italian. Erika caught Danny's eye in the bathroom mirror.

"I hate to ask you this," she said. "But do you think you could pick me up some St. John's Wort and kava combo from the health-food store?"

"Sure," Danny said.

"Get my brand. It's the best . . . I hope I don't sound like a rich-bitch princess. . . ."

"You do," Danny said, smiling as Erika ran her mother a bath. "But that's OK."

"I promise you I'll make this up to you," she said, nodding toward the bedroom.

"I'm used to waiting."

He hurried down the stairs, picking up pieces of Angela's clothes on every step—bra, big cotton bloomers, elastic stockings, and floral-patterned dress, her key chain with the keys to the house and the rolltop desk and the medical alert tag.

Danny placed all of the stuff on the recliner. He hung the key chain on the back of the chair, turned, grabbed his umbrella, and was reminded why he had come in the first place. Not in search of sex or love. But answers. The doubts he had about Erika had all but vanished in his lust. Now in the cold clarity of sexual frustration he retreated to his suspicions, the ones that could save his freedom. He put the umbrella back in the stand, the tape recorder locked and loaded for furtive information. And he grabbed Angela Malone's key chain from the chair and took it with him.

He left the keys to be duplicated at Slope Locksmith on First Street, went to the health-food store, paid for the bottle of Erika's Earth St. John's Wort and Kava Blend. He went back to the locksmith, picked up the duplicate keys, and was hurrying to his car when he heard his name being called.

He turned. Viviana Gonzalez leaned across the front seat of her Dodge Neon, wipers flapping. "Mr. Cassidy, got a minute?"

Danny jumped into the front seat. Viviana made a right and parked in a no-parking zone in front of a public school. She was very excited.

"Call me Danny, mister makes me feel old."

"That old man, Henry Bush, the one you told me to check into, Danny? I think you're right. I think he was poisoned. But the public relations people at Kings County wanted to know who gave me this information. They wouldn't confirm or deny it."

"I can confirm it," Danny said. "I'll give you an official to confirm it later today. You have time, you're working on a weekly. The dailies don't have the story yet."

"I'm so excited I can't control myself. I feel like . . . feel like kissing you."

"You don't kiss sources," Danny said. "And I hate to break this to you, but it's unethical to sleep with the people you're investigating."

"I told you I'm no bimbo."

"How much do you like Christie Strong?"

"Are you asking if I sleep with him?"

"It's none of my business but he might be part of this story."

"He wants me to sleep with him. But I haven't. He's attractive. He's nice to me. He's taken me to nice restaurants. Most of them he owns. He's given me keys to use his place in the Hamptons. To his place in the Bahamas. I never used them. He even gave me a key to his penthouse on Parkside West, the building where the senator lives. I've been to a few of his parties there. Gorgeous. Like a museum. But he already has so many girlfriends that it would just make me feel, ya know, like a bimbo if I became another one. He tells me he's not gonna pressure me, that when I'm ready to spend the night there with him that I should just use the key. I haven't used it."

"Are you afraid of him?"

"The only thing I'm afraid of is failure," she said.

"What if he's part of the story you're working on?"

"Is he?"

"Answer my question first," Danny said.

"The story has to come first, right?"

"Is that a question or a statement?"

"The story comes first."

"Which means you don't sleep with him. You investigate him."

"Right. Is he part of the story?"

He looked at Viviana, all brown eyes, white teeth, cinnamon skin, and beautiful sharp Latin features, and eager for "the story" to the point of obsession. He knew the look, knew the feeling. He took a gamble. Even if she went and told Christie Strong everything, he would be forced to make a reckless move. If she was serious about being a reporter and kept the confidence, she could be useful with contacts inside Strong's and Andersen's lives. "Yeah, Strong is part of the story," Danny said.

Viviana took out a notebook and scribbled notes as Danny gave her a quick rundown. He told her about Strong being a sixties dope pusher, who had some corrupt cops on his payroll, one of whom was murdered about two-thirty A.M. on November 21, 1969, and that the old cop who was poisoned yesterday had been the murdered cop's commanding officer. He gave her enough to whet her appetite and told her to go dig up some clips. He warned her again about not telling anyone what she was working on. Viviana got so excited he thought she was going to have a panic attack.

"God Almighty," she said. "I want to go up to the library on Grand Army Plaza, use the microfiche. I can't wait to get started on all of this. I want to talk to Christie before he leaves for the city."

"Be careful. He's smart, ruthless and I . . . there's no easy way to say this . . . I think Christie Strong had your father murdered."

Viviana's bright excited eyes narrowed and turned coal black in her wounded face, as if all the fatherless days of a little girl's life were playing behind them like some wispy home movie. In that dark instant, for Viviana, "the story" became family business.

"The trick here is not to let emotions overwhelm the intellect," Danny said.

"I can be cagey," she said, exhaling in a measured stream. "He's getting some award tonight from, get this, from the Society for Substance Abuse Counselors. He donates money to drug rehabs."

"Marvelous. He'll be out most of the night then?"

"Yeah, until midnight anyway. He asked me to go as his arm candy. I told him I was too busy. He was pissed off. But he'll bring one of his bimbos. Is there anything specific I should be looking for or asking him about?"

"If you get into his apartment see if you can find anything at all to do with Strong and Henry Bush, Strong and Jim Dugan, Strong and Helen Grabowski." He paused as Viviana wrote down these names.

"Anyone else?"

"Strong and Erika Malone," Danny said. Viviana looked up at him without moving her head, sensing by the way he said her name that she was somehow special.

"I've heard him mention her several times," she said.

"In what context?"

"I think he might have a, ya know, thing for her that goes back a lot of years. She's beautiful. I hope I look half as good as she does at her age."

"Call me at seven. Tell me what you've learned."

Viviana dropped him at his car, and Danny drove back up to see Erika Malone.

"Health-food store was packed," Danny said, handing Erika the St. John's Wort and kava blend. Angela Malone was still ranting in Italian, dressed in a fresh summer dress. She tried to spring out of her recliner when Erika led Danny into the living room.

Erika gave her mother two tablets with a glass of filtered water.

"I can't find Mama's goddamned keys anywhere," Erika said.

Danny felt the keys in his pocket and pretended to help her look for them.

"Maybe she left them in the yard," Erika said, banging through the screen door.

Danny thought it would be too suspicious if he happened to find the keys so took the opportunity to loop the keys around the Gucci woman's umbrella in the stand. So that Erika would find them.

"Nothing," Erika said, rushing in from the rain. "I have to go. Half the people won't be there because of the holiday weekend, but I want Mama to go so I can go clear up a few details at work. Want to meet me there for lunch? I'd like you to see my Manhattan condo."

"I'll call you."

"I'd like to finish what we started," she said, smiling like the Erika who used to be able to get him to do anything, handing him her business card with the address.

"It's ten-thirty now," she said. "I'll be there at one. Mama will be in the group until three. That'll give us two glorious hours alone. Then I have to get Mama home, let her change, rest, and get her to the five P.M. mass at St. Savior's."

Erika led her mother from the chair and out into the hallway. Danny was about to leave when Erika said, "Don't forget your umbrella."

"Oh, yeah," Danny said.

Erika lifted his and then lifted her own Gucci umbrella. Her mother's keys jangled from the handle.

"That's funny," she said, shaking her head. She looped the keys around her mother's neck and they stepped into the morning rain. Erika locked the door and the gate with the same key and shielded her mother with her umbrella to the red El Dorado, strapped her into the front passenger seat, and slammed the door.

"I'll be waiting for you," she said, kissing him. "This time we'll be all alone."

He became aroused again. Then Erika got in, and the Caddy squealed away.

Danny climbed into his Camry and started the engine. He took the tape recorder out of the umbrella and hit the rewind button. It spun backward for almost a minute, chipmunk voices squealing from the tape. When it finished rewinding he pressed PLAY. He heard Erika's phone ring. He heard high heels clicking on ceramic tiles. He heard Erika say: "Hello. Yes. No. No. Almost. . . . At the store. Of course not, you think I'm crazy. . . . That's what I'm trying to find out myself. . . . Well, I have a sick mother I'm taking care of here, on top of everything and every-fucking-one else. I take care of everyone, for Chrissakes. I have my fucking limits, you know. No . . . no don't hang up. Please. . . . All right, I'll do my best. He doesn't trust anyone. No, would you? He's smart. . . . No, you can't do that! You don't understand. I know it's ridiculous. But I can't help it. Maybe. Yes, as a matter of fact, I think I do. Yes, still, after all these years, yes. . . . That was never part of the fucking bargain. I fulfilled my end of this arrangement. No! I'll handle him. . . . OK. Let's leave it like that for now. Bye, always so fucking pleasant speaking to you, too."

Danny heard Erika slam down the phone. "Motherfucker!" she shouted. Then he heard her yell, "I'm coming, Mama. I'm coming. . . ." Then footsteps on the stairs. And then the tape stopped. Danny rewound and replayed the tape three times. He listened to the part that he was almost sure was about him. "I know it's ridiculous. But I can't help it. Maybe. Yes, as a matter of fact, I think I do. Yes, still, after all these years, yes. . . ."

He hoped she was talking about her love for him. But then maybe she thought he was an asshole after all these years. Still, he didn't think Erika Malone, who treated her body like a shrine, would ever have sex with anyone she didn't care about. And their unfinished romp was no act. She was into it. But Erika's conversation also sounded like she was involved in something dirty. Maybe even something beyond her control.

He was now more confused about Erika than ever. He thought about going right back in with the duplicate keys. But when he looked in his rearview and side mirrors, he saw a green Crown Victoria parked halfway down the block. O'Rourke was back on his ass. He'd return to Erika's house when he was sure he was alone.

Besides, there was someone else he wanted to see right away.

# twenty-seven

Who told you I was sick?" Hippie Helen said. "I'm not sick. Who told you that?"

"Everybody," Danny said, as a grandfather clock chimed 11 A.M.

Hippie Helen ate a handful of M&Ms with peanuts and gulped some lemonade. Danny scoured her eyes, searching for the lies he knew he'd find. He lied to expose her lies.

"Is there's anything I can do?"

"About what? I'm not sick."

"Gee, I hope you have health insurance," Danny said.

"I have full coverage," she said. "Not that I need it. . . ."

"With no full-time job? Must cost a fortune. Maybe you should take in a boarder."

"I don't need a boarder, I own—"

"I didn't know you owned the place, Helen," Danny said, walking to the telescope, peering up to Hippie Hill.

"Well, I got a great deal, ten years ago, so I took it."

"Good for you," Danny said, and then threw a curveball from the floor, reaching all the way back to the name of a lawyer he'd found the day before in Horsecock's old files. "Did you use Marvin Levy?"

"No, I used a different lawyer," she said. "I don't know who Marvin Levy is."

"How'd you know he was a lawyer?"

"I thought you said he was . . . I dunno."

"Oh," Danny said "Hey, Hel, you have any of the photos Dirty Jim took with the long lens camera from this window?"

He turned to her for a reaction. Her mouth was filled with peanuts, her lips stained with chocolate and food coloring. "I don't know anything about old photos."

"Did you watch Henry Bush die from strychnine poisoning yesterday, Helen? Convulsing. An old man dying in an agony you wouldn't inflict on a rodent?"

"No! I was out." She walked across the living room, lit three candles on the mantel, her sausage-thick fingers trembling. Sweat beaded her brow like a crystal rosary.

"Out at the clinic?"

"No, I go to the clinic on Tuesdays. . . ."

"I thought you weren't sick."

"For . . . for . . . you know, weight loss."

"They prescribe M&M peanuts, Helen? Insurance cover that?"

"Why are you grilling me like this, Danny? I'm not supposed to have stress."

"I think you know stuff, Hel."

"What kind of stuff?"

"Stuff that happened in the wee hours of November 21, 1969. . . ."

"I wasn't around. I was at the Fillmore East—"

"No, you sold your tickets to Kenny Byrne."

"I have the stubs—"

"Kenny signed an affidavit saying he gave them back to you," Danny said, pulling an empty microcassette from his shirt pocket. "I'm a reporter, Helen. I get facts. I cover my ass. I also have him on tape."

He watched her eyes skitter now. Saw her grab a handful of M&Ms, saw her stuff her mouth, gulp the lemonade, and wipe her brow.

"I think it's time for you to leave," she said. "I don't like your insinuations. I don't like that you've turned into an ingrate. When you were a little skell, running around paranoid on pills, you came to Helen. I was pretty! I was nice to you. I was kind. I sucked your cock! Helen taught you how to fuck, taught you how to be a man."

"You were an angel," Danny said. "But somewhere along the way you sold your soul, Helen. I don't know why but I think I know who you sold it to."

"You don't know anything about me. All I ever was to you was a pair of tits and a piece of ass. You have no idea where I came from or where I'm coming from now or where I'm going when you leave. All I ever was to you was a quick blow job and someone to feed you and wash your dirty hippie clothes. I was good to you, Danny. I was very good to you. Why are you being so fucking mean to me? Just go back home, go back to California, go away and forget all of us. Leave me alone."

Sobs jiggled her big body, tears coursing down her reddened face. Which threw Danny off track. The female machismo, Danny thought. *Works every fucking time.* He wanted to hug her, kiss her, to be good and kind to her like she had always been so very good and kind to him. Back in 1969.

"I'm sorry you're sick," Danny said. "But I'm in trouble. I have a daughter. I have a life I want to live. I don't want to spend it in a jail cell."

"I'm not sick," she said, tears coursing down her swollen face. "Please leave. . . ."

She pulled open the door. Danny stepped into the hallway. Leaving the umbrella with the running tape recorder in the umbrella stand inside the door. He turned to Helen and looked at her. Buried under the deep jowls and the chubby cheeks and the extra large muumuu Danny could see the beautiful young woman who had been his hippie earth mother when he was making the ephemeral transition from boy to man, from strung out mixed-up kid to a suspected cop killer.

He wiped the tears from her eyes, kissed her damp forehead. "Be good to yourself, Linc," he said and he saw a ripple of terror shimmer in her teary eyes. She made a motion to speak but no words formed.

Danny hurried down the stairs. In the vestibule he jammed Erika's folded business card into the automatic locking door mechanism so that it would not latch.

He dashed to the far side of the circle and down Fifteenth Road, where he had parked his car on the street, out of sight of Helen's window. The rain pounded as Danny raced to his rented car. He unlocked the door and climbed in. His heart leaped in his chest when he saw Pat O'Rourke sitting in the passenger seat, wearing a hooded rain slicker, sipping a container of steaming tea with the teabag floating in the cup.

"You trying to give me a goddamned heart attack?"

"I'm trying to give you a heads-up," she said. "The car was unlocked."

"Christ . . . what is it?"

"Henry Bush was murdered."

"No kidding?"

"I'm sure Ankles told you that already this morning. Also, there's a bimbo who is dating Christie Strong who works for the local newspaper who is calling up NYPD and asking about it."

"No kidding?"

"The last thing this whole case needs is publicity."

"Why?"

She looked at him as if he were crazy. "It could scare away the people we're looking for," she said. "Drive them underground."

"Could also stir up the hornet's nest, force them above ground. And just because she's a reporter doesn't make her a bimbo. Just like not all cops are corrupt."

O'Rourke looked at him, her eyes narrowing. "I can't ever figure you out. I guess that's what makes you interesting."

More diversionary bullshit, Danny thought. Good cop, hot cop.

"Look, I know you're going to take this with a grain of salt because you think I have some competitive thing going with her. But Erika Malone did more than contribute five thousand dollars to Christie Strong's campaign."

"Yeah? Like what?"

"She cosigned on several of his loans."

O'Rourke reached into her rain slicker and pulled out a manila envelope. She removed a printout from the county clerk's office, with columns of index numbers and real estate lot numbers and tax rates and purchases prices and owners' names. O'Rourke traced a thin soft finger with a mauve-painted nail down a stack of names. She stopped on the name Christie Strong. His name was hyphenated to Erika Malone's. Danny read Erika's familiar Social Security number, a number that like Helen's old phone number was engraved in his memory like a legend on a grave. He had gone with Erika the day she received that number and it was stuck in his brain.

"When?"

Her finger traced left to the date column. "As far back as twenty years ago. When your honey first became successful with her business, a mail-order operation then, she cosigned on several mortgages for old tenements in Prospect Gardens. Including that address you just came out of, where your friend Helen Grabowski lives. Strong bought that building, and it took him ten years, but he bought all the tenants out. Harassed most of the old ones. He made all his mortgage payments on time. Made a fortune converting it to condos. In that time Erika Malone cosigned on ten other buildings."

"All legal?"

"Oh, sure. Legal. Maybe lethal, too. Look at this piece of coziness."

She removed another document from the manila envelope, pushing in the cigarette lighter on the dashboard. Danny leaned closer to her to get a better gander.

"When Strong was rejected by the State Liquor Authority,"

O'Rourke said, lighting a cigarette with his car lighter, "she cosigned and they gave him his liquor licenses for all of Strong's restaurants."

She exhaled the smoke, showing Danny another document from the SLA bearing Erika Malone's and Christie Strong's signatures, side by side. His desire for a cigarette was uncontrollable. He wanted to snatch it out of her hand.

He patted himself, searching for the Zantac. He found them, pushed two through the tinfoil. O'Rourke handed him her container of tea, sweet with artificial sweetener, a rosy lipstick stain on the rim. He put his lip over the lipstick and sipped. The lipstick tasted good. He swallowed the pills.

"Why are telling me all this?"

"I don't want to see you get hurt," she said, pulling out another document from Columbia University, her words clouded in smoke as she spoke. "Your honey is also a liar. She didn't win a full schol- arship. She won a 25 percenter. The rest was paid out of pocket. No loans. Cash."

Danny looked at the document as the rain drummed on the car roof. He realized he was now leaning half out of his seat, she was tilting toward him. Their faces were inches apart. Their breath and body heat shrouded the rain-beaded windows. Steam from the tea and smoke from her cigarette commingled between them. He looked in her big blue eyes, her face smothered in curls under the rain hood. She raised the cigarette to his lips. He took a glorious drag. Closed his eyes. Exhaled.

She kissed him on the lips, very soft, very quick. "You deserve better than her," she whispered, yanking up the car door handle and rushing out into the rain.

Danny knocked on Helen's door. Helen opened it. "I forgot my umbrella," he said, reaching past her to retrieve it from the stand.

"How'd you get into the building?"

"Erika gave me a key," he said.

Helen blinked, slack-jawed.

He left the rental car where it was on Fifteenth Road, took the tape recorder out of his umbrella, stuffed it into his jacket pocket, and hurried across the street into Prospect Park. He opened the umbrella, rushed through the rain, doing pirouettes to be sure he wasn't followed on foot. He wasn't. He checked the Park Drive for O'Rourke's car and for signs of Christie Strong's aides. He was a lone figure in the soggy park.

At the Eleventh Street playground he ducked into the boys' bathroom to urinate. He rewound the tape as he stood alone at the urinal in the bathroom of the playground where he had spent so much joyous time as a kid, afternoons in the sprinklers and on the monkey bars and the swings and the slides. By the time he pulled up his zipper he hit the PLAY button. He fast-forwarded past the conversation he had had with Helen, until he got to the part where he called her Linc and told her to be good to herself.

Then he heard the beeps of a push-button phone being dialed. Helen was still crying. Then: "Hello. . . . Me. . . . Guess who just left? . . . Yeah. . . . Jesus Christ, he's back two days and already he knows half of everything. Maybe more. How do I know how? . . . I'm crying because I'm upset. I used to love that kid, you know. I was pretty then. I was sexy. Everybody loved Helen . . . Helen loved everybody back . . . like one big family. . . . Now he knows I'm sick. . . . He got me all kinds of tongue-tied. He knows about the condo. He knows about the stuff on film. No. Not that film . . . thank God. The stills Jim took later from the window was all he mentioned. He says Kenny Byrne signed an affidavit about the Doors tickets. Has it on tape, too. . . . Yes, he asked all about Henry Bush. . . . No, he didn't mention anything like that. Yes, I'm on the hard phone, you think I'm an asshole. . . . He's closing in. I'm scared. He even called me fucking Linc! I don't need this stress. I'm not well. You said you would always take care of me. Like family. I need you to take care of me. . . . Promise? I'm scared . . . what if he finds out everything? OK, OK, I won't panic . . . keep me updated . . . I can't sleep. . . ."

"Hey!"

Danny jumped. He turned. An old parkie stood at the door.

"Hi."

"You OK? Need paper or anything?"

"No," Danny said, washing his hands. Drying them on paper towels. "I'm fine."

"Some shit storm, huh?"

"You're not kidding."

"Supposed to rain all day and night."

"See ya."

Danny walked past the old parkie, their eyes meeting. Danny trusted no one. He stepped back into the rain, pulling up his rain hood, and splattered through the puddles toward the path snaking past Parkieville.

As he walked he tried to digest all that had happened. Horsecock had been murdered. He suspected Helen was Linc. The name spooked her. And the way she mentioned it to whomever it was she'd spoken to after he left. *Who was it she called,* he wondered. *Dirty Jim? I have to see that little turd again. And Erika is more than a liar. She's hip-deep in Christie Strong's bullshit. Cosigning loans and pretending she doesn't have anything to do with him. Something dirty is going on with her and Strong.*

He reached the bushes just inside the park, up the block from Erika's house, the place where he used to stand as a speed freak, watching the house for hours, paranoid that another guy would replace him in the Grindbox after he was gone. No one ever came. And then she broke off with him, and he used to watch Lars walk her home. But he never stayed long with her in the Grindbox. Not enough time to get the friction burns and squirt in his underwear. No, he waited until he could rape her. He got his. Danny was still glad he'd given him that beating. Because he was sure he had something to do with Horsecock's murder. Something to do with Pat O'Rourke. Who was playing both sides of the coin with him, lulling him, dickteasing him, setting him up for a fall.

He stood in the bushes for a full ten minutes, rain falling on the umbrella, to make certain that there was no green Crown Victoria, black Taurus, or silver Jaguar on his tail. *There are answers to some of my questions in that house,* he thought. He stood for another minute and then Danny sprinted through the rain with the keys to Erika Malone's house jingling in his hand.

# twenty-eight

Danny slammed the inside door and walked straight to the rolltop desk. He used the duplicate key to open it. He took out the phone records again and dialed some of the long-distance numbers. The most dialed number in the Hamptons was answered by a live service: "Mr. Strong's message line, may I help you?"

"Tell him Wally Fortune called, please," Danny said.

A caretaker answered the phone in the Bahamas, informing Danny that Mr. Strong only came down to his house in the winter months. He asked if Danny wanted to leave a message. "Yeah, tell him Vito Malone called," Danny said and hung up.

Danny went through some of Erika's canceled corporate checks. She was no idiot, Danny thought. This house was still in her mother's name. If the IRS were to ever get a warrant to enter Erika's home to seize records they would raid the condo in Manhattan, upstairs from the company's headquarters in Soho. There they would find one set of innocuous books. Meanwhile, he assumed, a second set of dirty books with corresponding canceled checks—most made out to cash—were stashed here in her feeble mother's house in Brooklyn.

He took an armload of paperwork from the rolltop desk, a stack of bills, canceled checks, two ledgers, and some bank books and carried them upstairs to the home office.

He opened three random Clubweb.com invoices to Erika Earth Inc. Each bill was for $300,000, adding up to $3.6 million a year.

In the late nineties so much money was spent on computer operations that $3.6 million a year was small potatoes for a company like Erika's, which made a fortune in Internet sales. But he suspected right away that Strong had used Erika's Earth and Clubweb.com as a double laundry, a way to launder his dirty money.

He made copies of everything, including the phone bills, corporate income tax returns, 1099s she'd sent to individuals who had done freelance and consulting work for her. He couldn't xerox every canceled check so he shuffled through them, hoping something would catch his eye. He found checks made out to stationery stores, travel agents, car-leasing companies, and freelance workers whose names he didn't recognize. Then Danny found several checks made out to Marvin Levy Jr., Esq. With a notation on the stub: "Consultation HG." He was certain Levy was the son of the lawyer to whom Henry Bush had sent his meager checks a long time ago. He suspected HG stood for Helen Grabowski.

His suspicions were confirmed when he found the corporate Blue Cross medical insurance paperwork for Helen Grabowski and James Dugan, aka Dirty Jim. Both of whom were listed as employees of Erika's Earth Inc.

*I've been in love with a stranger for thirty-two years,* he thought.

As he xeroxed the documents, he gazed up at a bulletin board above Erika's desk. Post-Its were thumbtacked all over the cork, with initials and phone numbers. None of them rang a bell. There were a few old photographs. Including one at an old party. Must be a christening, Danny thought. Jack Davis had his arm around his beautiful wife, who was holding a baby boy in a christening gown. Erika was about eleven or twelve in the picture, standing with Vito and Angela Malone. None of that was startling. Two cop partners, their wives and kids at Davis's christening for Pat O'Rourke's baby brother. In the photo he noticed a beautiful baby wearing a nameplate: Patricia. She was now a beautiful grown woman and an avenging angel, Danny thought. That alone was filled with blood-fueled ironies. It put a new spin on the exchange he'd witnessed between these two women, both daughters of dirty dead cops, who'd gone after each other like roller derby contestants the day before at the outdoor café.

But that wasn't the thing that caught Danny's eye. It was the face in the soft-focus background, much, much younger, the same age as Erika, about twelve or thirteen. But he recognized the unmistakable fair-haired male-model looks of Lars Andersen.

"Lying bitch," Danny said aloud, certain that Lars had been Erika's first boyfriend, even before Danny ever met her. Probably took him to the goddamned party. He was the same Lars Andersen who'd seen Horsecock just before he died. The one Danny suspected was the confidential informant who met Jack Davis every Thursday night while Boar's Head was with Linc, whom he was certain was Hippie Helen.

He made a color copy of the photo and placed it into a large Erika's Earth recycled-paper envelope. He pinned the original photo back onto the corkboard.

Next he searched the desk drawers. But they were filled with stationery and office supplies. He opened the file cabinets. They were empty. He sat at the desk and tried to log on to the computer but there was a security password barring his way.

He walked into her bedroom, careful not to disturb anything. He searched through the drawers, fingering her underwear, picking through makeup bags, stirring her jewelry box with a pen. There was nothing of true value in the jewelry box, which he found odd, since she always wore beautiful gems.

He looked under the mattress, under the bed, on the high shelves of the walk-in closet, which was jammed with designer clothes and maybe a hundred pairs of expensive European shoes. He found nothing of interest.

He climbed to the third floor, which consisted of two small rooms and a crawl space. Boxes of old photos, heirlooms, science award plaques, Erika's cheerleading, swimming, and gymnastic trophies, and old toys stuffed one room. Broken rocking chairs, a baby carriage, her father's police and army uniforms, discarded lamps and plain dusty old junk filled the other. In the crawl space Danny found Erika's blue-backed diaries, with her own name and calendar year hand-lettered on the cover of each one in blue, black, and gold ink. He had already read portions of the one for 1969. But Erika had not let him read more than she wanted him to, for fear that he would get a swollen head. He wanted to read those sections. He did and they were filled with a young girl's gushy scribbles. "I will love Danny with all my heart for all my life. It kills me that he's out getting experience but better her than me until I'm ready. Don't let him know you're jealous of this Hippie Helen bitch. She's just the town pump. I think I might have had an orgasm the other day but I'm not sure. I got shivers through my body as we made out in the Grindbox. I can't wait to go all the way with Danny. . . ."

Although he'd taped her, Danny felt creepy reading her private teenage thoughts.

There was more of the same throughout. He skipped past November to the December entries. There was only one. On Christmas Day. "I wonder what Danny is doing for Christmas. My heart breaks for him every day. Mama is so upset, all she does is cry and cry and cry. Mama gets the phone calls every day. I'm still shaking. One day Danny will come back. When all of this is forgotten. I'll be waiting for him. Merry Christmas, Danny, wherever you are. I love you always and forever. . . ."

He thumbed backward again, remembering when she'd broken up with him in late August. She started dating Lars Andersen. He leafed through the month of September and found the date. "First date with Lars. Dinner, movie. Kiss good night. Gorgeous as the day I first met him but boring. Too safe. I miss Danny. My only love. Maybe if he sees me with Lars he will get straight and become the old Danny again. . . ."

Danny closed the diary and picked up another one and counted backward five years. It took him a good ten minutes but he found the page corresponding to the photo he'd found on the wall. "Christening for Dad's boring partner's baby was boring. Met an absolutely gorgeous guy named Lars but he's also BORING. He didn't even try to kiss me. I must be ugly. Maybe if you're as gorgeous as him you only kiss gorgeous girls. So I must be ugly. . . ."

Danny took out the photo of Erika from the party. She was an exotic, mesmerizing-looking little girl, all red curls, dark eyes, and big cheekbones, as beautiful as she was now. He might have ignored her that day, Danny thought, but in five years Lars the lowlife would rape and deflower that grown-up little girl.

He took the diaries down to Erika's home office, copied some of the pages, and brought them back upstairs and put them back where he'd found them. When he tossed them into the box, he noticed that the final diary looked different than the others. The borders of the pages had not yellowed like the ones from previous years. It seemed much newer. He opened several of them and took them to the light of the window. He was right. There was a slight difference in Erika's 1969 diary. The lines were narrower. The paper was lighter. But the glaring thing that made Danny certain this was a much newer diary than the others was the computer bar code on the lower spine. There were no bar codes in 1969, Danny thought. They didn't start using them until the eighties.

Danny was about to leave when he passed another bedroom door. He tried turning the knob. It was locked. He tried one of the keys and it opened. He stepped into Angela Malone's room. More than a dozen old photos of her husband covered the walls, proud portraits of him in his police uniform, holding Erika as a baby, wedding photos, brandishing his gold shield. There were separate beds, the way couples used to sleep in the old days. Vito Malone's pajamas were laid out on his bed. Malone's reading glasses—the same ones he wore in some of the photos—rested on the nightstand on top of a TV guide from November 1969. A prescription jar dated November 3, 1969, from Balsam's Pharmacy stood next to the TV guide. Danny lifted it and saw that the instructions said take one Valium at bed-time to induce sleep.

*She still thinks he's coming home,* Danny thought. He looked in Angela's bureau, beneath Angela's bed, under her mattress. Nothing of value. Danny looked at a collection of Italian-language books in a small bookcase. Poetry by Gabriel D'Annunzio, Dante's *Inferno*, some crime novels, and books on the Vatican, self-help books. Another shelf sagged with Italian-language cookbooks. And some plain, blue-backed books like the ones Erika used as diaries. Angela's diaries stopped in 1982. Danny thumbed through a few of them and selected the one that was dated 1969. All the entries were in Italian.

Danny became startled when he heard the front gate slam, the inner door open, locks turning, hinges creaking, and footsteps in the hall. Heavy footsteps. Then a man's voice. "Erika?" the man called in a moderate tone. Danny recognized the voice right away. It was Christie Strong's voice. "Erika. You home? We need to talk. I didn't want to leave a message. You home?"

Danny carried his umbrella and the envelope with the Xerox copies and tiptoed across the second-floor landing. He opened the stoop door and stepped into the vestibule. He heard Strong climbing the stairs. Danny peeked out through the lace curtains to the double-parked silver Jaguar with the motor running.

"Erika, we need to talk!" Strong shouted. "Now!"

Danny let himself out into the pounding rain, clicking the stoop door behind him. He hurried down the stoop, out of the areaway, and ran for the wall of Prospect Park.

# twenty-nine

Danny bent above the wet headstone, tracing his fingers over the engraved legend: Margaret Murphy Cassidy. Born December 19, 1925. Died June 15, 1969. A quote from W. H. Auden's eulogy for William Butler Yeats adorned the headstone: "Earth, receive an honored guest."

Danny held the umbrella above his head, shielding himself from the tireless rain, gripping the wet stone in his hand. "The bastard will be with you soon," he whispered. "It's what you wanted. Truth is, I helped put you here as much as he did. Me, the old man, and that goddamned war. You were a queen. I love you."

He kissed the headstone and stood. The plot next to his mother's was dug, roped-off, and his father would soon be interred. He sloshed up the cobblestone path of Evergreen Cemetery to meet Ankles. The warm rain lashed in slanted sheets, needling the tress, dimpling the big pond, sponging the giant necropolis where the bodies of tens of thousands of Brooklyn's dead lay in muddy silence.

Over the rise and across the cemetery drive he spotted Ankles holding a green-and-white woman's floral design umbrella above a frail older woman, escorting her to his black Taurus, which was parked on the road thirty feet from the grave. Ankles eased her into the front seat, closed the door to the Taurus, and walked back to the gravesite, which was sheltered by a big yellowing maple. The old flatfoot stood on the hillock overlooking the twenty square blocks of Prospect Gardens that spilled toward Prospect Park like a warren of treachery, blood secrets, and old felonies. Danny knew that most of Ankles's life had been spent policing that urban grid, arresting people for killing victims, many of whom lay in this boneyard. One of them was his son, Tony Mauro, whose grave marker came into focus as Danny approached: Anthony Mauro. Born February 20, 1959. Died January 4, 1980.

Ankles wore a pea green trench coat, blotted with rain, and held his fedora in one hand and the small lady's umbrella in the other. The maple tree offered some small respite from the downpour, the umbrella shielding him from the stubborn drops that bled through the tapestry of sagging leaves. Danny squished toward him, the only other visitor to the cemetery. The bells of noon gonged through the Borough of Churches. Amid the falling rain and clanging bells Danny was reminded of the great Dickens ghost story "The Chimes," which had spooked him for months as a child after his brother, Brendan, read it to him at bedtime over three straight nights before Christmas of 1961. He thought of Brendan jetting home. He wished Darlene would call him.

"Visit your mother?" Ankles asked, staring out at his stomping ground, his watch, as he stood over the earth that held the murdered bones of his son.

"Yeah," Danny said. "Ya know, I knew who Tony was. But he was a kid. Eight years younger than me. So I never got to know him too well."

"He never got to know me that good, either," Ankles said. "Because of the situation. He thought, ya know, Mikey Mauro was his father. Me and Marsha, we let that go on too long. But I used to pick him up from the street, like the other guys, take him for rides, warn him that if he didn't stop fuckin' around, hanging with the wrong people, he could wind up in here before his time."

"You took me for a couple of those rides," Danny said. "Your line always was, 'There's people dying to get in there. Don't be one of 'em.' The ride always ended with kicks in the ankles so we couldn't walk all weekend. We hated you with a passion. But who knows? Maybe it did keep us out of trouble."

"I picked up Tony more than anyone else," Ankles said, turning toward the grave. "But I never put the cuffs on him. How could I? He was my son. My beautiful son."

"That's understandable."

"But it got him killed. The guy he ran with, that mutt Tommy Ryan—"

"Him I knew well. He ran with Christie Strong. You said you pinched him with Strong the night of Vito Malone's murder. They used you as their alibi."

"That's right," Ankles said. "Well, years after that, in 1979, I busted a bunch of them in a score. The only one I let go was Tony Mauro, whose real name should have been Tufano. Because of our situation, our secret, whatever you wanna call it, Marsha gave him my first name instead of my last. Anyway, I cut him loose and busted Ryan and another human switchblade named Cisco."

"So, by Brooklyn street logic," Danny said, "Tommy Ryan must've thought Tony could only have gotten cut loose if he was a rat?"

Ankles nodded, unwrapped a White Owl cigar, and put it in his mouth. He bit it until his face shivered. He didn't light it. "That woman started dying that same day," Ankles said, nodding toward Marsha Tufano, who sat behind the rain-beaded window of the Taurus, staring straight ahead.

"Jesus, Ankles, I'm sorry. I never knew."

"Either did he," Ankles said. "Never knew he was my kid. That kills me a little every fuckin' day of my life. Tony had a son, too. With a girl named Carol, cutest little guy you ever seen, name of Michael. But Carol split with the baby after the messy night Tommy Ryan got shot to death. Me and Marsha tried to make contact with Carol over the years, but she asked us to leave her alone. So did the kid, who's all grown up now, with the only father he remembers. Now Marsha's almost gone. She'll be right next to Tony. Jesus Christ, but it all went so fast. Fuckin' life, it lands running, straight for these gates. And in between people get themselves so friggin' tangled up in knots, crazy shit, life shit. Your heart gets led around by the dick, which gets you in the worst trouble of all. I must've investigated the murders of a hundred poor fucks buried in here like my son. Most of them got in trouble with their dicks. Half of them come from fucked-up families. I walk around in here some-times, on sunny days, looking at their headstones, and it seems like half the people in this neighborhood have skeletons in their closets that led to skeletons in this boneyard. I'm tellin' you all this because I don't take the moral high ground here. When I find out stuff, secret stuff, about people's lives, I don't judge them on it. My life ain't been Ozzie and Harriet. Bad shit just happens. I should know, because lotsa bad shit happened to me. Every day my son is dead is a day that bad shit happens to me. If I would have told my son I was his father I mighta saved him. But that ship sailed. I missed it. My kid missed it. I gotta deal with the cards on the table. I also like to give credit where it's due. Because of you I found some shit I never thought of looking for before. I'll give you the facts. But remember, I'm not judgmental."

He reached inside his coat and took out a large manila envelope, opened it, and took out some computer printouts.

"I made a bunch of calls," Ankles said. "I ran the personnel and Carr's computers. I called a guy I know in IAB. The shit I just found out, you won't believe. All these years, focusing on you, I never asked the right questions about other people. First off, Jack Davis. He got in trouble when he was a young cop. They sent him to the rubber-gun squad for a couple of months. I already knew that. But back in 1969 I could never find out for what. But now that all this time has passed, his files are more accessible. If you know how to use a computer. Which I learned how to do, so that I didn't become obsolete on this fucked-up job."

"What kind of problem did Davis have that they took away his gun for a few months?" Danny asked. "Rubber gun is for guys with booze problems, no?"

"They sent Davis for 'moral turpitude,' they called it then," Ankles said. "If he was still a rookie they woulda shit-canned him. But he was past his probationary period. So they sent him for counseling. A retreat, with priests and a shrink. This was in 1964."

"What for?"

"They raided a gay club in Brooklyn Heights," Ankles said. "In those days it was a big deal. There were drugs on the premises. A few guys pettin' pee-pees in the back room. Consenting adults. But in 1964, this was, like, a fuckin' scandal."

"Was Davis gay? Bisexual?"

"He said he didn't know it was a gay club, that someone brought him there after a bachelor party. Said he was half in the bag. He went along for a drink. He didn't notice that it was all guys. Most cop bars were all guys back then, he said. What did he know? One of the vice undercovers who raided the joint cut him loose but sent his name to his CO. The CO sent him for counseling to the retreat, to talk to shrinks and priests. That was the logic then. They treated it like it was a mental illness, or devil possession."

"Who was the undercover vice cop?"

Ankles smirked. "Vito Malone."

"Fuck," Danny said. "But Davis got married after that, didn't he?"

"Yeah. But I'd bet my pension that Vito Malone kept an eye on Davis over the years. Just like he kept an eye on me and found out about me and Marsha. I know how he operated because he tried to use the information against me. I starched him with one punch in the locker room. I told him to go ahead and file a complaint. Go ahead and tell Mikey Mauro. I wasn't gonna be fuckin' blackmailed by this lowlife. He backed down from me. But I had less to lose."

"Davis had more to lose?"

"Sure. Davis was married with one kid and another on the way when Malone came back to haunt him. The guy was bisexual. He had urges, desires, feelings. That don't make him a freak. It makes him human. But this was the midsixties. You hippie slobs mighta been into free love, but for a fag on the force it woulda been brutal. No one would wanna work with him. Woulda been ostracized. You think what they do to broads on the job is bad? A cop exposed as half a fag in the sixties woulda been tortured. Fag jokes, fag pranks, dildos in his locker, bouquets of flowers from guys named Ralph on Valentine's Day, applications to Cocksucker U. He woulda been crucified. Instead, Malone kept it to himself. He tracked Davis. I bet he had that fuckin' Dirty Jim Dugan, who he always used to shadow people around with a camera, catch him in the act. And I bet when he got the goods on Davis he used his seniority, and his dossiers on certain brass, to nab him as a partner. Then he used whatever new gay sex info he got on the poor son of a bitch to get Davis to go along with his drug racket with Strong."

"A straight blackmail," Danny said.

"You can't pull off renting your badge to a drug dealer unless your partner goes along with you," Ankles said. "Your partner is like a second spouse. He knows when you're hungry, when something's troublin' you, when you're broke, your sexual fantasies. You fart in each other's company. Your partner knows when you got extra dough in your pocket. And when you look the other way on an easy collar. And until Davis partnered with Malone he had an otherwise spotless folder. He was a very good cop. He was a loner, but he was clean, efficient, made collars, was not a malingerer. Never had a civilian complaint for brutality or disrespect or discrimination. Nothing. His Achilles' heel was that he was a gay cop in the wrong time. There hadda been plenty of gay cops, but everyone of them was in the closet."

"Today they recruit gay cops," Danny said.

"They had a fuckin' gay prom last year with nothin' but gay cops policin' it," Ankles said. "Who cares? Good for them. What, I should judge people on their sexual longings? As long as they're not doing it with kids, on the take to wise guys and dope dealers, they can patrol in pink uniforms for all I give a shit."

"Christ Almighty," Danny said. "Poor Davis. The poor, cornered son of a bitch didn't want to do more than scare Wally Fortune that night. He begged Boar's Head to stop beating Wally—"

Ankles looked at him, his stare as cold as squandered time. "You little fuck."

"What?"

"You just admitted you witnessed the Wally Fortune murder."

"I never said I didn't," Danny said, smiling. "I said I wasn't sure what I saw. I was on mescaline. I have a memory but it's an altered one. I was tripping."

"You just tripped over your own fuckin' tongue," Ankles said. "And you fucking will repeat what you just fucking said on a witness stand. If you don't I will repeat it for you and defy you to deny it."

Ankles bit into his cigar, flipped a page of his printouts. "Get a grip on your balls, it gets better," Ankles said. "As for Christie Strong, that ain't even his fuckin' name. Back in '69 we didn't have nationwide computer linkups so I never put this together back then. And then after he went legit I thought I'd missed the boat on Strong. He has all these new civic and political affiliations. But I told you this neighborhood had more inbreeding than a hillbilly mink farm. Christie Strong was born in New York City, but raised in Lincoln, Nebraska, by a woman named Fanny—get this—Grabowski."

Danny took out his Zantac, popped a pill. Swallowed it dry. "Are you telling me that Helen and Strong are brother and sister?"

"Twins. Same fuckin' DOB, same mother."

"Who's the father?"

"These computers today are amazing," Ankles said, flipping another page, rain dotting them. Danny moved closer, holding his bigger umbrella above them. "There are no holidays off for computers. So I run Fanny Grabowski's name through the computer. She has two pops for pros back in '51—the year that Thompson hit that fuckin' home run, with the stolen signs offa Branca. She was a dumb eighteen-year-old hayseed kid who came to New York to be an actress and wound up turning a few tricks. Both times she was busted by the same vice cop. Guess who?"

Danny grimaced and said, "Henry Bush?"

Ankles nodded and looked toward Marsha. She sat staring out at the rain like a woman who had accepted her fate as a kind of daily penance for her transgressions and waited to be rejoined with her son.

"Bush and Malone worked Vice together back then," Ankles said. "Malone musta known about Bush. Bush rose in the ranks. Malone was a great detective but shady. He reached detective and stayed there. But he had a dossier on Horsecock. Got himself transferred to his unit."

"Horsecock admitted to me his weakness was broads," Danny said. "Said he sometimes took some pleasure in trade."

"Only this one, this Fanny Grabowski, she got knocked up," Ankles said. "I checked that old garnishee you gave me. Fanny Grabowski might have turned tricks but she was a Catholic and didn't believe in abortion, which wasn't legal then anyway. She had the twins in Kings County Hospital. She fingered old Horsecock as the father. He told her to take a walk, that there were more dicks in and out of her than police headquarters. But she filed a paternity suit. The courts ordered blood tests. This was before DNA, but I guess they figured it was close enough to say he was the father. At first Henry refused to fucking pay. So the court garnisheed his check. The PD don't like that, a guy having to be garnisheed for child support. So he agreed to pay her eighteen dollars every two weeks—nine dollars a kid—if she would take the brats back to Nebraska. She did. But it looks like she told the kids all about their dear old dad before she died of cancer when they were just teenagers. After they buried mom, they headed east. The computer doesn't say what happened when they got here."

"Holy shit, but you can guess, can't you? I mean old Henry's wife had to know about the kids and it must have broken her heart because Horsecock said she couldn't have kids. So my guess is he rejected them when they showed up. They were legal age now. He had no more legal responsibility for them. But how would they get even? One would sell drugs all over his watch. The other would fuck every guy that moved. Follow the pathology."

"And, of course, Vito Malone probably busted Strong and figured it all out when the kid said his father was his CO," Ankles said. "Malone figured he could use that information to manipulate his commanding officer. Even Horsecock couldn't bring himself to lock up his own flesh and blood, the kids he brought into the world."

"The same way you cut loose Tony," Danny said, nodding toward the gravestone.

"So he turned his head," Ankles said, nodding. "Let Strong and Boar's Head do whatever they wanted to do. Malone voided the arrest and made a business deal with Strong. Then he needed a partner he could manipulate. So he had Horsecock get him Davis. He made a lot of fucking money. All of fuckin' which had to make

Malone giddy because Bush had gotten Malone in trouble a few times. Made him lose fifteen vacation days once for beating a prisoner so bad. Malone must have loved having Horsecock by the balls."

Danny thought about the long-ago Thursday night when he entered Helen's pad and discovered Vito Malone having S&M sex with Helen. *"When I'm fucking you I'm also fucking him," Vito Malone said.*

*"Fuck me," Helen said. "Fuck him."*

"Fucking mess," Danny said with a deep sigh. "When Horsecock was ready to tell me who Linc was, exposing the whole thing now that his wife was dead, they had him killed to keep him quiet."

"But their own father?" Ankles spit out a shred of tobacco.

"On the other hand, if you forgive my pop psychology, there had to be a deep, old Freudian hatred over the way Bush had knocked up and abandoned their prostitute mother."

"And later rejected them, treated them like a coupla bastards when their mother died and they came looking for their old man."

"And killing him had to be for practical reasons, too," Danny said. "Because Horsecock knew a lot more than who Linc was. It had to be because Horsecock knew who killed Wally Fortune and Vito Malone. It was probably Christie's decision."

"We have to prove all that," Ankles said. "The only thing we got Strong and Grabowski guilty of so far is being a pair of poor illegitimate kids, born from a horny cop who abused his badge and a silly young whore who didn't use a rubber. Making a leap from that to murder is a pole vault."

"Is that supposed to be a pun?"

"I also found out about our friend Patricia Davis O'Rourke," Ankles said, ignoring the question and flipping a few pages ahead in his printout sheath.

"And?"

"She's a savvy chick," Ankles said. "A helluva cop. But this kid started on a career path straight to here without being noticed as Jack Davis's kid."

"Yeah, I know," Danny said. "I figured that one out already."

"She went to John Jay College of Criminal Justice—"

"Not to be confused with John Jay High, where I went."

"One makes criminals," Ankles said. "The other makes crime fighters. Anyway, she gets married to a fellow student named

O'Rourke. The marriage tanks. They divorce. But she keeps the name. She graduates as Pat O'Rourke and joins the Suffolk police, which grabs her right away because she's a woman and has the college degree. She makes detective fast, doing undercover vice decoy and narc buys in the burbs. Then she does what nobody ever does. She transfers, at a loss of fuckin' pay, to NYPD, who is thrilled to fuckin' death to get her. And since she didn't come up the NYPD ranks she has no pals on the PD. No one who remembers Jack Davis knows who she is. And so when she volunteers for Internal Affairs the PD brass is tickled pink. She goes at the job like gangbusters. She rousts a bunch of dirty cops in the eighties who are involved in a crack cocaine ring in East New York. She busts a detective for repeated rape of his stepdaughter. She gets a first-grade status. And while she's there she starts pulling my folder and looking into the Vito Malone and Jack Davis case."

"And me," Danny said.

"You she gets into when she transfers to this new unit called the Cold-Case Squad," Ankles said. "But I learned only today that she's not even assigned to the Vito Malone case. See, she's too fuckin' savvy. She knows she'd get in trouble for working a case in which she had a vested interest. But they can't stop her from doing it on her spare time."

"This is her spare time?"

"O'Rourke saved all her vacation," Ankles said.

"She knew my father was dying," Danny said. "And figured I'd come home."

"Like I said, savvy," Ankles said. "Clean. No blemishes. But also ruthless. She'd put her own brother in the can if he wasn't already there."

"The brother is doing time?"

"Yeah. It's funny how kids go. One becomes hell-bent on clearing her father's name, to lift the stain from the family. The other just goes bad, so fucked up from seein' the old man blow his brains out that he ran for the drugs and the cheap stickups. This is Luke Davis's second armed robbery bit. Robbed a Sizzler steakhouse on Northern Boulevard. Seven to fifteen in Greenhaven for, like, three grand. But me and you know the life sentence started the second he watched his father's brains splat against the window."

"What about the mother?" Danny asked. "Whatever happened to her?"

"Dead. Looks like she became a rum pot," Ankles said. "Who could blame her? After the family lost the Mill Basin house, the Poconos house, the boat, the BMW, she dived off the high board into the bottle. She had five DWIs before she totaled a junker on the LIE on her way home from work as a barmaid in Hicksville. DOA Good Samaritan Hospital. Pat was just nineteen, the other guy was eighteen. They went down different roads from the funeral at Pinelawn, where she went in next to Jack Davis."

"What a fucking horror story," Danny said.

"That's the wonderful fuckin' sixties all you assholes love to celebrate so much."

"A lot of good things came out of the sixties, too."

"Not in this fuckin' neighborhood," Ankles said. "I better go. The fluids run into the lower extremities if Marsha sits too long. She needs to go home, put her legs up."

Danny was going to tell him about what he'd found in Erika's house and about Strong having a key. But Danny needed to see Erika again first. Needed to have a chance to cut her the same slack Ankles had cut for his son, Tony, the same slack Horsecock had cut for Helen and Christie Strong. Danny still cared for Erika Malone. He couldn't rat on her before she had the chance to defend herself.

"We need to see each other in a few hours," Ankles said. "We need to talk to some people."

"It's almost twelve-thirty now," Danny said. "Call me on my cell at three."

Ankles nodded and walked toward his car. Danny turned to walk down the winding road to the exit of the cemetery.

"Hey, Ankles," Danny said, pulling out the picture of Erika, her parents and Jack Davis and his wife and little Patricia Davis at newborn Luke's christening.

"Can you read Italian?"

"A little," he said. "A newspaper. A letter. Why?"

"I don't know yet."

"Don't fucking hold out on me. . . ."

"Oh, and about O'Rourke's mother."

"Yeah, what about her?" Ankles said, his driver's door pulled open, ready to climb in, getting soaked.

"You have a maiden name?"

"I dunno," he said. "Maybe. I just got this shit an hour ago. Lemme see."

Ankles held the sheath of computer printouts inside the shelter of the car, flipped through pages. He couldn't find it at first, getting frustrated as the rain drummed on his fedora.

"Hold on, it should be here somewheres. Here it is, maiden name."

He looked up at Danny and said, "Andersen. With an *e*."

# thirty

Lars Andersen bench-pressed 350 pounds for the tenth rep of his fourth set and dropped the bar on the steel rack. His muscles were pumped, pectorals bulging, upper-arms rippling, cables of vein pulsing in his forearms.

"No, I don't have a cousin named Pat," he said.

"How about a niece?" Danny asked.

Lars stood from the bench, walked across the gym on the top floor of the old Union Temple overlooking Grand Army Plaza. The place was busy with gym rats on treadmills, Stairmasters, stationary bikes, and weight-resistance machines. He bent over a water fountain and he took a long drink. Behind Lars, in a glass cube, four men in exceptional shape chased around a little black ball, beating it with racquets. In the next glass box chunky middle-aged women wearing leotards groaned through a step class led by a spear-thin woman instructor with a rump like a wildebeest.

"Yes, I have a niece named Patricia," Andersen said, impatient with Danny.

"And a nephew named Luke who is doing seven to fifteen for armed robbery?"

"Hey, pal, I don't have to even talk to you. I humor you because we come from the same time and place and because we both dated the same chick in the last century. And maybe because I'm extending a journalistic courtesy. But don't you dare come digging in my family's dirty laundry, or I'll get mad. I don't like me when I'm angry. You wouldn't either. I pay professional people good money to help me control my anger. I don't appreciate you trying to undo all the very expensive good they've done me."

Lars bent for another camel feed from the water fountain. Danny nodded, gaped at the wildebeest, and checked the clock on the wall. It was a quarter to one. He was going to be late for his appointment with Erika.

"I'm not digging into anyone's dirty laundry for kicks," Danny said. "And I'm too old to be threatened, big guy. I'm here about murder. A few of them. And your name is in the fucking mix. Big time. It's down on paper in Jack Davis's logbook. Every Thursday night, Evergreen cemetery."

Lars looked up from the water fountain, his eyes wide and glittering with anger.

"You trying to fucking blackmail me now, too?"

"What the fuck are you talking about?"

"Come with me," Lars said, grabbing Danny by the arm and banging through a door marked "sunroof" and up a flight of stairs. Lars hit the panic bar leading out to the roof that overlooked Prospect Park and the shrouded borough of Brooklyn from a fourteen-story vantage. Adirondak lounge chairs lined the rooftop. Danny did a pan of Brooklyn. It was immense, jammed with two and a half million people the last census knew about, most of them indoors today in the punishing rain. Lars led Danny under a green plastic canopy and began to pat him down, checking Danny's chest and back, and up and down his legs to his crotch. Danny had left the tape recorder in the rented car.

"A little paranoid, aren't you?"

"If you had spent half your life being blackmailed you would be paranoid, too," Lars said.

"Blackmailed by who about what?"

"Come on, fuck-o," Andersen said. "You already mentioned the fucking logbook. Don't pretend you don't know. Who sent you? The bastard with the photographs? I can't prove it, but my guess is it's that little fucking weasel Dirty Jim."

Andersen backed Danny to a damp brick wall with a chest butt. This big fuck raped Erika, he thought. He had something to do with Horsecock's murder. *And now I'm standing on a rooftop with him in the rain. He could toss me off like a bag of garbage.*

"Well, I paid and paid until I said fuck you," Andersen said. "His pictures aren't worth shit anymore. I don't care what he does with them. The day I came out of the closet his filthy pictures became worthless. So what? So I'm gay. Run me for congress. Sign me to a three-picture deal. Buy me a newspaper to run. Scratch that, I already have one."

He poked Danny in his chest, a finger that felt like a pool stick hitting a cue ball on a break. "Don't do that," Danny said, as the rain tattooed the plastic canopy, wind spinning a wet wash across the tar roof.

"Or what? You want to try me, Cassidy?"

"I didn't come here to fight with you, Andersen. But people know I'm here. Ankles knows I'm here. He knows about you and Davis now, too."

"So Dirty Jim uses the pictures. Ankles uses the logbook. And what? You point a finger at me for murder? Jack wasn't murdered. Jack blew his brains out."

Andersen's eyes glistened, looking across the park. "I loved him," Andersen said. "I would never have hurt Jack. Never."

"But you might have had a motive to kill Vito Malone. He knew about you and Jack, your sister's husband, didn't he? He knew that you and Jack met every Thursday night in the cemetery."

"He was no angel himself. He was always with that Hippie Helen slut at the same time I was with Jack. I was nineteen. Jack was twenty-five. We were in love. He loved my sister, too, but in a different way. It was just a shit time for people like us. Everybody talked about free love. What bullshit. There was no free love for people like me and Jack back then. A gay man on the police force was a fucking pariah, a moving target. He wanted to quit but Malone wouldn't even let him. He had him in a squeeze. Like an indentured servant. He never told me details, but I know they were involved in drugs."

"He didn't mind spending his money on nice things. Two houses. Cars. A boat, a boy toy."

"I think part of him wanted to get caught so it would all end," Andersen said, holding out his big hand, catching raindrops. "Part of him wanted to leave something for my sister and their kids in case something bad happened to him. He always hinted something might happen. He was haunted. I think Malone might have even killed a guy. He didn't want me to know the details. So all that died for me with Jack."

"Except for the photos."

"That bastard Dirty Jim had photos of everyone. He ran around at night popping flashes in everyone's face. He did it to Jack and me in the cemetery early in our relationship. Well, we were both naked, by the duck pond, on a blanket. We had a bottle of wine. He had some pot. We were making love under a big full moon. Very romantic. Then out of nowhere, like a lightning storm, there's this series of flashbulbs popping. And a spotlight blinding us. We thought it was a security patrol. We were terrified. Frozen. Scrambling for our clothes."

Danny remembered a spotlight himself, from November 21, 1969. . . .

*A white cone of blinding light, like the one in Bosch's painting. A series of flashes and then a long bright light. Then loud popping. Screaming. Moaning. . . .*

"Like a home movie sun gun," Danny said. "Super 8 surveillance film. Like the ones the cops used."

"That's what Jack said. He cursed Vito Malone. Said Malone must've put Dirty Jim up to it. First Malone followed us. Found out where we went. Then he had Dirty Jim take the pictures and the movie footage. Then Malone used the pictures to blackmail poor Jack into doing things he didn't want to do."

"They threatened to show the pictures to your sister?"

"Yeah," Andersen said. "And to police brass."

"What about Christie Strong?"

"What about him?"

"Malone and Davis rented their badges to him."

Andersen seemed amazed. "I don't think so," Andersen said. "I think you're wrong. Christie Strong is a great guy. In fact, he was the one who got the goddamned negatives for me. He never said from who, but I always thought it was from Dirty Jim. After my sister died, I pretty much lost contact with my niece and nephew. Luke went a little screwy, went to jail. Patricia became distant, as if she wanted to distance herself from Brooklyn and me and her father's name and reputation. She got married but I wasn't invited to the wedding. I heard she became a cop out in Long Island. I was shocked the other day when she picked me up in Prospect Park. I had no idea who she was. I get women coming on to me a lot, and they get disappointed when I have to tell them I'm not interested. I always joke and ask if they have any brothers."

Danny looked at him as the rain fell. "Does she know about you and her father?"

"I don't know," Andersen said. "I'm not going to tell my niece that me and her dad used to get it on. Hey, I'm not proud of it. It was wrong because he was my sister's husband. But guys have affairs with their sisters-in-law all the time. That's wrong, too. But no one thinks it's perverted. Were we wrong? Sure. Perverted? No way. We were two mixed-up young lovers. Jack was trapped in a job he hated. In a marriage he only half wanted. He loved my sister, as a companion, as the mother of his kids. He loved being a father, a family man, Disneyland, Christmas, Father's Day, all the traditional stuff. He even enjoyed straight sex with her. But he had other needs and desires. I filled those needs and desires. It was rather tame by today's standards."

"What if she does ask?"

"I don't know that I could ever make her understand. But if she asks I'll tell her the truth. We're not close. But when I met her in Prospect Park the other day she wanted to know what I knew about who killed Vito Malone. I told her I wished I knew who killed him. That I'd take out a full-page thank-you ad in my paper. As far as I'm concerned he drove Jack to suicide."

"What did your niece ask you about?"

"She asked a lot of questions about you. I told her I didn't know much, you'd been gone forever. She asked about Ankles the cop, who I thought was dead by now. He was a real prick. I remember he took me for a ride to the cemetery himself once when I was about seventeen. I hobbled home after he kicked the ankles off me. I'd like to pay him back sometime. But my doctor says I must control my anger."

"That's a very good idea," Danny said. "What else did she ask you?"

"She asked me to keep our blood relationship a secret, not to mention to anyone that she was Jack Davis's daughter. I said fine. But that I wouldn't be part of a criminal coverup. That I was a newspaper publisher. Since you already know, what's the difference? She knew an awful lot about me from stories I'd written in the past. She knew I was out of the closet."

"Did she ask you about Henry Bush?"

"She mentioned him. I told her I knew him but that he had never bothered me. He was just an old man who ran in the park every morning. A face from the past."

"Did you know that he knew all about you?"

"Where's this leading?"

"You lied to me, Lars. You told me you didn't meet Henry Bush in Prospect Park yesterday afternoon. But you did, didn't you?"

"Yeah, I met him," he said. "I just didn't want to get involved in all this old crap. Henry Bush was hyperactive on the phone. Like an old man on speed. He called me, asked me to meet him right away. Said it was life and death. Said he was going to reveal some old stuff. About Vito Malone and Jack Davis and his son and daughter. And it might affect me. So I drove straight up to meet him in the park. Right away I could smell the whiskey on his breath. He was babbling. He said he knew what Malone had on me and Jack Davis and that it was going to come out. He said he wanted to give me a heads-up so that I didn't get hurt. I told him it was yesterday's papers. I had nothing to fear. I told him I was an innocent background player in that whole dirty episode. Then he started gasping and lurching around. Then he sat on a bench and relaxed. He asked me not to touch him. Every time I did he would arch his back and rattle."

Danny knew that was the strychnine starting to hit him, the dose that was slipped into his drink up in Foley's. Before they jabbed him with the needle. At least now he knew how Horsecock wound up in the park. He walked there to meet Lars Andersen. He also knew JoJo Corcoran had been right about seeing the two of them together.

"So what happened?"

"I told him to go sleep it off. I jumped in my car and I went back to work. I'm sorry he died. But as far as I was concerned he was just an old rambling drunk."

"You didn't see him die?"

"No. Christ, I'm a human being. I would have helped him if I thought he was going to die. He looked smashed. That's all. He asked me not to touch him. I thought maybe he was an old homophobe, I dunno. A guy asks you not to touch him, you leave him alone."

Doing a Google.com search on the Internet, Danny had learned that people on strychnine can't tolerate being touched. Can't bear loud noises.

"Your niece didn't elaborate about Bush and Hippie Helen or Christie Strong?"

"Like I said she was more curious about you."

"Uh-huh," Danny said, finding Andersen disarming, refreshing, and if he didn't know better, he would have thought he was a likeable guy. "Why me, you think?"

"Well, everyone always said you were a suspect. I wasn't because I was in the fucking hospital from the beating that animal Malone ordered on me for going out with his daughter. Shit, I was just doing her a favor going out with her. She was just trying to make you jealous. But Boar's Head hit the roof when he found out his daughter was dating the same guy his partner was having a homosexual affair with. He went fucking berserk! I mean ballistic. He chased me for three blocks. If he'd caught me I think he would have killed me."

You would have deserved it for raping his daughter, Danny thought, afraid, here alone on the rooftop, to admit to Lars that he was the one who'd given him that beating.

"The very next day he had somebody give me a beating so bad I almost died," Andersen said, gazing into the rain. "Jack was convinced Malone ordered it. He was so upset I thought he might have killed Malone himself. I begged him not to. I didn't want him to get in trouble over me."

That thought had never occurred to Danny before. Maybe Davis killed Malone because he thought Malone had beaten up his young lover, Andersen.

"Maybe he did."

"Nah, he was home with my sister that night, all night," Andersen said. "But I promised myself in that hospital bed that I would become so big, so strong, so tough that no one could ever do that to me again. Tell you the truth I'm getting sort of tired keeping in this kind of shape. As you get into your fifties, it gets harder and harder. I'm thinking of settling down."

Danny looked at the clock on the phallic tower of the Williamsburg Bank that rose into the Brooklyn sky: 12:55.

"I have to go," Danny said.

Andersen blocked his way, standing in front of the door. "Did you kill Vito Malone?"

"Everybody asks me that," Danny said. "As soon as I know I'll let you know."

He put out his hand for Danny to shake. "I hope there's no hard feelings about the old days," he said.

"About what?" he asked before shaking his hand.

"About Erika."

"As a matter of fact—"

Danny thought of throwing caution to the storm, confronting Andersen about raping her. But Andersen cut him off. "I mean I was gay, man," he said.

"You were bisexual," Danny said. "Like Jack Davis. And you—"

"No, no, no," he said, laughing. "That's what me and Erika used to laugh about. I was then and still am 100 percent gay. We served each other well. I was still deep in the closet so I used Erika as a beard, a gorgeous girl on my arm. She liked being with me because I was, well, I was always kinda pretty, if I have to say so myself. And she thought being with me would make you mad jealous. You were the last guy I was afraid of because you were a strung out speed freak back then. I was a safe date for a holdout virgin in 1969. She was saving that for you."

Danny searched Lars's eyes for the big lie. But Lars looked earnest and truthful.

"You didn't take Erika's cherry?"

Andersen laughed. "Kinda comical—fiftysomething men standing on a rooftop in the rain talking about taking cherries," he said, catching his breath. "Jack Davis took mine, if you must know. But no, of course, I didn't take Erika Malone's cherry. I couldn't get it up for a girl if she looked like Mel Gibson. I've never had sex with a woman in my life, thank you very much."

# thirty-one

Erika Malone lay belly-down and naked on the king-size bed that sat on a raised platform in the center of her massive Soho loft. Rain drummed on three ten-foot-square skylights, thunder cracking over the city.

Danny had called her on his cell phone, told her he had been delayed by the rain. She told him that she had left keys under a mat in the vestibule of her building on Greene Street. She told him the big key would unlock the inside door and the second key would open the private express elevator that would take him to her loft above her Erika's Earth headquarters, which was closed for the holiday.

"Hurry," she'd said on the phone. "I have to pick up my mother in two hours. Park the car anywhere. Give me the ticket. Just get here. I need you. I'll be waiting."

He stepped off the elevator and walked across the gleaming oak plank floors of the loft, the walls covered in huge modern canvases, massive gilded mirrors, framed Warhols, and an original Monet. Two ten-foot bronze sculptures—one a naked man with out-stretched arms, the other a naked woman who seemed to be rushing into his arms—stood like sentries at the entrance of the loft. There were no walls separating the sections. A modern space-age kitchen was located against one far wall. A half-dozen leather couches and armchairs were scattered in haphazard but comfortable angles in the living room area, all facing windows that looked out on cityscapes and the Hudson River. Track lighting spotlighted the art and the kitchen and living room area.

But all the art and chic furnishings vanished from Danny's view as he approached the red-headed beauty lying naked on the big bed, a single magenta spotlight illuminating her tight, cut body. Six oval antique mirrors were stationed around the bed, tilted at strategic angles. Erika watched Danny approach, not uttering a single word, her arms and legs spread-eagle on the satin-sheeted bed, her hard round behind raised in anticipation. Danny undressed, piled his clothes on the raised platform, and he walked to her, aroused. He mounted her without foreplay. With a vengeance.

\*          \*          \*

They did everything. They did it for almost an hour. She was magnificent, Danny thought, as he separated himself from her. And yet, as he sat up, spent, he felt as if there had been another death in his life. The afterglow of sex with Erika after a three-decade wait was like the flickering of a funeral pyre. Another piece of him had died. The mystique had vanished. A lifelong fantasy had been gutted. The end of the hunt had ended in a kill. Erika Malone was just flesh and blood, and he'd made love to her. *La petite mort,* as the French said. The little death. He could never again look forward to the first time with Erika Malone. And so in a rueful, complicated way, a piece of her had perished in the bed. And a piece of himself.

"Was I worth the wait?" she asked.

"No." The loud word echoed in the big room like a gunshot. She lay in astonished naked silence as Danny hustled on his clothes and strode toward the elevator.

"Why?"

"Because you lied to me," he said. "Your lie changed my life."

"Lied about what?"

Danny pressed the elevator button.

"Lars Andersen is gay."

The elevator door opened.

"I never said he wasn't."

"You never said he was."

"It was a secret. His secret."

"You said he raped you, stole your virginity."

"I never said that. You assumed that."

"If not him, then who?"

"Maybe you should go," she said, getting up from the bed, tiptoeing like a ballerina across the floor, an insanity-provoking vision even with all the testosterone drained from his body. Even though he felt something between them had died.

"It was Christie Strong," he said. "Wasn't it?"

"Please, go."

"You have Helen Grabowski and Dirty Jim Dugan on your fucking staff! You deceived me when I was grilling that dirty fuck. You're up to your beautiful bare ass in these people's dirt and blood and treachery."

"You have no idea."

"Christie Strong has a key to your fucking house, Erika. He took your fucking cherry, and you've been fucking him since. You know all about what happened that night. Why are you involved with all these lowlifes?"

"Bury your father, Danny. Go back to where you've been. Take your daughter to a ball game. Send your ex-wife some flowers. You already know more than what's good for you. Quit while you're ahead."

She shoved him into the elevator, turned the key for the street. Danny blocked the closing door with his arm.

"Strong raped you, didn't he? And you let me beat up poor fucking Lars."

"I never told you Lars did it. I never asked you to hurt anyone. Go. You got what you came for. And you said I wasn't worth the wait. Now go."

He freed the elevator door.

"You were worth the wait for me," she said as the door rolled closed. He caught a final glimpse of her turning and walking naked across the loft. Gorgeous. As the elevator descended in the shaft he heard Erika Malone make a series of low muffled sounds but he could not tell if she was sobbing or laughing.

# thirty-two

Where's the film, you fuckin' freak?" Ankles said, stalking Dirty Jim around his desk in the Clubweb.com storefront.

"What fuckin' film?" Dirty Jim asked, yanking his retractable key ring.

"The eight-millimeter film you shot of Lars Andersen and Jack Davis," Danny said.

"Up with it before I snap you into fucking firewood, stick man," Ankles said.

"You, I got photos of," Dirty Jim said, pointing at Ankles. "All ready to go out on the Web if anything happens to me. Pictures of you and Mikey Mauro's bride getting it on in your detective car. All they're worth now is some cheap fuckin' laughs. But, you threaten me, asshole, I can threaten back. I'll make you and the missus a laughingstock."

Ankles made a lunge at him. Danny grabbed him. Dirty Jim clutched his stomach, belched, gagged, grabbed his bottle of prescription pills and his bottle of Pepto Bismol. He took a slug of the Pepto Bismol, his pink horse teeth gritting. He shook his head like a wet hound, stared at the bottle.

"Everybody calm the hell down," Danny said, holding his arms out full length, separating Ankles from Dirty Jim.

"You guys bust in here like gangbusters, you think I'm gonna cave?" Dirty Jim said, belching into his fist, then swinging his key ring and tapping his fingers across a computer keyboard. "Fuck you. I might be a skinny little fuck, but I got alliances. I got keys. I tap one computer key and shit starts flying on the Web like a squadron of Jap kamikazes. Pictures, dossiers, information, shit no one wants to see fly. I am not a stooge. Why you think I survived this long? I'm afraid of very few people. You guys aren't on the short list. Way I hear it, the fuckin' cold-case cop, the one with the champagne-glass-titties and the ass like two scoops of vanilla Häagen Dazs, she's closing in on both you dummies. I hit one key, I might just be the guy who could help her heat up her cold case against you. Then again, I hit a different key and I might be able to bum steer her a different way."

"I can bust you right now for withholding evidence," Ankles said.

"What evidence?" Dirty Jim said. "Go ahead, get a warrant, search the place. Before they crack the password one delete keystroke and everything on my hard drive vanishes into thin cybercacaland. You'll never find any of the negatives. Not even—"

"Not even what?" Danny said. "Not even the ones you took early in the morning of November 21, 1969? Stills from the eight-millimeter movie film?"

"I shot some film in a public park that night," Dirty Jim said, smirking. "That's right. I broke no laws. I told you I took pictures. I don't have them here. They're stashed. Safe. Where they been all these years, like money in the fuckin' bank."

"You told me you started taking pictures at two-thirty A.M.," Danny said. "But Kenny Byrne says you never even went to the Doors concert. Your alibi is bullshit."

"My word against his corpse," Dirty Jim said.

"How'd you know he was dead?" Danny said.

Dirty Jim looked at Danny, nervous for the first time, opened his pill bottle, tapped out a few pills, and washed them down with the Pepto Bismol. "I hear things."

"Good," Danny said. "Because that's what we wanted you to hear. That's the story we put out to see who would bite. That was our bum steer. But guess what?"

"Kenny Byrne is very much alive, asshole," Ankles lied. "You just bit. You swallowed hook, line, and rusty sinker. Just like they're gonna make you swallow joints in the joint. They see you walk into the cell they're gonna nickname you Hershey Park for all the fun and water sports they're gonna have with you."

"Bullshit," Dirty Jim said, slugging the Pepto Bismol.

Danny saw a river of panic running under Dirty Jim's taut skin, his skeletal face rollicking with tics. "Kenny Byrne is an upstanding, successful Vietnam veteran without a rap sheet," Danny said. "A family man. A real estate broker. Clean as a bean. He blows holes in your alibi, Jim."

"It makes you a suspect in Malone's murder," Ankles said. "He busted you a few times. You decided to get even. I'm bustin' you on it, Jim."

"He helped squash the charges in exchange for a little surveillance," Jim said.

"When I snap on the cuffs, I'm calling your PO to make it an instant parole violation," Ankles said, using the same scare tactic he'd tried on Danny back in 1969. "And then I'm gonna put you into a cage full of handpicked jailhouse pimps. Tonight."

"I got an appointment on Tuesday for surgery," Jim said, clutching his stomach now, staring at the Pepto Bismol bottle and holding it to the light, squinting. "You can't take me tonight. I'll fuckin' die in there. I'll fuckin' die if they work on my intestine."

"I've already told Eddie Fortune to expect you in Rikers, where he's a hack," Danny said. "We told him to expect a guy who is connected to his sister's and his brother's and Vito Malone's murders."

"He's got an impatient cage full of guys who like freaks built like Olive Oyl," Ankles said.

"You guys are bluffin'," Dirty Jim said, looking from one to the other. "But all bluffin' and bullshittin' aside, that Eddie Fortune's a fuckin' loony toon. You ain't puttin' me in his charge. He'll let the yoms go at me like I'm a fuckin' bucket of the colonel."

"Watch me," Ankles said, pulling out his handcuffs and reaching for Dirty Jim.

"OK, OK," Dirty Jim shouted, backing up. "But I want a fuckin' lawyer. I want a deal. I want a promise of immunity. All I did was take pictures, shoot some movies. I didn't shoot a gun. I'm a politician. A hustler. I ain't no fuckin' killer."

"Pictures of what?" Danny said. "Films of what?"

"My boss ain't buying less than top shelf," Ankles said. "What the fuck do you have to offer?"

"I can tell you who has an eight-millimeter film of Vito Malone getting whacked," Dirty Jim said. "Better quality than Zapruder. I got the combo to the safe. But I want it in writing, signed by the DA, that I don't spend one night in a monkey cage. Especially with Eddie Fortune on duty. My fuckin' stomach's already doing a prison riot thinkin' about it."

"It's a holiday weekend," Ankles said.

"I don't give a fuck," said Dirty Jim, slugging the Pepto Bismol. This time he clutched his stomach. Belched. Looked at the bottle and then he began to hyperventilate. The bottle smashed on the ground. He did a little dance, gasped for air, clutched his stomach. Then his chest. He lurched like a man being flung around by an angry ghost. He slammed against the wooden blinds covering the windows. His arms shot out in different directions like he was being electrocuted, his legs kicking.

He covered his ears, screamed. His eyes bulged and his face twisted as if caricatured in a funhouse mirror. And froze. His teeth clenched.

"Call nine-one-one!" Danny shouted. "Tell them it's strychnine!"

Ankles snatched up the telephone, dialed 911 as Dirty Jim arched his back and did a desperate tango across the office, crashing into computers, knocking over a lamp. Danny tried to hold him in his arms, but Dirty Jim, as skinny and weak as he was, flew into a violent convulsion provoked by Danny's touch, his big pink-coated horse teeth locked in a demented carousel-horse grin. His eyes bugged and locked as he flung himself to the floor and did an arched-back rattle, feet and arms drumming on the rug, face still fastened in a grin.

Then all at once Dirty Jim came to a rest. He gasped for air, trying to speak, but all that came from his mouth were gasps.

"Don't touch another fuckin' thing in this room," Ankles said. "I put in another call for uniforms and forensics. The 911 operator says don't touch him. That touch and noise can cause the convulsions. Also don't give him mouth to mouth. He can poison you. He could vomit in your mouth and kill you. They said to turn off the lights."

Danny lowered himself to Dirty Jim's ear. "We got an ambulance coming, Jim, help's on the way. Now where are the films?"

Dirty Jim tried to speak but before he could he burst into a second convulsion, fists balling, arms wrapping across his chest this time, his body arched in a convex bow, resting on his head and heels, the legs extended.

"Strooooong!" he shouted and then his face twisted into a Halloween mask again, distorted like a man who had just suffered a severe stroke. As Dirty Jim continued to clatter his bony shoulders and feet on the floor, Danny saw that he was not getting air into his lungs. He began to turn a sickening blue, his bulging eyes contracted and surreal. Danny had never seen a human so tormented in his life. Like a demonic possession, he thought.

Six brutal minutes passed before an EMS ambulance screeched to a halt outside the door of Clubweb.com.

The EMS crew rushed in and tried to paralyze Dirty Jim with an anticonvulsant drug. Danny asked if there was an antidote to strychnine.

"No, the only thing that works is clearing an air passageway," said the female EMS worker. "We have to maintain a clear airway with an endotracheal tube. And then oxygen to keep him from suffocating. But he looks bad."

"When can he talk?" Ankles asked.

"He might never talk," said the male EMS worker. "We get a half a dozen of these a week with ecstasy tablets. But those are low dosages. Back in the sixties it was acid and speed. Today the sick bastards cut the ecstasy with strychnine. But this looks like the old man from the other day in the park. This is a much higher dose than an ecstasy tab. You can tell by the deep blue color and the severity of the convulsions. Now we have to ask you guys to leave. We have to try to stop the convulsions with quiet and oxygen and then we have to get him to Methodist Hospital as fast as we can."

"Just don't touch anything you don't have to touch," Ankles said. "This is a crime scene."

Danny and Ankles stepped out of Clubweb.com into the easing rain. Standing on the sidewalk with the uniformed cops and the crime-scene cops was Pat O'Rourke.

"I'm gonna need statements from you guys," O'Rourke said.

"Who do you think you're kidding, sister?" Ankles said, walking twenty feet from the storefront, to the shelter of a sidewalk tree. Danny and O'Rourke followed.

"I'm not trying to kid anyone, Detective Tufano," O'Rourke said. "Just remember anything you guys say can and will be used against you."

"You're not even assigned to this case, toots," Ankles said.

"Oh yes, I am."

"Since when?"

"Since I heard this call come in," she said. "Which I told my boss could be connected to an old unsolved homicide in Prospect Park."

"He know you have a conflict of interest?"

"How's that?"

"Your maiden name is Davis," Ankles said. "As in Jack Davis."

O'Rourke looked at Danny, widened her eyes, and shrugged.

"I'm not investigating my father's death," she said.

"Vito Malone was his partner," Ankles said. "That's close enough for it to be offsides for you."

"But I'm not investigating Vito Malone's death either," she said, her tone coy and self-assured without being officious. "I'm working on the cold-case murders of Mary Fortune, a guy you knew as Rosario "Popcorn" Gonzalez, Lefty Mots, and Harry Bowles. And how those might be related to the death of Henry Bush yesterday from strychnine poisoning. And now with this second case of strychnine poisoning, involving an old denizen of Hippie Hill, I think I have clear connection. I think there might be a serial killer at work here."

"You know that Vito Malone is connected to all that," Ankles said. "You should recuse yourself."

Detective Pat O'Rourke took out her memo book and clicked a ballpoint pen. She scribbled some notes and looked Ankles in the eyes. "Care to elaborate?"

"Yeah," said Ankles as the EMS workers carried Dirty Jim out of Clubweb.com on a gurney and loaded him into a waiting ambulance. "Your old man was as dirty as his partner. Make that official."

O'Rourke's lower lip trembled, making Danny think of Dylan singing, *"You break just like a little girl."*

"That was uncalled for, Ankles," Danny said.

"So is treating me like a fuckin' suspect."

He turned and walked away, his orthopedic shoes squeaking on the wet sidewalk, his big old frame lurching toward the black Ford Taurus.

"How'd you find out?" O'Rourke asked Danny.

"You're trying to clear your father's name," he said. "I'm trying to clear my own. We both do what we have to do."

"You snooped in my apartment."

"You snooped in my life. My daughter's life. My ex-wife's life."

She nodded and said, "Touché."

"There's more going on than you know."

"Tell me," she said.

"So you can hang me with it?"

"Not unless you're dirty."

"I better go."

He turned to walk away. She touched his arm, looked into his eyes. "If you hadn't found the stuff in my apartment, would you have stayed?"

"I don't know. I know I wanted to."

"Do you think if I didn't want you to find it I would have let you?"

"You saying you wanted me to know?"

"I'm the one who took you there," she said, her eyes exploring his as the rain pattered the tree above them. "I did that because we're in this together. I'll see you."

She turned and Danny watched her walk back to the crime scene. He didn't know who or what to believe anymore. He knew he would have to find his own truth.

# thirty-three

Danny walked straight to Parkside West to Christie Strong's campaign storefront headquarters. He stepped into the beehive of ringing phones, bleeping fax machines, envelope stuffing, and the general excited din of young people trying to get older people elected to office for personal power.

Campaign workers, many of them wearing the same waitress uniforms they wore in the Strong Arms, answered phones: "Be Strong, vote Strong, may I help you?"

Danny looked past the outer office to a rear door with a smoked-glass panel that was marked "private." A pretty Team Strong receptionist asked, "May I help you?"

"I'd like to see the candidate," Danny said.

"I'm afraid Mr. Strong is busy at a strategy meeting right now. May I help you with something? Would you like to volunteer? Make a donation? Register to vote?"

Danny saw the black middleweight step out of the men's room. He spotted Danny, opened Strong's door, and leaned in. Danny rushed past the startled receptionist and pushed the black guy into the room in front of him. The black guy spun, set to throw punches. Danny flinched, stepped back.

"Easy, Carl," Strong said. "Come on in, Danny. Speak of the devil. . . ."

Hippie Helen bulged out of a straight-backed chair. Strong nodded to the black guy, who stepped back into the front office.

"Ms. Grabowski was just telling me about a rather interesting conversation you had with her earlier," Strong said.

Danny said, "It's good to see family stay so close."

Strong shot Helen a fierce look. She shook her head no.

"You're running for office, Christie Grabowski Strong," Danny said. "That puts you under glass. I told you shit would leak. Reporters dig. They unearth things. Like that you're the son of a whore and a horny old vice cop."

"That's not nice," Strong said.

"Mom teach you the tricks of the trade, Helen?" Danny asked. "Like the hog-tied rump roast you did with Vito Malone?"

Christie Strong glared at Helen and tried to maintain his composure.

"Don't you dare talk about my mother like that," Helen said. "Look how you were dragged up. Speed freak, murder suspect, shit son. You had a shit father and you are a shit father. The best things you ever learned in life you learned from me."

He had no replies for any of those things. Most of them were true.

"Our mother had youthful indiscretions," Strong said. "But she was a good and nurturing woman. She did what she had to do to survive. She couldn't give much—"

"Starting with a father," Danny said.

"Say what you will about me. But leave Mom out of it, OK?"

"OK," Danny said. "Let's talk instead about dear old dad."

"I never called him that," Strong said.

"I did," Helen said. "I even took him for a steak dinner on Father's Day. I wanted to make my peace with him. I wanted to bury the past. He didn't."

"He became belligerent and I had to ask him to leave," Strong said. "Helen tried. We failed to reach him. He was bitter toward us when it was we who were rejected by him."

"Hey," Danny said. "It's hard to forgive when the way you went about getting even with him was dealing drugs all over his precinct. And ordering murders. Maybe he was a prick to your mother. Maybe Henry Bush was as shitty a father as you think I am, Helen. But to get even, you chose to humiliate him. And, Christie, you exploited the son of a bitch. You made a deal with Vito Malone, who had an ax to grind with your father, and together you appropriated his precinct. You knew Henry Bush would never bust you because if he did you'd expose him as a whoremaster who was getting even with his illegitimate son. That scandal would have crushed his barren wife. It would have ended his career path in the NYPD or forced him out of the job altogether."

Strong laughed. Helen unwrapped a Nestlé's Crunch.

"What the hell are you talking about?" Strong said. "You make these outlandish accusations, reckless innuendoes, without an iota of evidence. You should write fiction, Danny. Your imagination runs away with you."

"I'll tell you what must have hurt," Danny said. "It must have stung when you arrived in Brooklyn from Lincoln, Nebraska, two bust outs looking for long-lost Dad. Only to find a flinty old cop nicknamed Horsecock, who told you both to take a hike."

"If this is an attempt to embarrass me," Strong said, "I'll just come clean about it. It didn't hurt Bill Clinton that he had dysfunctional parents, a violent alcoholic stepfather. An alcoholic mother. A junkie brother. The people of my district will admire me for overcoming such grim roots and making something of myself. They'll see a man who can turn rubble into rubies, the way I did with this neighborhood."

"Yeah," Danny said. "With loans and cosignatures from Erika Malone."

Strong squirmed, started building a paper clip chain at his desk, looked at Helen again, who bit into the Nestlé's Crunch.

"Put that away," Strong said. "I don't like watching you eat." He regained immediate control, modulating his tone, and said, "Please, don't eat stuff like that, honey. It's bad for you. I'll order you a salad, some grilled chicken, a fruit plate."

Helen withered under his lecture, balled the tinfoil around the chocolate.

"Yeah," Danny said. "But I'd get a food taster, Hel. Daddy dearest was poisoned yesterday. He died in desperation. Suffocated. Couldn't breathe. His eyes bulged, back arched, his jaws locked. He gasped for air. Like a crucifixion. Died like Jesus, betrayed by his own. A painful horrible death—"

"Stop it!" Helen shouted.

"I'm going to have to ask you to leave," Strong said.

"The same way I just watched poor Dirty Jim die," Danny said. "He threw five straight convulsions. Turned the color of Papa Smurf when he stopped breathing. His last breath was interesting. I think he was trying to say your name. 'Helen.' "

"No!" Helen pushed herself to her feet, her body rippling under her muumuu like a plastic garbage bag filled with water.

"Then he said, 'Film. Pictures. Christie Strong.' "

"This is absurd," Strong said.

"Ankles was there, witnessed it," Danny said, talking loud enough for those in the outer office to hear him. "They just took Dugan down Methodist Hospital. But the EMS people said he wasn't gonna make it. Someone spiked his medicine with strychnine. Same thing that killed your father. I hope you can explain it all on Judgment Day, *Hel*."

"Please, don't tell me this!" Helen shouted, staring at her brother, horrified. "Jim is not dead! Jim is all I have! Tell me he's OK, Christie."

"This is the first I've heard of this," Strong said.

"The room next to my father's in Dunne's is vacant," Danny said, in a flat monotone. "Unless your father fills it first."

"Danny, please leave," Strong said. "You're upsetting my sister. It's not nice."

"Poor Jim lurched all over the place," Danny said. "Like an eel on a dock. Right in the middle of telling Ankles and me about how your brother Christie here had his father killed yesterday. The same way he had Mary Fortune killed. And my old roommates. The way he was behind the Wally Fortune murder and Vito Malone's."

Strong pushed an intercom button. "Carl, can you come in a moment, please."

Helen sobbed, her hand covering her mouth, shuffling her feet across the floor. Mascara tears rushed in little rivers down the deep gullies of her face as she awaited a response from Strong, who added one paper clip to another on the chain.

"I know how much money Erika was billed by Dirty Jim's company," Danny said to Strong. "I know that he and Helen are on her company's health plan, good thing, too, for all the medical treatment they need. Forgive me, I'm still referring to Jim in the present tense. I hope Jim has burial insurance. I guess the only thing left to do is to get the photos and the eight-millimeter movies and then we're all set."

Carl entered the room as Helen moaned and collapsed onto her chair, breathing in and out in a panic attack. Christie ran around his desk to Helen, hovered over his ailing sister. Carl shot Danny the dead eye as he rushed to help his boss.

"Hit the fuckin' road," he said. Danny wasn't going to roll on the floor with an in-shape thirty-year-old ex-pug. *Even if I win he might kick the shit out me*, Danny thought, as he stuck out his foot. Carl tripped, spilled to the floor. As he pushed himself up to an all fours, his ass in the air like a center ready to snap a football, Danny saw him reach to the back of his belt for the handle of a pistol. Danny kicked him in the soft pouch between his parted legs, the toe of his boot crushing his testicles. Carl screamed in agony and writhed on the floor.

"Be strong," Danny said. "Vote strong."

And left.

# thirty-four

Danny hurried out of Christie Strong's storefront, checking his watch. It was 4:21 P.M. He hurried along the avenue, eager to get another look inside Erika's house. Erika had said she was bringing her mother to the five o'clock mass at St. Savior's. He needed to use that window of opportunity to get into the house, into the steel room, to see if he could find what he needed.

Dirty Jim had said the film he shot the night of the Vito Malone murder was in a safe all these years. Danny suspected it was Christie Strong's safe. But where? He was too smart to have it in a safe deposit box, where it could be subpoenaed. His real estate office was also a dumb place to keep it. He might have it hidden down in the Bahamas or out in the Hamptons.

But Danny figured Strong was arrogant enough to keep it at home, in his own penthouse condo on Parkside West near Grand Army Plaza. Close to the scene of the crime, the epicenter of Strong's world. He also suspected that Erika had gotten involved with Strong, had become a partner in his world. That her business was just a laundry for Strong's dirty money. He didn't have the time to do an audit, to account for all her wealth and Strong's wealth, to see how much she made from her beauty products. How much of it came from real estate swindles.

Danny had to find something solid, some exculpatory evidence. He needed answers. Needed them now.

He crossed Parkside West, walking toward Eleventh Avenue, where he'd parked his car, when a yellow Explorer pulled up beside him. "Danny, got a minute," Lars Andersen said, smiling from the driver's seat.

"I'm in kind of a hurry," Danny said.

"It's important," Lars said, leaning across the front seat and opening the passenger door. "Something I just learned. About 1969. Get in. I promise this won't take long."

Danny checked his watch, climbed in the front seat, and slammed the door on the storm. Lars spun away, made a hasty left through a yellow light, raced down Prospect Road to the schoolyard of a local public school on Eleventh Avenue.

"What's so important?" Danny asked.

"I got a phone call," Lars said. The Explorer entered the school-yard that was empty in the rain, whispered through the deep pud-dles formed by clogged storm drains to a blind alcove in the rear, known as the coop.

"Phone call from who?"

Lars jammed the gear into park, yanked up his driver's door handle, reached across the gear house, and clutched Danny by the shirtfront. In one ferocious motion he dragged Danny across the front seat and out the driver's door into the rain.

"Phone call from Erika Malone," Lars said, bull-charging Danny through the puddles toward a brick wall. "Apologizing for the mis-understanding back in 1969. For making you think I raped her! Which sent you looking for me. With a fucking blackjack."

Lars slammed Danny into the wall. All the air burst out of Danny's lungs. Lars swung a wide right hand onto Danny's ear. Bells banged in Danny's head, tiny stars spinning in front of his eyes. Lars swung another looping left into Danny's belly, doubling him over. Lars was big, strong as two men, but he had never learned to fight. Danny made him for a good-natured fella who hadn't had that many fights. He threw arm punches, heavy as mini wrecking balls, but no one had ever taught him how to throw proper punches with the force of the rest of his powerful body. Thank God, Danny thought, staggering through three inches of trapped water, slamming against a second wet brick wall as rain percolated in deep dirty puddles.

The hardest punch traveled six fierce inches, like a human pile driver. Lars threw looping overhand rights and wide roundhouses, a windmill of fists that lost their velocity and their pop before reaching Danny. But still he battered Danny around the brick coop, a brutal, vicious, old-fashioned schoolyard ass-kicking.

"You were the one who beat me," Lars said. "Not Vito Malone or one of his goons. You, you dirty little speed-freak bastard. You put me in the hospital where I couldn't even see my Jack. Couldn't go to his wake. Or his funeral. Now I'm gonna put you in the fucking hos-pital. I've been waiting all my life for this. You little . . . little . . . you little fucking faggot!"

He detonated a few final wallops on Danny's head and body. Then Danny set himself and threw one right hand back, waist, arms, and shoulders behind. It landed flush in the middle of Lars's perfect nose, cartilage and bone cracking like walnuts. Danny heard Lars moan in pain. Blood gushed from his nose, and he wiped tears from his eyes. But Lars didn't even stagger. The sight of his own blood only turbocharged him. He threw a hurricane of wild punches, his big arms never tiring. One of them caught a backpedaling Danny square on the jaw and he felt himself topple. He landed facedown in a puddle, the reflection of lightning in the sky reflecting in the dirty water.

Now Lars was on top of him, ramming a knee into the middle of Danny's back. *This is it,* Danny thought. *Payback. He's going to kill me. The running stops. The roads intersect. My life ends here. Now. Here. In a dirty fucking Brooklyn schoolyard. Like a little speed-freak skell.*

As Lars punched the back of his head Danny thought of Darlene, white-water rafting on a foamy clean river, rushing and rollicking and laughing through this wonderful thing called life. . . .

Lars grabbed a handful of Danny's hair, smashing his face into the ground. The three inches of puddle water around the clogged storm drain cushioned the bang. Danny's mouth filled with filthy water as Lars held him facedown as lowdown and dirty as Brooklyn gets. Tried to push his face through the concrete, into hell.

"You little motherfucker," Lars shouted in Danny's above-water ear, as bubbles blew from Danny's submerged nose and mouth. "You fucking little speed-freak bum. You hurt me. You hurt me. You hurt me and I never hurt anyone in my life. You almost killed me! I never raped anyone. You killed Vito Malone, which helped drive my Jack to hurt himself."

He lifted Danny's head up by the hair. Danny swallowed puddle water, retching from the stink and taste of filth and schoolyard piss. He gagged and coughed, his head an inanimate toy in a monster's paw. Lars smashed it down again. And again. And again. Each slam causing a loud dirty splash. The puddle buffered the blows, but the repetition and lack of oxygen were making Danny slip away. Danny could feel himself sliding into darkness. Brain battered. No air. Mouth and lungs filling with water. Nostrils plugged with puddle soot. *I'm being murdered,* Danny thought.

Lars rose to a half squat, his powerful knee lodged in Danny's back pushing harder and deeper into his lungs. Danny felt an eerie watery silence. He knew he was here, in the new century, but half of him was slipping back, melding into the rainy night Vito Malone died. The darkness. The blackness. The rain. The mud. Danny heard an explosion of thunder, as loud as the clap of creation. Sensed the glow of lightning. A brilliant flash. . . .

*The flash of lightning illuminates Hippie Hill. Several more flashes. Then a long ray of light. Like Bosch's blinding tunnel from purgatory to heaven separating the blessed and the damned. Danny looks up from the muddy grass. Dirty Jim stands half in, half out of Sewer 7, standing on the iron ladder, the trapdoor open, like a nocturnal mole creature, popping flashbulbs, snapping photos. Danny sees another face. It belongs to Erika Malone. And a third face he can't see in the dark and the rain. There are more flashes. But these are not from Dirty Jim's camera. These're from a gun. A gun fires into Boar's Head. Fired by the fourth person, whose face Danny cannot see. Vito Malone screams, begs for his life. Erika screams. Danny stands. His mouth full of mud and grass. Staggering, falling, and then he stumbles, and the blackness returns. . . .*

Danny felt the same blackness returning now as Lars slam-dunked him again, his forehead belting the cement. Just before he lost consciousness Danny heard the voice of Patricia O'Rourke. She was shouting.

"No fucking more, Uncle Lars! I said that's enough!"

"He tried to kill me, back in 1969," Lars screamed, holding Danny's head in his hand like a man brandishing a trophy. "He hurt me. He hurt me and I never did anything to him. He hurt me and it's hurt me ever since. So I'm hurting him back."

Lars lifted Danny's head a final time but O'Rourke cocked her pistol. "I'll more than hurt you if you make me pull this trigger," she said. "What you and my father did to hurt my mother is bad enough. Don't make this worse."

Lars froze, stared at her, tossed Danny's head aside. It splashed sideways in the puddle. Lars removed his knee from Danny's back and sat in the puddle in the teeming rain, clutching his knees, crying, as angry about his own outburst of anger as he was at Danny.

"I'm sorry," Lars said.

"It's OK," Danny gasped, coughing lungers of filth.

"I wasn't talking to you, you fucking piece of dogshit," Lars said. "I was talking to my beautiful niece."

"You finished playing victim, Lars?" O'Rourke said, snapping out a plastic contact sheet of pornographic photos of Lars and Jack Davis. "I found these when we tossed Jim Dugan's apartment. You're not so fucking innocent. You betrayed my mother, your own sister, you deceitful son of a bitch, and I half wish you would have made me pull this fucking trigger."

"You don't understand," he said. "It was the times. I was a kid—"

"You were fucking nineteen," she said. "So don't give me that 'kid' shit. Guys your age were dying all over Vietnam in a grown-up war. You were no kid. *I* was a kid. My brother, Luke, was a kid. Jack Davis's kids. You were a horny consenting adult having an affair with my adulterous father. You got out of the draft on a homosexual deferment and stayed home to betray my mother, your own sister, with her husband. The father of her children. Your niece and nephew. All of that helped lead to my father killing himself. My father was a fucking bastard too, for what he did to her. So don't you dare play fucking victim to me, Uncle Scumbag. Look at the pictures. Go ahead. Look at them!"

Lars glanced at them, then turned away, pulling his knees up tighter to his face, his big arms flexing with muscle.

"Please, stop," Lars said.

"Neither one of you look like you're riddled with guilt. You were both too busy laughing and grabbing each other, having a great old time while my mom was home raising two kids. Betrayed by the two men in her life that she loved and trusted most."

"Oh, God," Lars said, sobbing. "I loved him—"

"He wasn't fucking yours to love! He was mine to love! And my brother's! And my mother's! All this selfish, self-absorbed 1960s bullshit makes me fucking sick. Some people are not yours to love."

The rain fell and all three of them remained silent for a long moment. Danny gasped, coughed, and expectorated the muck.

"Thanks," Danny said to O'Rourke, who stood above him in the rain, gun at her side, photos in her other hand. He pushed himself to his feet.

"Fuck you, too," she said. "You've been holding out on me. I should have let him kill you and locked him up for murder. Two shitbirds with one stone."

"If it's any consolation to you," Danny said. "Your father might have been a shit husband. Big deal, they're a dime a dozen. Fact, you're looking at one. But he was no killer. I witnessed the Wally Fortune murder. It's pretty clear in my head now. He tried to stop

Malone. At one point Malone was gonna kill him for interfering with his fun."

Lars sat in the puddle, head between his knees, taking deep breaths, trying to control his emotions. O'Rourke looked at Danny through the showering rain, blinking.

"Are you sure?" Her voice was soft with hope and need.

Danny nodded. "He was a bad cop," Danny said. "But a decent man. I never saw him beat or plant anything on a single kid on Hippie Hill. Malone coerced him. Blackmailed him into his drug racket, the way he ruined everybody else's life he touched. He used the photos to blackmail your father. Jack Davis either went along with Vito Malone's schemes, or the photos went to your mom. And the PD. So he went along. And got sucked in deeper and deeper until it led to Mary Fortune getting hot-shotted. Then Wally Fortune. Malone was gonna kill your father that night, too."

"He was a beautiful, gentle man," Lars said.

"You shut the fuck up," O'Rourke said. "I don't want your opinion of my father. Any more than I would want his mistress's. In fact, get the hell out of my sight."

Lars got up from the puddle and sloshed to his car. "What we did was not dirty," Lars said. "But it was wrong. I'm sorry for that."

"Go tell it to my mother's—your sister's—grave."

Lars climbed into his Explorer, made a U-turn, and drove off. Danny was aching from head to toe, but he felt as sorry for Lars as he did for himself and O'Rourke.

"You OK?" she asked, touching the scrapes on his forehead.

"No, I feel like a bag of wet garbage."

"You are a bag of garbage."

"Don't blame me that you set out to find a perfect father and came up with a regular fucked-up human being like the rest of us," Danny said. "He was what he was. He was a young guy who had an affair. He took the dirty dollar. But he was not a killer. The only one he killed was himself. He thought he was doing that for your mom and you and your brother."

"His bullet went through my family like a dumdum," she said.

"That wasn't his intention."

She thought about this, wiped the rain from her face, but it didn't take away the freckles on her nose or the pain in her sea-blue eyes. "You sure he didn't help kill Wally Fortune?"

"Positive."

"Or Malone? He could have gotten up in the night, snuck out, came here, killed him, rushed home—"

"I think I have a big piece of that night back in my head now," Danny said. "There's a face that I can't see yet. But I don't think it's his."

"Is it yours?"

Danny thought she looked afraid of his answer.

"I think I went there to do it," he said. "But someone beat me to it. Because if what I'm starting to remember is right, it's a memory of someone else shooting him."

He told her about Hippie Helen and Strong being brother and sister, children of Henry Bush. He figured the more detours he could send her on the further she would stray from arresting him.

His cell phone rang. He answered. It was Viviana Gonzalez. She said she was in the newspaper office and that she'd been in Christie Strong's house in the afternoon and wanted to tell him about what she'd seen there.

"I'll be there in fifteen minutes," Danny said, and hung up.

O'Rourke looked at Danny, putting away the photos and her pistol. "Just a cursory look through this Dugan guy's photos is enough to make you shudder," she said. "He has dirt on everyone in the neighborhood. In cars. In the park. In motels. On rooftops. In people's apartments, taken with those hidden cameras in smoke alarms and Holy Bibles. He has tape of husbands banging the baby-sitters. Wives doing it with the baby-sitters. Teachers with students. Coaches with cheerleaders. Cops with hookers. Priests with altar boys. Mismatched husbands and wives. He must have hired one hooker for one bachelor party because he has videotape of her with every guy there. And the names, phone numbers, and E-mail addresses of all of the guys' wives. Clubweb.com is one big black-mail database of almost everyone in this neighborhood. The whole place has about three degrees of separation. If that."

"That's why they call him Dirty Jim." Danny knew there was also an eight-millimeter film taken the night Vito Malone was killed. He knew he was in the film. He didn't mention it to O'Rourke.

She stepped closer to him, raked wet hair from his eyes, and placed a ladies hankie on his raw forehead. "There was no file on you."

"I've been a long time gone," he said, grabbing the hankie, their hands touching.

"There was one on Erika Malone," O'Rourke said, removing her hand.

Danny looked at her, holding the hankie to his head, certain she was going to tell him there were compromising photographs of her with Christie Strong.

"And?"

"It was empty."

Relief whirlpooled through him. "You look disappointed."

"I am," she said. "Because I know she's as dirty as everyone else around here."

"I have to go see somebody."

"You're going to see her, aren't you?"

Danny stared into her eyes, this savvy woman who had just saved his ass, hell, his life, because he thought Lars would have killed him. He sighed and said, "I'm going to see about my future."

"If you still have one."

O'Rourke walked back to her Crown Victoria. She turned and said, "Need a lift?"

"I'm parked a block away."

"Thanks," she said, picking up what looked to Danny like a business card from a muddy puddle, glancing at it, and pocketing it.

"For what?"

"For telling me about my father. I needed to hear that."

"It's the truth," he said, shrugging. "That's all I'm looking for, too."

# thirty-five

Why didn't you tell me your boss was gay?" Danny asked.

"You didn't ask," Viviana said, letting him into the *Slope Sentinel*. "What the hell happened to you, anyway? You're filthy, you're all beat up. You look . . . *old*."

"I got hit with a boomerang," Danny said, the wall clock informing him it was 4:55. "And I am old. So I have no time to waste. Show me what you have."

He walked into the small bathroom, ran the hot water, washed his hands and face with antibacterial soap. He grabbed a bottle of Listerine from the medicine chest, poured some in a paper cup, gargled, and spit out the vile black remnants of the schoolyard.

Viviana recoiled as Danny grunted a comb through his wet sooty hair.

"I went up there today," she said. "He called me, invited me for brunch. When I'm in his company now, my skin crawls. But I play the game. When he left the room I poked around but I didn't find anything with the names you asked me about. But I did find out that he has a wall safe. Behind the Bosch painting."

"You know the combination?"

"Nope."

"He asked me again to go to this event with him tonight," she said. "I said no. He asked me to think about it. He said I could help him with the Hispanic vote."

"Go," Danny said.

"Yeah?"

"Yeah. Keep a tape recorder in your purse. Ask him questions. Pick his brains. It's legal to wire yourself in New York State."

"Oh, while I was there a lady detective came to see Christie," Viviana said.

"O'Rourke?"

"Yeah, Pat O'Rourke. A hottie. So flirty I thought she was going to tear off her jeans and jump his bones."

*Sounds familiar,* Danny thought. "What'd they talk about?"

"I don't know," Viviana said. "Christie asked me to leave. At the door he asked me again to please come with him tonight. He thinks who the hell he is, telling you, poppi. Fooling around with a hot young cop chick in front of me. And then asking me to be his date tonight."

Danny looked at the wall clock: 5:05.

"Go with Strong tonight," he said. "Call me before you leave."

"You got it," she said, dangling a set of keys. "You can also borrow these if you want. Won't be anyone home. I'll make sure I leave the delivery entrance on President Street unlocked; take the elevator from the basement." Danny took the keys from Viviana, thanked her, told her to be careful, and rushed back into the rain.

He left his car parked on Sixth Avenue, out of sight of Ankles, O'Rourke, Strong, and Erika, and splashed up Garvey Place toward Erika's house. The smell of Brooklyn in the cleansing summer rain flooded back childhood memories of being forced off the street, into tenement hallways on rainy days, playing Monopoly, a poor man's make-believe game of grown-up wealth, of disposable income, home ownership, and real estate empires. He'd never achieved anything close to those dreams. Erika had. Strong had. They could keep their money. All he wanted to know was if he would be a free man for the rest of his life. And a chance to salvage his relationship with Darlene.

He worried about what he would find in Erika's basement. Worried about what he'd learn about himself.

He scoped the street for the El Dorado. It wasn't at its usual place at the fire hydrant. He used the key to let himself into the house. He hurried upstairs, went into the mother's room, took the diary from the bookshelf, stuffed it in his rain slicker pocket, then ran straight for the cellar door, descended, and went to the removable section of the ceramic tile floor next to the hot water heater. He hoisted the three-by-four-foot ceramic tile rectangle the way he'd seen Vito Malone open it a lifetime ago, revealing the four-inch-thick steel-plate door with the combination dial. He dialed the month, day, and year of Erika Malone's birth and turned the handle. It opened. The combination hadn't been changed in thirty-two years, since the day of Erika's seventeenth birthday, when he watched Vito Malone turn the dial before leading Danny down to the steel room to read him the riot act of dos and don'ts of dating his daughter.

Danny flicked a wall switch and lights illuminated below him. As he descended the steel ladder Danny heard the loud whir of the underground exhaust fans that obliterated all other sound. He climbed down nine feet to the old 1950s underground bomb shelter.

The twelve-by-twelve-foot steel cube was wood-paneled with the same pressboard from the 1950s, part of the post-WWII plastic invasion that had ushered in the atomic age of aluminum siding, dropped ceilings, and anti-Communist preparedness. It was just as he remembered it the day Vito Malone had told him that if he ever laid a hand on his daughter he would take Danny down here, kill and mummify him with arsenic.

He lifted the only .45 on the wall from its peg. Danny had no real knowledge of guns so he held it at arm's length, pointing it away from himself to see if it was loaded. He thought that it was but didn't know how to push out the clip. He jammed it behind his belt at the back of his pants, covering it with his shirt. He'd give it to Ankles to check the ballistics.

Danny moved around the room. It had been updated since 1969. The cable TV and microwaves were giveaways. Erika's old clothes from 1969 hung in a wooden armoire next to the Castro, wrapped in clear plastic. Including the hip-hugger bell-bottoms with the Indian stitching that she'd worn just the other day. Danny picked through the clothes and then his eyes drifted to one plastic bag on the shoe rack at the base of the armoire.

His skin pebbled as he lifted it.

Through the clean plastic he saw a familiar pair of Danny's old bell-bottoms, the hems shredded from walking on the extra-long pants with his Frye boot heels, which was the grungy style back in '69. He also found his old John Jay sweatshirt. And his scuffed Frye boots. And his old army field jacket.

The hair on Danny's neck rose as he removed the clothes from the plastic bag. The jacket and sweatshirt were covered in mud and what looked like old, caked blood. The boots were freckled with blood. . . .

*Blood and gunshots everywhere. Vito Malone pumps blood. In the blinding light Danny sees Malone bucking in the grass, gagging on his own blood. Danny crawls through the mud to him. Lifts his head. Cradles him. Boar's Head rattles, teeth chattering. Danny calls for help. Thunder barks. Then the blinding light, the white tunnel from purgatory to heaven. The light dies. Darkness. Danny is pulled away from Malone. Dragged by the feet across the grass. Cold rain stings his face. Lightning splinters the sky over Prospect Park. He's yanked to his feet. Leaned against a car. A Cadillac. Red Cadillac. Lifted in sections. Dumped in the trunk. The trunk lid slams. Total darkness again. . . .*

Danny found two manila envelopes—one thin, one thick—in the plastic bag. He opened the thin one first, removed two eight-by-ten black-and-white photographs. The top one was a grainy but clear night shot taken with a flash with high-speed infrared film and then pushed in the lab. It showed Danny Cassidy standing on Hippie Hill with a .45 in his hand, his hair long and wet and stringy, wearing ragged bell-bottom jeans, an army coat, and old Frye boots. His face sagged like a dullard's. Stoned. Pathetic.

"Jesus Christ," he said, adrenaline surging in his central nervous system, his itching skin like a banquet to a million mites. Rancid bile rose, smelting his esophagus, as he faced the evidence that told Danny Cassidy that he was in fact a killer.

"I did it," he whispered.

He moved to the next picture. Erika Malone also stood on Hippie Hill, above the body of her dead father, holding a pistol, Danny in the background on all fours.

Confusion rioted in Danny head. *Which one of us shot the son of a bitch?* he wondered. There was one other item in the plastic bag with the old clothes. It was a blue-backed diary. He picked it up and saw Erika's name and the year 1969 in her fancy black, red, and gold hand-lettering. He examined the back of the book. There was no bar code.

*The other 1969 diary upstairs in the attic had been left lying around as a substitute prop,* he thought, *in case Ankles or me or someone else ever got a search warrant. This was her real 1969 diary.*

He turned to November 21, 1969. The page was blank. So were all the ones after it. He leafed backward, looking for September 24, 1969, the night Erika had said she was raped.

"Find what you were looking for?" Erika said, standing on the middle rung of the steel ladder.

Danny jumped, the book leaping from his hands. "Some of it," he said, bending to pick up the diary. "I imagine the rest is in here."

"Mama acted up at mass during the sermon." she said, descending the ladder, as if making small talk. "I had to take her home early. She's getting bad. They say she's going to the next level and she disrupts the group. She talks and talks, repeats the same story over and over, takes off all her clothes. They don't want her back."

"I'm sorry to hear that," Danny said.

"She forgets things. Loses things. But still, I knew there was something fishy this morning about her keys. I'd just looked in the umbrella rack minutes before they turned up there. But I didn't worry because I didn't think you knew about Daddy's steel room."

"He called it the Niggerproof Room," Danny said. "He wanted me to meet him here that night instead of on Hippie Hill."

She walked to him, took the diary from his hands. "You don't need this. I'll tell you everything you need to know."

"I'm in a fight for my life, Erika."

"I understand," she said. "You have no idea how well I understand that. Because we're in this together."

Danny held up the two photographs that Dirty Jim took on Hippie Hill on the night of November 20, 1969. "Those are just the sample frames from the film they shot that they sent me," Erika said.

" 'They' being?"

"Strong, Dirty Jim, and that pig Helen Grabowski," she said, pulling herself a cup of cooler water. "The irony is that I sent you to her for fucking experience. And she wound up fucking *me* for twenty-five years."

"Explain," Danny said, tapping his temple.

She walked to him and kissed him, her lips radiating heat. She gave him a sip of her cold water, as if to wash it down. "My father knew that you had witnessed the Wally Fortune murder. He figured it out because Ankles asked a million questions. Then some old rummy priest spilled the rest. So he pretended he wanted to see you about making a deal. He would let you continue to see me so long as you kept your mouth shut."

"How'd you know I spoke to your father? I called him, not vice versa."

"I listened on the extension," she said, lifting the old-fashioned wall phone receiver, screwing off the old-fashioned speaker cap. "In the old days, with old phones you could screw off the transmitter cap, take out the transmitter, and when you listened on the other end no one knew. But after you two made plans to meet on Hippie Hill at two A.M., he hung up. He made another call. This one to

Christie Strong. I listened again. He told Strong to send you to hang out with Wally Fortune. They laughed. I knew then that he planned to kill you."

She screwed the cap back on the phone.

"I planned to kill him," Danny said. "If he wouldn't leave us alone."

"I knew that, too, so I went looking for you," she said. "I found you stumbling out of Hippie Helen's building. I took you to your crash pad. With the promise that we'd sleep together, finally do it. And then I made sure you passed out."

"You gave me more goofballs."

"It was that or watching you get shot. You were already on acid and booze. What you needed was a good long sleep. So I gave you some of my father's Valiums. I stayed with you until you passed out. And then I went up there to Hippie Hill myself. With one of my father's guns."

She walked to the wall and saw that one rack was empty. Danny took out the .45.

"This one?"

"Yes. That one. And I went up there. And you showed up anyway. Somehow you woke up. Smashed. I knew Daddy was going to kill you. So I. . . ."

*Danny staggers toward Boar's Head in the rain. The acid and the goofballs yanking him this way and the other. He flails Brendan's .45. Waves it in the air. Boar's Head laughs. "Go ahead, try to shoot me, you twisted little hippie faggot," Vito Malone says. "You don't have the fuckin' balls." Danny raises the gun. Aims. But cannot fire. Malone backhands him. Danny falls to the mud. Malone raises his gun. Danny's blinded by a sudden ray of light just as the first bullet enters Vito Malone's chest. He hears a girl scream. "Stop! Stop!" Danny turns. Erika has a gun. . . .*

". . . So I was going to shoot him but my gun jammed. You shot him first. You turned your back. My father got up. I screamed to you. Warned you. You turned and shot him again and again and again and again. You crawled to him. Lifted his head in your arms. . . ."

Danny's flashbacks told him different murky details but how could he be sure? She was sober. He was stoned.

She stood silent for a moment and shrugged. "Anyway, then I

dragged you across the hill to my father's car. I got you in the trunk. I drove you to your apartment. I cleaned you up. I dressed you in the new clothes I'd bought you for your birthday but never gave you. And I took your old clothes with me. I also took the gun you used. We made a detour on the drive home and I flung the gun into the Big Lake."

"You helped cover it up," he said, pushing her father's gun back into his back waistband. "It's called aiding and abetting."

"Because we were there together it's also conspiracy and accomplice to murder. But I knew they could never prove you did it. There was no evidence."

"Why didn't you let me know?"

"I just thought it would be better for you to leave. To get away from me and Brooklyn and 1969. . . ."

"But when I came home you didn't tell me the truth either? Why?"

"Because I wanted to let sleeping dogs lie. I didn't want to implicate myself. If I told you the truth you would have to know it all, about me, too. I thought it was just better to let it lay buried. I tried to steer you away from the truth. Your own truth. I didn't want you to know you were a killer. Because deep down all you did was protect yourself. But you've dug so much of it up now, more people dying, that you have two cops on both of our asses now."

Danny wanted to believe her, but pieces were missing.

"Why'd you save my clothes?"

"So you would believe me one day," she said. "I got rid of the gun. I had nothing else to prove it with. I knew you'd have no memory of it."

"I'm starting to get one back now," he said.

"I'd be wary of what you remember from that night," she said.

"But there was a witness," Danny said, waving the photographs. "Dirty Jim, with his still camera and a Super 8 narco-surveillance camera that your father gave him to get compromising pictures of other people. People like Lars Andersen, with Jack Davis."

She seemed surprised by that.

"I didn't know about that, but Strong had that vile son of a bitch Dirty Jim taking pictures that night," Erika said. "Strong knew that my father planned to kill you. So he got Dirty Jim Dugan to get it on film. So that Strong could use the evidence to control my father for life. But instead he got you on film killing my father, aided and covered up by me. The film was useless to him for years. You were a speed-freak kid. You became a successful reporter, but you never made major money. I was just a teenage girl. And Strong tried using the photos to get in my pants."

"And?"

"I told him I'd rather die in the electric chair than let him lay one finger on me. He told me there was no statute of limitations on murder. That he'd be patient. Then he left me alone for years. I would see him and he would say hello, ogle me with a demented grin on his face, knowing that I knew that he knew that he had the sword of Damocles over my head. But he kept his distance. The weekly letters stopped. Then after college, when I became rich and half-assed famous, those pictures came in the mail."

"He wanted to use you as a laundry for his drug money?"

"I wish that's all it was," she said. "We met in person. He made me wear a mesh string bikini and meet him in the water at Brighton Beach so that he knew I wasn't wired. He wanted direct blackmail payoffs. He knew I was making over seven million a year in pure profit. He wanted half. Three-point-six million a year paid to Clubweb.com Inc. for alleged computer services. Or the pictures would go to Ankles or the district attorney. He also still wanted me. He tried using the photos to bed me again. I drew the line right there in the sand. Told him I would rather commit suicide than let him touch me. I told him that if I were dead he wouldn't get a dime. I convinced him I would kill myself rather than let him violate my body. I would have, too. He backed off on that part of the demand. I was worth too much to him alive. But still, during all these years, he's tried to charm me into his bed. He began writing his silly love letters again. The man is delusional. I threw them all in the garbage."

Danny listened to her. Looked at the photos. Much of what she was saying might've been true. But his memory was starting to tell him something different.

"Now that you know, are you going to turn yourself in?" Erika asked. "Implicate me? Who'll take care of Mama? All these years, the thing that worried me most was what would happen to Mama if I went to jail. She would have killed herself. She'd just lost my dad, and it would've killed her to know I was part of his murder."

Danny looked at her, her dark eyes as impenetrable and full of secrets as a midnight sea. He believed the part about her going out that night to save his life. Which in fact she did. And because she had saved his life, he was never going to tell Ankles or O'Rourke that she had helped him kill her father. But he wasn't going to implicate himself either, or take a fall for her or anyone else. He knew there were more answers. He knew the answers were on that film. Danny wasn't going to let his daughter, Darlene, live her life with her father in a jail cell if he was innocent. He wouldn't rat on Erika, but he was going to do whatever it took to prove his innocence.

Erika Malone had hidden all of this from him for thirty-two years, and he still didn't think she was giving him the whole story.

"Strong has the film," Danny said.

"I've been trying to get it back. I've asked Strong to let me make one final large payment, to end this once and for all. We're all getting too old."

"I'll get the film back," he said. "But you have to tell me the rest."

"I told you everything."

"You haven't been square with me, Erika. You've been lying to me for thirty-two fucking years."

"That's not true. I saved your life. I've protected you, protected us. Paid a fucking fortune—"

"Then tell me the rest. Who did it to you, Erika? Who raped you? If it was rape at all. Maybe you just fucked some hot guy? And just wanted to make me jealous the way you used Lars?"

She smacked him across the face. Danny grabbed Erika's wrist when a gunshot from behind them exploded in the steel room like the roar of a cannon. The bullet ricocheted around the room. Erika knocked Danny to the floor and then scrambled with athletic speed to her mother, who was standing on the steel ladder, clutching an upper rung, aiming to fire a second shot at Danny.

"Vaffanculo, you touch my daughter," Angela Malone screeched as Erika yanked her down from the ladder, wrestling the pistol from her mother's hand. Angela writhed and thrashed, kicking at Danny, her eyes wide and insane as she spit at him, cursing him in Italian.

"You should go," Erika said. "I've told you all I know—"

"Vaffanculo, you bastard, touching my daughter," Angela screamed, veins pulsing in her forehead like angry little vipers.

"I'm going to confront Christie Strong," he said. "It all has to end, Erika."

She looked at him and nodded. "It's time," Erika said, cradling her now whimpering mother. "It's time. Yes. Tell him I'll pay whatever he wants for the film."

Danny grabbed his old clothes, carried them with him as he climbed the steel ladder.

"Danny. . . ."

He looked down at her as she sat on the Castro with her mother in her arms, swallowed beneath a long-forgotten Brooklyn in her paranoid father's dungeon.

"I love you," she said.

He looked at her, didn't answer, and climbed out of the bomb shelter, up the stairs and let himself out of the house into the big rain.

# thirty-six

Danny met Ankles under the marquee of the Paragon multiplex a little before six P.M. Middle-aged yuppies left a foreign art film, popping brand-name umbrellas as another young, wet throng inched in to see an action picture featuring black and Asian actors. Approaching from several blocks down the parkside, Danny could hear a campaign flatbed truck with mounted speakers promoting Christie Strong for city council.

"You look like you got run over by a street sweeper," Ankles said, sniffing Danny and taking a step back. "Smell like it too. That girl of yours throw you a beatin' for coppin' a feel?"

"I don't think you want to get into a girlfriend rank-out contest, old man."

"What the fuck you got for me?"

"You first."

"Dirty Jim didn't make it," Ankles said.

"Does anyone know yet?"

"I put a lid on it. But it'll get out. Doctors are gossips. Strong knows everyone down there. They eat in his restaurant Pasta Bello at a discount."

Danny hadn't known when he was eating there that Pasta Bello was Strong's place, too. It was one of two Brooklyn restaurants where Erika ate. The other was the Strong Arms. He popped two Rolaids. Ankles held out his hand and Danny gave him a pair and Ankles chomped them like peanuts.

"Can you put out a wire that between convulsions Dirty Jim gave me an exclusive deathbed confession naming names? On tape. That you're going to subpoena that tape. But that I'm using the journalist's shield law."

"For what?"

Danny hesitated.

"To smoke Strong out. Make him do something. I have to force his hand. See if he wants to deal with me—"

"I think you're holding out on me, Danny."

"On what?"

"You know something you're not sharing with me. Something to do with your dame. Dirty Jim talked about films. Maybe you know where they are. That O'Rourke broad impounds all the computers. What's she tellin' you? You show up looking like someone just played T-ball with your face. What did you find out about Christie Strong?"

"I think he had Dirty Jim shoot a film the night of Malone's killing."

Ankles's eyes widened. "Where is it?"

"My guess he has it in a safe. Maybe I can horse-trade him Dirty Jim's deathbed tape for the Dirty Jim film."

"Good luck, because you know how many warrants I'd need to search all Strong's premises? Condos? Bim pads, which he gotta have a dozen? And stores? And safety deposit boxes? I'd need an all-premises, all-purpose pass. Ixnay that idea. I don't think I could even get one for his primary residence, because Strong knows more judges than my boss. He gives to their campaigns. He sells them houses and condos. He rents them apartments, and second ones half price for their goomattas. Who he sets them up with. Gives jobs to their college kids. It's better to know a judge than the law, but it's better still when you feed the judge on the arm. And fix them up with a broad. You just ain't gettin' a warrant for Christie Strong in this county without a smokin' gun."

Danny hesitated then reached into his rain slicker jacket, took out Angela Malone's diary, and handed it to Ankles. Ankles opened it, squinting at the scratchy foreign writing.

"This looks like a book of recipes, asshole. I'll have to take it home and use the paisan dictionary," he said, turning pages. "Looks like a hodgepodge of shit. Recipes. Little prayers. Girlhood memories. . . ." He turned more pages. "Wait, there are some sorta diary entries. But nothin's dated. All over the map. . . ."

"She's got Alzheimer's."

"*Du bots* is what we always called it when old fucks started shooting crap with baby blocks," Ankles said. "You don't havta say it, I'll be bettin' at that table soon."

"I'm telling you what I know." He just wasn't telling him everything. Yet. Ankles was still a cop who had been trying to nail him for most of his life. Ankles looked over Danny's shoulder as the flatbed campaign sound truck grew louder.

He grabbed Danny by the shirtfront, slammed him against his black Taurus, pointing a finger in his face. Moviegoers jumped back and formed startled knots, watching the confrontation like it was a coming attraction.

"The fuck you doing?"

The campaign flatbed truck passed, covered in red, white, and blue bunting, plastered with posters: BE STRONG: VOTE STRONG FOR A STRONGER CITY. Strong sat in the front seat, waving to people entering and exiting the movie house. He waved to Danny and Ankles, before looping around the circle, a recorded message blaring, "Be Strong, vote Strong on the Independent ticket on November 3."

"I'm making it look like I want something from you, asshole," Ankles said. "You been in that California too long. Street smarten up."

Ankles let go of him. Curious onlookers murmured and laughed as the flatbed truck swished around the circle.

"You didn't have to overdo it," Danny said. "My back is already killing me."

Ankles watched the Strong-for-city-council campaign truck disappear up Parkside West, the loudspeaker still blaring the same slogan.

"You give me a diary written in siggie by a *du botz*, which you musta stole from your tomata's house, which means it'll be inadmissible in a courtroom, anyways. Plus, I think you got the hots for this O'Rourke broad, who's trying to deep-freeze both of us. I'm giving you a play. I'm treating you down the middle, straight pool. You don't square with me, it's suicide. Warnin' ya—"

"Then we'll have to get the smoking gun. Decipher that book and call me later. I'll be at the hotel."

Ankles climbed into his Taurus and pulled away. Danny jaywalked across the parkside to get into his rented car in the park lot. He stopped when he saw the familiar gait of a hooded figure rush through the rain, stopping just past Hippie Hill and bending to unlock the Transit Authority access door to Sewer 7, Pipe 11.

Danny watched JoJo Corcoran pull up the steel door and begin to descend. Danny called his name, glanced over his shoulder at Helen's window, and JoJo stopped halfway down the ladder, holding the metal door open.

Danny sloshed up the hill toward JoJo, who smiled when he saw Danny coming.

"Happnin', Danny? I know I owe you fourteen dollars but—"

"Forget the money, I wanna ask you a few questions."

"Come on in," he said. "I'll make you a cup of tea. Red Rose, it's on sale up Key Food at $2.99 for 100 bags with a ceramic dolphin to add to my menagerie of Red Rose animals. . . ."

Danny laughed. He was already filthy so he followed JoJo down the steel ladder to Sewer 7, Pipe 11. As he descended, Danny saw all the old graffiti from three decades ago spray-painted on the sooty stone walls. Most of the names belonged to people who were now dead—Wally Fortune, Kenny Byrne, Tony Mauro, Tommy Ryan, Cisco, Popcorn Gonzalez, Ocarman, Slappy, Gordon. He saw his own name spray-painted in silver letters in a big heart along with Erika's name. He had no memory of spraying it. Too fucking weird, he thought, deafened by the incessant humming of the huge electronic generator and the rumble of an F train roaring through the black subterranean veins of the city.

JoJo led him into the roaring main generator room, pushed wide a big heavy steel door that opened onto the black tunnel. An F train whipped past like videotape on fast-forward. "That's the catwalk to the station," JoJo yelled. "Remember?"

Danny nodded, recalling coming up from here the night he witnessed Vito Malone murdering Wally Fortune.

Danny recoiled from the train as it lashed by in a white-and-silver streak. . . .

*November 21, 1969*

*Danny stumbles up from his crash pad on Fifteenth Road. Dressed in his old clothes, the .45 pistol in his army jacket pocket. He enters the subway. Smashed. Acid contortions. Goofball spasms. Boozy blur. Danny pays for a token so no one gets suspicious. The token booth clerk warns him about falling into the tracks. Danny plunges into the platform, which is empty at two-fifteen A.M. He walks to the end. Thinking he's slick, he wobbles down the catwalk. When a train thunders past, loud and enormous, fast and ferocious, Danny totters, woozy, swaying. He sees astonished faces in the subway cars. And then it is gone. He enters the main generator room of Sewer 7, Pipe 11. JoJo Corcoran slams the door to the tool storage room that serves as his little bedroom. "What the hell are you doing here?"*

"Who's in the other room?" *Danny asks.*

"Nobody. A bim. Where you going?"

*"To kill Boar's Head."*

*"Danny, don't be a stooge. . . ."*

*Danny climbs the steel ladder to the rear of Hippie Hill to sneak up on Boar's Head in the rain. Slick. . . .*

JoJo slammed the big door and led him to another heavy door that opened into a back tool storage room, where it was much quieter and air-conditioned. This was the sanctuary where trackwalkers, maintenance men, and TA electricians took coffee breaks. JoJo had it set up like a studio apartment. John Jay High School gym mats covered the walls to muffle the sound and an inlaid wall-to-wall shag rug covered the floor of the room. It was furnished with a folding bed, table, and chairs, an old boom box, a microwave, and a small fridge. A twelve-inch color TV sat on top of a tiny dresser with a cable wire that snaked up the wall and through the stone ceiling toward the street. An air conditioner was fitted into the cinderblock wall above the bed. Two bruiser-looking tomcats slept on the foot of the bed, stirring when JoJo gave each a pet. The room was immaculate.

"How long you been living here in Sewer 7 now?"

"Thirty-four years, on and off, with stops in nuthouses like Creedmore, Pilgrim State, and KCH G building here and there."

"No one ever kicked you out?"

"For what? I keep the place spotless," JoJo said, putting a tea bag into a Styrofoam cup and filling it with water from a small sink. He placed it into the microwave, pressed some numbers and the START button. "I always have coffee or tea for the guys and Entenmanns cake. They can take a nap. Get laid. Goof off. Kill time. One of the electricians spliced into a cable TV pole in the street, ran the cable underground, drilled a hole into this room, and hooked it up down here to a pirate box so that they can watch big fights, pay-per-view movies, and porno when they're supposed to be working. I'm the caretaker. They know there wouldn't be a rat within two miles of Brook and Lynne, my two felines. They can meow in five lingos, including Arabic, Korean, Spanish, Haitian, and Ebonics. I remember one time, July 13, 1977, ninety-two degrees, humidity 86 percent, and the lights went out all over the city, the great blackout. They started walking people down the track to escape from the stalled trains. People fainting, screaming, shitting in their pants in thirty-nine foreign languages. I sat in here, air conditioner going, legs up, reading Archie comics because there's a small alternative generator to light the emergency tunnel lights in the next room and—"

"JoJo, the night of November 20, 1969, where were you?"

"Home."

"Home where?"

"Home here, I just finished telling you, I moved in here on June 12, 1967, the Summer of Love. It's not for the faint of heart, but Dr. Christian Barnard performed the first heart transplant that year. You guys hung out in the outer generator room. I lived in here. This was the only place I could get my head together, because down here, there was nowhere else to go but up, which was still a step above where the army left me. You ever get electroshock on LSD? You'd rather butter your feet and step on the third rail—"

"JoJo, November 20, 1969—"

The microwave beeped and JoJo removed the Styrofoam cup. "You just said that. Milk and sugar?"

"Christ . . . yeah, milk and fucking sugar."

"That was the night Vito Malone was murdered upstairs on Hippie Hill at 2:43 A.M.," JoJo said, adding milk and sugar and stirring the tea with a swizzle stick and handing it to Danny. "So in reality it was November 21, but nobody counts the hours when people are asleep unless you have F trains rushing past you all night on their way to Manhattan and Queens or Coney Island, where you should know they started a minor league baseball team since you were gone called the Brooklyn Cyclones and—"

"You were here that night?" Danny asked, sipping the hot tea, which was delicious, warming his esophagus.

"Sure. It was raining. Only a fucking nut job stays out at 2:43 A.M. in the rain. My brains were french-fried that year from acid, which I thought might reverse what the army did to me, but only exacerbated it, but I still knew when to come in from the rain."

"Did you see the shooting?"

"Sure."

"You saw Malone get murdered?" Danny was excited.

"You bet your ass I did. So did you."

Danny took another sip, stared at JoJo through the steam underneath the approximate scene of the old murder.

"Hold it. Let me get this straight. Where were you standing?"

"Next to Dirty Jim, upstairs on the ladder of Sewer 7," he said.

"We were half in, half out of the hatch. I held his sun gun light while he filmed with the Super 8 camera. I was his assistant."

"How come you never told me this before?"

"First of all, you were here, I figured you knew. You passed right through here to sneak up on Boar's Head on Hippie Hill. You were smashed. But I figured you'd remember that. And you never once asked me about it so I never said nothing. But also because Dirty Jim swore me to secrecy. He paid me fifty bucks. Your word is your honor when there's a half a yard involved. You know how much fifty bucks was in '69? Uppies were three for a buck, so were downs. Blue cheer acid was five bucks. You could get a six-pack of Schlitz in Bohack for ninety-nine cents. A gallon of Guinea red Chianti was two-ninety-nine in Sammy's Liquors. Milk was thirty-three cents, butter was eighty-five cents a pound, coffee was seventy-five cents a pound, and Wonder Bread was twenty-seven cents. A fuckin' stamp was six cents. So fifty bucks meant something back then. It meant keep your fuckin' mouth shut. . . ."

"You saw who killed Boar's Head, JoJo?"

"I didn't say that," he said. "I saw him get shot but I didn't see who shot him."

"Why not? I'm not following—"

"I was too busy holding up the light and watching you," JoJo said. "I had the light trained on you and Boar's Head when I saw you aim your gun at him. I saw him taunting you, daring you to shoot. But you kept falling on your ass, stoned. And when you had the chance, you just didn't pull the trigger."

"Who the fuck did?"

"I dunno," JoJo said. "It was all really fast. Maybe thirty, forty seconds, the most. I was watching you, holding the light, then I heard the woman's voice—"

"Woman's voice?"

"Yeah, then I heard the first shot. Blam! And I just ducked down below the stairway entrance, holding the light up with one arm as Dirty Jim kept shooting the film. Then I heard blam, blam, blam, blam, blam. Dirty saw it all. Got it all on film. . . ."

"Who was the woman . . . how do you know I didn't shoot him—"

"I know it wasn't you who fired the shots because by that time you were facedown in the mud," JoJo said.

Danny looked at him, a celestial shiver washing through him like a spiritual absolution, as if he'd just been washed clean of his life's greatest mortal sin.

"So why are you telling me this now?" Danny asked.

"Like I sez, because you asked. Plus, I like what you sez about what I owed your pop, death ending all contracts and all that. Dirty Jim died two hours and twelve minutes ago in Methodist Hospital, and so my fifty-dollar dummy-up contract with him is up now, too."

Danny was startled, dread replacing the absolution. "Who told you he died?"

"I was down the Methodist Hospital where I go to wash up every day in the men's room and I heard two guys say they had a guy named James Dugan had to go to KCH for an autopsy. I know he was strychnined."

Danny looked around the room, realizing that the only place to find the Brooklyn he remembered was with an archeological dig. He knew JoJo talked to everybody. If he wanted to spread a wire, the way to do it was to have JoJo put it on the neighborhood tom-toms. He wanted Christie to contact him so that he didn't think it was a setup.

"News travels fast," Danny said. "Did you hear that I got a deathbed confession on tape from Dirty Jim? All about the murders of Wally Fortune, Mary Fortune, Vito Malone, and how Christie Strong and Dirty Jim and Hippie Helen used all the info to black-mail people. . . ."

"They didn't get dime fuckin' one from me."

"I have it all on tape," Danny said. "I want what Christie has on film. Fair exchange."

"You must sure love this Erika broad, huh?"

"Why do you say that?"

"Because you're willing to go to the mat with a fucking savage like Christie Strong just to get back a film that shows Erika Malone was there that night when her father was killed. I don't know if she did the shooting, but Erika was the last person I saw before I ducked my head."

JoJo confirmed what Danny had recalled in his LSD-induced state-dependent memory. "There was a fourth person on the hill that night," Danny said. "There was me, Boar's Head, Erika—"

"You're right."

"Who was it, JoJo?"

"I had my head ducked," he said. "So your guess is as good as mine."

Danny's guess was Christie Strong.

# thirty-seven

Danny drove downtown in total silence. No radio. Just the rain on the steel roof and JoJo Corcoran's information exploding in his brain.

If what JoJo said and what Danny now remembered was true, and Danny had no reason to doubt it because JoJo stored details like a human hard drive, it explained everything. It also changed everything.

JoJo was holding the light for Dirty Jim that night. No one had ever taken him serious enough to even question him as a witness. The man was a certifiable lunatic. He had a history of schizophrenic behavior, and a psychiatric military discharge. He was a repository for every psychotropic drug ever pushed across a pharmacy counter. He had case-history folders bearing his name in every puzzle factory in the metropolitan area.

Put him on a witness stand and he would put on a hell of a show. But his word wasn't going to help Danny Cassidy walk out of a courtroom as a free man. Still, Danny believed him. JoJo had been right about Horsecock and Lars Andersen. He'd been right about Mary Fortune. He was nuts and he knew he was nuts. But JoJo Corcoran wasn't stupid. He knew what was going on in this neighborhood, which had been his entire world for most of his life. You just didn't survive for thirty-four years living in a subterranean hovel and hustling on the street unless you knew what was going on.

What was going on was that Erika Malone had spent the last thirty-two years covering up her own presence at her father's murder. Or her participation in it. But why would Erika kill her father? To save Danny? Maybe, he thought. But he suspected the answer was darker.

He wanted to confront Erika, but he needed time to think. He was dirty, filthy, beat up, tired, and confused. He needed to stand under a boiling-hot shower, let the water pulsate on his neck and his back, let the whole dirty, smarmy jumble sluice down the drain. He needed to lay his head down, listen to the beat of his own heart. And think.

Erika had been protecting herself all this time, maybe protecting someone else, too, but she had also left Danny out there to take the fall.

Just as Danny was parking the car at the hotel traffic loop his cell phone rang. Viviana Gonzalez said, "Christie's picking me up in twenty minutes with his Mercedes limousine."

"Good," Danny said. "Tell him you heard from me that Jim Dugan gave me a deathbed confession. On tape. That he implicated him in Dugan's and several other murders. Tell him that I also have Kenny Byrne's affidavit and his interview on tape."

"How should I say you contacted me?"

"Tell him I tracked you down. That I got your number from the sign-in book at the wake. That I told you all of this. Tell him you also heard from Ankles the cop. Tell him you also heard it from one of the nurses or doctors at the hospital."

"I'll make him believe it's all over the neighborhood."

"Thanks, Viv. Be careful."

"He wants to get in my pants too bad to hurt me. What's going on?"

"I can tell you a lot more tomorrow."

"Can I print it all?"

"The parts you can confirm with triple sourcing."

"Where do I get those?"

"Working the story," Danny said. "I can point you in the right direction. You have to get the rest with shoe leather, phone calls, and ball-busting."

"I'll call you after I tell him what you said."

"OK," Danny said. "But don't tell him for a couple of hours. I need a nap and some time to think."

They said good-bye, Danny parked the car. He checked for his key card, but couldn't find it. Must've lost it in the schoolyard, he thought.

Filthy, bruised, and battered he went to the front desk and asked for a replacement. The clerk eyed him with a raised eyebrow and asked for ID. Danny showed him some and he got the new card. He took the elevator up to his floor. He had the .45 jammed under his waistband, covered by his shirt, and when he walked down the corridor he looked over his shoulder to be sure no one was following him. No one was.

He opened his door with the key card, and Pat O'Rourke sat in a chair looking out over a Manhattan skyline that was still shrouded in rain. He was startled and looked behind him down the hallway again.

"This official? If it is, I'd like to see a warrant. If it's not—"

"It's not," she said, holding up the key card. "You dropped this when you were getting your ass kicked. I thought I'd return it."

"Why are you here?"

"I'm worried about you," she said, rising from the chair, sipping a seven-ounce bottle of Diet Coke she'd swiped from his minibar, walking toward him, her tight damp jeans clinging to her strong, small hips and thighs. "I know you think time is running out. I know Ankles is in a foot race with me to close the Malone case."

"That true?"

"I'm gonna close it. I can't say for sure, but I don't think you did it. People are dying. Something tells me they aren't done dying yet. I don't want to see you become a collateral casualty. I'm asking you to back off, let me do this."

"I can't. It's about me. My life."

"I think your girlfriend is in hip-deep and I know—"

"She used to be my girlfriend."

Pat O'Rourke stood in front of him now, all freckled nose, blond curls, and blue eyes, in counterpoint to the serious nature of her visit. She rolled the mouth of the bottle on her lower lip, leaving a lipstick smudge.

"I like you. . . ."

"That the same line of shit you used to disarm Christie Strong?"

"Yeah, I flirted with Strong," she said. "I played dumb blonde for him. He asked me out. We went out. I ate his food. I picked his brain. It's how I learned your used-to-be girlfriend was dirty. She called twice while I was there. I know because I saw her company's name and number on his caller ID box."

"She knows him, sure, but—"

"They were talking about millions of dollars."

"That's what millionaires talk about."

"I already lost a father and a mother to things that happened in 1969," O'Rourke said. "My brother went downhill from that point on. It's haunted most of my life—"

"Join the club," he said. "Club Dead."

"I don't want to see you go down."

"Why are you so concerned about me?"

"I didn't lie to you the night I met you," she said. "I started liking you before I even met you. I like your writing. I like that you love your kid. I like that you regret what you did to your wife. I like the way you look, the way you walk and talk. I like the way you listen. I like your balls, um, guts. I like everything about you except that you like, or love, Erika Malone."

If O'Rourke were standing any closer she would be in his shirt pocket, looking up into his eyes. "I can't trust you," he said. "You're a cop. . . ."

"I left my gun and badge in the car because I didn't want it to come between us."

She looped her hand around his neck and kissed him.

"I need a shower, bad."

"So do I. Can I join you?"

"It could taint your testimony against me. Sure you want to do this?"

She answered by pulling her Mets T-shirt over her head. She wore no bra. She was hard and toned, her breasts small and flawless, an ice tray of muscle in her belly.

"Consider me legally neutralized," she said.

She opened her pewter belt buckle and worked the wet jeans over her tight hips when the knock came upon the door. O'Rourke looked trapped.

"Expecting someone?"

Danny shook his head. She reached into her bag for her gun. It wasn't there, which for Danny made her seem all the more naked and vulnerable and sexy. He didn't want her to know he had the .45. O'Rourke pulled up and buckled her pants. Before she could pull on her shirt Danny reached out and touched her breasts. He put each nipple in his mouth, headlocked her, and kissed her. Her tongue was small and hot. A much different tongue than Erika Malone's. She sighed. "Oh, God. . . ."

Another knock came on the door. O'Rourke, looking more vulnerable than ever, pulled on her Mets shirt and nodded for him to answer. Her aroused nipples protruded through the shirt.

Danny opened the door. His daughter, Darlene, said, "Hi, Dad. Oh, shit . . . hope I'm not interrupting. . . ."

Darlene backed away from the door. O'Rourke walked to her, smiling, holding out a hand. "Detective Pat O'Rourke, NYPD. I was here on official business and I was just leaving. I gotta tell you, your father is one hell of a guy. All he ever talks about is you. Brags about you all the time. You're a lucky chick. I wish I would've had an old man like him. Listen, your pop was just about to have a shower. Why don't you and me go down and grab a coffee?"

"Um, thanks . . . I guess . . . all right. Dad?"

"Good idea, pussycat," Danny said, using the nickname he'd called her by until she reached puberty and she'd asked him to stop. "I'm a mess right now."

"You're not kidding. What the hell happened to you?"

O'Rourke looked at Danny, as if asking permission to fill his daughter in on some of the details. He nodded.

"It's time she knew," Danny said.

"I'll tell you what I know," O'Rourke said. "Maybe he'll tell you the stuff he doesn't tell me."

"This is, like, bizarro," Darlene said.

"I'll only be a few minutes," Danny said.

Darlene smiled at her father, shrugged, and walked down the corridor with O'Rourke.

Danny closed the door, shut his eyes, trembling.

When he got down to the lobby, scrubbed and changed, he found Darlene and O'Rourke sitting on a settee, gabbing over ceramic cups of coffee. Darlene was even laughing, which made Danny's heart soar. Darlene saw her father walk across the lobby, a limp in his gait, a robotic stiffness in his back. Danny wondered if she thought he looked old. Their eyes met and Darlene stopped smiling. A look of concern spread across her face as she rose from the couch and crossed the champagne-colored rug. O'Rourke stood, hands jammed in her back jeans pockets, taking a step backward toward the exit.

"Hey, you have a great kid here, Cassidy," O'Rourke said. "I'm sure you two have lots to talk about. Sorry for your loss. Both of you. See ya."

O'Rourke walked past Darlene, looked back, nodded at Danny, and was gone.

Danny stared into his daughter's eyes, hoping he had the courage to hold the stare. He did. Darlene, his little girl, was all grown up, her eyes crammed with earnest concern, the kind that comes from uncompromising love.

"I wish you would have told me all of this a long, long time ago," she said, biting her lower lip. He took her in his sore arms. She looped her arms around his chest. Danny's body was a touch pad of pain, bruises, and knots in every muscle, joint, and bone. But Darlene's embrace was like a salve, the miracle drug of filial love and forgiveness. *God Almighty,* he thought. *What have I done with this kid's childhood? I didn't show up for the middle of my daughter's life. . . .*

"Can we walk?"

"You bet," he said and he led her outside into the rain, opening the umbrella. Darlene grabbed his hand and yanked him across Adams Street, dodging traffic, laughing, his umbrella turning inside out. On the sidewalk he fixed the umbrella and they walked down rain-hammered Montague Street toward the Brooklyn Heights promenade, passing bookstores, health-food stores, restaurants, and streets lined with brownstones built a couple of centuries earlier. A foot cop stood under an awning of a Baskin Robbins, licking an ice cream.

Darlene told Danny that O'Rourke had filled her in on the old murders and the new ones, all about Vito Malone and his daughter, Erika Malone, and O'Rourke's father, Jack Davis, who was blackmailed over an affair he'd had with her uncle.

"She told me you gave this Lars guy an ass-whipping today," Darlene said.

"Is that what she said?" he asked, laughing.

"Yeah," Darlene said. "But looking at you I'd love to see the other guy."

"It was the other way around," Danny said, holding the umbrella above them, passing storm-logged yuppies gazing at the fifty-year-old man with the beautiful twenty-year-old arm candy.

"I look like a cradle snatcher."

"Maybe they think you're a congressman and I'm your intern."

He laughed and then he asked, "How's your mom?"

"She's good. . . ."

"Well. . . ."

"She's the best."

"I know."

"You never mentioned Erika Malone before."

"Would it have made a difference when you were fourteen?"

"No. I guess it would have made it worse. Did you see her back then?"

"No."

"You lived with all these secrets."

"I'm not alone, believe me."

"It explains a lot. . . ."

He stopped, turned to her under the umbrella, rainwater rolling off onto their shoulders as foghorns grumped from the shrouded harbor, and looked her in the hazel star-burst eyes. She looked like her mother had when he first started dating her, which filled him with regret and loss. *Emptiness is an ache that can't be located because it is and isn't there at the same time.*

"Darlene, pussycat, I'm so sorry. No, I'm *shit* and—"

She stepped out from under the umbrella, rain dancing on the thin hood of her zippered jacket. "You're my father. If you ever say that about yourself again, I'll get pissed off."

He put the umbrella over her head again. He kissed her forehead and took a deep breath. "I'd give anything to have a second shot at raising you."

"Hey, it ain't like there's a terminal illness here," she said as they resumed walking, passing a playground that was as empty as the last five years of his life. They stepped out onto the promenade, overlooking the rain-shrouded skyline that looked like the gray hull of an immense ship. "When I was on the river floating, one of the kids who was white-watering with us almost drowned."

"I know, your mother told me."

"I never came that close to death before. I thought, Holy shit, that could be me. What if I died before I patched things up with Dad? How shitty would that be? So then when I got your message, I was, like, so happy that you wanted me to be with you when your father had died. It felt good. I was elated, even in what should be a sad time."

"You have no idea how good it is to see you, pussycat."

"And as for the wasted time. I dunno, hey, I'm only nineteen. You're what, fifty? Old but not decrepit yet. We have plenty of time. You wanna take me to Disneyland, I'm game. Wanna go to Europe, I'm already packed. Wanna be just, like, ya know, father and daughter, and go for pizza, I'm ready. We blew the high school years, so what? I have friends whose fathers are dead or in jail for tax scams. I could've drowned yesterday. . . ."

"Jesus Christ, don't say that. And I'm not out of this trouble yet."

"O'Rourke doesn't think you'll go to jail. Unless you do something stupid."

*O'Rourke also told you I kicked Lars's ass,* he thought. "I hope she's right."

"How come you never saw your own dad in all these years?"

"He drove my mom to her grave."

"That's heavy baggage, old man," Darlene said. "To hell with everybody else, but when it's family, you're supposed to forgive even when you can't forget. You should have made your peace with him when there was still time."

Danny looked at his kid, who was making her peace with him. He shuddered as a wet wind lashed off the harbor.

"I guess I wasn't as good a son as you are a daughter," he said.

"I wish I would have met him. I guess. But the way you talked about him, I thought maybe he was some kind of monster."

"I was wrong about not letting you meet him. I should have let you make up your own mind. I guess I made more mistakes than I did things right."

"Can I confess something?" she asked.

"Sure."

"All these years I sort of prayed that you'd get sick, or hurt, or in trouble, and that I could come and help you because that's what a daughter is supposed to do with her father in a time of need. So I could put aside all our resentments and feuds and just be family. I wanted to find a way to tell you I love you without making it seem like I was a wimp or betraying mom, ya know?"

"Jesus, pussycat, I'm so—"

Darlene put her finger on her father's lips, looked into his eyes under the umbrella, as the wind whipped and foghorns bellowed and cars whooshed through the flooded Brooklyn-Queens Expressway beneath them. For a minute he could see his father in her frown, and pieces of Brendan. And Tammy in the eyes. He couldn't see himself in her face at all.

"All these years, I was angry," she said. "But at the same time I ached for you to get sick or in trouble so I could come to you and help you in a vulnerable time when even Mom would understand."

"I should have tried harder to reach out to you, pussycat. I was a flop at fatherhood. I should have done better. I cared more about my own demons than yours."

"You were human. You're my father. I'm your kid. I want you to know that no matter what happens now, I'm here. I still think what you did to Mom and me sucks a big one. I always will. But it's done. So I'll always be here. I mean, what the f—hell."

He knew that if he looked at her he would lose it, so he stared off at Lady Liberty. He put his arm around his daughter's shoulder and pulled her to him.

"I think that cop got the hots for you," Darlene said.

"Has, not got . . . yeah?"

"Tell you what, she ain't . . . *isn't* bad for an old man like you."

"Last thing on my mind."

But she wasn't, he thought. *I think about her a lot. About her and Erika Malone.*

"Know what I'd like to see?"

"Name it."

"I want to see where you grew up," she said. "Granddad's place."

He looked at her, ghosts whipping past him on the rain.

# thirty-eight

Brendan said, "You look like shit, bro." He stood by the sink in the eat-in kitchen of their old Prospect Road tenement apartment, sipping a beer from a bottle. Danny's heart thumped, his palms sweated, and his mouth was dry. He noticed a pink envelope on the kitchen table, propped between the blue delft salt and pepper shakers, addressed in his father's script to Brendan and Danny.

"You look good," Danny said.

"*Well,*" Darlene said, elbowing Danny, slamming the door behind them. "Hi, I'm Darlene. . . ."

Brendan walked to her, kissed her on the cheek. "Nice to meet you. I'm your long in the tooth and very lost Uncle Brendan." He looked at Danny, put his palms up, and said, "So, what happened to Brooklyn, bro? It looks like a cross between the Village in the sixties and Boston's Back Bay."

"Gone."

Brendan stared at Danny, their eyes exploring one another, trying to peel away the decades, searching for the inseparable brothers who once shared this apartment and their lives. "Thanks for calling."

"Thanks for coming."

They shook hands, almost embraced but just bumped shoulders.

"Yo, I see a pizza store across the street," Darlene said. "You guys want me to bring any back?"

"Get a whole pie," Brendan said, pulling out a fistful of cash, peeling off a hundred-dollar bill. "And a large orange soda and a Diet Coke, honey."

Darlene took the money and shuffled back out the door, leaving the Cassidy brothers alone in their old apartment.

"You OK?"

"Yeah."

Brendan opened the fridge, took out a pair of beers, put them on the table. They both sat down and popped the brews. They stared at the letter on the table, which sat there like a ticking bomb, a living thing left by a dead man who helped give both of them life.

"How come you haven't opened this yet?" Brendan asked.

"First time I set foot back in here since I'm back."

"Why?"

"Too many memories. Mom. . . ."

Brendan nodded, looked around the kitchen. Danny followed his gaze past the old burnt pot holders, the ancient black cast-iron frying pan that had cooked them thousands of pancakes, and sizzling bacon. Their mother had dropped dead cooking hamburgers at that stove. He looked past the old owl clock that said it was 9:35 P.M. Past the ancient Emerson radio their mother used to put on when she ironed, singing along with Kitty Kelly and Perry Como. Past the windows that looked out at the Manhattan skyline and the pizza parlor across the street. Past the portraits of the Sacred Heart of Jesus and the crucifix and the photograph of Pope John XXIII. The photo of JFK that went along with those like a set package was missing, shit-canned by Mickey Cassidy after their mother died because he thought Kennedy was a liberal asshole. The yellowed vinyl wallpaper was the same as Danny remembered it, a Parisian outdoor-café design with a plump waiter delivering a bottle of wine to an elegant couple.

"He never changed Mom's favorite wallpaper," Danny said.

Brendan picked up the envelope from the table. "I'm the oldest, which is still a pain in the ass, so I guess I have to do the honors."

Danny nodded as Brendan opened the pink envelope, stationery left over from when their mother was alive, thinking it might've been the only letter Mickey Cassidy had written in all those years.

"He ever write you in Asia?"

"You fucking crazy? I never sent him an address. He was the prototype for Archie Bunker. He would have written back, the envelope addressed to 'Brendan Cassidy, Commie and Chink Lover, No Tickee No Shirtee, Red Chinkland.' You know him."

"No, I don't think I ever did."

Brendan nodded, took out a pair of prescription bifocals, balanced them on his nose, and held the letter in his hands. "Ready for this shit?"

"No, but go ahead anyway."

"Dear Guys:
I know I stunk as a father and a husband. I can't even say I did my best because I didn't. I drank too much. I was too

mean. I treated your mother like shit instead of a queen, which is what she was. She was the best thing that ever happened to me. I was the worst thing ever happened to her. But she stayed with me. I don't know why. Being Catholic, I guess. Maybe if she didn't stay with me she'd still be here. I loved her. I loved you guys, too. I guess I realized all of this too late. What can I say? I screwed it all up. I'm old and I'm dying now. It sucks and I'm scared of hell. If I had to do it all over again I don't know if I could do anything different. So, all I ask, because I know your mother would have wanted this more than anything, is that you guys forgive each other for whatever happened back in 1969 when the wheels came off this family, this neighborhood. You two used to love each other like brothers should. When you bury me, bury the hatchet. You do that and I won't be a complete failure and your mother will sing in heaven. That's it. The docs say I'm out of here anytime now.

Love,
Dad."

Brendan looked at Danny over his bifocals and said, "Whadda ya think?"

"It doesn't make me love him," Danny said. "But there's enough to hang your hat on there to make me want to forgive him."

"I'm with you."

They raised their beers, swigged, and nodded.

"Good, that's out of the friggin' way," Brendan said, folding his bifocals and putting them in his shirt pocket. "Wait'll you see our bedroom. It's a wax museum."

Danny followed Brendan to the archway of their old bedroom and looked in at the bunk beds, made with tight hospital corners, the walls covered with old posters of Mickey Mantle, Y.A. Tittle, Joe Namath, Tom Seaver, and Muhammad Ali. Board games—Monopoly, Parcheesi, Civil War, Chance, Clue—were stacked on top of a brown tin armoire. Baseball bats, gloves, hockey sticks, boxing gloves, and a catcher's mask protruded from an old toy box. A bookcase overflowed with the collected Hardy Boys and Encyclopaedia Britannica from 1960, and Brendan's collection of classic books like *Huckleberry Finn*, *The Iliad* and *The Odyssey*, *A Thousand and One*

*Arabian Nights, The Collected Edgar Allan Poe, Ivanhoe, The Count of Monte Cristo, The Three Musketeers.*

"We did an awful lot of dreaming in here," Brendan said.

"None of them came true."

"Doesn't matter. Sometimes dreams are better left as dreams. Think about it, those days of dreaming, they're the dream now."

Brendan lifted the old Wilson football off the top of the bookcase, spiraled it in his hands, and then buried it in Danny's gut. And in the same fluid motion he grabbed his little brother in his arms and hugged him, smothering him, clutched him so tightly to his chest that Danny thought he'd break some bones. The wordless heat of their bodies said more than words could ever convey. Brendan kissed the top of Danny's head, smacked the back of his head, gave him a noogie, kissed him again, and hugged him closer.

"I missed the shit out of you, Brendan."

"What happened happened," Brendan whispered.

They separated and stood for a long silent moment frozen in time in the room where they never once thought of someday being old.

"What happens now?" Danny asked.

"We bury the old man and we live what's left as well as we can."

"That's it?"

"You have a kid there, man. I wish I had one of them. You're blessed. We don't need each other like she needs you."

"Why don't you have any kids?"

"I guess I was always a little afraid I'd be too much like him," he said, nodding toward the pink envelope out on the kitchen table. "Let's skip the rest of the maudlin Irish family horseshit for now. We can get around to that later, after the funeral. Right now tell me the fucking truth. What's going on, Danny?"

So they sat on the lower bunk bed and Danny told him about most of it, about Erika Malone and Christie Strong, about Horsecock and Kenny Byrne, about Ankles and Pat O'Rourke, and getting his ass kicked by Lars Andersen and dosed with a bad trip. He told him that the two cops were in a foot race to bring a circumstantial case against him to the Brooklyn DA, who was itching to indict a newspaper reporter for an old cold-case cop killing, which would be sexy news in an election year.

"You think I shot him, Brendan?"

"I saw kids in Nam who were wimps all their lives and turned into monsters," he said. "Saw monsters who turned into wimps.

When push comes to shove, anyone is capable of murder. All I know is that at the time, that night, for me, killed any future you and me might have had together. I just wanted you to hit the road, to get away. Then I did too, in the opposite direction. I thought it was the best way to confuse the law."

"Why didn't you answer my letters?"

"It would have encouraged you to write more."

"You hated me that much?"

"I love you that much, asshole. But you'd gotten yourself into one of those black holes where even if you tried to get out of it, you'd only dig yourself deeper. Because you didn't know what the truth was. I was afraid our mail or telephone calls would be monitored. If we didn't communicate, you couldn't incriminate yourself. I was your big brother, home from the war, and there was nothing I could do to help you. Made me feel like shit. I was pissed at feeling inadequate. Useless. Except to stay out of your way, out of your life, and hope you dodged the bullet. Mom was dead. Dad was a swine. You'd boxed yourself into a trap. I sent you one way and I went the other to forget and to find a life."

"You have a wife?"

"I see a few dames . . . Jesus Christ, I can't believe you're still chasing Erika Malone."

"Lots of people rediscover their childhood sweethearts."

"Not one whose father you might've killed."

"For the first time, I can say I don't think I did."

Brendan looked at him with a long silent stare, his face still strong, iron-gray hair laying in soft thick curls on his head, pretty trim and muscular for a guy almost fifty-one.

"You remember, now?"

"I'm getting pieces of it back. Believe it or not the LSD might have triggered—"

"State-dependent memory?"

"Yeah, how'd you know?"

"A lot of amnesiacs in Nam and China are treated with opium to recall atrocities that were blocked out in the war."

"Brendan, did you ever kill anyone?

"I'm not sure either," he said. "There were firefights at night in the Central Highlands when I fired into the dark. I have no idea if any of the bullets hit anyone. I've often wondered about it, though. Then I take a deep breath and get on with the day."

They fell silent again, looking around the room. "Did you really get dosed?" Brendan asked.

"Yup."

"Good shit?" he asked, laughing.

"Good acid, bad trip. They spiked a bowl of sherbet."

"Could've killed you."

"That was probably the intention."

"Strong's a bad fucking guy," Brendan said. "Always was."

"I'll get him."

"Not without me you won't."

"Just one of us is in trouble," Danny said. "Let's keep it that way. I don't want to fuck up your second homecoming."

They stood again and this time Danny saw fear in Brendan's eyes. He turned toward the window, looked through the bars of the fire escape at the drizzly Brooklyn sprawl. Danny turned to him and this time Danny held Brendan in his arms. "I'm so sorry, Danny. I. . . ."

"Me too."

When Danny looked over Brendan's shoulder he saw Darlene standing in the bedroom doorway with the pizza, blinking, as if discovering a vital hidden part of her father she'd never known before. Danny and Brendan separated.

"Let's eat," she said.

Danny and Brendan entered the kitchen. Brendan sat and Danny walked to the overhead cabinets, remembering which had the plates, which one had the glasses, which drawer held the yellow bone-handled silverware. Nothing had changed.

"Get me a knife and fork," Darlene said.

"This is New York," Danny said. "There's a law against eating pizza with a knife and fork. You fold it in half lengthwise and eat it like this."

He bit into a folded slice of pie, looked at his smiling daughter and his grinning brother all eating the pizza. Three Cassidys sitting around the old Formica kitchen table.

"I've been traveling for twenty-one hours," Brendan said. "I gotta get some z's."

"I have to iron my black dress and take a bath," Darlene said. "Can we stay here tonight?"

"Sure," Danny said. "You can sleep in Mom's bed. Me and Brendan'll sleep in the bunk beds. I just have to go check out of the hotel later. Then I'll come back."

They finished the pizza and Darlene went into the bathroom, started drawing a bath, and entered the bedroom to unpack.

Danny looked at his watch. It was almost ten o'clock. Brendan yawned, stretched, and walked into the living room, plopped on the hard plaid couch that was bought in the last decade and turned on the color TV. He yawned again.

"What've you been doing all these years?" Danny asked as a promo for the ten o'clock news came on Channel 5.

"I've been living a life. Teaching. Reading. I have friends, girl-friends. I have a nice pad. I read your stuff on-line. . . ."

"Yeah?"

"You're pretty good," Brendan said, yawning again.

"Thanks. You ever do any writing? Brendan?"

Brendan answered with a snore, followed by another and another.

# thirty-nine

Danny pulled on the Brooklyn Cyclones batting gloves, grabbed the metal Brooklyn Cyclones baseball bat from the trunk of his Camry, stuffed the .45 into his back waistband, and entered the building through the delivery entrance on President Street. The gate was jammed open as Viviana had promised. Danny hurried down the ramp that ran with drainpipe rain. He entered the basement. He walked to the small private elevator and summoned it with the key. Within seconds the elevator door opened, and Danny used the special key to ride it up to the penthouse. He turned the key to the locked position so that it would hold the elevator door open.

He walked to the middle of the beautiful Kuwaiti rug, wiped his wet shoes, unzipped his pants and urinated, spinning in a circle to give it a good steaming soak. He strolled to the white lacquered Louis XV grand Steinway and hefted the ball bat, smashed every crystal figurine, hammered them into gleaming splinters, and diamond dust, splitting the wooden top of the Steinway grand.

He smashed the metal bat down on the three-and-a-quarter-inch hard rock maple rim, chipping away the eighteen laminations, smashed it until the wood dented and split. He wiped his brow, opened the lid, and beat the guts until the strings, braces, pin blocks, hammers, soundboards, and ribs were a joyous mangle. He beat the piano from every angle, a deafening, gratifying symphony of demolition and destruction and revenge. He smashed the keys, bridges, scales, tuning pins, dampers. Then he beat off one of the gilt carved piano legs, collapsing it sideways onto the floor like a battered white fighter driven to one knee. *Call me a Philistine*, he thought. *This is a fucking ball.*

He took out every vase in the room with home run swings, marvelous *thwocking* mini explosions that rippled sweet satisfying vibrations through his wrists and up into his aching shoulders. He swung at every expensive vase and Tiffany lamp in sight until his arms began to hurt. He walked out onto the terrace for a breather, took gulps of the wet night air. "Who's the fucking boss, bitch?" asked the mynah bird.

"I am, motherfucker," Danny said and opened all the fancy gold gilded cages, setting loose a carnival of excited birds.

Behind him the cuckoo clocks chirped in midnight unison, and Danny smashed each one with the bat, singing a Chambers Brothers tune he used to hear them sing in the Electric Circus: "Time has come today / Young hearts can go their way. . . ." He batted the clocks until they were silent, stopping time itself with each soothing bash.

He entered the kitchen, grabbed a butcher knife, looked around, and said, "Be right back." Then he stalked into the living room and carved large X's in each cushion of the white leather sectional couch, the same for the matching chairs and ottomans. He turned on the TV, checked the weather report that said the rain would continue to fall until six A.M., and then dug his feet into the rug, waited for the right pitch, and swung the baseball bat through the sixty-inch screen.

On the way out of the living room he pounded the stereo system until it lay in useless sections on the hardwood floor.

Passing through the dining room, Danny toppled the china cabinet, a great cymbal crash of glass and dishware, and clubbed every single elegant china piece to garden gravel on the parquet floor. He stood on the table and took out the chandelier with five good swings, hurtling a crystal ice storm across the room.

Then he invaded the bedroom, where he had seen the two bimbos collapse onto Strong's king-size water bed. He punctured holes in three sides, hundreds of gallons of water running out onto Strong's handpicked carpets. He picked up a jewelry box filled with diamond cuff links and tie clasps, opened the window, and tossed them out into the street.

He discovered king-size water beds in four more bedrooms, the fuck rooms for his judge and politico pals, and Danny punctured every one of them as if lancing pus from infected boils.

He'd worked up a healthy sweat and paused for a respite in the kitchen, filling himself a cool glass of water from the faucet. He drank half, shattered the dangling Tiffany lamps over the butcher block island, and pulverized a set of English condiment crockery, a soup tureen, delicate French wine and champagne glasses and brandy snifters. And finished his glass of tap water. He tossed the glass in the air and swung and smashed it in flight.

Then he walked into Christie Strong's office as renegade water invaded all the rooms. He rooted in Christie Strong's desk, looking for any kind of exculpatory evidence for his case, or incriminating evidence against Christie. He knew that anything of value would be in the wall safe behind the Bosch painting. So he rummaged through the desk drawers and desktop, looking for check stubs, bills, anything linking him to Clubweb.com or Erika's Earth. He found a large key ring with dozens of keys to various properties. Each key had a white tag attached with the corresponding address. He found one for Clubweb.com, one for Erika's house on Garvey Place, and two for Helen Grabowski's building and apartment on the parkside. He didn't find any documents but he pocketed the keys to Helen's place.

He was about to exit the office when he saw one hand-lettered envelope in Christie Strong's outgoing mailbox, amid a stack of typed bills and correspondence. The envelope was addressed to Erika Malone, waiting to be mailed after the holiday.

He tore open the envelope, took out the letter:

Dear Erika:

It now seems appropriate to end a long and noble chase that began in the last century. Alas, you are a truly beautiful, old-fashioned girl, and so this will be my last and final love letter to you. Please cherish it.

I still love you. I always have. But it's clear to me now that I will never have you. I have chased you for a lifetime to no avail. I suppose I could have pressured you, done an unfriendly takeover (ha ha), but that is no way to win a human heart, especially one as dear and strong as yours.

Now that the man you love is back in town and you still want him above all others, I will gracefully accept that I never will have a place in your heart or your life. For this reason, and because neither of us is getting any younger, I suggest we end our business arrangement ASAP. Cut all ties. Call it even. I am moving on to my third act, and you to yours, so I suggest we meet after Danny leaves town, hammer out our final numbers, and civilly go our separate ways. I will give you what you want. You will give me what is rightfully mine. No need for any further animus or hostility.

However, I urge you to use whatever charms or influence you possess to make Danny back off. It serves neither of our interests to have him opening old wounds, awakening old dogs better left sleeping.

I wish you well in your life with Danny. If it is of any flattering value to you, you are the only woman I ever pursued with such fervor whose charms I failed to win. Congratulations.

I will contact you next week.

> Love always,
> C.

Asshole, Danny thought, rattling the letter in his hands. Confused.

Danny's cell phone rang as water rushed into the room from five punctured water beds, carrying with it a cargo of shattered glass and pulverized ceramics like a rumbling cascade of river gravel. He answered the phone. It was Viviana. They exchanged hellos and then she said, "I told Christie that you contacted me and said you had the two tapes. He looked worried. He said that if I could reach you I should tell you he has something you want. Something that will set you free. He wants to make an exchange. He said to meet him. Alone or else everything is off, at his penthouse tonight. . . ."

"Sure, so his goons can be there. Forget that. Write this down and quote me verbatim. Tell him I said, 'Fuck you, meet me in the wide-open. In Prospect Park. Two A.M. You know where.' "

# forty

Erika Malone answered the door, vacuum-packed into a black micromini dress and high heels with ankle straps. She grabbed Danny by the belt buckle and pulled him into the Grindbox. She took his hands and put them on her bare behind and buried her tongue in his mouth. She licked her way to his ear and whispered, "Mama's asleep, come inside and take inappropriate advantage of me."

He pushed her away, flaccid.

"First, tell me who fucked you first."

Danny backed a bewildered Erika into the house, kicking the door closed behind him.

"What are you talking about?" she asked.

"It wasn't Lars, we know that."

"I never said it was—"

"I thought for a while there it was Christie Strong," Danny said, taking out Strong's unmailed letter to Erika. "Why else would you be so cozy with him? Why else would he have a key to your house? But then I read this pathetic note—"

"He still has a key? That *is* pathetic. When he first started black-mailing me he demanded to search the house from top to bottom. He was certain my father had stashed a bundle of his cash here in the house. That my mother and I used it to live on after he died. To send me to school. To start my business. I told him there was no cash. That we were living on Dad's pension and his life insurance. I gave him the key, told him to go ahead and search. He never found the steel room. Or the half million in cash. I was saving it. For my tuition. And to start my business. Why not? I deserved it. After he searched for two days, I asked for the key back. He must've had another one made. But I didn't fear physical harm from him. It was in his interests that I live a long and healthy life. But like I said, no, I never once had sex with that pig."

"It sure wasn't me who got you first."

"It should have been you. I offered myself, my virginity to you on my seventeenth birthday. But you couldn't get it up. That's in the real diary. Go read it. It's also in my head. I was humiliated. I was ready, willing, and able. You weren't any of the above. I thought it was my fault."

He stalked her into the living room, toward the kitchen, passing the eagles and the empty reclining chair and the rolltop desk.

"That's right," Danny said. "I couldn't get it up because your father took me down into the basement that night. Then into the subbasement, the bomb shelter, into what he called the Niggerproof Room. He sat there cleaning a gun, polishing a bayonet, as he told me what he would do if I ever laid a hand on you. He told me that he promised himself that no nigger, spic, Jew, or dirty hippie would ever deflower his little girl. He scared the living shit out of me. He mentally castrated me—"

"He was protective to a fault, yes . . . what is this all ab—"

Danny stood above her, peering into her bitter-chocolate eyes that retreated deeper into the sockets, looking for places to hide. Then as she swallowed hard, her face seemed to crack, a tiny fault line zigzagging down the middle like a fracture in fine porcelain.

"And he made sure no one violated his precious daughter," Danny said, lifting her chin to make her look him in the eyes. "No one else, that is except . . ."

"You have no idea."

Erika backed into the kitchen. Danny reached past her, opened the basement door and pointed. She glanced, then looked away, as if reacting to the single greatest horror of her life.

Her whisper was a little girl's plea, "Stop."

"He took you down there, didn't he? After he found out that I was the long-haired hippie speed freak who'd witnessed him murder Wally Fortune. After he found out his daughter's boyfriend was the kid who stood between him making a fortune with Christie Strong and jail. So he decided to take your cherry so I never would."

Erika stood still, tears drooling down her face, her back against the open cellar door. She wrapped her arms around herself, cowering from the words. There wasn't enough dress to hide behind. He'd never seen Erika more naked. For the first time, as her face collapsed with emotion, she looked her age. As if all the pain of all the years had caught up with her all at once, collapsing her jowls, drooping her eyes, and cracking her trembling upper lip.

"You have no idea what it was like," she whispered, hiding her face in her soft small hands. Her tears did it to him again, took Danny out at the knees.

"Uh-uh, this time it's not just about you, Erika. It's about me, too. It's about what your father did to *me*, too. To my family. To my kid. So no fucking feel-sorry-for-myself tears, this time. This isn't just about you. There are other victims here, too. . . ."

She balled a fist and pounded her open palm, her rings cutting into her flesh.

"Don't talk to me about being a fucking victim," she said, her face now clenching into another fist. "He took me down there! He showed me the secret room. I got so excited. I was so flattered that he used my birthday as the combination to his lock. I followed him down on a secret adventure. Even my mom didn't know about this room. Daddy closed the steel door. Locked it. And then he pretended to show me what he did to the skells he arrested. He handcuffed me to the headboard railing. I laughed. But then he . . . he tied my legs apart to the foot railings. I told him it wasn't funny anymore. And he put tape over my mouth—"

"Oh, Jesus Christ, please don't tell me all of it—"

"He cut off my clothes with his prized bayonet—"

"Erika, don't—"

"My fucking father stared down at me naked, spread-eagle on the bed, in an underground bomb shelter, surrounded by guns and weapons. And then my father took off all his clothes. As if I were someone else. Some hooker. Some bimbo. Some slut from the street. My father talked to me like I was a subhuman. And then *my father* got on top of me. Big and hairy and fat and old and sweaty and smelly and my own flesh and blood. My fucking father! It felt like the world just landed on top of me, like the house landing on the Wicked Witch. He stared me in the face. He smelled like my mother's garlicky tomato sauce. And wine. And cigars. And the aftershave he smacked on every morning when I used to watch him shave, when he used to dot my face with shaving cream. And then my father, my own father took his big hard hairy *thing,* the dick that had made me! And my father hurt me with it. Rammed me with it. He didn't just want to take my virginity. My father, who had never lifted a finger to me in his life, wanted to hurt and punish me. He kept saying this was my fault. He was doing this to save me. From you!"

"Don't you fucking dare make this about me! Not this part, Erika . . . oh, Jesus Christ, no fucking way. . . ."

"He pushed it into me like a weapon. I felt like I was being stabbed. The pain was so horrible. I can't explain it. I felt the blood running out of me, down my legs, into the crack of my butt, onto the bed, I thought I would bleed to death. I was never so scared in my life. It was one of those moments when the first thing that comes to your mind is that you want to call for your father. And when I looked up there was my daddy's face, the man I loved and trusted, the man who'd always protected me since I was an infant. And he was fucking raping me! He whispered in my ear as he plunged into me, 'I gave you your virginity, and I'll be the one who takes it.' All so that *you* couldn't have me first!"

"I don't need to know any more. Stop. Please, in the name of God, Erika, just stop fucking talking. . . ."

Danny walked away from her, drew a deep breath, raked his fingers through his hair, and rubbed his eyes. He couldn't make the images disappear.

"I wanted to vomit but I knew I would choke to death if I did," she said. "He whispered to me as he did it. Told me he was doing this because he loved me. So that some dirty nigger or filthy hippie like you would never be able to say he took Vito Malone's daughter's cherry. He told me he was doing what a father who loved his daughter was supposed to do. And he got so excited by that idea that he didn't pull out in time. . . ."

Danny marbled in horror, turned to her as the sassy woman stood statue still, her face red and ravaged like a woman fighter who'd just fought to a grueling draw. Whatever anger Danny had for her emptied out of him. He reached for her. Held her in his arms as her body trembled like a woman whose hardwiring was short-circuiting.

"I'm sorry," Danny said. He didn't know what else to say.

"So am I," she whispered. "I'm sorry, too. I'm so sorry I ruined your life."

"I'm still here. So are you. . . ."

She wrapped her arms around him. He stroked her long red hair.

"Make love to me," she whispered. "Make me feel clean."

He held her at arm's length. "Tell me the rest."

She looked at him, her face sagging, the pain reflecting a tortured soul.

"Abortion was still illegal," she said. "Except if the mother's life was in danger. After I missed my second period I told Mama. Told her everything. She didn't want to believe me at first. But then when I showed her the room downstairs, the handcuffs, the bloodstained mattress, she believed me. She didn't confront my father about it. She controlled her rage. At first. But there was a plan in her head. I knew it. Her Sicilian mind was plotting. She didn't want anyone else to know about what my father had done to me. The shame was too great, she said. She said I would forever be known as the girl who was raped by her father. No doctors. No illegal quacks. But the real reason she didn't want anyone else to know was because she had a plan in her head. So she did the abortion herself. She killed that poor baby, who was just another unnamed victim. And because she didn't know what she was doing, she also killed any chance that I'd ever have another one . . . and then. . . ."

Danny looked at her, nodded. Jogged by the recent LSD experience into state-dependent memory, Danny could now see the fourth figure on Hippie Hill on the night of November 20, 1969. . . .

*It's the number one neighborhood MILF, Angela Malone, wearing a hooded sweatshirt, tight jeans, carrying a .45. She storms up Hippie Hill as the rain falls, and Danny stumbles, holding his brother Brendan's .45 on Boar's Head. Vito Malone scoffs at him, dares him to shoot him, and is alarmed when he sees his wife appear out of the cold November rain.*

*"What the hell are you doing here?" Vito Malone shouts.*

*"I'm here to kill you for what you did to Erika," Angela Malone says.*

*And then Angela Malone raises her .45 and shoots. And shoots. And shoots. And shoots and shoots. And shoots him once more in the groin. All as the big white light from purgatory to heaven blinds the night and he hears Erika come running, screaming, "Mama, Mama, Mama. . . ."*

"And then she went and killed that son of a bitch, didn't she?" Danny said, squinting into Erika's fidgety eyes. "Mama took care of her daughter first. Made sure she got rid of the incest bastard baby in your belly. Then your mother found out your father was going to kill me on Hippie Hill that night. And that you planned to kill him first. But to save you from killing him, to save you from the awfulness of the deed and maybe jail, she got there first. And Mama emptied the gun into the bastard, didn't she? She had as much if not more motive than the rest of us to kill your father."

"She got there a minute before I did. When I arrived she was just shooting him. He tried to crawl, tried to hide. But she shot him again. And again. Jim Dugan's big light was shining and his film was rolling. I didn't know what that was at the time. It just scared the hell out of me. I thought maybe it was a police spotlight. You were stumbling and falling all over the place, with a gun in your hand. Stoned. Babbling. Falling. After my mother finished shooting him you tried to hold my father in your arms, for chrissakes. When the light went out, my mother helped me drag you into our car, we got you away from there. We took you home. We washed and changed you into new clothes I'd bought for your birthday. Then we took you back to your own apartment, dumped you on the couch. I was never so scared in my life . . . except for the night when he raped me. . . ."

Danny drew a deep breath, took a few steps away. "Why didn't you or your mother just go to the cops, go to Ankles? Tell them the truth? You had cause for justifiable homicide."

"Are you kidding? My mother didn't want the shame! But even if we did, no one would have believed me or her. You don't claim that your father, a decorated cop, raped your daughter. He would have said the bloodstains were from you and me. That you deflowered me. Besides, I waited two months to tell my mother because I was afraid of his threats. And then if you wait two months, until after the abortion, to kill the bastard, it's murder. Premeditated. It was murder, Danny. So was the abortion at the time. But I couldn't let my mother go to jail. The best thing to do was just cover it up. When it came between you having to go away from Brooklyn, losing you, or losing my mother to jail, I chose her. I needed her, Danny. I had no father now. She had no husband. We needed each other. I'm sorry. But I would never have let you go to jail. If we wanted to frame you, we would have just left you there that night. But I loved you. I still do."

He surprised himself by not saying he loved her too. "And Strong blackmailed you by threatening to expose your mother?"

She nodded. "Of course I would have gone down, too, for aiding and abetting and accessory and the coverup. So I paid him half of everything Erika's Earth made because he said it was founded with money that belonged to him, money that was stolen from him by my father. He took half. I'm not complaining. I haven't missed any meals. I have no kids to support."

"Ah, Christ—"

"But, hey, the upside is my mother never went to jail. She only has five, maybe six years before she needs to be institutionalized. One day she will just forget how to stay alive. One day she'll inhale her food instead of swallowing, like many Alzheimer's victims, which will cause pneumonia, and she will just die. She will already have disappeared. She will not know who I am. Will not remember my father or the murder. She will not remember who she is. She will vanish into her own skin. So there will be no heroic measures, even the church goes along with that. But I can't let them take these final years from her. But if she remembers me for only minutes a day, it will be all the family I will ever have. There are still moments in every day when she knows who I am and I cherish those moments. Because she is my mama."

Danny sighed. The images of Vito Malone bull-raping his daughter, of her mother shooting him for revenge, of him cradling Vito Malone all bubbled in his head like a tainted gumbo.

"I'm getting the film tonight."

"How, where?" She seemed excited. "I'll pay him anything. One final lump. . . ."

"I have something he wants. I want the film."

"You're going to use it to exonerate yourself, aren't you?" she said, the excitement turning to dread. "Which will incriminate me and my mother."

"I think once Ankles sees the film and hears the whole story, he'll either bury the whole thing or persuade the DA to cut a no-jail deal."

"I can't risk that, Danny. Just give me the film. I'll pay for the best legal team in America for you. . . ."

"I won't use the film unless I have to. I'm not doing anything to hurt you, Erika. But the same way you needed your mother, I want my kid to have me."

Erika nodded. She trembled and took short breaths and then she said, "I understand."

She embraced Danny, kissed him. Then he picked Erika up in his sore arms and carried her up the stairs to her bedroom. They made love for almost an hour. Danny postponed his orgasm, fearing that *la petite mort*, or the little death, might be but a prelude.

# forty-one

Danny didn't bother to knock. He opened Hippie Helen's door with the key he'd taken from Christie Strong's desk. A jumble of rage, pity, revenge, regret, and sadness bubbled in his head about Hippie Helen. She had been so generous to him as a kid, teaching him the basic grammar of sex and love, a kind and gentle woman who fed, sheltered, and nursed Danny in days when he was a near zombie.

But somewhere along the way Helen had turned bad. She was party to a blackmail racket, and the blood of more people than Danny wanted to count was on her hands. Her coverup of what had happened on November 20, 1969, had plagued most of Danny's life.

He stepped inside her apartment as the old Columbia vinyl platter of Dylan's "Sad-Eyed Lady of the Lowlands" spun on the old-fashioned stereo turntable. The needle was stuck in a groove and Dylan kept singing ". . . or, sad-eyed la-dy, should I wait. . . ."

"Helen?"

There was no response in the candlelit room. Dozens of candles burned on the mantelpiece in front of the photo collage of Hippie Hill circa 1969. More candles and incense burned in little brass holders all over the room. A black light ignited the old Day-Glo posters on the bare brick walls.

Danny could see the back of Helen's head as she sat on the big cushioned sofa, her bewildered white long-haired cat on her lap.

"Helen?"

But all he heard was Dylan repeating the same line over and over, the same song that had played the day she had taken part of Danny's virginity in the back of Wally Fortune's Volkswagen bus.

"Hel," Danny said again, walking around the couch to face Helen. "I just wanted to warn you that the cops will be coming for you. You're sick, Helen. You can probably cut a deal if you testify, if you give up Christie. My advice is—"

He stopped in midsentence when he looked at Helen Grabowski on the couch, as dead as the sixties. Her blue denim muumuu and the cushions under her were soaking wet where she had eliminated her bodily fluids. A little trickle of vomit coursed from her lower lip to her chin. The empty bottle of Clozapine lay in Helen's limp right hand. Rosary beads intertwined her left hand, which clutched a framed photo of Dirty Jim Dugan. Danny grabbed her right wrist. It was cold. He felt for a pulse. There wasn't one. He lifted an eyelid. Her eyeball was the color of an oyster.

As sad as she looked, Danny felt an odd shiver of relief. He straightened out the needle on the stereo and as Dylan continued the song, he left.

# forty-two

Christie Strong was already there.

As Danny parked his Camry alongside Strong's Jaguar in the park lot, he saw Strong standing on Hippie Hill, still dressed in a tuxedo from the testimonial dinner, holding a big umbrella.

Danny scoped the rest of the area. He saw no one. He climbed out into the rain, the hood of his rain slicker covering his head. He kept his gloved hands in his jacket pocket, one holding two blank tapes. The other wrapped around the .45.

He squished up the hillock where Vito Malone had died. He faced Strong.

"The crystal collection was unnecessary," Strong said. "It was started by my mother."

"The LSD wasn't my idea of a dream vacation, either."

"And you pissed on my Kuwaiti rug."

"You shit on my life."

"So I dosed you a few times. Big deal. That's it. My beef was with your lady friend. Not you. She and her mother robbed me. Took my nest egg. Malone had all my cash hidden. They wouldn't give it back. But I had the upper hand."

Strong waved a reel of Super 8-millimeter film.

"I had nothing personal against you," Strong said.

"You told Vito Malone to kill me," Danny said. "When that went wrong you let me run and hide for over thirty years. It ruined my life. That's personal."

"You shouldn't feel that way. It was business. I always liked you, Danny. You were smart, cultured, creative. You turned me on to the poetry and drawings of William Blake, the masterpieces of Hieronymus Bosch, the visions of Coleridge. I thought *Huckleberry Finn* was a kid's book until you showed that life was a raft on a big river. Until you enlightened me, I thought *Moby Dick* was a story about a whale. The *Garden of Earthly Delights* by Bosch and Samuel Taylor Coleridge's "Kubla Khan" changed my life, man."

"In Xanadu did Kubla Khan
   A stately pleasure-dome decree:
Where Alph, the sacred river, ran
Through caverns measureless to man
   Down to a sunless sea.

"Hey, man, because of you I *became* Kubla Khan. I built my Xanadu, my own dynasty. I lived in the center panel of the *Garden of Earthly Delights*. I'm Huck Finn on my raft on the sacred river Alph. You introduced me to true geniuses. Not like the ersatz poets and artists of the sixties, Allen Ginsberg couldn't empty Coleridge's trash basket. Peter Max wasn't good enough to wash Bosch's brushes. You helped point me the way. You gave me poetry, you gave me art, you gave me vision. So I liked you, Danny. You were smarter than all the other little assholes on this pathetic little hill. Problem was you were too smart. And you got in the way. I thank you for the culture, but you became clutter."

"Just like Mary and Wally Fortune—"

"An ingrate bimbo and a two-bit con artist," he said, waving a dismissive hand. "Two fruit flies hovering over my golden apples."

Danny took out two microcassette tapes and held them up. "I have two interviews that could relocate you from Xanadu to Attica, Christie," Danny said. "One with Kenny Byrne and one with Dirty Jim Dugan."

"How do I know you haven't made copies?"

"Oh, but I have, just like you've made copies of the film," Danny said, eager to get his hands on any copy of the film. "All I want is to prove that I didn't kill Vito Malone. Once I have that, I'll be satisfied. I'm not after a headline. I just want my life back. We each have something the other wants."

Strong looked around, did a 360 on the hill. "You really did come alone."

"It's been my problem—alone for thirty-two years," Danny said.

Danny walked to him and held out the two blank tapes. Strong held out his film. They exchanged.

"Good-bye, Danny," Strong said.

Danny pocketed the film and saw Strong glance toward the parking lot. Danny flung himself to the ground. Just as he saw the black middleweight climb out of the trunk of the silver Jaguar. Pumping a double-barrel shotgun.

Danny pulled the .45 from his back waistband. The middleweight came on a run, firing his first shot. It lashed over Danny's head. Now from behind Danny the big Russian jumped from a tree near the retaining fence. He aimed a big handgun with his left hand, his right hand bandaged from Danny's bite wound. Strong hurried toward his Jaguar, a man late for an appointment with destiny.

Danny yanked the safety of his .45 but couldn't figure it out. Then he freed it. But didn't know if there was a bullet in the chamber. He fumbled with it, pointed it at himself, twisted it, and almost dropped it, like a man wrangling a captured rat. Danny fired at the charging middleweight. The muzzle flash stunned his eyes, the recoil surprising him, pins-and-needles stitching his arm. The bullet went awry. Now the Russian raced at Danny.

"Focking die, moddafockah!" he screamed, aiming his elaborate-looking pistol.

Eddie Fortune emerged from Sewer 7, Pipe 11, and dropped the Russian with three fast shots. He turned toward Strong and aimed.

Before Eddie could fire the middleweight fired at him, the blast sending up clumps of grass and mud in front of Sewer 7. Some of the deflected shotgun pellets tore into Eddie Fortune, but he made no discernable sound, his silence like another weapon. Danny gripped and pointed his gun with two hands, sweat dampening his palms inside the batting gloves. He sucked air. Held it, swallowed hard, and squeezed the trigger. Nothing happened. The gun jammed. "Fuck!"

Eddie rolled across the shadowy grass, his Special Forces training like a parallel set of instincts. He fired once in midroll, shattering the middleweight's knee. The middleweight hollered and dived behind the trunk of an old maple.

Danny saw Strong sprint in his patent-leather shoes for his Jaguar. Danny was up and running after him, his jammed .45 at his side. Before Danny could reach him the red 1969 El Dorado sped out of the black belly of the park, aiming straight for Christie Strong.

Strong stopped. Gaped. Dived behind his Jaguar. Erika smashed into the car, all crunching metal and exploding glass. Strong scrambled away as a bleeding Erika pried herself loose from the mangled car.

"I want the film," she screamed, brandishing her .38 police special.

"He has it," Strong shouted.

Danny chased after Strong, who raced up the knoll toward the retaining fence on the far side of Hippie Hill. The middleweight popped from behind the maple and aimed at Danny, a cruel little smile spreading. Erika shot him in the face. Dead. Danny stood, stunned. He turned to Erika, blinking, swallowing hard.

"Watch!" Erika shouted. Danny turned and saw Strong pointing a small pistol at him. Erika ran right at Strong, firing. Strong fired at Danny. Her shot flashed high when her powerful body was ripped open by Strong's bullet that was intended for Danny. She died before she reached the ground. Danny rushed to her and he heard Eddie Fortune screaming. "Danny!"

Danny turned and saw Strong ready to shoot him, too. Danny snatched Erika's .38 and fired like a kid testing a new Christmas toy. His bullet pierced Christie Strong's right eye. He dropped straight down, like someone had just pushed an off switch. Danny flung the gun out of his hand.

*I came back to Brooklyn to see if I was a killer and if I still loved my first love,* he thought as he cradled Erika. *And now that woman has died saving my life.*

*And for the first time I have killed a man. The very first time.*

He wished he could weep, wished he could unleash a deep and sobbing cry. But he felt as lifeless as Erika's body in his arms.

Danny was still cradling Erika when Ankles arrived with Brendan ten minutes later. Eddie Fortune had summoned him with his cell phone. Ankles separated Danny from Erika.

Eddie Fortune filled in Ankles on almost everything. Danny told him about the film and the blackmail and that Erika's mother was the one who'd killed Vito Malone. Eddie Fortune detailed the shootings, small purple polka dots of blood staining his pants and jacket.

"I know you said you were driving home from work, Eddie," Ankles said, pulling the batting gloves from Danny's hands. "And you saw Danny in trouble and so you used your service revolver to kill one attacker, and to wound a second. And then you said Erika Malone shot the black guy that you'd already wounded?"

"Affirmative," Eddie said.

"Which means the ME will find cordite gunshot residue on Erika Malone's hands, correct?"

"I assume so," Eddie said.

"Remember, because of your law-enforcement status and your spotless record and military-hero background, your statement on this incident will be golden, Eddie. So tell me again, fast, on the fucking record, who shot Christie Strong?"

Eddie Fortune looked at Danny Cassidy, nodded, and said, "Erika Malone."

"Oh, OK, that clears that up, then," Ankles said, stuffing Danny's batting gloves into the same pocket as the .45 Danny had carried. Without speaking another word, Ankles wiped Erika's gun with a hankie and stuffed it back in her dead hand.

The forensic crew arrived ten minutes later. They taped off the crime scene, chalked the body outlines, put small paper tents over the bullet casings. They took gunshot residue scrapings from Danny's hands, examining them under a special battery operated lamp. He was clean because he'd worn gloves.

Danny saw the green Crown Victoria pull into the lot. Pat O'Rourke walked up the hill, her face puffy and vulnerable with interrupted sleep. She looked at Erika Malone, Christie Strong, and Strong's two bodyguards. Then she looked at Danny with sleepy eyes. "OK, what do we have?"

"We have nothing," Ankles said. "Four bodies. And an old film that might exonerate Cassidy and implicate Erika Malone's nutso mother with the old-timers disease, for the murder on November 21, 1969. It looks like a long-running blackmail racket came to a head. . . ."

Pat O'Rourke smirked. Danny knew that she knew that she was being at least half bullshitted.

"Good," she said. "Copy me your report. The press will be all over it for a week or two but as far as I'm concerned let's close this son of a bitch down."

"Yeah," Ankles said. "Pure pleasure workin' with ya, toots."

Brendan led Danny down the hill. O'Rourke followed a few steps, lighting a cigarette, pushing the Mets hat up higher to reveal more of her sweet and pretty face. Bittersweet relief filled her blue eyes, a look of final acceptance that made her look less like a cop and more like a woman. A woman who'd searched, found an important answer, and slammed a heavy door. And who was now ready to open a new door.

"Danny?"

He turned to her. "I'm sorry about your girlfriend," she said.

Danny nodded. "I'm sorry about your father."

"I'll see ya, huh?"

He nodded again and then Danny Cassidy walked home in the rain with his brother.

# epilogue

Danny, Darlene, and Brendan stood above the grave as Mickey Cassidy's coffin was lowered into the gash in the earth next to the headstone of Maggie Cassidy. The priest said a few kind and solemn words that Danny did not listen to and then Brendan and Darlene threw clumps of dirt onto the gleaming mahogany box.

Danny stepped to the edge of the grave and dangled his head bag. Inside were all his 1960s memorabilia and the case file with his name on it, which Ankles had given to him at the church after the mass. Danny dropped it on top of his father's coffin and watched the gravediggers shovel six feet of dark Brooklyn soil on top of his father and the year 1969.

"Forgiven," Danny said.

Brendan wiped away a tear and Darlene wept for her father's loss as they strolled out of the cemetery. As he left Danny saw Ankles and Marsha Mauro standing above the grave of their murdered son. Danny and Ankles nodded. The next day Erika Malone would be cremated, as she requested, in the crematorium here in the cemetery. She'd always said she wanted her ashes scattered in the lake of Prospect Park. Danny would stay one extra day to carry out her last wishes. And in a few months Ankles would be burying his wife. Angela Malone would be placed in an institution, until the plaque and tangles of Alzheimer's buried her alive in the gullies of her own brain.

Viviana Gonzalez stood off to the side, elegant and beautiful in a tasteful black dress and low heels. She held a bouquet of flowers that she said she was going to put on her father's grave. "I never did that before," she said. "He was a Christie Strong victim, too. I owe it to him to find out more about him now. . . ."

Danny introduced Viviana to Darlene and asked her how her story was coming. She said there was so much to write that it was overwhelming her. But she had faxed a query letter to Danny's friend at the *Village Voice* who was interested in seeing the piece when she was finished.

"Can I show it to you before I send it in?" she asked.

"Of course," Danny said.

"I need to interview you, too. . . ."

"Sure."

"I'm sure you're gonna write about it, too. . . ."

"Probably."

"It's really your story," Viviana said.

Danny ruffled the bouquet of flowers in Viviana's hand. "It's yours, too, Viv. My recommendation, write a story about how and why you came to put flowers on your father's grave after all these years. Use that as a portal to the bigger story. It'll make it personal, touching, about something. But for chrissakes don't make it weepy and sentimental. The flowers should be in the lead and the kicker. The rest of the story you know. If you have the story, tell it."

Viviana smiled and nodded. "I like that."

"Thanks for your help."

"Thank you, I'll E-mail it to you before I turn it in."

Danny, Brendan, and Darlene ate breakfast at the Squared One across from Prospect Park. There was a lingering emptiness inside Danny that would not go away.

"Give me the keys to your car," Brendan said. "I gotta go home to get something."

Danny handed him his keys and Brendan ran out to the car and sped off. Father and daughter sat sipping coffee, his black suit making him sweat.

"How does it feel to be free from all the baggage?" Darlene asked.

"Just sitting here with you is like getting out of jail."

"Did you love her, Dad?"

"Once, at least," he said. "I'm still not sure about the second time."

"If there's doubt it couldn't have been love."

"There wasn't enough time to find out. Besides, I was pretty distracted."

"But she must have loved you."

"In her own crazy way, maybe she did."

"What now?"

"I have a job I have to get back to, back home."

"I'm glad you're going back because when I'm finished with school, I'm coming back home. Maybe I'll get an apartment near you. We could have a beer or lunch or catch a flick now and then."

"That'd be a dream come true."

She fell silent for a few moments and then looked up at him. "You shouldn't live alone anymore, Dad. You're fifty. You need a babe."

He smiled. "Someone to push the wheelchair, huh?"

"Something like that. You have plenty of life left, old man. Party."

Danny nodded and saw a green Crown Victoria pass the restaurant in a slow crawl, Pat O'Rourke peering through her side window. She caught Danny's eye.

"I'll say this and I'll say no more about it," Darlene said. "Pat seems cool. At least she'd feel your pain. Other than that, you're on your own."

Danny laughed as the waitress brought the check. He left a 30 percent tip and he and Darlene walked outside as Brendan parked the car across the street in the park lot, waving for Danny.

The two brothers looked at each other. Brendan cocked the football. And Danny broke into a run, all the sore muscles igniting in his legs and shoulders. He ran right across the traffic circle, motorists honking horns, citizens stopping to stare, JoJo Corcoran cheering him on. Darlene shouted, "Go, old man!" And Danny kept on running, deep into the park, high up onto Hippie Hill, past the discarded crime-scene tape as Brendan let loose a towering spiral that came out of the past, out of 1969, spinning above the trees and above Brooklyn, breaking into a perfect descent as Danny tracked it over his shoulder.

The ball whizzed down toward him as he picked up speed. Danny outstretched his arms and his fingertips felt the smooth magical hide of the football that told him that the war and the sixties and the dying and the running were over. He clutched the ball in his big hands. He crushed it into the crook of his arm. He ran past Sewer 7 and into an imaginary end zone. He tumbled to the ground, doing a somersault and a double roll. And then Danny Cassidy sat up, holding the ball aloft. He saw Brendan give him the upended arms of a touchdown. He saw Darlene smiling and shaking her fist into the sky. He saw Patricia O'Rourke standing with one foot propped up on the fender of her car, her Mets hat on backward. Smiling.

Danny thought about his dead father saying he was sorry and about his daughter accepting his apology and about Brendan being home and about the bullet Erika Malone took for him the night before.

And then Danny Cassidy walked down Hippie Hill toward the people he cared for most in the world, and for no particular reason except that he was fifty and free at last, he just started to laugh.